JUDGE DEE AT WORK

These eight stories, featuring the master-detective of
Ancient China and his assistants Ma Joong, Sergeant
Hoong and Chiao Tai, cover a decade during which the
judge served in four different provinces of the T'ang
Empire. From the suspected treason of a general in the
Chinese army facing the Tartar hordes on the western
frontier to the murder of a lonely poet in his garden
pavilion in Han-yuan, the cases presented here are
among the most memorable of Judge Dee's long and
distinguished career.

Judge Dee Mysteries available from Chicago:

The Chinese Bell Murders
The Chinese Gold Murders
The Chinese Lake Murders
The Chinese Nail Murders
Judge Dee at Work
The Lacquer Screen
The Monkey and the Tiger
Necklace and Calabash

JUDGE DEE AT WORK

Eight Chinese Detective Stories

by

ROBERT VAN GULIK

*With illustrations
drawn by the author in Chinese style*

DISCARD

The University of Chicago Press

This edition is reprinted by arrangement with
Charles Scribner's Sons, an imprint of
Macmillan Publishing Company.

The University of Chicago Press, Chicago 60637
Copyright © 1967 by Robert van Gulik
All rights reserved. Published 1967
University of Chicago Press edition 1992
Printed in the United States of America
99 98 97 96 95 94   6 5 4 3 2

ISBN 0-226-84866-3 (pbk.)

Library of Congress Cataloging-in-Publication Data

Gulik, Robert Hans van, 1910–1967.
    Judge Dee at work : eight Chinese detective stories / by
Robert van Gulik ; with illustrations drawn by the author
in Chinese style. — University of Chicago Press ed.
        p.   cm.
    1. Ti, Jen-chieh, 629–700—Fiction.   2. Detective and
mystery stories, English.   3. China—History—T'ang
dynasty, 618–907—Fiction.   I. Title.
PR9130.9.G8J8   1992
823—dc20   92-18598
                                                      CIP

♾ The paper used in this publication meets the minimum
requirements of the American National Standard for
Information Sciences—Permanence of Paper for Printed
Library Materials, ANSI Z39.48-1984

CONTENTS

1. Five Auspicious Clouds   1

2. The Red Tape Murder   20

3. He Came with the Rain   44

4. The Murder on the Lotus Pond   73

5. The Two Beggars   94

6. The Wrong Sword   115

7. The Coffins of the Emperor   140

8. Murder on New Year's Eve   163

   Colophon   174

   Judge Dee Chronology   175

ILLUSTRATIONS

The design of the incense-clock   7

'You are shielding someone, Meng!' Judge Dee said angrily   32

Then she dropped to her knees, trembling violently   57

She was standing in the doorway, her torso naked   87

Raising the candle, the judge stared at the lifeless, haggard face   99

'I am the daughter of a noble king and his chaste queen! How's that for a joke?'   129

'You are good at riddles, they say, eh, Dee?' the Marshal growled   155

As soon as the pedlar saw his wife and son . . .   172

FIVE AUSPICIOUS CLOUDS

*This case occurred in A.D. 663 when Judge Dee had been
serving only a week in his first independent official post—
Magistrate of Peng-lai, a remote district on the north-east
coast of the Chinese Empire. Directly upon his arrival there
he had been confronted with three mysterious crimes, described in my novel* The Chinese Gold Murders. *In that story
mention was made of the flourishing shipbuilding industry of
Peng-lai, and of Mr Yee Pen, the wealthy shipowner. The
present story opens in Judge Dee's private office in the tribunal, where he is in conference with Yee Pen and two other
gentlemen; they have just finished discussing at length Judge
Dee's proposal for bringing the shipbuilding industry under
government control.*

'Well, gentlemen,' Judge Dee said with a satisfied smile to his
three guests, 'that settles it then, I think.'

The conference in his private office had begun at about two
o'clock, and now it was already past five. But he thought that
the time had been well spent.

'The rules we drafted seem to cover all possible contingencies,'
Mr Ho remarked in his precise voice. He was a soberly dressed,
middle-aged man, a retired secretary of the Minister of Justice.
Looking at Hwa Min, the wealthy shipowner on his right, he
added, 'You'll agree, Mr Hwa, that our draft provides for an equitable settlement of your differences with your colleague Mr Yee
Pen here.'

Hwa Min made a face. ' "Equitable" is a nice word,' he said
dryly, 'but as a merchant I like the word "profitable" even better!
If I had been given a free hand in competing with my friend Mr
Yee, the result might not have been exactly equitable, no. . . .
But it would have been eminently profitable—for me!'

'Shipbuilding affects our coastal defence,' Judge Dee observed
stiffly. 'The Imperial Government does not allow a private mono-
poly. We have spent the entire afternoon on this matter and,

1

thanks also to the excellent technical advice of Mr Ho, we have now drafted this document setting forth clearly the rules all ship-owners are to follow. I shall expect both of you to keep to those rules.'

Mr Yee Pen nodded ponderously. The judge liked this shrewd, but honest businessman. He thought less of Mr Hwa Min, who he knew was not averse to shady deals, and who often had woman-trouble. Judge Dee gave a sign to the clerk to refill the teacups, then he leaned back in his chair. It had been a hot day, but now a cool breeze had risen, wafting into the small office the scent of the magnolia tree outside the window.

Mr Yee set his cup down and gave Ho and Hwa Min a question-ing look. It was time for them to take their leave.

Suddenly the door opened and Sergeant Hoong, Judge Dee's trusted old adviser, came in. He stepped up to the desk and said: 'There's someone outside with an urgent message, Your Honour.'

Judge Dee had caught his look. 'Excuse me for one moment,' he said to his three guests. He rose and followed the sergeant outside.

When they were standing in the corridor, the sergeant told him in a low voice, 'It's Mr Ho's house steward, sir. He came to report to his master that Mrs Ho has committed suicide.'

'Almighty heaven!' the judge exclaimed. 'Tell him to wait. I'd better break this bad news to Ho myself. How did she do it?'

'She hanged herself, Your Honour. In their garden pavilion, during the siesta. The steward came rushing out here at once.'

'Too bad for Mr Ho. I like the fellow. A bit on the dry side, but very conscientious. And a clever jurist.'

He sadly shook his head, then re-entered his office. After he had sat down again behind his desk, he addressed Ho gravely: 'It was your house steward, Mr Ho. He came with shocking news. About Mrs Ho.'

Ho grasped the armrests of his chair. 'About my wife?'

'It seems that she committed suicide, Mr Ho.'

Mr Ho half-rose, then let himself sink back again into his chair. He said in a toneless voice, 'So it happened, just as I feared. She . . . she was very depressed, these last weeks.' He passed his hand over his eyes, then asked: 'How . . . how did she do it, sir?'

'Your steward reported that she hanged herself. He is waiting now to take you home, Mr Ho. I'll send the coroner along at once, to draw up the death certificate. You will want to have the formalities over and done with as quickly as possible, of course.'

Mr Ho did not seem to have heard him. 'Dead!' he muttered. 'Only a few hours after I had left her! What shall I do?'

'We'll help you with everything of course, Mr Ho,' Hwa Min said consolingly. He added a few words of condolence, in which Yee Pen joined. But Ho did not seem to have heard them. He was staring into space, his face drawn. Suddenly he looked up at the judge and spoke after some hesitation:

'I need time, sir, a little time to . . . I don't like to presume upon your kindness, sir, but . . . would it perhaps be possible for Your Honour to get someone to attend to the formalities on my behalf? Then I can go home after . . . after the autopsy, and when the dead body has been . . .' He let his voice trail off, giving the judge a pleading look.

'Of course, Mr Ho!' Judge Dee replied briskly. 'You remain here and have another cup of tea. I'll go personally to your house with the coroner, and a temporary coffin will be prepared. It's the least I can do. You have never grudged me your valuable advice, and today again you have devoted your entire afternoon to the business of this tribunal. No, I insist, Mr Ho! You two look after our friend, gentlemen. I'll be back here in half an hour or so.'

Sergeant Hoong was waiting in the courtyard, together with a small rotund man with a black goatee. Hoong presented him as Ho's house steward. Judge Dee told him, 'I have informed Mr Ho already; you can return now, steward. I'll be along presently.' He added to Sergeant Hoong, 'You'd better go back to the chancery, Hoong, and sort out the official papers that have come in. We'll have a look at them together after I get back. Where are my two lieutenants?'

'Ma Joong and Chiao Tai are in the main courtyard, sir, putting the guards through their drill.'

'Good. I need only the headman and two of his men to go to

Mr Ho's house. They'll place the dead body in the coffin. When Ma Joong and Chiao Tai are through with the drill, they can retire. I shan't need them tonight. Get the coroner and have my official palankeen brought out!'

In the small front courtyard of Mr Ho's modest residence the small, obese steward stood waiting for the judge. Two red-eyed maids were hovering near the gatehouse. The headman helped Judge Dee to alight from his palankeen. The judge ordered him to wait with the two constables in the courtyard, then told the steward to conduct him and the coroner to the pavilion.

The small man led them along the open corridor that circled the house to an extensive garden, surrounded by a high wall. He took them down a well-kept path winding among the flowering shrubs to the farthest corner. There, in the shade of two tall oak trees, stood an octagonal pavilion, built on a round brick platform. The pointed, green-tiled roof was topped by a gilded globe, and the pillars and the intricate lattice-work of the windows were lacquered a bright red. The judge went up the four marble steps and pulled the door open.

It was hot in the small but high room, the pungent smell of some outlandish incense hung heavily in the close air. Judge Dee's eyes went at once to the bamboo couch against the wall on the right. The still figure of a woman was stretched out on it. The face was turned to the wall; he saw only the thick strands of glossy hair spilling out over her shoulders. She was clad in a summer robe of white silk, her small feet were shod in white satin shoes. Turning round to the coroner, Judge Dee said:

'You go ahead and examine her while I prepare the death certificate. Open the windows, steward, it is very stuffy in here.'

The judge took an official form from his sleeve and put it ready on the side table beside the door. Then he idly surveyed the room. On the centre table of carved rosewood stood a tea-tray with two cups. The square teapot had been knocked over; it was lying with its spout half across a flat brass box. A length of red silk cord was lying next to it. Two high-backed chairs stood by the table. Except for two racks of spotted bamboo between the windows, holding books and a few small antiques, there was no other furniture.

4

The upper half of the walls was covered with wooden tablets, inscribed with famous poems. There was an atmosphere of quiet, elegant taste.

The steward had pushed open the last window. Now he came up to the judge and pointed to the thick, red-lacquered beams running across the dome-shaped ceiling. From the central beam dangled a red cord, its end frayed.

'We found her hanging there, sir. The chambermaid and I.'

Judge Dee nodded. 'Was Mrs Ho depressed this morning?'

'Oh no, sir, she was in high spirits at the noon meal. But when Mr Hwa Min came to visit the master, she . . .'

'Hwa Min, you say? What did he come here for? He was going to meet Mr Ho in my office at two!'

The steward looked embarrassed. After some hesitation he replied, 'While I was serving tea to the two gentlemen in the reception room, sir, I couldn't help hearing what was being said. I understand that Mr Hwa wanted my master to give Your Honour advice during the conference that would be advantageous to him. He even offered my master a substantial ah . . . reward. My master refused indignantly, of course. . . .'

The coroner stepped up to the judge. 'I'd like to show Your Honour something rather odd!' he said.

Noticing the coroner's worried expression, Judge Dee ordered the steward curtly: 'Go and fetch Mrs Ho's chambermaid!' Then he went over to the couch. The coroner had turned the dead woman's head round. The face was badly distorted, but one could still see that she had been a handsome woman. The judge put her age at about thirty. The coroner pushed the hair aside and showed the judge a bad bruise above the left temple.

'This is one point that worries me, sir,' he said slowly. 'The second is that the death was caused by strangulation, but none of the vertebrae of the neck has been dislocated. Now I measured the length of the cord dangling from that beam up there, of the noose lying on the table and of the woman herself. It's easy to see how she could have done it. She stepped on that chair, then onto the table. She threw the cord over the beam, tied one end in a slip-knot and pulled it tight round the beam. Then she made the other end into a noose, put it round her neck and jumped

5

from the table, upsetting the teapot. While she was hanging there, her feet must have been only a few inches from the floor. The noose slowly strangled her, but her neck was not broken. I can't help wondering why she didn't put the other chair on the table, then jump down from it. A drop like that would have broken her neck, ensuring a quick death. If one combines this fact with the bruise on her temple. . .' He broke off and gave the judge a meaningful look.

'You are right,' Judge Dee said. He took the official form and put it back in his sleeve. Heaven only knew when he would be able to issue the death certificate! He sighed and asked: 'What about the time of death?'

'That's hard to say, Your Honour. The body is still warm, and the limbs haven't yet begun to stiffen. But in this hot weather, and in this closed room . . .'

The judge nodded absentmindedly. He was staring at the brass box. It had the shape of a pentagon with rounded corners, measuring about a foot in diameter, and about an inch high. The brass cover showed a cut-out design of five interconnected spirals. Through it one could see the brown powder that filled the box to the brim.

The coroner followed his glance. 'That's an incense-clock,' he remarked.

'It is indeed. The pattern excised in the cover is that of the Five Auspicious Clouds, each cloud being represented by one spiral. If one lights the incense at the beginning of the design, it'll slowly burn on along the spirals of the pattern, as if it were a fuse. Look, the tea spilling from the spout of the teapot moistened the centre of the third spiral, extinguishing the incense about halfway through that part of the design. If we could find out when exactly this incense-clock was lit, and how long it took the fire to reach the centre of the third spiral, we would be able to establish the approximate time of the suicide. Or rather of the . . .'

Judge Dee checked himself, for the steward had come in. He was accompanied by a portly woman of about fifty, in a neat brown dress. Her round face still showed traces of tears. As soon as she had seen the still figure on the couch, she burst out in sobs.

6

'How long has she been with Mrs Ho?' Judge Dee asked the steward.

'More than twenty years, Your Honour. She belonged to Mrs Ho's own family, and three years ago followed her here, after Mr Ho had married her. She is not too bright, but a good woman. The mistress was very fond of her.'

THE DESIGN OF THE INCENSE-CLOCK

'Calm yourself!' the judge addressed the maid. 'This must be a terrible shock for you, but if you answer my questions promptly, we'll be able to have the body properly placed in a coffin very soon. Tell me, are you familiar with this incense-clock?'

She wiped her face with her sleeve and replied listlessly, 'Of course I am, sir. It burns exactly five hours, each spiral taking one hour. Just before I left, the mistress complained of the musty air here, and I lit the incense.'

7

'What time was that?'

'It was getting on for two, sir.'

'That was the last time you saw your mistress alive, wasn't it?'

'Yes, sir. When Mr Hwa was talking with the master in the reception room, over in the house, I took my mistress here. Soon after the master came in, to see that she was comfortably established for her siesta. She told me to pour two cups of tea, adding that she wouldn't need me again until five o'clock, and that I'd better take a nap also. She was always so considerate! I went back to the house and told the steward to lay out in the main bedroom the master's new grey dress, for the conference in the tribunal. Then the master came too. After the steward had helped him to change, the master told me to fetch Mr Hwa. They left the house together.'

'Where was Mr Hwa?'

'I found him in the garden, sir, admiring the flowers.'

'That's right,' the steward remarked. 'After the conversation in the reception room I just told Your Honour about, the master asked Mr Hwa to excuse him while he said good-bye to Mrs Ho in the pavilion and changed. It seems that Mr Hwa, left alone in the reception room, got bored and went outside to have a look at the garden.'

'I see. Now who discovered the body first, you or this maid?'

'I did, sir,' the maid replied. 'I came here a little before five o'clock, and I . . . I saw her hanging there, from that beam. I rushed out and called the steward.'

'I stood on the chair at once,' the steward said, 'and cut the cord while the maid put her arms round her. I prised the cord loose, and then we carried her to the couch. Breathing and heart-beat had stopped. We tried to revive her with vigorous massage, but it was too late. I hurried to the tribunal to report to the master. If I had discovered her earlier . . .'

'You did what you could, steward. Let me see now. You told me that during the noon meal Mrs Ho was in high spirits, until the arrival of Mr Hwa, right?'

'Yes, sir. When Mrs Ho heard me announce Mr Hwa's arrival to the master, she turned pale and quickly withdrew to the side room. I saw that she . . .'

8

'You must be mistaken!' the maid interrupted crossly. 'I accompanied her when she went from the side room to the pavilion, and I didn't notice that she was upset!'

The steward was about to make an angry retort, but Judge Dee held up his hand and said curtly to him: 'Go to the gatehouse, and ask the gatekeeper what persons he admitted to the house after your master and Mr Hwa had left—why they came and how long they stayed. Hurry up!'

When the steward had scurried away, Judge Dee sat down at the table. Slowly caressing his sidewhiskers, he silently studied the woman who was standing in front of him with downcast eyes. Then he spoke: 'Your mistress is dead. It is your duty to tell us everything that might help to find the person who either directly or indirectly caused her death. Speak up, why did the arrival of Mr Hwa distress her?'

The maid darted a frightened look at him. She replied diffidently: 'I really don't know, sir! I only know that in the past two weeks she went twice to visit Mr Hwa, without Mr Ho knowing it. I wanted to go with her, but Mr Fung said . . .' She suddenly broke off. Growing red in the face, she angrily bit her lip.

'Who is Mr Fung?' Judge Dee asked sharply.

She deliberated for a while, her forehead creased in a deep frown. Then she shrugged her shoulders and answered, 'Well, it's bound to come out, and they didn't do anything wrong anyway! Mr Fung is a painter, sir, very poor and in bad health. He used to live in a small hovel near our house. Six years ago the father of my mistress, the retired prefect, engaged Mr Fung to teach my mistress to paint flowers. She was only twenty-two then, and he was such a handsome young man. . . . No wonder they fell in love with each other. Mr Fung is such a nice man, Your Honour, and his father was a famous scholar. But he lost all his money, and . . .'

'Never mind that! Were they lovers?'

The maid shook her head emphatically and replied quickly, 'Never, sir! Mr Fung had planned to ask somebody to approach the old prefect regarding a marriage. It's true that he was desperately poor, but since he belonged to such an illustrious family

9

there was hope that the prefect would consent. Just at that time, however, Mr Fung's cough grew worse. He consulted a physician and was told that he was suffering from an incurable lung disease, and would die young. . . . Mr Fung told her that they could never marry, it had all been but a brief dream of spring. He would go away to a distant place. But she implored him to stay; she said they could still remain friends, and that she wanted to be near him should the disease grow worse. . . .'

'Did they continue to meet after Mr Ho had married your mistress?'

'Yes, sir. Here in the pavilion. But only during the daytime, and I was always there. I swear that he never even touched her hand, sir!'

'Did Mr Ho know about those visits?'

'No, of course not! We would wait till the master was away for the day, then I would take a note from my mistress to Mr Fung, and he would slip inside by the garden door and have a cup of tea with her here in the pavilion. I know these occasional visits were the only thing that kept Mr Fung going, all through the last three years, after my mistress married. And she enjoyed their talks so much! And I was there, always. . . .'

'You connived at clandestine meetings,' the judge said harshly. 'And probably at murder. For your mistress did not commit suicide, she was killed. At half past four, to be precise.'

'But how could Mr Fung have anything to do with that, Your Honour?' the maid wailed.

'That's what I am going to find out,' the judge said grimly. He turned to the coroner. 'Let's go to the gatehouse!'

The headman and his two constables were sitting on the stone bench in the front courtyard. Springing to attention, the headman saluted and asked, 'Shall I tell my men to fetch a temporary coffin, sir?'

'No, not yet,' the judge said gruffly, and walked on.

In the doorkeeper's lodge the small steward was cursing a wizened old man in a long blue gown. Two grinning palankeen-bearers were looking inside through the window, and listening with relish.

'This man maintains that nobody came to the house, Your Honour,' the steward said angrily. 'But the old fool confessed that he took a nap between three and four. Disgraceful!'

Disregarding this remark, the judge asked abruptly: 'Do you know a painter called Fung?'

The astonished steward shook his head, but the elder coolie called out, 'I know Mr Fung, Excellency! He often buys a bowl of noodles at my father's stall round the corner. He rents an attic over the grocery, behind this house. I saw him standing about near our garden gate an hour or so ago.'

Judge Dee turned to the coroner and said: 'Let this coolie take you to Mr Fung's place, and bring him here. On no account let Mr Fung know about Mrs Ho's demise!' Then he ordered the steward: 'Lead me to the reception room. I shall see Mr Fung there.'

The reception room proved to be rather small, but the simple furniture was of good quality. The steward offered the judge a comfortable armchair at the centre table, and poured him a cup of tea. Then he discreetly withdrew.

Slowly sipping the tea, Judge Dee reflected with satisfaction that the murderer had now been traced. He hoped the coroner would find the painter in, so that he could interrogate him at once.

Sooner than he had expected the coroner entered with a tall, thin man of about thirty, clad in a threadbare but clean blue robe, fastened with a black cotton sash. He had a rather distinguished face, with a short black moustache. A few locks of hair came out from under the faded black cap he was wearing. The judge took in his large, rather too brilliant eyes, and the red spots on the hollow cheeks. He motioned him to take the chair on the other side of the table. The coroner poured a cup of tea for the guest, then remained standing behind his chair.

'I have heard about your work, Mr Fung,' the judge began affably. 'I have been looking forward to making your acquaintance.'

The painter straightened his robe with a long, sensitive hand. Then he spoke in a cultured voice: 'I feel most flattered by your interest, sir. Yet I find it hard to believe that Your Honour ur-

11

gently summoned me here to Mr Ho's house just to engage in a leisurely talk about artistic matters.'

'Not in the first place, no. An accident has occurred in the garden here, Mr Fung, and I am looking for witnesses.'

Fung sat up in his chair. He asked worriedly: 'An accident? Not involving Mrs Ho, I trust?'

'It did indeed involve her, Mr Fung. It occurred between four and five, in the pavilion. And you came to see her at that time.'

'What has happened to her?' the painter burst out.

'You ought to know the answer to that yourself!' Judge Dee said coldly. 'For it was you who murdered her!'

'She is dead!' Fung exclaimed. He buried his face in his hands. His narrow shoulders were shaking. When after a long time he looked up, he had himself under control again. He asked in a measured voice: 'Would you kindly inform me, sir, why I should have murdered the woman I loved more than anything else in the world?'

'Your motive was fear of exposure. After her marriage you continued to force your attentions on her. She grew tired of it and told you that if you didn't stop seeing her she would inform her husband. Today you two had a violent quarrel, and you killed her.'

The painter nodded slowly. 'Yes,' he said resignedly, 'that would be a plausible explanation, I suppose. And I was indeed at the garden gate at the time you mentioned.'

'Did she know you were coming?'

'Yes. This morning a street urchin brought me a note from her. It said that she had to see me, on an urgent matter. If I would come at about half past four to the garden gate, and knock four times as usual, the maid would let me in.'

'What happened after you had gone inside?'

'I didn't go inside. I knocked several times, but the gate remained closed. I walked up and down there for a while, and having made one more fruitless attempt, I went back home.'

'Show me her note!'

'I can't, for I destroyed it. As she told me to.'

'So you deny having killed her?'

Fung shrugged his shoulders. 'If you are certain that you won't be able to discover the real criminal, sir, I am perfectly willing to say I killed her, just to help you dispose of the case. I'll be dead before long anyway, and whether I die in bed or on the scaffold is all the same to me. Her death has robbed me of my last reason for prolonging this miserable life. For my other love, my art, has already left me long ago—this lingering illness seems to destroy the creative impulse. If, on the other hand, you think it possible to trace the cruel fiend who murdered this innocent woman, then there's no earthly reason why I should confuse the issue by confessing to a crime I did not commit.'

Judge Dee gave him a long look, pensively tugging at his moustache. 'Was Mrs Ho in the habit of sending you her messages through a street urchin?'

'No, sir. Her maid always brought the notes, and this was the first time it contained the request to burn it. But it was hers all right, I am familiar with her style and her handwriting.' A violent attack of coughing interrupted him. He wiped his mouth with a paper handkerchief, looked for a moment indifferently at the flecks of blood, then resumed, 'I can't imagine what urgent matter she wanted to discuss. And who would have wanted her dead? I have known her and her family for more than ten years, and I can assure you that they didn't have an enemy in the world!' Fingering his moustache, he added, 'Her marriage was a reasonably happy one. Ho is a bit dull, but he is genuinely fond of her, always kind and considerate. Never spoke of taking a concubine, although she hadn't born him a child. And she liked and respected him.'

'Which did not prevent her from continuing to meet you behind his back!' the judge remarked dryly. 'Most reprehensible behaviour for a married woman. Not to mention you!'

The painter gave him a haughty look.

'You wouldn't understand,' he said coldly. 'You are caught in a net of empty rules and meaningless conventions. There was nothing reprehensible about our friendship, I tell you. The only reason we kept our meetings secret was because Ho is a rather old-fashioned man who would interpret our relations as wrongly as you seem to do. We didn't want to hurt him.'

'Most considerate of you! Since you knew Mrs Ho so

well, you can doubtless tell me why she was often depressed of late?'

'Oh yes. The fact is that her father, the old prefect, didn't manage his finances too well, and got deeply in debt with that wealthy shipowner Hwa Min. Since a month or so that heartless usurer has been pressing the old man to transfer his land to him, in lieu of payment, but the prefect wants to keep it. It has belonged to his family for heaven knows how many generations, and moreover he feels responsible for the welfare of the tenant farmers. Hwa would squeeze the last copper out of those poor devils! The old man begged Hwa to wait till after the harvest, then he'd be able to pay Hwa at least the atrocious interest due. But Hwa insists on foreclosing, so as to get that land into his hands cheaply. Mrs Ho kept worrying about this affair, she made me take her to see Hwa twice. She did her best to persuade him to drop his demand for immediate payment, but the dirty rat said he would consider that only if she let him sleep with her!'

'Did Mr Ho know about those visits?'

'He didn't. We knew how much it would distress him to hear that his father-in-law was in financial trouble while he could do nothing to help him. Mr Ho has no private means, you know. He has to depend on his modest pension for his living.'

'You two were indeed very kind towards Mr Ho!'

'He deserved it; he is a decent fellow. The only thing he couldn't give his wife was intellectual companionship, and that she found in me.'

'I never saw such a complete lack of the most elementary morality!' the judge exclaimed disgustedly. He got up and ordered the coroner: 'Hand this man over to the headman, to be locked up in jail as a murder suspect. Thereafter you and the two constables convey Mrs Ho's dead body to the tribunal, and conduct a thorough autopsy. Report to me as soon as you are through. You'll find me in my private office.'

He left, angrily shaking his long sleeves.

Mr Ho and the two shipowners were waiting in Judge Dee's private office, attended upon by a clerk. They wanted to rise when

14

the judge came in, but he motioned them to remain seated. He took the armchair behind his desk, and told the clerk to refill the teacups.

'Has everything been settled, Your Honour?' Mr Ho asked in a dull voice.

Judge Dee emptied his cup, then rested his forearms on the desk and replied slowly, 'Not quite, Mr Ho. I have bad news for you. I found that your wife did not commit suicide. She was murdered.'

Mr Ho uttered a suppressed cry. Mr Hwa and Mr Yee exchanged an astonished look. Then Ho blurted out, 'Murdered? Who did it? And why, in the name of heaven?'

'The evidence points to a painter, by the name of Fung.'

'Fung? A painter? Never heard of him!'

'I warned you the news was bad, Mr Ho. Very bad. Before you married your wife, she had friendly relations with this painter. After the marriage the two kept on seeing each other secretly, in the garden pavilion. It is possible that she grew tired of him and wanted to end the liaison. Knowing that you would be here all afternoon, she may have sent Fung a note asking him to come and see her. And if she then told him that they were through, he may well have killed her.'

Ho sat there staring straight ahead, his thin lips compressed. Yee and Hwa looked embarrassed; they made to get up and leave the judge and Ho alone. But Judge Dee gave them a peremptory sign to stay where they were. At last Mr Ho looked up and asked: 'How did the villain kill her?'

'She was knocked unconscious by a blow on her temple, then strung up by the neck to a beam and strangled. The murderer upset a teapot, and the tea from it extinguished the fire of the incense-clock, establishing half past four or thereabouts as the time he committed his evil deed. I may add that a witness saw the painter Fung loitering about at that time near your garden gate.'

There was a knock on the door. The coroner came in and handed a document to the judge. Quickly glancing through the autopsy report, he saw that the cause of death had indeed been slow strangulation. Beyond the bruise on the temple the body

15

bore no other marks of violence. She had been in the third month of pregnancy.

Judge Dee folded the paper up slowly and put it into his sleeve. Then he said to the coroner, 'Tell the headman to set free the man he put in jail. That person will have to wait a while in the guard-room, though. I may want to question him again later.'

When the coroner had left, Mr Ho got up. He said in a hoarse voice, 'If Your Honour will allow me, I'll now take my leave. I must . . .'

'Not yet, Mr Ho,' the judge interrupted. 'I want to ask you a question first. Here in front of Mr Hwa and Mr Yee.'

Ho sat down again with a perplexed look.

'You left your wife in the pavilion at about two o'clock, Mr Ho,' Judge Dee resumed. 'And you were here in this office till five, when your steward came to report your wife's demise. For all we know she could have died any time between two and five. Yet when I told you about her suicide you said: "Only a few hours after I had left her . . ." as Mr Hwa and Mr Yee here will attest. How did you know that she died at about half past four?'

Ho made no answer. He stared at the judge with wide, un-believing eyes. Judge Dee went on, his voice suddenly harsh:

'I'll tell you! Because when you had killed your wife at two o'clock, directly after the maid had left the pavilion, you inten-tionally spilled the tea over the incense-clock. You apparently consider me a fairly competent investigator—thank you. You knew that if I visited the scene I would discover that your wife had been murdered, and deduct from the incense-clock that the deed had been done at about half past four. You also assumed that I would find out sooner or later that Fung had been at the garden gate at about that time—lured there by the faked note you had sent him. It was a clever scheme, Ho, worthy of an expert in juridical affairs. But the carefully faked time element proved to be your undoing. You kept telling yourself: I can never be suspected, because the time of the murder is clearly established at half past four. And so you inadvertently made that slip about "a few hours after I had left her". At that time the remark didn't strike me as odd. But as soon as I realized that if Fung was not the murderer it had to be you, I remembered those

16

words, and that provided the final proof of your guilt. The Five Auspicious Clouds didn't prove very auspicious for you, Mr Ho!'

Ho righted himself. He asked coldly: 'Why should I want to murder my wife?'

'I'll tell you. You had found out about her secret meetings with Fung, and when she told you she was pregnant you decided to destroy them both, with one and the same blow. You assumed that Fung was the father of the unborn child and . . .'

'He was not!' Ho suddenly shrieked. 'Do you think that miserable wretch could ever have . . . No, it was *my* child, do you hear? The only thing those two were capable of was sickening, sentimental drivel! And all the kind words I overheard them saying about me! . . . the decent but rather dull husband, who was entitled to her body, mind you, but who could of course never understand her sublime mind. I could, I could have . . .' He began to stutter in impotent rage. Then he took hold of himself and went on in a calmer voice, 'I didn't want the child of a woman with the mind of a streetwalker, a woman who . . .'

'That'll do!' Judge Dee said curtly. He clapped his hands. When the headman came in he said, 'Put this murderer into chains and lock him up. I shall hear his full confession tomorrow, in the tribunal.'

After the headman had led Ho away, the judge continued to Yee Pen, 'The clerk shall see you out, Mr Yee.' Turning to the other shipowner, he added, 'As for you, Mr Hwa, you'll stay a few moments: I want a word with you in private.'

When the two men were alone, Hwa said unctuously, 'Your Honour solved this crime in a remarkably short time! To think that Ho . . .' He sadly shook his head.

Judge Dee gave him a sour look. 'I was not too happy with Fung as a suspect,' he remarked dryly. 'The evidence against him fitted too neatly together, while the manner of the murder was totally inconsistent with his personality. I made my palankeen bearers bring me back here by a roundabout way, so as to have a little time to think. I reasoned that since the evidence could only have been rigged by an insider, it had to be Ho—the well-known motive of the deceived husband who wants to take vengeance on his adulterous wife and her lover, both at the same

17

time. But why did Ho wait so long? He knew everything about Mrs Ho sending messages to Fung; he must have discovered all about their secret meetings long ago. When I saw from the autopsy report that Mrs Ho had been pregnant, I took it that it was this news that had made her husband resolve to act. And I was right, though we now know that his emotional reaction was different from what I had assumed.' Fixing the shipowner with his sombre eyes, he continued, 'The false evidence could have been fabricated only by an insider, familiar with the incense-clock and with Mrs Ho's handwriting. That saved you from being accused of this murder, Mr Hwa!'

'Me, sir?' Hwa exclaimed aghast.

'Of course. I knew about Mrs Ho's visits to you, and about her refusing your disgusting proposal. Her husband was ignorant of this, but Fung knew. That gave you a motive for wanting both her and Fung out of the way. And you also had the opportunity, for you were in the garden towards two o'clock, while Mrs Ho was alone in the pavilion. You are innocent of murder, Mr Hwa, but guilty of attempted seduction of a married woman, as will be attested by Mr Fung, and of attempted bribery, as will be attested by Ho's steward, who overheard your conversation while you were visiting Ho at noon. Tomorrow I shall charge you with these two offences in the tribunal, and sentence you to a term in prison. That will be the end of your career here in Peng-lai, Mr Hwa.'

Hwa jumped up and was about to kneel down and beg for mercy, but Judge Dee went on quickly:

'I shan't have you up on those two charges, provided you agree to pay two fines. First, you shall this very night write a formal letter to Mrs Ho's father, duly signed and sealed, informing him that he can pay back the money you lent him any time that suits him, and that you renounce all interest on that loan. Second, you shall commission Mr Fung to paint a picture of every single boat in your shipyard, paying him one silver piece for each drawing.' He cut short Hwa's protestations of gratitude by raising his hand. 'This fine gets you only a reprieve, of course. As soon as I hear that you are again importuning decent women, you shall be indicted on the charges mentioned. Go now to the guardroom. You'll find Mr Fung there, and you'll place your order with him.

Pay him then and there five silver pieces as an advance. Good-bye!'

When the frightened shipowner had hurriedly taken his leave, the judge got up from his chair and went to stand in front of the open window. He enjoyed the subtle fragrance of the magnolia blossoms for a while, then he muttered to himself: 'Disapproval of a man's moral standards is no reason for one to allow him to die in misery!'

He turned round abruptly and left for the chancery.

THE RED TAPE MURDER

The coastal district of Peng-lai, where Judge Dee began his career as a magistrate, was jointly administered by the judge, in his capacity as the highest local civil servant, and by the commander of the Imperial Army unit stationed there. The extent of their respective jurisdiction was fairly clearly laid down; civilian and military affairs seldom overlapped. When Judge Dee had been serving in Peng-lai for just over a month, however, he was drawn unexpectedly into a purely military affair. My novel The Chinese Gold Murders *mentions the large fort, three miles downstream from the city of Peng-lai, which was built at the mouth of the river to prevent the land-ings of the Korean navy. It was within the walls of this formidable stronghold that the military murder described in this story took place: a proper men's affair, with no ladies present—but featuring yards and yards of red tape!*

Judge Dee looked up from the file he was leafing through and peevishly addressed the two men on the other side of his desk:

'Can't you two sit still? Stop fidgeting, will you?'

As the judge turned to his file again his two hefty lieutenants, Ma Joong and Chiao Tai, made a determined effort to keep still on their stools. Soon, however, Ma Joong stealthily gave Chiao Tai an encouraging nod. The latter placed his large hands on his knees and opened his mouth to speak. But just then the judge pushed the file away and exclaimed disgustedly:

'This is most annoying; document P-404 is indeed missing! For a moment I thought that Sergeant Hoong must have inserted it in the wrong folder, since he was in rather a hurry yesterday before he left for the prefecture. But P-404 simply isn't there!'

'Couldn't it be in the second file, Magistrate?' Ma Joong asked. 'That folder is also marked with the letter P.'

'Nonsense!' Judge Dee snapped. 'Haven't I explained to you that in the archives of the fort they have two files marked P, P for Personnel and P for Purchases? In the latter file, paper P-405 concerning a purchase of leather belts is clearly marked: "Refer back to P-404". That proves beyond doubt that P-404 belongs to Purchases, and not to Personnel.'

'This red tape business is a bit beyond me, sir! Besides, those two P files contain only information-copies sent on to us by the fort. Now as regards the fort, sir, we . . .'

'This is *not* mere red tape,' Judge Dee interrupted him sourly. 'It concerns the close observation of an established office routine, without which the entire administrative machinery of our Empire would get clogged.' Noticing the unhappy look on the deeply-tanned faces of his two lieutenants, the judge smiled despite himself and went on in a more friendly tone, 'In the four weeks that you two have been working for me here in Peng-lai, you have proved yourselves able to deal efficiently with the rough work. But the task of an officer of the tribunal comprises more than the arrest of dangerous criminals. He must keep abreast of the office routine, harbour a feeling for its finer points, and realize the importance of adhering to those finer points—a practice sometimes referred to by ignorant outsiders as red-tapery. Now this missing paper P-404 may well be quite unimportant in itself. But the fact that it is missing makes it of supreme importance.'

Folding his arms in his wide sleeves, he continued, 'Ma Joong correctly observed that these two files marked P contain nothing but copies, namely of the correspondence of the fort with the Board of Military Affairs in the capital. Those papers deal with purely military matters that don't concern us directly. What does concern us, however, is that every single file in this tribunal, whether important or unimportant, must be kept in good order, and must above all be complete!' Raising his forefinger for emphasis, the judge went on, 'Remember now, once and for all: you must be able to rely unreservedly on your files, and you can do so only when you are absolutely sure they are complete. An incomplete file has no place in a well-run office. An incomplete file is worthless!'

'Let's heave that P-file out of the window, then!' Ma Joong exclaimed. Then he added quickly: 'Beg your pardon, sir, but the fact is that Brother Chiao and I are rather upset. This morning we heard that our best friend here, Colonel Meng Kwo-tai, was

21

found guilty last night of having murdered Colonel Soo, the Vice-Commander of the fort.'

Judge Dee straightened himself. 'So you two know Meng, eh? I heard about that murder the day before yesterday. Since I was very busy writing the report Hoong took to the capital, I didn't make inquiries. Anyway it's a military case that exclusively concerns the commander of the fort. How did you two come to know Colonel Meng?'

'Well,' Ma Joong replied, 'a couple of weeks ago we ran into him in a wine-house when he was spending his evening off here in town. The fellow is a fine athlete, excellent boxer, and the fort's champion archer. We became fast friends, and he made it a practice to spend all his free evenings with us. And now they say he shot the Vice-Commander! Of all the silly nonsense . . .'

'Don't worry,' Chiao Tai comforted his friend. 'Our magistrate'll straighten it all out!'

'It was like this, sir,' Ma Joong began eagerly. 'Day before yesterday the Vice-Commander . . .'

Judge Dee stopped him by raising his hand.

'In the first place,' he said dryly, 'I can't meddle with the affairs of the fort. Second, even if I could, I wouldn't be interested in hearsay of the murder. However, since you know the accused, you may as well tell me something more about him, for my orientation.'

'Colonel Meng is an upright, straightforward fellow!' Ma Joong burst out. 'We have boxed with him, got drunk with him and gone wenching with him. Let me tell you, Magistrate, that that's the way to get to know a man inside out! Now Vice-Commander Soo was a martinet and a bully, and Meng got his share of his foul mouth. I can imagine that some day Meng might fly into a rage and strike Soo down. But Meng would give himself up at once, and face the consequences. To shoot a man in his sleep, then deny he did it . . . No, sir, Meng wouldn't do that. Never!'

'Do you happen to know how Commander Fang feels about it?' the judge asked. 'He presided at the court martial, I presume.'

'He did,' Chiao Tai replied. 'And he confirmed the verdict of premeditated murder. Fang is a haughty, taciturn fellow. But rumour has it that he isn't too happy about the verdict—despite the fact that all the evidence points straight to Meng. Goes to show how popular the man is, even with his commanding officer!'

'When did you two last see Meng?' Judge Dee asked.

'The very night before Soo was murdered,' Ma Joong said. 'We had our supper together in the crab restaurant on the quay. Later that night two Korean merchants joined us, and the five of us had a real good drinking bout. It was long past midnight when Brother Chiao dropped Meng at the military barge that was to take him back to the fort.'

Judge Dee sat back in his chair and slowly tugged at his long sidewhiskers. Ma Joong quickly rose and poured him a cup of tea. The judge took a few sips, then he set his cup down and said briskly:

'I haven't yet returned Commander Fang's courtesy call. It's still early in the morning; if we leave now we'll be at the fort well before the noon rice. Tell the headman to have my official palankeen ready in the courtyard to carry us to the quay. In the meantime I'll change into ceremonial dress.' He got up from his chair. Seeing the satisfied looks of his two lieutenants, he added, 'I must warn you that I can't force my assistance on the Commander. If he doesn't ask for my advice, then that's the end of it. In any case I'll take the opportunity to ask him for an extra copy of that missing document.'

The sturdy rowers drove the heavy military barge to the north of the river in less than an hour. On the low bank to the left rose the forbidding walls of the fortress; ahead was the muddy water of the estuary, broadening out into the wide expanse of sunlit sea beyond.

Ma Joong and Chiao Tai jumped onto the quay under the towering front gate. When the captain of the guard discovered Judge Dee's identity, he at once took him across the paved courtyard to the main building. Ma Joong and Chiao Tai stayed behind in the gatehouse, for the judge had instructed them to pick up any gossip about the sensational murder.

Before stepping inside, Judge Dee cast an admiring glance at the thick, solid walls. The fort had been built only a few years before, when Korea had revolted against the T'ang Empire, and her fleet was preparing to invade China's north-east coast. The revolt had been crushed in two difficult campaigns by a Chinese expeditionary force, but the Koreans were still smarting from their defeat, and the possibility of a surprise attack had to be reckoned with. The river-mouth, and the fort guarding it, had been declared an emergency zone, and although it was located inside Peng-lai, Judge Dee had no authority in this particular area.

Commander Fang came to meet him at the bottom of the stairs, and took him up to his private office. He made the judge sit down by his side on the large couch against the back wall.

Fang was just as formal and sparing of words as when he had come to call on Judge Dee in the tribunal of Peng-lai. He sat stiffly erect, encased in his heavy coat of mail with the iron breast- and shoulder-pieces. Looking morosely at the judge from under his grey, tufted eyebrows, he brought out haltingly a few words of thanks for the visit.

Judge Dee made the usual polite inquiries. The Commander replied gruffly that he still thought his present post unsuitable for an old combat soldier. He didn't think the Koreans would start making trouble again; it would take them years to recoup their losses. And in the meantime he, Fang, had to keep order among more than a thousand officers and men cooped up idle in the fort.

The judge expressed his sympathy, then added, 'I hear that a murder occurred here recently. The criminal has been found and convicted, but I am eager to hear more about the case. As you know, Peng-lai is my first post, and I would welcome an opportunity to enlarge my experience.'

The Commander gave him a sharp look. He fingered his short grey moustache for a moment, then he got up abruptly and said curtly:

'Come along, I'll show you where and how it happened.'

While passing the two orderlies who stood stiffly at attention by the door, he barked at them:

'Get me Mao and Shih Lang!'

The Commander led the way across the inner courtyard to a large, two-storeyed building. As they ascended the broad staircase, he muttered, 'Case worries me, to tell you the truth!' At the head of the stairs four soldiers were sitting on a bench. They sprang to attention. The Commander guided Judge Dee down the long, empty corridor to the left. It ended at a heavy door; over its lock was pasted a strip of paper bearing the Commander's seal. Fang tore it off, kicked the door open and said:

'This was Vice-Commander Soo's room. He was murdered on the couch over there.'

Before crossing the threshold, the judge quickly surveyed the spacious, bare room. On his right was an open window arch, about five foot high and seven foot broad. In the recess below it lay a quiver of lacquered leather, containing a dozen or so iron-tipped arrows with red shafts. Four more had spilled out of the quiver. The room had no other window or door. On the left stood a simple desk of scarred, unpainted wood, on which lay an iron helmet and another arrow. Against the back wall stood a large bamboo couch. The reed mat covering it was stained with ominous, brownish spots. The floor consisted of roughly hewn boards; there was no rug or floor mat.

After they had gone inside, the Commander said:

'Soo used to come up here every afternoon about one o'clock, after drill, to take a brief nap till two, when he would go down to the officers' mess for the noon rice. Day before yesterday Colonel Shih Lang, who assists Soo with the administrative paperwork, comes up here a little before two. Planned to go down to the mess together with Soo, and have a few words with him in private about a breach of discipline concerning a Lieutenant Kao. Shih Lang knocks. No answer, so he thinks maybe Soo has gone down already. He steps inside to make sure, and sees Soo lying on that couch over there. He has his mail jacket on, but an arrow is sticking out of his unprotected stomach, and his leather trousers are covered with blood. Soo's hands are round the arrow's shaft —apparently he made a vain attempt to pull it out. But the tip is barbed, you see. Soo's as dead as a doornail.'

The Commander cleared his throat, then went on, 'You see what happened, don't you? Soo comes in here, throws his quiver in that recess, his helmet on that desk, then lies down on the couch, doesn't bother to take off his mail jacket or his boots. When he has dozed off . . .'

Two men entered and saluted smartly. The Commander motioned the tall man in the brown-leather uniform to step forward and grunted:

'This is Colonel Shih Lang, who discovered the body.'

Judge Dee took in Shih Lang's heavy, deeply lined face, his broad shoulders and long ape-like arms. He wore a short moustache and ring-beard. His lacklustre eyes stared sullenly at the judge.

Indicating the squat man who wore the short mail jacket, pointed helmet and baggy trousers of the mounted military police, the Commander added: 'And this is Colonel Mao, who was in charge of the investigation. Used to be my chief of military intelligence during the Korea campaign. Able fellow.'

The judge made a perfunctory bow. He thought Mao's thin, cynical face had a rather foxy expression.

'I was just explaining the facts to the magistrate here,' Commander Fang told the two men. 'Thought we might as well have his opinion.'

The two newcomers remained silent. Then Colonel Shih Lang broke the awkward pause. He said in a deep, rather hoarse voice, 'I hope the magistrate'll find another solution. In my opinion Meng is not a murderer. Let alone one who foully shoots a man in his sleep.'

'Opinions don't matter,' the military police chief remarked dryly. 'We only deal with facts. And on that basis we reached a unanimous verdict of guilty.'

The Commander hitched up his sword belt. He took Judge Dee to the large window arch and pointed at the three-storeyed building opposite. 'The ground floor and the second floor across the yard there have no windows—our storerooms are located there. But do you see that big window up on the top floor? That's the armoury.'

Judge Dee saw that the window indicated was of the same type and size as the one he was standing at. The Commander turned round and resumed, 'Now then, Soo was lying with his

26

towards this window. Experiments with a[...] ed that the arrow must have been shot fro[...] [...] the armoury there. And at that time there wa[...] : Colonel Meng.'

[...] a distance,' Judge Dee remarked. 'About sixty feet, I[...] say.'

'Colonel Meng is our champion archer,' Mao observed.

'Not a job for a beginner,' Commander Fang admitted, 'but quite feasable for an expert with a crossbow.'

The judge nodded. After a few moments' thought he asked, 'The arrow couldn't have been shot from within this room, I suppose?'

'No,' the Commander replied curtly. 'Four soldiers stand guard day and night at the head of the stairs, at the other end of the corridor. They testified that after Soo had come up here and before Shih Lang's arrival, no one passed them.'

'Couldn't the murderer have scaled the wall, entered through the window and stabbed Soo with the arrow?' Judge Dee asked. 'I am just trying to cover all possibilities,' he added quickly as he saw the pitying looks of the others.

'The wall is perfectly smooth, no human could ever scale it,' Fang said. 'Not even Shih Lang here, and he is our expert in that art. Besides, there are always soldiers about in the yard below, so nobody could perform antics on the wall unnoticed.'

'I see,' Judge Dee said. He stroked his long black beard, then asked: 'Why should Colonel Meng want to kill the Vice-Commander?'

'Soo was an able officer, but short-tempered and a bit rough in the mouth. Four days ago he cursed Meng in front of the troops, because Meng had taken sides with Lieutenant Kao.'

'I was present,' Mao said. 'Meng kept himself under control, but his face was livid. He brooded over this insult, and . . .' He paused significantly.

'Meng had been bawled out by Soo before,' Shih Lang remarked. 'He was accustomed to it, didn't take it seriously.'

Judge Dee said to the Commander: 'You mentioned this breach of discipline by Lieutenant Kao before. What did he do?'

'Soo cursed Kao because his leather belt was cracked. Kao

...ed back and Soo was going to have him se....
....hed. Colonel Meng spoke up for Kao, and then Soo went
...g.'

'I was going to put in a word for Kao too,' Shih Lang said.
'.hat's why I came up here, directly after the morning drill. I
.hought that if I talked to Soo privately, I could make him drop
the case. And to think that fate ordained Kao as the main witness against Colonel Meng, his protector!'

'How was that?' the judge asked.

Commander Fang sighed. 'Everybody knew that Soo always
used to come up here for a nap after the morning drill. And
Colonel Meng was in the habit of going up to the armoury to
exercise with the heavy spear before going down to the mess hall.
Fellow is as strong as an ox, doesn't know the word fatigue. But
day before yesterday Meng tells his colleagues that he has a hangover, he's not going up to the armoury after drill. Yet Meng did
go! Look, do you see that smaller window up there, about twenty
feet to the left of the armoury window? Well, that belongs to a
room where leather goods are stored. Only the quartermaster goes
up there, and only once in a fortnight or so. But Kao gets it into
his head to look for a new leather belt there, because Soo had
reprimanded him so severely about his old one. The fastidious
beggar takes quite a time selecting a belt he likes. When he turns
to the door connecting the room with the armoury, he happens
to look out of the window. He sees Shih Lang enter Soo's room
here. Shih Lang suddenly halts in his tracks right in front of the
window arch, stoops, then starts waving his hands and rushes
out of the room, shouting. Kao opens the door of the armoury
to run down and find out what's wrong in the building opposite,
and nearly collides with Colonel Meng, who is standing there
fiddling with a crossbow. Both men rush down together and come
up here directly behind the soldiers of the guard, who have been
alarmed by Shih Lang. Then Shih Lang fetches me and Colonel
Mao. When we arrive here, we know at once where that arrow
came from, and I place Meng under arrest as the most likely
suspect.'

'What about Lieutenant Kao?' Judge Dee asked.

Mao silently took him to the window and pointed outside.

Judge Dee looked up and realized that though from the window of the storeroom one could cover the door of Soo's room and the space in front of the window arch, the part of the room beyond, where the couch stood, was out of range.

'How did Meng explain his presence in the armoury?' Dee asked the Commander. 'He said clearly that he wouldn't go up there that day, didn't he?'

Fang nodded unhappily. 'The idiot said that after he had gone up to his room to lie down, he found there a note from Soo, ordering him to meet him in the armoury at two. When asked to produce the note, he said he had thrown it away! We considered that story as strong proof of Meng's guilt.'

'It does indeed look bad for him,' Judge Dee agreed. 'Meng didn't know that Kao would go up to the leather room. If Kao hadn't surprised him, he would have sneaked back to his own room after the deed, and no one would have suspected him.' He stepped up to the desk and picked up the arrow lying next to the iron helmet. It was about four foot long, and much heavier than he expected. Its long, needle-sharp iron point, provided at the base with two wicked barbs, showed some brownish spots. 'I suppose this was the arrow that killed Soo?'

The Commander nodded. 'We had a messy job getting it out,' he remarked, 'because of the barbs.'

Judge Dee examined the arrow carefully. The shaft was lacquered red, with black feathers attached to the end. Just below the iron point, the shaft had been reinforced by red tape tightly wound around it.

'Nothing special about the arrow,' Mao said impatiently. 'Regular army issue.'

'I see that the red tape is torn,' Judge Dee remarked. 'There is a jagged tear, parallel with the shaft.'

The others made no comment. The judge's remarks didn't seem to strike them as very brilliant. He didn't think much of them himself, either. With a sigh he put the arrow back on the desk and said:

'I must admit there's a strong case against Colonel Meng. He had the motive, the opportunity, and the particular skill required to utilize the opportunity. I'll have to think this over. Before leaving the fort, though, I'd like to see Colonel Meng. Perhaps Lieutenant Kao could take me to him, then I'll have seen all persons concerned in this vexing affair.'

The Commander gave the judge a searching look. He seemed to hesitate, then he barked an order at Colonel Mao.

While Lieutenant Kao was conducting him to the prison at the rear of the fort, Judge Dee unobtrusively studied his companion. Kao was a good-looking youngster, very trim in his close-fitting mail coat and round helmet. The judge tried to make him talk about the murder, but got only very curt answers. The young man was either overawed or extremely nervous.

A giant of a man was pacing the cell, his hands behind his back. As he saw the two men arrive in front of the heavy iron bars, his face lit up and he said in a deep voice: 'Good to see you, Kao! Any news?'

'The magistrate is here, sir,' Kao said rather diffidently. 'He wants to ask you a few questions.'

Judge Dee told Kao that he could leave. Then he addressed the prisoner:

'Commander Fang told me that the court martial pronounced you guilty of premeditated murder. If there is anything you might adduce for a plea for clemency, I should be glad to help you formulate that plea. My two lieutenants Ma and Chiao spoke highly of you.'

'I didn't murder Soo, sir,' the giant said gruffly. 'But they found me guilty, so let them chop my head off. That's the army statute, and a man has to die sooner or later anyway. There's no occasion for any plea.'

'If you are innocent,' the judge resumed, 'it means that the murderer must have had a compelling reason for wanting both Soo and you out of the way. For it was he who sent you the faked note, to make you the scapegoat. So that narrows down the number of suspects. Can you think of anybody who had reason to hate both you and Vice-Commander Soo?'

'There were too many who hated Soo. He was a good administrator but a real martinet; he had the men flogged at the slightest provocation. As for me, well, I always thought I had only friends

30

here. If I offended someone, I did it unwittingly. So that doesn't help very much.'

Judge Dee silently agreed. He thought for a while, then resumed, 'Tell me exactly what you did after you came back to the fort, the night before the murder.'

'The morning, rather!' Meng said with a wry smile. 'It was long after midnight, you know! The boat trip back had sobered me up a bit, but I was still in a happy mood. The captain of the guard, a good fellow, helped me to get up to my room. I made a bit of a nuisance of myself, and wouldn't let him go, insisting on telling him in considerable detail about the good time we'd had, what nice fellows those two Koreans were, and about their splendid hospitality. Pak and Yee their names were—funny pronunciation those people have!' He scratched his unruly head, then went on, 'Yes, I remember that I let the captain go only after he had solemnly promised me that he would come along too, next week. I had told him that Pak and Yee had said they'd have even more money to spend then, and were determined to throw a real party for me and all my friends. I laid myself down on my bed fully dressed, feeling perfectly happy. But the next morning I didn't feel happy any more! I had the father and mother of all headaches. Somehow or other I managed to get through the morning drill, but I was glad when it was over and I could go up to my room for a nap. Then, just as I was going to throw myself on my bed, I saw that note. I . . .'

'Couldn't you see it was faked?' the judge interrupted.

'Heavens no, I am no student of calligraphy! Besides, it was just a few scrawled words. But Soo's seal was on it and that was genuine—I have seen it a hundred times on all sorts of papers. If the seal hadn't been on it, I would have thought it a prank by a colleague and would have checked with Soo. But that seal made it genuine all right, and I went up to the armoury at once. Soo didn't relish people questioning his orders! And that's how my trouble started!'

'You didn't look out of the window while you were in the armoury?'

'Why should I? I expected Soo to come up at any moment. I examined a couple of crossbows, that's all.'

'YOU ARE SHIELDING SOMEONE, MENG!' JUDGE DEE SAID ANGRILY

Judge Dee studied Meng's broad honest face. Suddenly he stepped up to the bars and shouted angrily:

'You are shielding someone, Meng!'

Meng grew red in the face. Gripping the bars with his large powerful hands, he growled, 'You are talking nonsense! You are a civilian. You'd better not meddle in military affairs!' He turned round and resumed his pacing.

'Have it your own way!' Judge Dee said coldly. He walked down the corridor. The turnkey opened the heavy iron door, and Lieutenant Kao took him to the Commander's office.

'Well, what do you think of Meng?' Fang asked.

'I admit he doesn't seem the type that murders a man in his sleep,' Judge Dee replied cautiously. 'But one never knows, of course. By the way, I have mislaid one of the copies of the official correspondence you always let me have so kindly. Could I have an extra copy, just to complete my file? The number of the document is P-404.'

The Commander looked astonished at this unexpected request, but he ordered his aide to get the paper from the archives.

The officer was back in a remarkably short time. He handed the Commander two sheets. Fang glanced them through, then gave them to the judge, saying, 'Here you are! Routine matter.'

Judge Dee saw that the first page contained a proposal that Kao and three other lieutenants be promoted to the rank of captain, together with a list of their names, ages and terms of service. It was stamped with the impression of Soo's seal. The second sheet contained only a few lines, wherein the Commander expressed the hope that the Board of Military Affairs would speedily approve his proposal. It bore the Commander's large seal, the date and the number P-404.

The Judge shook his head. 'There must be a mistake somewhere. The missing paper must have dealt with the purchase of material, for the next number, P-405, a request for the supply of leather belts, refers back to P-404. Therefore P in P-404 must stand for Purchases, and not for Personnel.'

'Holy heaven!' the Commander exclaimed, 'clerks do make mistakes sometimes, don't they? Well, thanks very much for your visit, Magistrate. Let me know when you have formulated your opinion on Soo's murder.'

While the judge was stepping outside he vaguely heard the Commander muttering something to his aide about 'silly red tape'.

The fiery midday sun had transformed the quay in front of the gate into a brick oven, but as soon as the barge was well out into the river, there was an agreeably cool breeze. The sergeant in charge of the barge had seen to it that the judge and his two lieutenants had comfortable seats on the platform at the stern, under an awning of green cloth.

As soon as the orderly, who had brought a large teapot, had disappeared into the hold, Ma Joong and Chiao Tai stormed the judge with questions.

'I really don't know what to think,' Judge Dee said slowly. 'All appearances are against Meng, but I have a vague suspicion that the fool is shielding someone. Did you two learn anything?'

Ma Joong and Chiao Tai shook their heads. The latter said:

'We had a long talk with the captain of the guard who was on duty when Meng came back to the fort after his spree with us. He likes Meng, the same as everybody else in the fort. He didn't mind practically carrying Meng up to his room, though that was by no means an easy job! And Meng kept on singing bawdy songs at the top of his voice. He must have wakened up all his colleagues, I fear! The captain said also that Meng was no special friend of Soo's, but that Meng respected him as an able officer, and didn't take Soo's frequent fits of anger too seriously.'

Judge Dee made no comment. He remained silent for a long time. Sipping his tea, he looked at the peaceful scenery floating by. Both banks were lined with green rice fields, dotted here and there with the yellow straw hats of the farmers working there. Suddenly he said, 'Colonel Shih Lang also thinks that Meng is innocent. But Colonel Mao, the chief of the military police, believes he's guilty.'

'Meng often told us about Shih Lang,' Ma Joong said. 'Meng is the champion archer, but Shih Lang is the champion at scaling walls! The fellow is one bunch of muscle! He is in charge of drilling the soldiers in this art. They strip down to their underclothes, and with bare feet they have to tackle an old wall. They learn to use their toes as if they were fingers. When they have found a hold, they work their toes into a crack below, then reach up to find a higher hold, repeating this till they get to the top of the wall. I'd like to try it myself some day ! As for that Colonel Mao, he is a nasty suspicious specimen; everybody is agreed on that !'

Judge Dee nodded. 'According to Meng, the two Koreans footed the bill for your party.'

'Oh,' Chiao Tai said a little self-consciously, 'that was because of a rather silly prank we played on them ! We were in a gay mood, and when Pak asked us about our professions, we said all three of us were highwaymen. The two fellows believed us; they said they might have work for us some day ! When we wanted to pay our share, it turned out that they had settled the whole bill already.'

'But we are going to meet them again next week when they are back from the capital,' Ma Joong said. 'Then we'll tell them the truth and the evening'll be on us. We hate sponging.'

'It may disappoint them,' Chiao Tai added, 'for Pak and Yee are expecting payment for three junks, and they are all set on having a big celebration then. Did you get the joke about those three boats by the way, Brother Ma? After Pak and Yee had told us about that business deal, both of them got such a fit of laughter that they nearly rolled under the table !'

'That's where I nearly landed too !' Ma Joong said ruefully.

The judge had not heard the last remark, he was deep in thought, slowly stroking his black beard. Suddenly he said to Ma Joong, 'Tell me more about that night ! Especially how Meng acted, and what he said.'

'Well,' Ma Joong replied, 'Brother Chiao and I go to the crab restaurant on the quay, it's nice and cool there. About dinner time we see the military barge come alongside, and Meng and another fellow get out. They say good-bye, then Meng comes strolling over to us on the terrace. He says he has had rather a heavy day at the fort, so we should have a really good meal. And that's what we did. Then . . .'

35

'Did Meng say anything about the Vice-Commander, or about Lieutenant Kao?' the judge interrupted him.

'Not a word!'

'Did he seem to have anything on his mind?'

'Nothing beyond a base desire for a nice girl!' Ma Joong replied with a grin. 'Accordingly we go to the flowerboats, and there Meng gets that particular problem off his mind. While we are having a few rounds on deck, those two fellows Pak and Yee arrive in a boat, drunk as can be. The madame can't get them interested in business, although she trots out the best she has. The only thing Pak and Yee want is more wine, and lots of it, and some congenial conversation. So the five of us start on a protracted drinking bout. I am not clear about the rest—Brother Chiao had better take up the story from there!'

'You disappeared from sight, let's leave it at that,' Chiao Tai said dryly. 'As for me, a couple of hours after midnight I helped Meng lower the two Koreans into a rowboat, to be taken back to the Korean quarter on the other side of the canal. Then Meng and I whistled for another boat, and had ourselves rowed to the quay. When I had put Meng on the military barge waiting there, I felt rather tired, and since the crab restaurant was so near, I asked them to put me up for the night. That's all.'

'I see,' said Judge Dee.

He drank a few more cups of tea, then he suddenly set his cup down and asked, 'Where are we here?'

Ma Joong looked at the river bank, then answered, 'About half-way to Peng-lai, I'd say.'

'Tell the sergeant to turn the barge round and take us back to the fort,' the judge ordered.

Ma Joong and Chiao Tai tried to elicit from the judge the reason for his sudden decision, but he only said he wanted to verify two or three points he had overlooked.

Back at the fort an aide-de-camp informed them that the Commander was in a secret staff conference, discussing important intelligence reports that had just come in.

'Don't disturb him!' Judge Dee told him. 'Get me Colonel Mao!'

He explained to the astonished chief of the military police that he wanted to have another look at the scene of the murder, and that he wished him to be present, as a witness.

Looking more cynical than ever, Colonel Mao led the three men upstairs. He broke the paper strip that had again been pasted over the lock on the door of Soo's room, and bade the judge enter.

Before stepping inside, Judge Dee told Ma Joong and Chiao Tai, 'I am looking for something small and sharp, say a splinter, or the head of a nail, and roughly within this area.' He indicated a square space of the floor, beginning at the door and ending halfway across the room in front of the window arch. Then he squatted down and began to examine the floorboards inch by inch. His two lieutenants joined him.

'If you are looking for a secret trap-door or any such hocus-pocus,' Colonel Mao said with heavy irony, 'I must disappoint you. This fort was built only a few years ago, you know!'

'Here—I have something!' Ma Joong exclaimed. He pointed at a spot in front of the window where the sharp edge of the head of a nail protruded from the floorboard.

'Excellent!' the judge exclaimed. He knelt down and scrutinized the nail-head. Then he got up and asked Mao, 'Would you mind prying loose that tiny fragment of red material sticking to the head of the nail? And at the same time have a good look at those small brownish spots on the wood there!'

Mao straightened himself, looking doubtfully at the small piece of red tape on his thumbnail.

'In due time,' Judge Dee said gravely, 'I shall ask you to testify that the fragment of red tape was indeed found stuck to the head of the nail. Also, that the brown spots found near it are most probably traces of human blood.' Ignoring the Colonel's excited questions, Judge Dee took the arrow from the desk and drove it into the floorboard next to the nail-head. 'This'll mark the exact spot!' He thought for a while, then asked, 'What happened to the dead man's personal effects, and to the contents of that desk drawer?'

Irritated by Judge Dee's peremptory tone, Mao replied coldly:

'Those objects were collected in two separate containers, which I asked the Commander to seal. They are locked away in my office. We of the military police are, of course, not as clever and experienced as officers of the tribunal, but we know our job, I trust!'

'All right, all right!' the judge said impatiently. 'Take us to your office!'

Colonel Mao asked Judge Dee to sit down at his large desk, which was littered with papers. Ma Joong and Chiao Tai remained standing by the door. Mao unlocked an iron chest and took from it two packages wrapped up in oiled paper. Placing one in front of the judge, he said:

'This is what we found in the leather folder the Vice-Commander carried on a string round his neck, under his mail jacket.'

Judge Dee broke the seal and arranged on the desk a folded identification card of the Imperial Army, a receipted bill for the purchase of a house dated seven years before, and a small square brocade carrying-case for a personal seal. He opened the latter, and seemed pleased when it proved to be empty. 'I presume,' he said to Mao, 'that the seal itself was found in the drawer of the dead man's desk?'

'It was. It's in the second package, together with the papers we found in the drawer. I thought it rather careless of Soo to let his personal seal lie about in that unlocked drawer. As a rule people always carry their seal on their person.'

'They do indeed,' Judge Dee said. He rose and added, 'I don't need to inspect the other package. Let's go and see whether the Commander is through with his conference.'

The two sentries who stood guard outside the door of the council room informed them that the conference had just ended and that tea would soon be brought in. Judge Dee brushed past them without more ado.

Commander Fang was seated at the main table in the centre of the room. At the side table on his left sat Colonel Shih Lang, and another officer the judge did not know. At the table on the other side two senior officers were sitting, and Lieutenant Kao was sorting out a pile of papers on a small table apart; evidently he had been taking notes of the proceedings. All rose from their chairs when they saw the judge enter.

'Please excuse this intrusion,' Judge Dee said calmly as he advanced to the Commander's table. 'I came to report my findings regarding the murder of Vice-Commander Soo. Am I right in assuming that the officers assembled here form the quorum for a court martial?'

'If you include Colonel Mao over there, they do,' Fang replied slowly.

'Excellent! Please let Colonel Meng be brought in, so that we can have a regular session of the court martial.'

The Commander gave an order to his aide, then he pulled a chair up to his table and invited Judge Dee to sit down by his side. Ma Joong and Chiao Tai went to stand behind their master's chair.

Two orderlies came in with trays. All drank their tea in silence.

Then the door opened again. Four military police in full armour came in with Colonel Meng in their midst. Meng stepped up to the central table and saluted smartly.

The Commander cleared his throat. 'We are convened today to hear a report by Magistrate Dee, drawn up at my request, and to decide whether the said report shall necessitate a review of the case against Colonel Meng Kwo-tai, convicted of the premeditated murder of Soo, Vice-Commander of this fort. I request Magistrate Dee to make his report.'

'The motive for this murder,' Judge Dee began in an even voice, 'was to prevent the Vice-Commander from starting an investigation of a clever fraud, by which a criminal hoped to acquire a large amount of money.

'I must remind you of the office routine regarding requests for the purchase of military supplies needed for this fort. After a request has been drafted by the Commander in council, a clerk writes the text out on official paper and it is passed on to the Vice-Commander, who checks its contents and impresses his seal on every page. He then gives the document to the Commander who rechecks it and impresses his seal at the end. When the customary number of copies have been made, the original is put in an envelope addressed to the Board of Military Affairs in the capital, sealed and forwarded there by despatch riders.'

Judge Dee took a sip of his tea, then went on, 'This system has only one loophole. If the document consists of more than one sheet, a dishonest person here who has access to the official correspondence may destroy all sheets but the last one that bears the Commander's seal, substitute spurious ones and then send the document to the capital, including the authentic last page.'

'Impossible!' Commander Fang interrupted. 'The other sheets must bear the seal of the Vice-Commander!'

'That's why he was murdered!' the judge said. 'The criminal purloined Soo's seal, and Soo discovered it. However, before going further into that, I'll first explain how the laudable devotion to office routine of a clerk here put me on the criminal's track.

'Three days ago, a request for the promotion of four lieutenants offered the criminal his chance. The proposal, as written out in its final form, consisted of two sheets. The first contained the request together with the names, ages, etc. of the four persons concerned. The second sheet contained only the Commander's recommendation for speedy action (in general terms, mind you!), the date and the file number: P for Personnel and the figure 404. The first page bore Soo's seal, the second that of the Commander.

'The criminal got hold of this paper on its way to the despatch section. He destroyed the first sheet and replaced it by one on which he had written an urgent request for the purchase of three war junks from the Korean merchants Pak and Yee, adding that the Board of Military Affairs was to pay out the purchase price— a small fortune!—to the said two merchants. After the criminal had marked this spurious page with Soo's purloined seal, he himself put it in an envelope and addressed it: Board of Military Affairs, Section of Supplies. Finally he wrote in a corner of the envelope the number of the paper it contained, namely P-404, as prescribed. He gave the closed envelope to the despatch clerk; the extra copies of the original letter containing the request for the promotion of the four lieutenants he himself entered into the archives. Since he was not familiar with the new rules for distribution, he omitted to have one of those copies sent to my tribunal.

'Now it so happened that the same despatch clerk who sent out the sealed envelope marked P-404 received that same day another letter numbered P-405 containing a request for the purchase of leather goods. He remembered that the two Ps for Purchase and

Personnel sometimes gave rise to confusion in the archives. Therefore, being a good bureaucrat, he added to this number P-405 a note saying, "Refer back to P-404"; for although he had not seen the paper P-404, he remembered that the Section of Supplies had been mentioned on the envelope. The clerk distributed the copies of P-405 correctly, including one extra copy for me. But when I checked my Purchases file, I found P-404 missing. That annoyed me, for I believe in keeping my files complete. Therefore I asked the Commander here to let me have an extra copy. He gave me a letter concerning the promotion of four lieutenants, which belonged therefore to Personnel.'

The Commander, who had been shifting impatiently on his chair, now burst out: 'Couldn't you skip all these details? What is all that nonsense about three war junks?'

'The criminal,' Judge Dee replied calmly, 'was in collusion with the merchants Pak and Yee. Having received in the capital the money for this imaginary purchase, they were going to share it with the criminal. Since it would be many weeks before the routine checks in the Board of Military Affairs revealed the discrepancy with your reports on supplies received, the criminal had plenty of time to prepare his abscondence with the money.

'It was a clever scheme, but he had bad luck. On the night preceding the murder, Colonel Meng and my two assistants met the two Korean merchants in the city and they got drunk together. The merchants thought the three men were highway robbers, and said something about the junks and the money they were going to get for them in the capital. My assistants reported that to me, and I put two and two together. I may add that when Meng came back to the fort he boasted to the captain of the guard about the munificence of Pak and Yee, and that there was more to come. The murderer overheard this and concluded—wrongly— that Meng knew too much, which fortified him in his plan to make Meng the scapegoat. When the criminal learned the next morning that Meng had a hangover and had decided not to go up to the armoury, he sent him a faked message, sealing it with Soo's seal which he still had in his possession.'

'I don't follow all this!' the Commander exclaimed crossly. 'What I want to know is: who shot Soo, and how?'

'Fair enough!' the judge said. 'Colonel Shih Lang murdered Soo.'

It was very still. Then the Commander spoke angrily:

'Utterly impossible! Lieutenant Kao saw Colonel Shih Lang enter and leave Soo's room; Shih Lang didn't even go near Soo's couch!'

Judge Dee continued calmly, 'Colonel Shih Lang went up to Soo's room a little before two, directly after wall-scaling drill. That means that he was clad only in an undergarment, and was bare-foot. He couldn't take any weapon, and he didn't need to. For he knew that Soo was in the habit of throwing his quiver into the window recess, and his plan was to grab an arrow and stab Soo to death in his sleep.

'However, when Shih Lang came in he saw that Soo had got up. He had stepped into his boots and was standing in front of his couch, wearing his mail jacket. Thus Shih Lang couldn't stab him as planned. But then the murderer saw that one arrow had dropped out of the quiver and lay on the floor pointing at Soo. Shih Lang stepped on it, put his big toe and the next around the shaft directly behind the point, and with a powerful kick sent it flying into Soo's unprotected abdomen. At the same time he put on an act for Meng, in case he was looking out of the armoury window: he waved his arms and started to shout—drowning the cries of his victim as he fell backwards on the couch. When he had made sure his victim was dead, he went outside and called the guards. Then, having come back to the room together with the Commander and Colonel Mao, he slipped Soo's seal into the drawer of the desk during the general confusion. It was neatly done; he overlooked only one fact, namely that the dead man would be found with his boots on. That suggested to me that Soo had not been killed in his sleep. It was understandable that Soo should have kept his mail jacket on while taking a brief nap, for it's quite a job to get it off. But he had thrown his helmet on the desk, and one would have expected him also to have stepped out of his boots before lying down.'

The judge paused. All eyes were now on Colonel Shih Lang. He gave Judge Dee a contemptuous look and asked with a sneer: 'And how do you propose to prove this fantastic theory?'

'For the time being,' the judge replied calmly, 'by the fact that you have a nasty scratch on the big toe of your right foot. For where the arrow was lying, the sharp edge of a nail head protruded from the floorboards. It tore the red tape round the arrow's shaft when you kicked it up, and also scratched your toe. Small bloodstains mark the spot. The final proof will be here later, when Pak and Yee have been arrested, and the false document traced in the Board of Military Affairs.'

Shih Lang's face had become livid, his lips were twitching. But he pulled himself together and said in a steady voice, 'You needn't wait for that. I murdered Soo. I am in debt and needed the money. In ten days I'd have applied for sick leave, and never come back. It hadn't been my intention to kill Soo. I had hoped to be able to return the seal by leaving it on his desk. But he discovered the loss too soon, so I decided to stab him with an arrow while he was asleep. But when I came in I saw that Soo was up and about. He shouted at me: "Now I have verified my suspicions, it was you who stole my seal!" I thought I was lost, for tackling Soo armed only with an arrow would be a difficult proposition, and if Meng looked out of the window he would see our struggle. Then my eye fell on the arrow on the floor, and I kicked it up into Soo's guts.' He wiped the perspiration from his brow and concluded: 'I am not sorry, for Soo was a mean bastard. I regret that I had to make you the scapegoat, Meng, but it couldn't be helped. That's all!'

The Commander rose from his chair. 'Your sword, Shih Lang!'

As the colonel unbuckled his swordbelt he said bitterly to the judge: 'You sly devil! How did you get on to me?'

Judge Dee replied primly: 'Mainly by red tape!'

HE CAME WITH THE RAIN

The scene of this third story is also laid in Peng-lai about half a year later. In the meantime Judge Dee's two wives and their children arrived in Peng-lai, and settled down in the magistrate's private residence at the back of the tribunal compound. Shortly afterwards, Miss Tsao joined the household. In Chapter XV of The Chinese Gold Murders *the terrible adventure from which Judge Dee extricated Miss Tsao has been described in detail. When Judge Dee's First Lady met Miss Tsao, she took an instant liking to her and engaged her as her lady-companion. Then, on one of the hottest, rainy days of mid-summer, there occurred the strange case related in the present story.*

'This box won't do either!' Judge Dee's First Lady remarked disgustedly. 'Look at the grey mould all along the seam of this blue dress!' She slammed the lid of the red-leather clothes-box shut, then turned to the Second Lady. 'I've never known such a hot, damp summer. And the heavy downpour we had last night! I thought the rain would never stop. Give me a hand, will you?'

The judge, seated at the tea-table by the open window of the large bedroom, looked on while his two wives put the clothes-box on the floor, and went on to the third one in the pile. Miss Tsao, his First Lady's friend and companion, was drying robes on the brass brazier in the corner, draping them over the copper-wire cover above the glowing coals. The heat of the brazier, together with the steam curling up from the drying clothes, made the atmosphere of the room nearly unbearable, but the three women seemed unaware of it.

With a sigh he turned round and looked outside. From the bedroom here on the second floor of his residence one usually had a fine view of the curved roofs of the city, but now everything was shrouded in a thick leaden mist that blotted out all contours. The mist seemed to have entered his very blood, pulsating dully in his veins. Now he deeply regretted the unfortunate impulse that, on rising, had made him ask for his grey summer robe. For that request had brought his First Lady to inspect the four clothes-boxes, and finding mould on the garments, she had at once summoned his Second and Miss Tsao. Now the three were completely engrossed in their work, with apparently no thought of morning tea, let alone breakfast. This was their first experience of the dog-days in Peng-lai, for it was just seven months since he had taken up his post of magistrate there. He stretched his legs, for his knees and feet felt swollen and heavy. Miss Tsao stooped and took a white dress from the brazier.

'This one is completely dry,' she announced. As she reached up to hang it on the clothes-rack, the judge noticed her slender, shapely body. Suddenly he asked his First Lady sharply: 'Can't you leave all that to the maids?'

'Of course,' his First replied over her shoulder. 'But first I want to see for myself whether there's any real damage. For heaven's sake, take a look at this red robe, dear!' she went on to Miss Tsao. 'The mould has absolutely eaten into the fabric! And you always say this dress looks so well on me!'

Judge Dee rose abruptly. The smell of perfume and stale cosmetics mingling with the faint odour of damp clothes gave the hot room an atmosphere of overwhelming femininity that suddenly jarred on his taut nerves. 'I'm just going out for a short walk,' he said.

'Before you've even had your morning tea?' his First exclaimed. But her eyes were on the discoloured patches on the red dress in her hands.

'I'll be back for breakfast,' the judge muttered. 'Give me that blue robe over there!' Miss Tsao helped the Second put the robe over his shoulders and asked solicitously: 'Isn't that dress a bit too heavy for this hot weather?'

'It's dry at least,' he said curtly. At the same time he realized with dismay that Miss Tsao was perfectly right: the thick fabric clung to his moist back like a coat of mail. He mumbled a greeting and went downstairs.

He quickly walked down the semi-dark corridor leading to the small back door of the tribunal compound. He was glad his old friend and adviser Sergeant Hoong had not yet appeared. The sergeant knew him so well that he would sense at once that he was in a bad temper, and he would wonder what it was all about.

The judge opened the back door with his private key and slipped out into the wet, deserted street. What was it all about, really? he asked himself as he walked along through the dripping mist. Well, these seven months on his first independent official post had been disappointing, of course. The first few days had been exciting, and then there had been the murder of Mrs Ho, and the case at the fort. But thereafter there had been nothing but dreary office routine: forms to be filled out, papers to be filed, licences to be issued. . . . In the cap:tal he had also had much paperwork to do, but on important papers. Moreover, this district was not really his. The entire region from the river north was a strategic area, under the jurisdiction of the army. And the Korean quarter outside the East Gate had its own administration. He angrily kicked a stone, then cursed. What had looked like a loose boulder was in fact the top of a cobblestone, and he hurt his toe badly. He must take a decision about Miss Tsao. The night before, in the intimacy of their shared couch, his First Lady had again urged him to take Miss Tsao as his Third. She and his Second were fond of her, she had said, and Miss Tsao herself wanted nothing better. 'Besides,' his First had added with her customary frankness, 'your Second is a fine woman but she hasn't had a higher education, and to have an intelligent, well-read girl like Miss Tsao around would make life much more interesting for all concerned.' But what if Miss Tsao's willingness was motivated only by gratitude to him for getting her out of the terrible trouble she had been in? In a way it would be easier if he didn't like her so much. On the other hand, would it then be fair to marry a woman one didn't really like? As a magistrate he was entitled to as many as four wives, but personally he held the view that two wives ought to be sufficient unless both of them proved barren. It was all very difficult and confusing. He pulled his robe closer round him, for it had begun to rain.

He sighed with relief when he saw the broad steps leading up to the Temple of Confucius. The third floor of the west tower had been converted into a small tea-house. He would have his morning tea there, then walk back to the tribunal.

In the low-ceilinged, octagonal room a slovenly dressed waiter was leaning on the counter, stirring the fire of the small tea-stove with iron tongs. Judge Dee noticed with satisfaction that the youngster didn't recognize him, for he was not in the mood to acknowledge bowing and scraping. He ordered a pot of tea and a dry towel and sat down at the bamboo table in front of the the counter.

The waiter handed him a none-too-clean towel in a bamboo basket. 'Just one moment please, sir. The water'll be boiling soon.' As the judge rubbed his long beard dry with the towel, the waiter went on, 'Since you are up and about so early, sir, you'll have heard already about the trouble out there.' He pointed with his thumb at the open window, and as the judge shook his head, he continued with relish, 'Last night a fellow was hacked to pieces in the old watchtower, out there in the marsh.'

Judge Dee quickly put the towel down. 'A murder? How do you know?'

'The grocery boy told me, sir. Came up here to deliver his stuff while I was scrubbing the floor. At dawn he had gone to the watchtower to collect duck eggs from that half-witted girl who lives up there, and he saw the mess. The girl was sitting crying in a corner. Rushing back to town, he warned the military police at the blockhouse, and the captain went to the old tower with a few of his men. Look, there they are!'

Judge Dee got up and went to the window. From this vantage-point he could see beyond the crenellated top of the city wall the vast green expanse of the marshlands overgrown with reeds, and further on to the north, in the misty distance, the grey water of the river. A hardened road went from the quay north of the city straight to the lonely tower of weather-beaten bricks in the middle of the marsh. A few soldiers with spiked helmets came marching down the road to the blockhouse halfway between the tower and the quay.

'Was the murdered man a soldier?' the judge asked quickly. Although the area north of the city came under the jurisdiction of the army, any crime involving civilians there had to be referred to the tribunal.

'Could be. That half-witted girl is deaf and dumb, but not too bad-looking. Could be a soldier went up the tower for a private

47

conversation with her, if you get what I mean. Ha, the water is boiling!'

Judge Dee strained his eyes. Now two military policemen were riding from the blockhouse to the city, their horses splashing through the water that had submerged part of the raised road.

'Here's your tea, sir! Be careful, the cup is very hot. I'll put it here on the sill for you. No, come to think of it, the murdered man was no soldier. The grocery boy said he was an old merchant living near the North Gate—he knew him by sight. Well, the military police will catch the murderer soon enough. Plenty tough, they are!' He nudged the judge excitedly. 'There you are! Didn't I tell you they're tough? See that fellow in chains they're dragging from the blockhouse? He's wearing a fisherman's brown jacket and trousers. Well, they'll take him to the fort now, and . . .'

'They'll do nothing of the sort!' the judge interrupted angrily. He hastily took a sip from the tea and scalded his mouth. He paid and rushed downstairs. A civilian murdered by another civilian, that was clearly a case for the tribunal! This was a splendid occasion to tell the military exactly where they got off! Once and for all.

All his apathy had dropped away from him. He rented a horse from the blacksmith on the corner, jumped into the saddle and rode to the North Gate. The guards cast an astonished look at the dishevelled horseman with the wet house-cap sagging on his head. But then they recognized their magistrate and sprang to attention. The judge dismounted and motioned the corporal to follow him into the guardhouse beside the gate. 'What is all this commotion out on the marsh?' he asked.

'A man was found murdered in the old tower, sir. The military police have arrested the murderer already; they are questioning him now in the blockhouse. I expect they'll come down to the quay presently.'

Judge Dee sat down on the bamboo bench and handed the corporal a few coppers. 'Tell one of your men to buy me two oilcakes!'

The oilcakes came fresh from the griddle of a street vendor and had an appetizing smell of garlic and onions, but the judge did not enjoy them, hungry though he was. The hot tea had burnt his tongue, and his mind was concerned with the abuse of power by the army authorities. He reflected ruefully that in the capital one didn't have such annoying problems to cope with: there, detailed rules fixed the exact extent of the authority of every official, high or low. As he was finishing his oilcakes, the corporal came in.

'The military police have now taken the prisoner to their watch-post on the quay, sir.'

Judge Dee sprang up. 'Follow me with four men!'

On the river quay a slight breeze was dispersing the mist. The judge's robe clung wetly to his shoulders. 'Exactly the kind of weather for catching a bad cold,' he muttered. A heavily armed sentry ushered him into the bare waiting-room of the watchpost.

In the back a tall man wearing the coat of mail and spiked helmet of the military police was sitting behind a roughly made wooden desk. He was filling out an official form with laborious, slow strokes of his writing-brush.

'I am Magistrate Dee,' the judge began. 'I demand to know . . .' He suddenly broke off. The captain had looked up. His face was marked by a terrible white scar running along his left cheek and across his mouth. His misshapen lips were half-concealed by a ragged moustache. Before the judge had recovered from this shock, the captain had risen. He saluted smartly and said in a clipped voice:

'Glad you came, sir. I have just finished my report to you.' Pointing at the stretcher covered with a blanket on the floor in the corner, he added, 'That's the dead body, and the murderer is in the back room there. You want him taken directly to the jail of the tribunal, I suppose?'

'Yes. Certainly,' Judge Dee replied, rather lamely.

'Good.' The captain folded the sheet he had been writing on and handed it to the judge. 'Sit down, sir. If you have a moment to spare, I'd like to tell you myself about the case.'

Judge Dee took the seat by the desk and motioned the captain to sit down too. Stroking his long beard, he said to himself that all this was turning out quite differently from what he had expected.

'Well,' the captain began, 'I know the marshland as well as the palm of my hand. That deaf-mute girl who lives in the tower is a harmless idiot, so when it was reported that a murdered man was lying up in her room, I thought at once of assault and robbery, and sent my men to search the marshland between the tower and the riverbank.'

'Why especially that area?' the judge interrupted. 'It could just as well have happened on the road, couldn't it? The murderer hiding the dead body later in the tower?'

'No, sir. Our blockhouse is located on the road halfway between the quay here and the old tower. From there my men keep an eye on the road all day long, as per orders. To prevent Korean spies from entering or leaving the city, you see. And they patrol that road at night. That road is the only means of crossing the marsh, by the way. It's tricky country, and anyone trying to cross it would risk getting into a swamp or quicksand and would drown. Now my men found the body was still warm, and we concluded he was killed a few hours before dawn. Since no one passed the blockhouse except the grocery boy, it follows that both the murdered man and the criminal came from the north. A pathway leads through the reeds from the tower to the riverbank, and a fellow familiar with the layout could slip by there without my men in the blockhouse spotting him.' The captain stroked his moustache and added, 'If he had succeeded in getting by our river patrols, that is.'

'And your men caught the murderer by the waterside?'

'Yes, sir. They discovered a young fisherman, Wang San-lang his name is, hiding in his small boat among the rushes, directly north of the tower. He was trying to wash his trousers which were stained with blood. When my men hailed him, he pushed off and tried to paddle his boat into midstream. The archers shot a few string arrows into the hull, and before he knew where he was he was being hauled back to shore, boat and all. He disclaimed all knowledge of any dead man in the tower, maintained he was on his way there to bring the deaf-mute girl a large carp, and that he got the blood on his trousers while cleaning that carp. He was waiting for dawn to visit her. We searched him, and we found this in his belt.'

50

The captain unwrapped a small paper package on his desk and showed the judge three shining silver pieces. 'We identified the corpse by the visiting-cards we found on it.' He shook the contents of a large envelope out on the table. Besides a package of cards there were two keys, some small change, and a pawn-ticket. Pointing at the ticket, the captain continued, 'That scrap of paper was lying on the floor, close to the body. Must have dropped out of his jacket. The murdered man is the pawnbroker Choong, the owner of a large and well-known pawnshop, just inside the North Gate. A wealthy man. His hobby is fishing. My theory is that Choong met Wang somewhere on the quay last night and hired him to take him out in his boat for a night of fishing on the river. When they had got to the deserted area north of the tower, Wang lured the old man there under some pretext or other and killed him. He had planned to hide the body somewhere in the tower—the thing is half in ruins, you know, and the girl uses only the second storey—but she woke up and caught him in the act. So he just took the silver and left. This is only a theory, mind you, for the girl is worthless as a witness. My men tried to get something out of her, but she only scribbled down some incoherent nonsense about rain spirits and black goblins. Then she had a fit, began to laugh and to cry at the same time. A poor, harmless half-wit.' He rose, walked over to the stretcher and lifted the blanket. 'Here's the dead body.'

Judge Dee bent over the lean shape, which was clad in a simple brown robe. The breast showed patches of clotted blood, and the sleeves were covered with dried mud. The face had a peaceful look, but it was very ugly: lantern-shaped, with a beaked nose that was slightly askew, and a thin-lipped, too large mouth. The head with its long, greying hair was bare.

'Not a very handsome gentleman,' the captain remarked. 'Though I should be the last to pass such a remark!' A spasm contorted his mutilated face. He raised the body's shoulders and showed the judge the large red stain on the back. 'Killed by a knife thrust from behind that must have penetrated right into his heart. He was lying on his back on the floor, just inside the door of the girl's room.' The captain let the upper part of the body drop. 'Nasty fellow, that fisherman. After he had murdered

Choong, he began to cut up his breast and belly. I say *after* he had killed him, for as you see those wounds in front haven't bled as much as one would expect. Oh yes, here's my last exhibit! Had nearly forgotten it!' He pulled out a drawer in the desk and unwrapped the oiled paper of an oblong package. Handing the judge a long thin knife, he said, 'This was found in Wang's boat, sir. He says he uses it for cleaning his fish. There was no trace of blood on it. Why should there be? There was plenty of water around to wash it clean after he had got back to the boat! Well, that's about all, sir. I expect that Wang'll confess readily enough. I know that type of young hoodlum. They begin by stoutly denying everything, but after a thorough interrogation they break down and then they talk their mouths off. What are your orders, sir?'

'First I must inform the next of kin, and have them formally identify the body. Therefore, I . . .'

'I've attended to that, sir. Choong was a widower, and his two sons are living in the capital. The body was officially identified just now by Mr Lin, the dead man's partner, who lived together with him.'

'You and your men did an excellent job,' the judge said. 'Tell your men to transfer the prisoner and the dead body to the guards I brought with me.' Rising, he added, 'I am really most grateful for your swift and efficient action, captain. This being a civilian case, you only needed to report the murder to the tribunal and you could have left it at that. You went out of your way to help me and . . .'

The captain raised his hand in a deprecatory gesture and said in his strange dull voice, 'It was a pleasure, sir. I happen to be one of Colonel Meng's men. We shall always do all we can to help you. All of us, always.'

The spasm that distorted his misshapen face had to be a smile. Judge Dee walked back to the guardhouse at the North Gate. He had decided to question the prisoner there at once, then go to the scene of the crime. If he transferred the investigation to the tribunal, clues might get stale. It seemed a fairly straightforward case, but one never knew.

He sat down at the only table in the bare guardroom and settled down to a study of the captain's report. It contained little beyond what the captain had already told him. The victim's full name was Choong Fang, age fifty-six; the girl was called Oriole, twenty years of age, and the young fisherman was twenty-two. He took the visiting-cards and the pawn-ticket from his sleeve. The cards stated that Mr Choong was a native of Shansi Province. The pawn-ticket was a tally, stamped with the large red stamp of Choong's pawnshop; it concerned four brocade robes pawned the day before by a Mrs Pei for three silver pieces, to be redeemed in three months at a monthly interest of 5 per cent.

The corporal came in, followed by two guards carrying the stretcher.

'Put it down there in the corner,' Judge Dee ordered. 'Do you know about that deaf-mute girl who lives in the watchtower? The military police gave only her personal name—Oriole.'

'Yes, sir, that's what she is called. She's an abandoned child. An old crone who used to sell fruit near the gate here brought her up and taught her to write a few dozen letters and a bit of sign language. When the old woman died two years ago, the girl went to live in the tower because the street urchins were always pestering her. She raises ducks there, and sells the eggs. People called her Oriole to make fun of her being dumb, and the nickname stuck.'

'All right. Bring the prisoner before me.'

The guards came back flanking a squat, sturdily built youngster. His tousled hair hung down over the corrugated brow of his swarthy, scowling face, and his brown jacket and trousers were clumsily patched in several places. His hands were chained behind his back, an extra loop of the thin chain encircling his thick, bare neck. The guards pressed him down on his knees in front of the judge.

Judge Dee observed the youngster in silence for a while, wondering what would be the best way to start the interrogation. There was only the patter of the rain outside, and the prisoner's heavy breathing. The judge took the three silver pieces from his sleeve.

'Where did you get these?'

53

The young fisherman muttered something in a broad dialect that the judge didn't quite understand. One of the guards kicked the prisoner and growled: 'Speak louder!'

'It's my savings. For buying a real boat.'

'When did you first meet Mr Choong?'

The boy burst out in a string of obscene curses. The guard on his right stopped him by hitting him over his head with the flat of his sword. Wang shook his head, then said dully, 'Only knew him by sight because he was often around on the quay.' Suddenly he added viciously: 'If I'd ever met him, I'd have killed the dirty swine, the crook . . .'

'Did Mr Choong cheat when you pawned something in his shop?' Judge Dee asked quickly.

'Think I have anything to pawn?'

'Why call him a crook then?'

Wang looked up at the judge who thought he caught a sly glint in his small, bloodshot eyes. The youngster bent his head again and replied in a sullen voice: 'Because all pawnbrokers are crooks.'

'What did you do last night?'

'I told the soldiers already. Had a bowl of noodles at the stall on the quay, then went up river. After I had caught some good fish, I moored the boat on the bank north of the tower and had a nap. I'd planned to bring some fish to the tower at dawn, for Oriole.'

Something in the way the boy pronounced the girl's name caught Judge Dee's attention. He said slowly, 'You deny having murdered the pawnbroker. Since, besides you, there was only the girl about, it follows it was she who killed him.'

Suddenly Wang jumped up and went for the judge. He moved so quickly that the two guards only got hold of him just in time. He kicked them but got a blow on his head that made him fall down backwards, his chains clanking on the floor-stones.

'You dog-official, you . . .' the youngster burst out, trying to scramble up. The corporal gave him a kick in the face that made his head slam back on the floor with a hard thud. He lay quite still, blood trickling from his torn mouth.

The judge got up and bent over the still figure. He had lost consciousness.

'Don't maltreat a prisoner unless you are ordered to,' the judge told the corporal sternly. 'Bring him round, and take him to the jail. Later I shall interrogate him formally, during the noon session. You'll take the dead body to the tribunal, corporal. Report to Sergeant Hoong and hand him this statement, drawn up by the captain of the military police. Tell the sergeant that I'll return to the tribunal as soon as I have questioned a few witnesses here.' He cast a look at the window. It was still raining. 'Get me a piece of oiled cloth!'

Before Judge Dee stepped outside he draped the oiled cloth over his head and shoulders, then jumped into the saddle of his hired horse. He rode along the quay and took the hardened road that led to the marshlands.

The mist had cleared a little and as he rode along he looked curiously at the deserted, green surface on either side of the road. Narrow gullies followed a winding course through the reeds, here and there broadening into large pools that gleamed dully in the grey light. A flight of small water birds suddenly flew up, with piercing cries that resounded eerily over the desolate marsh. He noticed that the water was subsiding after the torrential rain that had fallen in the night; the road was dry now, but the water had left large patches of duck-weed. When he was about to pass the blockhouse the sentry stopped him, but he let him go on as soon as the judge had shown him the identification document he carried in his boot.

The old watchtower was a clumsy, square building of five storeys, standing on a raised base of roughly hewn stone blocks. The shutters of the arched windows had gone and the roof of the top storey had caved in. Two big black crows sat perched on a broken beam.

As he came nearer he heard loud quacking. A few dozen ducks were huddling close together by the side of a muddy pool below the tower's base. When the judge dismounted and fastened the reins to a moss-covered stone pillar, the ducks began to splash around in the water, quacking indignantly.

The ground floor of the tower was just a dark, low vault, empty

55

but for a heap of old broken furniture. A narrow, rickety flight of wooden stairs led up to the floor above. The judge climbed up, seeking support with his left hand from the wet, mould-covered wall, for the bannisters were gone.

When he stepped into the half-dark, bare room, something stirred among the rags piled up on the roughly made plank-bed under the arched window. Some raucous sounds came from under a soiled, patched quilt. A quick look around showed that the room only contained a rustic table with a cracked teapot, and a bamboo bench against the side wall. In the corner was a brick oven carrying a large pan; beside it stood a rattan basket filled to the brim with pieces of charcoal. A musty smell of mould and stale sweat hung in the air.

Suddenly the quilt was thrown to the floor. A half-naked girl with long, tousled hair jumped down from the plank-bed. After one look at the judge, she again made that strange, raucous sound and scuttled to the farthest corner. Then she dropped to her knees, trembling violently.

Judge Dee realized that he didn't present a very reassuring sight. He quickly pulled his identification document from his boot, unfolded it and walked up to the cowering girl, pointing with his forefinger at the large red stamp of the tribunal. Then he pointed at himself.

She apparently understood, for now she scrambled up and stared at him with large eyes that held an animal fear. She wore nothing but a tattered skirt, fastened to her waist with a piece of straw rope. She had a shapely, well-developed body and her skin was surprisingly white. Her round face was smeared with dirt but was not unattractive. Judge Dee pulled the bench up to the table and sat down. Feeling that some familiar gesture was needed to reassure the frightened girl, he took the teapot and drank from the spout, as farmers do.

The girl came up to the table, spat on the dirty top and drew in the spittle with her forefinger a few badly deformed characters. They read: 'Wang did not kill him.'

The judge nodded. He poured tea on the table-top, and motioned her to wipe it clean. She obediently went to the bed, took a rag and began to polish the table top with feverish haste. Judge Dee

THEN SHE DROPPED TO HER KNEES, TREMBLING VIOLENTLY

walked over to the stove and selected a few pieces of charcoal. Resuming his seat, he wrote with the charcoal on the table-top: 'Who killed him?'

She shivered. She took the other piece of charcoal and wrote: 'Bad black goblins.' She pointed excitedly at the words, then scribbled quickly: 'Bad goblins changed the good rain spirit.'

'You saw the black goblins?' he wrote.

She shook her tousled head emphatically. She tapped with her forefinger repeatedly on the word 'black', then she pointed at her closed eyes and shook her head again. The judge sighed. He wrote: 'You know Mr Choong?'

She looked perplexedly at his writing, her finger in her mouth. He realized that the complicated character indicating the sur-name Choong was unknown to her. He crossed it out and wrote 'old man'.

She again shook her head. With an expression of disgust she drew circles round the words 'old man' and added: 'Too much blood. Good rain spirit won't come any more. No silver for Wang's boat any more.' Tears came trickling down her grubby cheeks as she wrote with a shaking hand: 'Good rain spirit always sleep with me.' She pointed at the plank-bed.

Judge Dee gave her a searching look. He knew that rain spirits played a prominent role in local folklore, so that it was only natural that they figured in the dreams and vagaries of this over-developed young girl. On the other hand, she had referred to silver. He wrote: 'What does the rain spirit look like?'

Her round face lit up. With a broad smile she wrote in big, clumsy letters: 'Tall. Handsome. Kind.' She drew a circle round each of the three words, then threw the charcoal on the table and, hugging her bare breasts, began to giggle ecstatically.

The judge averted his gaze. When he turned to look at her again, she had let her hands drop and stood there staring straight ahead with wide eyes. Suddenly her expression changed again. With a quick gesture she pointed at the arched window, and made some strange sounds. He turned round. There was a faint colour in the leaden sky, the trace of a rainbow. She stared at it, in childish delight, her mouth half open. The judge took up the piece of charcoal for one final question: 'When does the rain spirit come?'

She stared at the words for a long time, absentmindedly combing her long, greasy locks with her fingers. At last she bent over the table and wrote: 'Black night and much rain.' She put circles round the words 'black' and 'rain', then added: 'He came with the rain.'

All at once she put her hands to her face and began to sob convulsively. The sound mingled with the loud quacking of the ducks from below. Realizing that she couldn't hear the birds, he rose and laid his hand on her bare shoulder. When she looked up he was shocked by the wild, half-crazed gleam in her wide eyes. He quickly drew a duck on the table, and added the word 'hunger'. She clasped her hand to her mouth and ran to the oven. Judge Dee scrutinized the large flagstones in front of the entrance. He saw there a clean space on the dirty, dust-covered floor. Evidently it was there that the dead man had lain, and the military police had swept up the floor. He remembered ruefully his unkind thoughts about them. Sounds of chopping made him turn round. The girl was cutting up stale rice cakes on a primitive chopping board. The judge watched with a worried frown her deft handling of the large kitchen knife. Suddenly she drove the long, sharp point of the knife in the board, then shook the chopped up rice cakes into the pan on the oven, giving the judge a happy smile over her shoulder. He nodded at her and went down the creaking stairs.

The rain had ceased, a thin mist was gathering over the marsh. While untying the reins, he told the noisy ducks: 'Don't worry, your breakfast is under way!'

He made his horse go ahead at a sedate pace. The mist came drifting in from the river. Strangely shaped clouds were floating over the tall reeds, here and there dissolving in long writhing trailers that resembled the tentacles of some monstrous water-animal. He wished he knew more about the hoary, deeply rooted beliefs of the local people. In many places people still venerated a river god or goddess, and farmers and fishermen made sacrificial offerings to these at the waterside. Evidently such things loomed large in the deaf-mute girl's feeble mind, shifting continually from fact to fiction, and unable to control the urges of her full-blown body. He drove his horse to a gallop.

Back at the North Gate, he told the corporal to take him to the pawnbroker's place. When they had arrived at the large, prosperous-looking pawnshop the corporal explained that Choong's private residence was located directly behind the shop and pointed at the narrow alleyway that led to the main entrance. Judge Dee told the corporal he could go back, and knocked on the black-lacquered gate.

A lean man, neatly dressed in a brown gown with black sash and borders, opened it. Bestowing a bewildered look on his wet, bearded visitor, he said: 'You want the shop, I suppose. I can take you, I was just going there.'

'I am the magistrate,' Judge Dee told him impatiently. 'I've just come from the marsh. Had a look at the place where your partner was murdered. Let's go inside, I want to hand over to you what was found on the dead body.'

Mr Lin made a very low bow and conducted his distinguished visitor to a small but comfortable side hall, furnished in conventional style with a few pieces of heavy blackwood furniture. He ceremoniously led the judge to the broad bench at the back. While his host was telling the old manservant to bring tea and cakes, the judge looked curiously at the large aviary of copper wire on the wall table. About a dozen paddy birds were fluttering around inside.

'A hobby of my partner's,' Mr Lin said with an indulgent smile. 'He was very fond of birds, always fed them himself.'

With his neatly trimmed chin-beard and small, greying moustache Lin seemed at first sight just a typical middle-class shop-keeper. But a closer inspection revealed deep lines around his thin mouth, and large, sombre eyes that suggested a man with a definite personality. The judge set his cup down and formally expressed his sympathy with the firm's loss. Then he took the envelope from his sleeve and shook out the visiting-cards, the small cash, the pawn-ticket and the two keys. 'That's all, Mr Lin. Did your partner as a rule carry large sums of money on him?'

Lin silently looked the small pile over, stroking his chin-beard. 'No, sir. Since he retired from the firm two years ago, there was no need for him to carry much money about. But he certainly had more on him than just these few coppers when he went out last night.'

'What time was that?'

'About eight, sir. After we had had dinner together here downstairs. He wanted to take a walk along the quay, so he said.'

'Did Mr Choong often do that?'

'Oh yes, sir! He had always been a man of solitary habits, and after the demise of his wife two years ago, he went out for long walks nearly every other night and always by himself. He always had his meals served in his small library upstairs, although I live here in this same house, in the left wing. Last night, however, there was a matter of business to discuss and therefore he came down to have dinner with me.'

'You have no family, Mr Lin?'

'No, sir. Never had time to establish a household! My partner had the capital, but the actual business of the pawnshop he left largely to me. And after his retirement he hardly set foot in our shop.'

'I see. To come back to last night. Did Mr Choong say when he would be back?'

'No, sir. The servant had standing orders not to wait up for him. My partner was an enthusiastic fisherman, you see. If he thought it looked like good fishing weather on the quay, he would hire a boat and pass the night up river.'

Judge Dee nodded slowly. 'The military police will have told you that they arrested a young fisherman called Wang San-lang. Did your partner often hire his boat?'

'That I don't know, sir. There are scores of fishermen about on the quay, you see, and most of them are eager to make a few extra coppers. But if my partner rented Wang's boat, it doesn't astonish me that he ran into trouble, for Wang is a violent young ruffian. I know of him, because being a fisherman of sorts myself, I have often heard the others talk about him. Surly, uncompanionable youngster.' He sighed. 'I'd like to go out fishing as often as my partner did, only I haven't got that much time. . . . Well, it's very kind of you to have brought these keys, sir. Lucky that Wang didn't take them and throw them away! The larger one is the key of my late partner's library, the other of the strongbox he has there for keeping important papers.' He stretched out his hand to take the keys, but Judge Dee scooped them up and put them in his sleeve.

'Since I am here,' he said, 'I shall have a look at Mr Choong's papers right now, Mr Lin. This is a murder case, and until it is solved, all the victim's papers are temporarily at the disposal of the authorities for possible clues. Take me to the library, please.'

'Certainly, sir.' Lin took the judge up a broad staircase and pointed at the door at the end of the corridor. The judge unlocked it with the larger key.

'Thanks very much, Mr Lin. I shall join you downstairs presently.'

The judge stepped into the small room, locked the door behind him, then went to push the low, broad window wide open. The roofs of the neighbouring houses gleamed in the grey mist. He turned and sat down in the capacious armchair behind the rosewood writing-desk facing the window. After a casual look at the iron-bound strongbox on the floor beside his chair, he leaned back and pensively took stock of his surroundings. The small library was scrupulously clean and furnished with simple, old-fashioned taste. The spotless whitewashed walls were decorated with two good landscape scrolls, and the solid ebony wall table bore a slender vase of white porcelain, with a few wilting roses. Piles of books in brocade covers were neatly stacked on the shelves of the small bookcase of spotted bamboo.

Folding his arms, the judge wondered what connection there could be between this tastefully arranged library that seemed to belong to an elegant scholar rather than to a pawnbroker, and the bare, dark room in the half-ruined watchtower, breathing decay, sloth and the direst poverty. After a while he shook his head, bent and unlocked the strongbox. Its contents matched the methodical neatness of the room: bundles of documents, each bound up with green ribbon and provided with an inscribed label. He selected the bundles marked 'private correspondence' and 'accounts and receipts'. The former contained a few important letters about capital investment and correspondence from his sons, mainly about their family affairs and asking Mr Choong's advice

62

and instructions. Leafing through the second bundle, Judge Dee's practised eye saw at once that the deceased had been leading a frugal, nearly austere life. Suddenly he frowned. He had found a pink receipt, bearing the stamp of a house of assignation. It was dated back a year and a half. He quickly went through the bundle and found half a dozen similar receipts, the last dated back six months. Apparently Mr Choong had, after his wife's demise, hoped to find consolation in venal love, but had soon discovered that such hope was vain. With a sigh he opened the large envelope which he had taken from the bottom of the box. It was marked: 'Last Will and Testament'. It was dated one year before, and stated that all of Mr Choong's landed property—which was considerable—was to go to his two sons, together with two-thirds of his capital. The remaining one-third, and the pawnshop, was bequeathed to Mr Lin 'in recognition of his long and loyal service to the firm'.

The judge replaced the papers. He rose and went to inspect the bookcase. He discovered that except for two dog-eared dictionaries, all the books were collections of poetry, complete editions of the most representative lyrical poets of former times. He looked through one volume. Every difficult word had been annotated in red ink, in an unformed, rather clumsy hand. Nodding slowly, he replaced the volume. Yes, now he understood. Mr Choong had been engaged in a trade that forbade all personal feeling, namely that of a pawnbroker. And his pronouncedly ugly face made tender attachments unlikely. Yet at heart he was a romantic, hankering after the higher things of life, but very self-conscious and shy about these yearnings. As a merchant he had of course only received an elementary education, so he tried laboriously to expand his literary knowledge, reading old poetry with a dictionary in this small library which he kept so carefully locked.

Judge Dee sat down again and took his folding fan from his sleeve. Fanning himself, he concentrated his thoughts on this unusual pawnbroker. The only glimpse the outer world got of the sensitive nature of this man was his love of birds, evinced by the paddy birds downstairs. At last the judge got up. About to put his fan back into his sleeve, he suddenly checked himself. He looked at the fan absentmindedly for a while, then laid it on

63

the desk. After a last look at the room he went downstairs.

His host offered him another cup of tea but Judge Dee shook his head. Handing Lin the two keys, he said, 'I have to go back to the tribunal now. I found nothing among your partner's papers suggesting that he had any enemies, so I think that this case is exactly what it seems, namely a case of murder for gain. To a poor man, three silver pieces are a fortune. Why are those birds fluttering about?' He went to the cage. 'Aha, their water is dirty. You ought to tell the servant to change it, Mr Lin.'

Lin muttered something and clapped his hands. Judge Dee groped in his sleeve. 'How careless of me!' he exclaimed. 'I left my fan on the desk upstairs. Would you fetch it for me, Mr Lin?'

Just as Lin was rushing to the staircase, the old manservant came in. When the judge had told him that the water in the reservoir of the birdcage ought to be changed daily, the old man said, shaking his head, 'I told Mr Lin so, but he wouldn't listen. Doesn't care for birds. My master now, he loved them, he . . .'

'Yes, Mr Lin told me that last night he had an argument with your master about those birds.'

'Well yes, sir, both of them got quite excited. What was it about, sir? I only caught a few words about birds when I brought the rice.'

'It doesn't matter,' the judge said quickly. He had heard Mr Lin come downstairs. 'Well, Mr Lin, thanks for the tea. Come to the chancery in, say, one hour, with the most important documents relating to your late partner's assets. My senior clerk will help you fill out the official forms, and the registration of Mr Choong's will.'

Mr Lin thanked the judge profusely and saw him respectfully to the door.

Judge Dee told the guards at the gate of the tribunal to return his rented horse to the blacksmith, and went straight to his private residence at the back of the chancery. The old housemaster informed him that Sergeant Hoong was waiting in his private office. The judge nodded. 'Tell the bathroom attendant that I want to take a bath now.'

In the black-tiled dressing-room adjoining the bath he quickly stripped off his robe, drenched with sweat and rain. He felt soiled,

64

in body and in mind. The attendant sluiced him with cold water, and vigorously scrubbed his back. But it was only after the judge had been lying in the sunken pool in hot water for some time that he began to feel better. Thereafter he had the attendant massage his shoulders, and when he had been rubbed dry he put on a crisp clean robe of blue cotton, and placed a cap of thin black gauze on his head. In this attire he walked over to his women's quarters.

About to enter the garden room where his ladies usually passed the morning, he halted a moment, touched by the peaceful scene. His two wives, clad in flowered robes of thin silk, were sitting with Miss Tsao at the red-lacquered table in front of the open sliding doors. The walled-in rock garden outside, planted with ferns and tall, rustling bamboos, suggested refreshing coolness. This was his own private world, a clean haven of refuge from the outside world of cruel violence and repulsive decadence he had to deal with in his official life. Then and there he took the firm resolution that he would preserve his harmonious family life intact, always.

His First Lady put her embroidery frame down and quickly came to meet him. 'We have been waiting with breakfast for you for nearly an hour!' she told him reproachfully.

'I am sorry. The fact is that there was some trouble at the North Gate and I had to attend to it at once. I must go to the chancery now, but I shall join you for the noon rice.' She conducted him to the door. When she was making her bow he told her in a low voice, 'By the way, I have decided to follow your advice in the matter we discussed last night. Please make the necessary arrangements.'

With a pleased smile she bowed again, and the judge went down the corridor that led to the chancery.

He found Sergeant Hoong sitting in an armchair in the corner of his private office. His old adviser got up and wished him a good morning. Tapping the document in his hand, the sergeant said, 'I was relieved when I got this report, Your Honour, for we were getting worried about your prolonged absence! I had the prisoner locked up in jail, and the dead body deposited in the mortuary. After I had viewed it with the coroner, Ma Joong and

Chiao Tai, your two lieutenants, rode to the North Gate to see whether you needed any assistance.'

Judge Dee had sat down behind his desk. He looked askance at the pile of dossiers. 'Is there anything urgent among the incoming documents, Hoong?'

'No, sir. All those files concern routine administrative matters.'

'Good. Then we shall devote the noon session to the murder of the pawnbroker Choong.'

The sergeant nodded contentedly. 'I saw from the captain's report, Your Honour, that it is a fairly simple case. And since we have the murder suspect safely under lock and key . . .'

The judge shook his head. 'No, Hoong, I wouldn't call it a simple case, exactly. But thanks to the quick measures of the military police, and thanks to the lucky chance that brought me right into the middle of things, a definite pattern has emerged.'

He clapped his hands. When the headman came inside and made his bow the judge ordered him to bring the prisoner Wang before him. He went on to the sergeant, 'I am perfectly aware, Hoong, that a judge is supposed to interrogate an accused only publicly, in court. But this is not a formal hearing. A general talk for my orientation, rather.'

Sergeant Hoong looked doubtful, but the judge vouchsafed no further explanation, and began to leaf through the topmost file on his desk. He looked up when the headman brought Wang inside. The chains had been taken off him, but his swarthy face looked as surly as before. The headman pressed him down on his knees, then stood himself behind him, his heavy whip in his hands.

'Your presence is not required, Headman,' Judge Dee told him curtly.

The headman cast a worried glance at Sergeant Hoong. 'This is a violent ruffian, Your Honour,' he began diffidently. 'He might . . .'

'You heard me !' the judge snapped.

After the disconcerted headman had left, Judge Dee leaned back in his chair. He asked the young fisherman in a conversational tone, 'How long have you been living on the waterfront, Wang?'

'Ever since I can remember,' the boy muttered.

'It's a strange land,' the judge said slowly to Sergeant Hoong. 'When I was riding through the marsh this morning, I saw weirdly shaped clouds drifting about, and shreds of mist that looked like long arms reaching up out of the water, as if . . .'

The youngster had been listening intently. Now he interrupted quickly: 'Better not speak of those things!'

'Yes, you know all about those things, Wang. On stormy nights, there must be more going on in the marshlands than we city-dwellers realize.'

Wang nodded vigorously. 'I've seen many things,' he said in a low voice, 'with my own eyes. They all come up from the water. Some can harm you, others help drowning people, sometimes. But it's better to keep away from them, anyway.'

'Exactly! Yet you made bold to interfere, Wang. And see what has happened to you now! You were arrested, you were kicked and beaten, and now you are a prisoner accused of murder!'

'I told you I didn't kill him!'

'Yes. But did you know who or what killed him? Yet you stabbed him when he was dead. Several times.'

'I saw red . . .' Wang muttered. 'If I'd known sooner, I'd have cut his throat. For I know him by sight, the rat, the . . .'

'Hold your tongue!' Judge Dee interrupted him sharply. 'You cut up a dead man, and that's a mean and cowardly thing to do!' He continued, calmer, 'However, since even in your blind rage you spared Oriole by refraining from an explanation, I am willing to forget what you did. How long have you been going with her?'

'Over a year. She's sweet, and she's clever too. Don't believe she's a half-wit! She can write more than a hundred characters. I can read only a dozen or so.'

Judge Dee took the three silver pieces from his sleeve and laid them on the desk. 'Take this silver, it belongs rightly to her and to you. Buy your boat and marry her. She needs you, Wang.' The youngster snatched the silver and tucked it in his belt. The judge went on, 'You'll have to go back to jail for a few hours, for I can't release you until you have been formally cleared of the murder charge. Then you'll be set free. Learn to control your temper, Wang!'

He clapped his hands. The headman came in at once. He had been waiting just outside the door, ready to rush inside at the first sign of trouble.

'Take the prisoner back to his cell, headman. Then fetch Mr Lin. You'll find him in the chancery.'

Sergeant Hoong had been listening with mounting astonishment. Now he asked with a perplexed look, 'What were you talking about with that young fellow, Your Honour? I couldn't follow it at all. Are you really intending to let him go?'

Judge Dee rose and went to the window. Looking out at the dreary, wet courtyard, he said, 'It's raining again! What was I talking about, Hoong? I was just checking whether Wang really believed all those weird superstitions. One of these days, Hoong, you might try to find in our chancery library a book on local folklore.'

'But you don't believe all that nonsense, sir!'

'No, I don't. Not all of it, at least. But I feel I ought to read up on the subject, for it plays a large role in the daily life of the common people of our district. Pour me a cup of tea, will you?'

While the sergeant prepared the tea, Judge Dee resumed his seat and concentrated on the official documents on his desk. After he had drunk a second cup, there was a knock at the door. The headman ushered Mr Lin inside, then discreetly withdrew.

'Sit down, Mr Lin!' the judge addressed his guest affably. 'I trust my senior clerk gave you the necessary instructions for the documents to be drawn up?'

'Yes, indeed, Your Honour. Right now we were checking the landed property with the register and . . .'

'According to the will drawn up a year ago,' the judge cut in, 'Mr Choong bequeathed all the land to his two sons, together with two-thirds of his capital, as you know. One-third of the capital, and the pawnshop, he left to you. Are you planning to continue the business?'

'No, sir,' Lin replied with his thin smile. 'I have worked in that pawnshop for more than thirty years, from morning till night. I shall sell it, and live off the rent from my capital.'

'Precisely. But suppose Mr Choong had made a new will? Containing a new clause stipulating that you were to get only the shop?' As Lin's face went livid, he went on quickly, 'It's a prosperous business, but it would take you four or five years to assemble enough capital to retire. And you are getting on in years, Mr Lin.'

'Impossible! How . . . how could he . . .' Lin stammered. Then he snapped, 'Did you find a new will in his strongbox?'

Instead of answering the question, Judge Dee said coldly: 'Your partner had a mistress, Mr Lin. Her love came to mean more to him than anything else.'

Lin jumped up. 'Do you mean to say that the old fool willed his money to that deaf-mute slut?'

'Yes, you know all about that affair, Mr Lin. Since last night, when your partner told you. You had a violent quarrel. No, don't try to deny it! Your manservant overheard what you said, and he will testify in court.'

Lin sat down again. He wiped his moist face. Then he began, calmer now, 'Yes, sir, I admit that I got very angry when my partner informed me last night that he loved that girl. He wanted to take her away to some distant place and marry her. I tried to make him see how utterly foolish that would be, but he told me to mind my own business and ran out of the house in a huff. I had no idea he would go to the tower. It's common knowledge that that young hoodlum Wang is carrying on with the half-wit. Wang surprised the two, and he murdered my partner. I apologize for not having mentioned these facts to you this morning, sir. I couldn't bring myself to compromise my late partner. . . . And since you had arrested the murderer, everything would have come out anyway in court. . . .' He shook his head. 'I am partly to blame, sir. I should have gone after him last night, I should've . . .'

'But you did go after him, Mr Lin,' Judge Dee interrupted curtly. 'You are a fisherman too, you know the marsh as well as your partner. Ordinarily one can't cross the marsh, but after a heavy rain the water rises, and an experienced boatman in a shallow skiff could paddle across by way of the swollen gullies and pools.'

'Impossible! The road is patrolled by the military police all night!'

'A man crouching in a skiff could take cover behind the tall reeds, Mr Lin. Therefore your partner could only visit the tower on nights after a heavy rain. And therefore the poor half-witted girl took the visitor for a supernatural being, a rain spirit. For he came with the rain.' He sighed. Suddenly he fixed Lin with his piercing eyes and said sternly, 'When Mr Choong told you about his plans last night, Lin, you saw all your long-cherished hopes of a life in ease and luxury go up into thin air. Therefore you followed Choong, and you murdered him in the tower by thrusting a knife into his back.'

Lin raised his hands. 'What a fantastic theory, sir! How do you propose to prove this slanderous accusation?'

'By Mrs Pei's pawn-ticket, among other things. It was found by the military police on the scene of the crime. But Mr Choong had completely retired from the business, as you told me yourself. Why then would he be carrying a pawn-ticket that had been issued that very day?' As Lin remained silent, Judge Dee went on, 'You decided on the spur of the moment to murder Choong, and you rushed after him. It was the hour after the evening rice, so the shopkeepers in your neighbourhood were on the lookout for their evening custom when you passed. Also on the quay, where you took off in your small skiff, there were an unusual number of people about, because it looked like heavy rain was on its way.' The glint of sudden panic in Lin's eyes was the last confirmation the judge had been waiting for. He concluded in an even voice, 'If you confess now, Mr Lin, sparing me the trouble of sifting out all the evidence of the eyewitnesses, I am prepared to add a plea for clemency to your death sentence, on the ground that it was unpremeditated murder.'

Lin stared ahead with a vacant look. All at once his pale face became distorted by a spasm of rage. 'The despicable old lecher!' he spat. 'Made me sweat and slave all those years . . . and now he was going to throw all that good money away on a cheap, half-witted slut! The money I made for him. . . .' He looked steadily at the judge as he added in a firm voice, 'Yes, I killed him. He deserved it.'

70

Judge Dee gave the sergeant a sign. While Hoong went to the door the judge told the pawnbroker, 'I shall hear your full confession during the noon session.'

They waited in silence till the sergeant came back with the headman and two constables. They put Lin in chains and led him away.

'A sordid case, sir,' Sergeant Hoong remarked dejectedly.

The judge took a sip from his teacup and held it up to be refilled. 'Pathetic, rather. I would even call Lin pathetic, Hoong, were it not for the fact that he made a determined effort to incriminate Wang.'

'What was Wang's role in all this, sir? You didn't even ask him what he did this morning!'

'There was no need to, for what happened is as plain as a pikestaff. Oriole had told Wang that a rain spirit visited her at night and sometimes gave her money. Wang considered it a great honour that she had relations with a rain spirit. Remember that only half a century ago in many of the river districts in our Empire the people immolated every year a young boy or girl as a human sacrifice to the local river god—until the authorities stepped in. When Wang came to the tower this morning to bring Oriole her fish, he found in her room a dead man lying on his face on the floor. The crying Oriole gave him to understand that goblins had killed the rain spirit and changed him into an ugly old man. When Wang turned over the corpse and recognized the old man, he suddenly understood that he and Oriole had been deceived, and in a blind rage pulled his knife and stabbed the dead man. Then he realized that this was a murder case and he would be suspected. So he fled. The military police caught him while trying to wash his trousers which had become stained with Choong's blood.'

Sergeant Hoong nodded. 'How did you discover all this in only a few hours, sir?'

'At first I thought the captain's theory hit the nail on the head. The only point which worried me a bit was the long interval between the murder and the stabbing of the victim's breast. I didn't worry a bit about the pawn-ticket, for it is perfectly normal for a pawnbroker to carry a ticket about that he has made

71

out that very same day. Then, when questioning Wang, it struck me that he called Choong a crook. That was a slip of the tongue, for Wang was determined to keep both Oriole and himself out of this, so as not to have to divulge that they had let themselves be fooled. While I was interviewing Oriole she stated that the "goblins" had killed and *changed* her rain spirit. I didn't understand that at all. It was during my visit to Lin that at last I got on the right track. Lin was nervous and therefore garrulous, and told me at length about his partner taking no part at all in the business. I remembered the pawn-ticket found on the murder scene, and began to suspect Lin. But it was only after I had inspected the dead man's library and got a clear impression of his personality that I found the solution. I checked my theory by eliciting from the manservant the fact that Lin and Choong had quarreled about Oriole the night before. The name Oriole meant of course nothing to the servant, but he told me they had a heated argument about birds. The rest was routine.'

The judge put his cup down. 'I have learned from this case how important it is to study carefully our ancient handbooks of detection, Hoong. There it is stated again and again that the first step of a murder investigation is to ascertain the character, daily life and habits of the victim. And in this case it was indeed the murdered man's personality that supplied the key.'

Sergeant Hoong stroked his grey moustache with a pleased smile. 'That girl and her young man were very lucky indeed in having you as the investigating magistrate, sir! For all the evidence pointed straight at Wang, and he would have been convicted and beheaded. For the girl is a deaf-mute, and Wang isn't much of a talker either!'

Judge Dee nodded. Leaning back in his chair, he said with a faint smile:

'That brings me to the main benefit I derived from this case, Hoong. A very personal and very important benefit. I must confess to you that early this morning I was feeling a bit low, and for a moment actually doubted whether this was after all the right career for me. I was a fool. This is a great, a magnificent office, Hoong! If only because it enables us to speak for those who can't speak for themselves.'

THE MURDER ON THE LOTUS POND

This case occurred in the year A.D. 667 in Han-yuan, an ancient little town built on the shore of a lake near the capital. There Judge Dee has to solve the murder of an elderly poet, who lived in retirement on his modest property behind the Willow Quarter, the abode of the courtesans and singing-girls. The poet was murdered while peacefully contemplating the moon in his garden pavilion, set in the centre of a lotus pond. There were no witnesses—or so it seemed.

From the small pavilion in the centre of the lotus pond he could survey the entire garden, bathed in moonlight. He listened intently. Everything remained quiet. With a satisfied smile he looked down at the dead man in the bamboo chair, at the hilt of the knife sticking up from his breast. Only a few drops of blood trickled down the grey cloth of his robe. The man took up one of the two porcelain cups that stood by the pewter wine jar on the round table. He emptied it at one draught, then muttered to the corpse, 'Rest in peace! If you had been only a fool, I would probably have spared you. But since you were an interfering fool . . .'

He shrugged his shoulders. All had gone well. It was past midnight; no one would come to this lonely country house on the outskirts of the city. And in the dark house at the other end of the garden nothing stirred. He examined his hands—there was no trace of blood. Then he stooped and scrutinized the floor of the pavilion, and the chair he had been sitting on opposite the dead man. No, he hadn't left any clue. He could leave now, all was safe.

Suddenly, he heard a plopping sound behind him. He swung round, startled. Then he sighed with relief; it was only a large, green frog. It had jumped up out of the pond on to the marble steps of the pavilion. Now it sat there looking up at him solemnly with its blinking, protruding eyes.

'You can't talk, bastard!' the man sneered. 'But I'll make

double-sure!' So speaking, he gave the frog a vicious kick that smashed it against the table leg. The animal's long hindlegs twitched, then it lay still. The man picked up the second wine cup, the one his victim had been drinking from. He examined it, then he put it in his wide sleeve. Now he was ready. As he turned to go, his eye fell on the dead frog.

'Join your comrades!' he said with contempt and kicked it into the water. It fell with a splash among the lotus plants. At once the croaking of hundreds of frightened frogs tore the quiet night.

The man cursed violently. He quickly crossed the curved bridge that led over the pond to the garden gate. After he had slipped outside and pulled the gate shut, the frogs grew quiet again.

A few hours later three horsemen were riding along the lake road, back to the city. The red glow of dawn shone on their brown hunting-robes and black caps. A cool morning breeze rippled the surface of the lake, but soon it would grow hot, for it was mid-summer.

The broad-shouldered, bearded man said with a smile to his thin, elderly companion, 'Our duck-hunt suggested a good method for catching wily criminals! You set up a decoy, then stay in hiding with your clap-net ready. When your bird shows up, you net him!'

Four peasants walking in the opposite direction quickly set down the loads of vegetables they were carrying, and knelt down by the roadside. They had recognized the bearded man: it was Judge Dee, the magistrate of the lake-district of Han-yuan.

'We did a powerful lot of clapping among the reeds, sir,' the stalwart man who was riding behind them remarked wryly. 'But all we got was a few waterplants!'

'Anyway it was good exercise, Ma Joong!' Judge Dee said over his shoulder to his lieutenant. Then he went on to the thin man riding by his side: 'If we did this every morning, Mr Yuan, we'd never need your pills and powders!'

The thin man smiled bleakly. His name was Yuan Kai, and he was the wealthy owner of the largest pharmacy in Judge Dee's district. Duck-hunting was his favourite sport.

Judge Dee drove his horse on, and soon they entered the city

74

of Han-yuan, built against the mountain slope. At the market place, in front of the Temple of Confucius, the three men dismounted; then they climbed the stone steps leading up to the street where the tribunal stood, overlooking the city and the lake.

Ma Joong pointed at the squat man standing in front of the monumental gate of the tribunal. 'Heavens!' he growled, 'I have never seen our good headman up so early. I fear he must be gravely ill!'

The headman of the constables came running towards them. He made a bow, then said excitedly to the judge, 'The poet Meng Lan has been murdered, Your Honour! Half an hour ago his servant came rushing here and reported that he had found his master's dead body in the garden pavilion.'

'Meng Lan? A poet?' Judge Dee said with a frown. 'In the year I have been here in Han-yuan I have never even heard the name.'

'He lives in an old country house, near the marsh to the east of the city, sir,' the pharmacist said. 'He is not very well known here; he rarely comes to the city. But I heard that in the capital his poetry is praised highly by connoisseurs.'

'We'd better go there at once,' the judge said. 'Have Sergeant Hoong and my two other lieutenants come back yet, Headman?'

'No sir, they are still in the village near the west boundary of our district. Just after Your Honour left this morning, a man came with a note from Sergeant Hoong. It said that they hadn't yet found a single clue to the men who robbed the treasury messenger.'

Judge Dee tugged at his long beard. 'That robbery is a vexing case!' he said testily. 'The messenger was carrying a dozen gold bars. And now we have a murder on our hands too! Well, we'll manage, Ma Joong. Do you know the way to the dead poet's country place?'

'I know a short-cut through the east quarter, sir,' Yuan Kai said. 'If you'll allow me . . .'

'By all means! You come along too, Headman. You sent a couple of constables back with Meng's servant to see that nothing is disturbed, I trust?'

75

'I certainly did, sir!' the headman said importantly.

'You are making progress,' Judge Dee observed. Seeing the headman's smug smile, he added dryly, 'A pity that the progress is so slow. Get four horses from the stables!'

The pharmacist rode ahead and led them along several narrow alleys, zigzagging down to the bank of the lake. Soon they were riding through a lane lined with willow trees. These had given their name to the Willow Quarter, the abode of the dancing-girls and courtesans that lay to the east of the city.

'Tell me about Meng Lan,' the judge said to the pharmacist.

'I didn't know him too well, sir. I visited him only three or four times, but he seemed a nice, modest kind of person. He settled down here two years ago, in an old country house behind the Willow Quarter. It has only three rooms or so, but there is a beautiful large garden, with a lotus pond.'

'Has he got a large family?'

'No sir, he was a widower when he came here; his two grown-up sons live in the capital. Last year he met a courtesan from the Willow Quarter. He bought her out, and married her. She didn't have much to commend herself besides her looks—she can't read or write, sing or dance. Meng Lan was able to buy her cheaply, therefore, but it took all his savings. He was living on a small annuity an admirer in the capital was sending him. I am told it was a happy marriage, although Meng was of course much older than she.'

'One would have thought,' Judge Dee remarked, 'that a poet would choose an educated girl who could share his literary interests.'

'She is a quiet, soft-spoken woman, sir,' the pharmacist said with a shrug. 'And she looked after him well.'

'Meng Lan was a smart customer, even though he wrote poetry,' Ma Joong muttered. 'A nice, quiet girl that looks after you well—a man can hardly do better than that!'

The willow lane had narrowed to a pathway. It led through the high oak trees and thick undergrowth that marked the vicinity of the marsh behind the Willow Quarter.

The four men dismounted in front of a rustic bamboo gate. The two constables standing guard there saluted, then pushed the gate open. Before entering, Judge Dee surveyed the large garden. It was not very well kept. The flowering shrubs and bushes round the lotus pond were running wild, but they gave the place a kind of savage beauty. Some butterflies were fluttering lazily over the large lotus leaves that covered the pond's surface.

'Meng Lan was very fond of this garden,' Yuan Kai remarked.

The judge nodded. He looked at the red-lacquered wooden bridge that led over the water to a hexagonal pavilion, open on all sides. Slender pillars supported the pointed roof, decked with green tiles. Beyond the pond, at the back of the garden, he saw a low, rambling wooden building. Its thatched roof was half covered by the low foliage of the tall oak trees that stood behind the house.

It was getting very hot. Judge Dee wiped the perspiration from his brow and crossed the narrow bridge, the three others following behind him. The small pavilion offered hardly enough space for the four men. Judge Dee stood looking for a while at the thin figure, clad in a simple house-robe of grey cloth, lying back in the bamboo armchair. Then he felt the shoulders, and the limp arms. Righting himself, he said, 'The body is just getting stiff. In this hot, humid weather it's hard to fix the time of death. In any case after midnight, I would say.' He carefully pulled the knife out of the dead man's breast. He examined the long, thin blade and the plain ivory hilt. Ma Joong pursed his lips and said, 'Won't help us much, sir. Every ironmonger in town keeps these cheap knives in stock.'

Judge Dee silently handed the knife to him. Ma Joong wrapped it up in a sheet of paper he had taken from his sleeve. The judge studied the thin face of the dead man. It was frozen in an eery, lopsided grin. The poet had a long, ragged moustache and a wispy grey goatee; the judge put his age at about sixty. He took the large wine jar from the table and shook it. Only a little wine was left. Then he picked up the wine cup standing next to it, and examined it. With a puzzled look he put it in his sleeve. Turning to the headman he said:

'Tell the constables to make a stretcher of some branches, and convey the body to the tribunal, for the autopsy.' And to Yuan Kai: 'You might sit on that stone bench over there near the

77

fence for a while, Mr Yuan. I won't be long.' He motioned Ma Joong to follow him.

They crossed the bridge again. The thin planks creaked under the weight of the two heavy men. They walked round the lotus pond and on to the house. With relief Judge Dee inhaled the cool air in the shadow under the porch. Ma Joong knocked.

A rather handsome but surly-looking youngster opened. Ma Joong told him that the magistrate wanted to see Mrs Meng. As the boy went hurriedly inside, Judge Dee sat down at the rickety bamboo table in the centre of the sparsely furnished room. Ma Joong stood with folded arms behind his chair. The judge took in the old, worn furniture, and the cracked plaster walls. He said, 'Robbery can't have been the motive, evidently.'

'There—the motive is coming, sir!' Ma Joong whispered. 'Old husband, pretty young wife—we know the rest!'

Judge Dee looked round and saw that a slender woman of about twenty-five had appeared in the door opening. Her face was not made up and her cheeks showed the traces of tears. But her large, liquid eyes, gracefully curved eyebrows, full red lips and smooth complexion made her a very attractive woman. The robe she wore was of faded blue cloth, but it did not conceal her splendid figure. After one frightened look at the judge she made an obeisance, then remained standing there with downcast eyes, waiting respectfully till he would address her.

'I am distressed, madam,' Judge Dee said in a gentle voice, 'that I have to bother you so soon after the tragedy. I trust that you'll understand, however, that I must take swift action to bring the vile murderer to justice.' As she nodded he went on: 'When did you see your husband last?'

'We had our evening rice here in this room,' Mrs Meng replied in a soft, melodious voice. 'Thereafter, when I had cleared the table, my husband read here for a few hours, and then said that since there was a beautiful moon he would go to the garden pavilion and have a few cups of wine there.'

'Did he often do that?'

'Oh yes, he would go out there nearly every other night, enjoying the cool evening breeze, and humming songs.'

'Did he often receive visitors there?'

'Never, Your Honour. He liked to be left alone, and did not encourage visitors. The few people who came to see him he always received in the afternoon, and here in the hall, for a cup of tea. I loved this peaceful life, my husband was so considerate, he . . .'

Her eyes became moist and her mouth twitched. But soon she took hold of herself and went on, 'I prepared a large jar of warm wine, and brought it out to the pavilion. My husband said that I need not wait up for him, since he planned to be sitting there till a late hour. Thus I went to bed. Early this morning the servant knocked frantically on the door of our bedroom. I then saw that my husband wasn't there. The boy told me that he had found him in the pavilion. . . .'

'Does this boy live here in the house?' Judge Dee asked.

'No, Your Honour, he stays with his father, the gardener of the largest house in the Willow Quarter. The boy only comes for the day; he leaves after I have prepared the evening rice.'

'Did you hear anything unusual during the night?'

Mrs Meng frowned, then answered, 'I woke up once, it must have been shortly after midnight. The frogs in the pond were making a terrible noise. During the daytime one never hears them, they stay under water. Even when I wade into the pond to gather lotus flowers they remain quiet. But at night they come out, and they are easily startled. Therefore I thought that my husband was coming inside, and had dropped a stone or so into the pond. Then I dozed off again.'

'I see,' Judge Dee said. He thought for a while, caressing his long sidewhiskers. 'Your husband's face didn't show any signs of terror or astonishment; he must have been stabbed quite unexpectedly. He was dead before he knew what was happening. That proves your husband knew his murderer well; they must have been sitting there drinking wine together. The large jar was nearly empty, but there was only one cup. I suppose that it would be difficult to check whether a wine cup is missing?'

'It's not difficult at all,' Mrs Meng replied with a thin smile. 'We have only seven cups, a set of six, of green porcelain, and one larger cup of white porcelain, which my husband always used.'

The judge raised his eyebrows. The cup he had found was of green porcelain. He resumed: 'Did your husband have any enemies?'

'None, Your Honour!' she exclaimed. 'I can't understand who . . .'

'Do *you* have enemies?' Judge Dee interrupted.

She grew red in the face, and bit her lip. Then she said contritely, 'Of course Your Honour knows that until a year ago I worked in the quarter over there. Occasionally I refused a person who sought my favours, but I am certain that none of them would ever . . . And after all that time . . .' Her voice trailed off.

The judge rose. He thanked Mrs Meng, expressed his sympathy, and took his leave.

When the two men were walking down the garden path Ma Joong said, 'You ought to have asked her also about her *friends*, sir!'

'I depend on you for that information, Ma Joong. Have you kept in contact with that girl from the quarter—Apple Blossom is her name, I think.'

'Peach Blossom, sir. Certainly I have!'

'Good. You'll go to the quarter right now, and get her to tell you everything she knows about Mrs Meng at the time she was still working there. Especially about the men she used to associate with.'

'It's very early in the day, sir,' Ma Joong said doubtfully. 'She'll still be asleep.'

'Then you wake her up! Get going!'

Ma Joong looked dejected, but he hurried to the gate. Judge Dee reflected idly that if he sent his amorous lieutenant often enough to interview his lady-friends before breakfast, he might yet cure him of his weakness. As a rule such women don't look their best in the early morning after a late night.

Yuan Kai was standing by the lotus pond talking earnestly with a newcomer, a tall, neatly dressed man with a heavy-jowled, rather solemn face. The pharmacist introduced him as Mr Wen Shou-fang, newly elected master of the tea-merchants' guild. The guildmaster made a low bow, then began an elaborate apology for not having called on the judge yet. Judge Dee cut him short, asking, 'What brings you here so early in the morning, Mr Wen?'

Wen seemed taken aback by this sudden question. He stammered, 'I . . . I wanted to express my sympathy to Mrs Meng, and . . . to ask her whether I could help her in any way. . . .'

'So you knew the Mengs well?' Judge Dee asked.

'I was just talking this matter over with my friend Wen, sir,' Yuan Kai interposed hurriedly. 'We decided to report to Your Honour here and now that both Wen and I myself sought Mrs Meng's favours when she was still a courtesan, and that neither of us was successful. Both of us want to state that we perfectly understood that a courtesan is free to grant or withhold her favours, and that neither of us bore her any malice. Also that we had a high regard for Meng Lan, and were very glad that their marriage proved to turn out so well. Therefore . . .'

'Just to get the record straight,' the judge interrupted, 'I suppose that both of you can prove that you weren't in this vicinity last night?'

The pharmacist gave his friend an embarrassed look. Wen Shou-fang replied diffidently, 'As a matter of fact, Your Honour, both of us took part in a banquet, held in the largest house in the Willow Quarter last night. Later we ah . . . retired upstairs, with ah . . . company. We went home a few hours after midnight.'

'I had a brief nap at home,' Yuan Kai added, 'then changed into hunting-dress and went to the tribunal to fetch Your Honour for our duck-hunt.'

'I see,' Judge Dee said. 'I am glad you told me, it saves me unnecessary work.'

'This lotus pond is really very attractive,' Wen said, looking relieved. While they were conducting the judge to the gate, he added: 'Unfortunately such ponds are usually infested with frogs.'

'They make an infernal noise at times,' Yuan Kai remarked as he opened the gate for Judge Dee.

The judge mounted his horse, and rode back to the tribunal.

The headman came to meet him in the courtyard and reported

81

that in the side hall everything was ready for the autopsy. Judge Dee went first to his private office. While the clerk was pouring him a cup of hot tea the judge wrote a brief note to Ma Joong, instructing him to question the two courtesans Yuan Kai and Wen Shou-fang had slept with the night before. He thought a moment, then added: 'Verify also whether the servant of the Mengs passed last night in his father's house.' He sealed the note and ordered the clerk to have it delivered to Ma Joong immediately. Then Judge Dee quickly munched a few dry cakes, and went to the side hall where the coroner and his two assistants were waiting for him.

The autopsy brought to light nothing new: the poet had been in good health; death had been caused by a dagger thrust that had penetrated the heart. The judge ordered the headman to have the body placed in a temporary coffin, pending final instructions as to the time and place of burial. He returned to his private office and set to work on the official papers that had come in, assisted by the senior clerk of the tribunal.

It was nearly noon when Ma Joong came back. After the judge had sent the clerk away, Ma Joong seated himself opposite Judge Dee's desk, twirled his short moustache and began with a smug smile, 'Peach Blossom was already up and about, sir! She was just making her toilet when I knocked. Last night had been her evening off, so she had gone to bed early. She was looking more charming than ever, I . . .'

'Yes, yes, come to your point!' the judge cut him short peevishly. Part of his stratagem had apparently miscarried. 'She must have told you quite a lot,' he continued, 'since you were gone nearly all morning.'

Ma Joong gave him a reproachful look. He said earnestly, 'One has to handle those girls carefully, sir. We had breakfast together, and I gradually brought her round to the subject of Mrs Meng. Her professional name was Agate, her real name Shih Mei-lan; she's a farmer's daughter from up north. Three years ago, when the big drought had caused famine and the people were dying like rats, her father sold her to a procurer, and he in turn sold her to the house where Peach Blossom is working. She was a pleasant, cheerful girl. The owner of the house confirmed that

Yuan Kai had sought Agate's favours, and that she had refused. He thinks she did so only in order to raise her price, for she seemed rather sorry when the pharmacist didn't insist but found himself another playmate. With Wen Shou-fang it was a little different. Wen is a rather shy fellow; when Agate didn't respond to his first overtures, he didn't try again but confined himself to worshipping her from a distance. Then Meng Lan met her, and bought her then and there. But Peach Blossom thinks that Wen is still very fond of Agate, he often talks about her with the other girls and recently said again that Agate had deserved a better husband than that grumpy old poetaster. I also found out that Agate has a younger brother, called Shih Ming, and that he is a really bad egg. He is a drinker and gambler, who followed his sister out here and used to live off her earnings. He disappeared about a year ago, just before Meng Lan married her. But last week he suddenly turned up in the quarter and asked after his sister. When the owner told him that Meng Lan had bought and married her, Shih Ming went at once to their country house. Later Meng's servant told people that Shih Ming had quarrelled with the poet; he hadn't understood what it was all about, but it had something to do with money. Mrs Meng cried bitterly, and Shih Ming left in a rage. He hasn't been seen since.'

Ma Joong paused, but Judge Dee made no comment. He slowly sipped his tea, his bushy eyebrows knitted in a deep frown. Suddenly he asked: 'Did Meng's servant go out last night?'

'No, sir. I questioned his father, the old gardener and also their neighbours. The youngster came home directly after dinner, fell down on the bed he shares with two brothers, and lay snoring there till daybreak. And that reminds me of your second point, sir. I found that Yuan Kai stayed last night with Peony, a friend of Peach Blossom. They went up to her room at midnight, and Yuan left the house two hours later, on foot—in order to enjoy the moonlight, he said. Wen Shou-fang stayed with a girl called Carnation, a comely wench, though she was in a bit of a sullen mood this morning. It seems that Wen had drunk too much during the banquet, and when he was up in Carnation's room he laid himself down on the bed and passed out. Carnation tried to rouse him in vain, went over to the girls in the next room for a card game and forgot all about him. He came to life three hours later, but to Carnation's disappointment he had such a hangover that he went straight home, also on foot. He preferred walking to sitting in a sedan chair, because he hoped the fresh air would clear his brain—so he said. That's all, sir. I think that Shih Ming is our man. By marrying his sister, Meng Lan took Shih Ming's rice-bowl away from him, so to speak. Shall I tell the headman to institute a search for Shih Ming? I have a good description of him.'

'Do that,' Judge Dee said. 'You can go now and have your noon rice, I won't need you until tonight.'

'Then I'll have a little nap,' Ma Joong said with satisfaction. 'I had quite a strenuous morning. What with the duck-hunt and everything.'

'I don't doubt it!' the judge said dryly.

When Ma Joong had taken his leave Judge Dee went upstairs to the marble terrace that overlooked the lake. He sat down in a large armchair, and had his noon rice served there. He didn't feel like going to his private residence at the back of the tribunal; preoccupied as he was with the murder case, he wouldn't be pleasant company for his family. When he had finished his meal he pulled the armchair into a shadowy corner on the terrace. But just as he was preparing himself for a brief nap, a messenger came up and handed him a long report from Sergeant Hoong. The sergeant wrote that the investigation in the western part of the district revealed that the attack on the treasury messenger had been perpetrated by a band of six ruffians. After they had beaten the man unconscious and taken the package with the gold bars, they coolly proceeded to an inn near the district boundary, and there they had a good meal. Then a stranger arrived; he kept his neckcloth over his nose and mouth, and the people of the inn had never seen him before. The leader of the robbers handed him a package, and then they all left in the direction of the forests of the neighbouring district. Later the body of the stranger had been found in a ditch, not far from the inn. He was recognized by his dress; his face had been beaten to pulp. The local coroner was an experienced man; he examined the contents of the dead man's stomach, and discovered traces of a strong drug. The package with

84

the gold bars had, of course, disappeared. 'Thus the attack on the treasury messenger was carefully planned,' the sergeant wrote in conclusion, 'and by someone who has remained behind the scenes. He had his accomplice hire the ruffians to do the rough work, then sent that same accomplice to the inn to collect the booty. He himself followed the accomplice, drugged him and beat him to death, either because he wanted to eliminate a possible witness against him, or because he didn't want to pay him his share. In order to trace the criminal behind this affair we'll have to ask for the co-operation of Your Honour's colleague in the neighbouring district. I respectfully request Your Honour to proceed here so as to conduct the investigation personally.'

Judge Dee slowly rolled up the report. The sergeant was right, he ought to go there at once. But the poet's murder needed his attention too. Both Yuan Kai and Wen Shou-fang had had the opportunity, but neither of them seemed to have a motive. Mrs Meng's brother did indeed have a motive, but if he had done the deed he would doubtless have fled to some distant place by now. With a sigh he leaned back in his chair, pensively stroking his beard. Before he knew it he was sound asleep.

When he woke up he noticed to his annoyance that he had slept too long; dusk was already falling. Ma Joong and the headman were standing by the balustrade. The latter reported that the hue and cry was out for Shih Ming, but that as yet no trace of him had been found.

Judge Dee gave Ma Joong the sergeant's report, saying, 'You'd better read this carefully. Then you can make the necessary preparations for travelling to the west boundary of our district, for we shall go there early tomorrow morning. Among the incoming mail was a letter from the Treasury in the capital, ordering me to report without delay on the robbery. A missing string of coppers causes them sleepless nights, let alone a dozen good gold bars!'

The judge went downstairs and drafted in his private office a preliminary report to the Treasury. Then he had his evening meal served on his desk. He hardly tasted what he ate, his thoughts were elsewhere. Laying down his chopsticks, he reflected with a sigh that it was most unfortunate that the two crimes should have occurred at approximately the same time. Suddenly he set down his tea cup. He got up and started to pace the floor. He thought he had found the explanation of the missing wine cup. He would have to verify this at once. He stepped up to the window and looked at the courtyard outside. When he saw that there was no one about, he quickly crossed over to the side gate and left the tribunal unnoticed.

In the street he pulled his neckcloth up over the lower half of his face, and on the corner rented a small sedan chair. He paid the bearers off in front of the largest house in the Willow Quarter. Confused sounds of singing and laughter came from the brilliantly lit windows; apparently a gay banquet was already in progress there. Judge Dee quickly walked on and started along the path leading to Meng Lan's country house.

When he was approaching the garden gate he noticed that it was very quiet here; the trees cut off the noise from the Willow Quarter. He softly pushed the gate open and studied the garden. The moonlight shone on the lotus pond, the house at the back of the garden was completely dark. Judge Dee walked around the pond, then stooped and picked up a stone. He threw it into the pond. Immediately the frogs started to croak in chorus. With a satisfied smile Judge Dee went on to the door, again pulling his neckcloth up over his mouth and nose. Standing in the shadow of the porch, he knocked.

A light appeared behind the window. Then the door opened and he heard Mrs Meng's voice whispering, 'Come inside, quick!'

She was standing in the doorway, her torso naked. She only wore a thin loin-cloth, and her hair was hanging loose. When the judge let the neckcloth drop from his face she uttered a smothered cry.

'I am not the one you were expecting,' he said coldly, 'but I'll come in anyway.' He stepped inside, shut the door behind him and continued sternly to the cowering woman, 'Who were you waiting for?'

Her lips moved but no sound came forth.

'Speak up!' Judge Dee barked.

Clutching the loin-cloth round her waist she stammered, 'I wasn't waiting for anyone. I was awakened by the noise of the

86

SHE WAS STANDING IN THE DOORWAY, HER TORSO NAKED

frogs, and feared there was an intruder. So I came to have a look and . . .'

'And asked the intruder to come inside quickly! If you must lie, you'd better be more clever about it! Show me your bedroom where you were waiting for your lover!'

Silently she took the candle from the table, and led the judge to a small side room. It only contained a narrow plank-bed, covered by a thin reed mat. The judge quickly stepped up to the bed and felt the mat. It was still warm from her body. Righting himself, he asked sharply: 'Do you always sleep here?'

'No, Your Honour, this is the servant's room, the boy uses it for his afternoon nap. My bedroom is over on the other side of the hall we passed just now.'

'Take me there!'

When she had crossed the hall and shown the judge into the large bedroom he took the candle from her and quickly looked the room over. There was a dressing-table with a bamboo chair, four clothes-boxes, and a large bedstead. Judge Dee pulled the bedcurtains aside. He saw that the thick bedmat of soft reed had been rolled up, and that the pillows had been stored away in the recess in the back wall. He turned round to her and said angrily, 'I don't care where you were going to sleep with your lover, I only want to know his name. Speak up!'

She didn't answer, she only gave him a sidelong glance. Then her loin-cloth slipped down to the floor and she stood there stark naked. Covering herself with her hands, she looked coyly at him.

Judge Dee turned away. 'Those silly tricks bore me,' he said coldly. 'Get dressed at once, you'll come with me to the tribunal and pass the night in jail. Tomorrow I shall interrogate you in court, if necessary under torture.'

She silently opened a clothes-box and started to dress. The judge went to the hall and sat down there. He reflected that she was prepared to go a long way to shield her lover. Then he shrugged. Since she was a former courtesan, it wasn't really such a very long way. When she came in, fully dressed, he motioned her to follow him.

They met the night watch at the entrance of the Willow Quarter. The judge told their leader to take Mrs Meng in a sedan chair to the tribunal, and hand her to the warden of the jail. He was also to send four of his men to the dead poet's house, they were to hide in the hall and arrest anyone who knocked. Then Judge Dee walked back at a leisurely pace, deep in thought.

Passing the gatehouse of the tribunal, he saw Ma Joong sitting in the guardroom talking with the soldiers. He took his lieutenant to his private office. When he had told him what had happened in the country house, Ma Joong shook his head sadly and said, 'So she had a secret lover, and it was he who killed her husband. Well, that means that the case is practically solved. With some further persuasion, she'll come across with the fellow's name.'

Judge Dee took a sip from his tea, then said slowly, 'There are a few points that worry me, though. There's a definite connection between Meng's murder and the attack on the treasury messenger, but I haven't the faintest idea what it means. However, I want your opinion on two other points. First, how could Mrs Meng conduct a secret love affair? She and her husband practically never went out, and the few guests they received came during the day. Second, I verified that she was sleeping tonight in the servant's room, on a narrow plank-bed. Why didn't she prepare to receive her lover in the bedroom, where there is a large and comfortable bedstead? Deference to her dead husband couldn't have prevented her from that, if she had been merrily deceiving him behind his back! I know, of course, that lovers don't care much about comfort, but even so, that hard, narrow plank-bed . . .'

'Well,' Ma Joong said with a grin, 'as regards the first point, if a woman is determined on having her little games, you can be dead sure that she'll somehow manage to find ways and means. Perhaps it was that servant of theirs she was playing around with, and then her private pleasures had nothing to do with the murder. As to the second point, I have often enough slept on a plank-bed, but I confess I never thought of sharing it. I'll gladly go to the Willow Quarter, though, and make inquiries about its special advantages if any.' He looked hopefully at the judge.

Judge Dee was staring at him, but his thoughts seemed to be elsewhere. Slowly tugging at his moustache, he remained silent for some time. Suddenly the judge smiled. 'Yes,' he said, 'we might try that.' Ma Joong looked pleased. But his face fell as Judge Dee continued briskly, 'Go at once to the Inn of the Red Carp, behind the fishmarket. Tell the head of the beggars there to get you half a dozen beggars who frequent the vicinity of the Willow Quarter, and bring those fellows here. Tell the head of the guild that I want to interrogate them about important new facts that have come to light regarding the murder of the poet Meng Lan. Make no secret of it. On the contrary, see to it that everybody knows I am summoning these beggars, and for what purpose. Get going!'

As Ma Joong remained sitting there, looking dumbfounded at the judge, he added, 'If my scheme succeeds, I'll have solved both Meng's murder and the robbery of the gold bars. Do your best!'

Ma Joong got up and hurried outside.

When Ma Joong came back to Judge Dee's private office herding four ragged beggars he saw on the side table large platters with cakes and sweetmeats, and a few jugs of wine.

Judge Dee put the frightened men at their ease with some friendly words of greeting, then told them to taste the food and have a cup of wine. As the astonished beggars shuffled up to the table looking hungrily at the repast, Judge Dee took Ma Joong apart and said in a low voice:

'Go to the guardroom and select three good men from among the constables. You wait with them at the gate. In an hour or so I'll send the four beggars away. Each of them must be secretly followed. Arrest any person who accosts any one of them and bring him here, together with the beggar he addressed!'

Then he turned to the beggars, and encouraged them to partake freely of the food and wine. The perplexed vagabonds hesitated long before they fell to, but then the platters and cups were empty in an amazingly brief time. Their leader, a one-eyed scoundrel, wiped his hands on his greasy beard, then muttered resignedly to his companions, 'Now he'll have our heads chopped off. But I must say that it was a generous last meal.'

To their amazement, however, Judge Dee made them sit down on tabourets in front of his desk. He questioned each of them about the place he came from, his age, his family and many other innocent details. When the beggars found that he didn't touch upon any awkward subjects, they began to talk more freely, and soon an hour had passed.

Judge Dee rose, thanked them for their co-operation and told them they could go. Then he began to pace the floor, his hands clasped behind his back.

Sooner than he had expected there was a knock. Ma Joong came in, dragging the one-eyed beggar along.

'He gave me the silver piece before I knew what was happening, Excellency!' the old man whined. 'I swear I didn't pick his pocket!'

'I know you didn't,' Judge Dee said. 'Don't worry, you can keep that silver piece. Just tell me what he said to you.'

'He comes up to me when I am rounding the street corner, Excellency, and presses that silver piece into my hand. He says: "Come with me, you'll get another one if you tell me what that judge asked you and your friends." I swear that's the truth, Excellency!'

'Good! You can go. Don't spend the money on wine and gambling!' As the beggar scurried away the judge said to Ma Joong: 'Bring the prisoner!'

The pharmacist Yuan Kai started to protest loudly as soon as he was inside. 'A prominent citizen arrested like a common criminal! I demand to know . . .'

'And I demand to know,' Judge Dee interrupted him coldly, 'why you were lying in wait for that beggar, and why you questioned him.'

'Of course I am deeply interested in the progress of the investigation, Your Honour! I was eager to know whether . . .'

'Whether I had found a clue leading to you which you had overlooked,' the judge completed the sentence for him. 'Yuan Kai, you murdered the poet Meng Lan, and also Shih Ming, whom you used to contact the ruffians that robbed the treasury messenger. Confess your crimes!'

Yuan Kai's face had turned pale. But he had his voice well under control when he asked sharply: 'I suppose Your Honour has good grounds for proffering such grave accusations?'

'I have. Mrs Meng stated that they never received visitors at night. She also stated that the frogs in the lotus pond never croak during the day. Yet you remarked on the noise they make—sometimes. That suggested that you had been there at night. Further, Meng had been drinking wine with his murderer, who left his own cup on the table, but took away Meng's special cup. That, together with Meng's calm face, told me that he had been drugged before he was killed, and that the murderer had taken his victim's cup away with him because he feared that it would still smell after the drug, even if he washed it there in the pond. Now the accomplice of the criminal who organized the attack on the treasury messenger was also drugged before he was killed. This suggested that both crimes were committed by one and the same person. It made me suspect you, because as a pharmacist you know all about drugs, and because you had the opportunity to kill Meng Lan after you had left the Willow Quarter. I also remembered that we hadn't done too well on our duck-hunt this morning—we caught nothing. Although an expert hunter like you led our party. You were in bad form, because you had quite a strenuous night behind you. But by teaching me the method of duck-hunting with a decoy, you suggested to me a simple means for verifying my suspicions. Tonight I used the beggars as a decoy, and I caught you.'

'And my motive?' Yuan Kai asked slowly.

'Some facts that are no concern of yours made me discover that Mrs Meng had been expecting her brother Shih Ming to visit her secretly at night, and that proved that she knew that he had committed some crime. When Shih Ming visited his sister and his brother-in-law last week, and when they refused to give him money, he became angry and boasted that you had enlisted his help in an affair that would bring in a lot of money. Meng and his wife knew that Shih Ming was no good, so when they heard about the attack on the treasury messenger, and when Shih Ming didn't show up, they concluded it must be the affair Shih Ming had alluded to. Meng Lan was an honest man, and he taxed you with the robbery—there was your motive. Mrs Meng wanted to shield her brother, but when presently she learns that it was you who murdered her husband, and also her brother, she'll speak, and her testimony will conclude the case against you, Yuan Kai.'

The pharmacist looked down; he was breathing heavily. Judge Dee went on, 'I shall apologize to Mrs Meng. The unfortunate profession she exercised hasn't affected her staunch character. She was genuinely fond of her husband, and although she knew that her brother was a good-for-nothing, she was prepared to be flogged in the tribunal for contempt of court, rather than give him away. Well, she'll soon be a rich woman, for half of your property shall be assigned to her, as blood-money for her husband's murder. And doubtless Wen Shou-fang will in due time ask her to marry him, for he is still deeply in love with her. As to you, Yuan Kai, you are a foul murderer, and your head will fall on the execution ground.'

Suddenly Yuan looked up. He said in a toneless voice, 'It was that accursed frog that did for me! I killed the creature, and kicked it into the pond. That set the other frogs going.' Then he added bitterly : 'And, fool that I was, I said frogs can't talk !'

'They can,' Judge Dee said soberly. 'And they did.'

THE TWO BEGGARS

This story explains why Judge Dee was late for his family dinner on the Feast of Lanterns. This feast is the concluding phase of the protracted New Year's celebrations; in the evening an intimate family dinner is held, and the ladies of the household consult the oracle on what the New Year has in store for them. The scene of this story is laid in Poo-yang, well-known to readers of the novel The Chinese Bell Murders. *Chapter IX of that book mentions Magistrate Lo, Judge Dee's volatile colleague in the neighbouring district of Chinhwa, who now figures in this tale about the sad fate that befell two beggars.*

When the last visitor had left, Judge Dee leaned back in his chair with a sigh of relief. With tired eyes he looked out over his back garden where in the gathering dusk his three small sons were playing among the shrubbery. They were suspending lighted lanterns on the branches, painted with the images of the Eight Genii.

It was the fifteenth day of the first month, the Feast of Lanterns. People were hanging gaily painted lanterns of all shapes and sizes in and outside their houses, transforming the entire city into a riot of garish colours. From the other side of the garden wall the judge heard the laughter of people strolling in the park.

All through the afternoon the notables of Poo-yang, the prosperous district where Judge Dee had now been serving one year as magistrate, had been coming to his residence at the back of the tribunal compound to offer him their congratulations on this auspicious day. He pushed his winged judge's cap back from his forehead and passed his hand over his face. He was not accustomed to drinking so much wine in the daytime; he felt slightly sick. Leaning forward, he took a large white rose from the bowl on the tea-table, for its scent is supposed to counteract the effects of alcohol. Inhaling deeply the flower's fresh fragrance, the judge reflected that his last visitor, Ling, the master of the goldsmiths' guild, had really overstayed his welcome, had seemed glued to his chair. And Judge Dee had to change and refresh himself before going to his women's quarters, where his three wives were now supervising the preparations for the festive family dinner.

Excited children's voices rang out from the garden. The judge looked round and saw that his two eldest boys were struggling to get hold of a large coloured lantern.

'Better come inside now and have your bath!' Judge Dee called out over to them.

'Ah-kuei wants that nice lantern made by Big Sister and me all for himself!' his eldest son shouted indignantly.

The judge was going to repeat his command, but out of the corner of his eye he saw the door in the back of the hall open. Sergeant Hoong, his confidential adviser, came shuffling inside. Noticing how wan and tired the old man looked, Judge Dee said quickly, 'Take a seat and have a cup of tea, Hoong! I am sorry I had to leave all the routine business of the tribunal to you today. I had to go over to the chancery and do some work after my guests had left, but Master Ling was more talkative than ever. He took his leave only a few moments ago.'

'There was nothing of special importance, Your Honour,' Sergeant Hoong said, as he poured the judge and himself a cup of tea. 'My only difficulty was to keep the clerks with their noses to the grindstone. Today's festive spirit had got hold of them!'

Hoong sat down and sipped his tea, carefully holding up his ragged grey moustache with his left thumb.

'Well, the Feast of Lanterns is on,' the judge said, putting the white rose back on the table.' As long as no urgent cases are reported, we can afford to be a little less strict for once.'

Sergeant Hoong nodded. 'The warden of the north quarter came to the chancery just before noon and reported an accident, sir. An old beggar fell into a deep drain, in a back street not far from Master Ling's residence. His head hit a sharp stone at the bottom, and he died. Our coroner performed the autopsy and signed the certificate of accidental death. The poor wretch was clad only in a tattered gown, he hadn't even a cap on his head, and his greying hair was hanging loose. He was a cripple. He must have stumbled into the drain going out at dawn for his

95

morning rounds. Sheng Pa, the head of the beggars, couldn't identify him. Poor fellow must have come to the city from up-country expecting good earnings here during the feast. If nobody comes to claim the corpse, we'll have it burned tomorrow.'

Judge Dee looked round at his eldest son, who was moving an armchair among the pillars that lined the open front of the hall. The judge snapped: 'Stop fiddling around with that chair, and do as I told you! All three of you!'

'Yes, sir!' the three boys shouted in chorus.

While they were rushing away, Judge Dee said to Hoong: 'Tell the warden to have the drain covered up properly, and give him a good talking to! Those fellows are supposed to see to it that the streets in their quarter are kept in good repair. By the way, we expect you to join our small family dinner tonight, Hoong!'

The old man bowed with a gratified smile.

'I'll go now to the chancery and lock up, sir! I'll present myself at Your Honour's residence again in half an hour.'

After the sergeant had left, Judge Dee reflected that he ought to go too and change from his ceremonial robe of stiff green brocade into a comfortable house-gown. But he felt loath to leave the quiet atmosphere of the now empty hall, and thought he might as well have one more cup of tea. In the park outside it had grown quiet too; people had gone home for the evening rice. Later they would swarm out into the street again, to admire the display of lanterns and have drinking bouts in the roadside wine-houses. Putting his cup down, Judge Dee reflected that perhaps he shouldn't have given Ma Joong and his two other lieutenants the night off, for later in the evening there might be brawls in the brothel district. He must remember to tell the headman of the constables to double the night watch.

He stretched his hand out again for his teacup. Suddenly he checked himself. He stared fixedly at the shadows at the back of the hall. A tall old man had come in. He seemed to be clad in a tattered robe, his head with the long flowing hair was bare. Silently he limped across the hall, supporting himself on a crooked staff. He didn't seem to notice the judge, but went straight past with bent head.

Judge Dee was going to shout and ask what he meant by coming in unannounced, but the words were never spoken. The judge froze in sudden horror. The old man seemed to flit right through the large cupboard, then stepped down noiselessly into the garden.

The judge jumped up and ran to the garden steps. 'Come back, you!' he shouted angrily.

There was no answer.

Judge Dee stepped down into the moonlit garden. Nobody was there. He quickly searched the low shrubbery along the wall, but found nothing. And the small garden gate to the park outside was securely locked and barred as usual.

The judge remained standing there. Shivering involuntarily, he pulled his robe closer to his body. He had seen the ghost of the dead beggar.

After a while he took hold of himself. He turned round abruptly, went back up to the hall and entered the dim corridor leading to the front of his private residence. He returned absent-mindedly the respectful greeting of his doorman, who was lighting two brightly coloured lanterns at the gate, then crossed the central courtyard of the tribunal compound and walked straight to the chancery.

The clerks had gone home already; only Sergeant Hoong was there, sorting out a pile of papers on his desk by the light of a single candle. He looked up astonished as he saw the judge come in.

'I thought that I might as well have a look at that dead beggar after all,' Judge Dee said casually.

Hoong quickly lit a new candle. He led the judge through the dark, deserted corridors to the jail at the back of the courtroom. In the side hall a thin form was lying on a deal table, covered by a reed mat.

Judge Dee took the candle from Hoong, and motioned him to remove the mat. Raising the candle, the judge stared at the lifeless, haggard face. It was deeply lined, and the cheeks were hollow, but it lacked the coarse features one would expect in a beggar. He seemed about fifty; his long, tousled hair was streaked with grey. The thin lips under the short moustache were distorted in a repulsive death grimace. He wore no beard.

The judge pulled open the lower part of the tattered, patched gown. Pointing at the misshapen left leg, he remarked, 'He must have broken his knee once, and it was badly set. He must have walked with a pronounced limp.'

Sergeant Hoong picked up a long crooked staff standing in the corner and said, 'Since he was quite tall, he supported himself on this crutch. It was found by his side, at the bottom of the drain.'

Judge Dee nodded. He tried to raise the left arm of the corpse, but it was quite stiff. Stooping, he scrutinized the hand, then righting himself, he said, 'Look at this, Hoong! These soft hands without any callouses, the long, well-tended fingernails! Turn the body over!'

When the sergeant had rolled the stiff corpse over on its face Judge Dee studied the gaping wound at the back of the skull. After a while he handed the candle to Hoong, and taking a paper handkerchief from his sleeve, he used it to carefully brush aside the matted grey hair, which was clotted with dried blood. He then examined the handkerchief under the candle. Showing it to Hoong, he said curtly: 'Do you see this fine sand and white grit? You wouldn't expect to find that at the bottom of a drain, would you?'

Sergeant Hoong shook his head perplexedly. He replied slowly, 'No, sir. Slime and mud rather, I'd say.'

Judge Dee walked over to the other end of the table and looked at the bare feet. They were white, and the soles were soft. Turning to the sergeant, he said gravely, 'I fear that our coroner's thoughts were on tonight's feast rather than on his duties when he performed the post-mortem. This man wasn't a beggar, and he didn't fall accidentally into the drain. He was thrown into it when he was dead already. By the person who murdered him.'

Sergeant Hoong nodded, ruefully pulling at his short grey beard. 'Yes, the murderer must have stripped him, and put him in that beggar's gown. It should have struck me at once that the man was naked under that tattered robe. Even a poor beggar would have been wearing something underneath; the evenings are still rather chilly.' Looking again at the gaping wound, he asked: 'Do you think the head was bashed in with a heavy club, sir?'

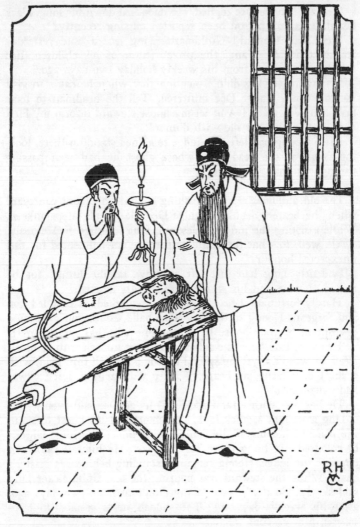

RAISING THE CANDLE, THE JUDGE STARED AT THE LIFELESS,
HAGGARD FACE

'Perhaps,' Judge Dee replied. He smoothed down his long, black beard. 'Has any person been reported missing recently?'

'Yes, Your Honour! Guildmaster Ling sent a note yesterday stating that Mr Wang, the private tutor of his children, had failed to come back from his weekly holiday two days ago.'

'Strange that Ling didn't mention that when he came to visit me just now!' Judge Dee muttered. 'Tell the headman to have my palankeen ready! And let my house steward inform my First Lady not to wait for me with dinner!'

After Hoong had left, the judge remained standing there, looking down at the dead man whose ghost he had seen passing through the hall.

The old guildmaster came rushing out into his front courtyard when the bearers deposited Judge Dee's large official palankeen. While assisting the judge to descend, Ling inquired boisterously, 'Well, well, to what fortunate occurrence am I indebted for this unexpected honour?'

Evidently Ling had just left a festive family dinner, for he reeked of wine and his words were slightly slurred.

'Hardly fortunate, I fear,' Judge Dee remarked, as Ling led him and Sergeant Hoong to the reception hall. 'Could you give me a description of your house tutor, the one who has disappeared?'

'Heavens, I do hope the fellow didn't get himself into trouble! Well, he wasn't anything special to look at. A tall thin man, with a short moustache, no beard. Walked with a limp, left leg was badly deformed.'

'He has met with a fatal accident,' Judge Dee said evenly.

Ling gave him a quick look, then motioned his guest to sit in the place of honour at the central table under the huge lantern of coloured silk hung there for the feast. He himself sat down opposite the judge. Hoong remained standing behind his master's chair. While the steward was pouring the tea, Guildmaster Ling said slowly, 'So that's why Wang didn't turn up two days ago, after his weekly day off!' The sudden news seemed to have sobered him up considerably.

'Where did he go to?' Judge Dee asked.

'Heaven knows! I am not a man who pries into the private

affairs of his household staff. Wang had every Thursday off; he would leave here Wednesday night before dinner, and return Thursday evening, also at dinner time. That's all I know, and all I need to know, if I may say so, sir!'

'How long had he been with you?'

'About one year. Came from the capital with an introduction from a well-known goldsmith there. Since I needed a tutor to teach my grandsons, I engaged him. Found him a quiet, decent fellow. Quite competent too.'

'Do you know why he chose to leave the capital and seek employment here in Poo-yang? Did he have any family here?'

'I don't know,' Ling replied crossly. 'It was not my habit to discuss with him anything except the progress of my grandchildren.'

'Call your house steward!'

The guildmaster turned round in his chair and beckoned the steward who was hovering about in the back of the spacious hall.

When he had come up to the table and made his obeisance, Judge Dee said to him, 'Mr Wang has met with an accident and the tribunal must inform the next of kin. You know the address of his relatives here, I suppose?'

The steward cast an uneasy glance at his master. He stammered, 'He . . . as far as I know Mr Wang didn't have any relatives living here in Poo-yang, Your Honour.'

'Where did he go then for his weekly holidays?'

'He never told me, sir. I suppose he went to see a friend or something.' Seeing Judge Dee's sceptical expression, he quickly went on, 'Mr Wang was a taciturn man, Your Honour, and he always evaded questions about his private affairs. He liked to be alone. He spent his spare hours in the small room he has in the back yard of this residence. His only recreation was brief walks in our garden.'

'Didn't he receive or send any letters?'

'Not that I know of, sir.' The steward hesitated a moment. 'From some chance remarks of his about his former life in the capital I gathered that his wife had left him. It seemed that she was of a very jealous disposition.' He gave his employer an anxious glance. As he saw that Ling was staring ahead and didn't seem to be listening, he went on with more self-assurance: 'Mr Wang had no private means at all, sir, and he was very parsimonious. He hardly spent one cent of his salary, never even took a sedan chair when he went out on his day off. But he must have been a wealthy man once, I could tell that from some small mannerisms of his. I think that he was even an official once, for sometimes when caught off guard he would address me in rather an authoritative tone. I understand he lost everything, his money and his official position. Didn't seem to mind, though. Once he said to me: "Money is of no use if you don't enjoy life spending it; and when your money is spent, official life has lost its glamour." Rather a frivolous remark coming from such a learned gentleman, I thought, sir—if I may make so bold, sir.'

Ling glared at him and said with a sneer, 'You seem to find time hanging heavily on your hands in this household! Gossiping instead of supervising the servants!'

'Let the man speak!' the judge snapped at Ling. And to the steward: 'Was there absolutely no clue as to where Mr Wang used to go on his days off? You must know; you saw him go in and out, didn't you?'

The steward frowned. Then he replied, 'Well, it did strike me that Mr Wang always seemed happy when he went, but when he came back he was usually rather depressed. He had melancholy moods at times. Never interfered with his teaching, though, sir. He was always ready to answer difficult questions, the young miss said the other day.'

'You stated that Wang only taught your grandchildren,' the judge said sharply to Ling. 'Now it appears that he also taught your daughter!'

The guildmaster gave his steward a furious look. He moistened his lips, then replied curtly, 'He did. Until she was married, two months ago.'

'I see.' Judge Dee rose from his chair and told the steward: 'Show me Mr Wang's room!' He motioned to Sergeant Hoong to follow him. As Ling made a move to join them, the judge said: 'Your presence is not required.'

The steward led the judge and Hoong through a maze of corridors to the back yard of the extensive compound. He unlocked a narrow door, lifted the candle and showed them a small, poorly furnished room. There was only a bamboo couch, a simple writing-desk with a straight-backed chair, a bamboo rack with a few books and a black leather clothes-box. The walls were covered with long strips of paper, bearing ink-sketches of orchids, done with considerable skill. Following Judge Dee's glance, the steward said:

'That was Mr Wang's only hobby, sir. He loved orchids, knew everything about tending them.'

'Didn't he have a few potted orchids about?' the judge asked.

'No, sir. I don't think he could afford to buy them they are quite expensive, sir!'

Judge Dee nodded. He picked up a few of the dog-eared volumes from the book rack and glanced through them. It was romantic poetry, in cheap editions. Then he opened the clothes-box. It was stuffed with men's garments, worn threadbare. but of good quality. The cash box at the bottom of the box contained only some small change. The judge turned to the desk. The drawer had no lock. Inside were the usual writing materials, but no money and not a scrap of inscribed paper, not even a receipted bill. He slammed the drawer shut and angrily asked the steward, 'Who has rifled this room during Mr Wang's absence?'

'Nobody has been here, Your Honour!' the frightened steward stammered. 'Mr Wang always locked the door when he went out, and I have the only spare key.'

'You yourself told me that Wang didn't spend a cent, didn't you? What has happened to his savings over the past year? There's only some small change here!'

The steward shook his head in bewilderment. 'I really couldn't say, Your Honour! I am sure nobody came in here. And all the servants have been with us for years. There has never been any pilfering, I can assure you, sir!'

Judge Dee remained standing for a while by the desk. He stared at the paintings, slowly tugging at his moustache. Then he turned round and said: 'Take us back to the hall!'

While the steward was conducting them again through the winding corridors, Judge Dee remarked casually, 'This residence is situated in a nice, quiet neighbourhood.'

'Oh yes, indeed, sir, very quiet and respectable!'

'It's exactly in such a nice, respectable neighbourhood that one finds the better houses of assignation,' the judge remarked dryly. 'Are there any near here?'

The steward seemed taken aback by this unexpected question. He cleared his throat and replied diffidently, 'Only one, sir, two streets away. It's kept by a Mrs Kwang—very high class, visited by the best people only, sir. Never any brawls or other trouble there, sir.'

'I am glad to hear that,' Judge Dee said.

Back in the reception hall he told the guildmaster that he would have to accompany him to the tribunal to make the formal identification of the dead man. While they were being carried out there in Judge Dee's palankeen, the guildmaster observed a surly silence.

After Ling had stated that the dead body was indeed that of his house tutor and filled out the necessary documents, Judge Dee let him go. Then he said to Sergeant Hoong, 'I'll now change into a more comfortable robe. In the meantime you tell our headman to stand by in the courtyard with two constables.'

Sergeant Hoong found the judge in his private office. He had changed into a simple robe of dark-grey cotton with a broad black sash, and he had placed a small black skull-cap on his head.

Hoong wanted to ask him where they were going, but seeing Judge Dee's preoccupied mien, he thought better of it and silently followed him out into the courtyard.

The headman and two constables sprang to attention when they saw the judge.

'Do you know the address of a house of assignation in the north quarter, close by Guildmaster Ling's residence?' Judge Dee asked.

'Certainly, Your Honour!' the headman answered officiously. 'That's Mrs Kwang's establishment. Properly licensed, and very high class, sir, only the best . . .'

'I know, I know!' the judge cut him short impatiently. 'We'll walk out there. You lead the way with your men!'

Now the streets were crowded again with people. They were milling around under the garlands of coloured lanterns that spanned the streets and decorated the fronts of all the shops and restaurants. The headman and the two constables unceremoniously elbowed people aside, making way for the judge and Sergeant Hoong.

Even in the back street where Mrs Kwang lived there were many people about. When the headman had knocked and told the gatekeeper that the magistrate had arrived, the frightened old man quickly conducted the judge and Hoong to a luxuriously appointed waiting-room in the front court.

An elderly, sedately dressed maidservant placed a tea-set of exquisite antique porcelain on the table. Then a tall, handsome woman of about thirty came in, made a low bow and introduced herself as Mrs Kwang, a widow. She wore a straight, long-sleeved robe, simple in style but made of costly, dark-violet damask. She herself poured the tea for the judge, elegantly holding up with her left hand the trailing sleeve of the right. She remained standing in front of the judge, respectfully waiting for him to address her. Sergeant Hoong stood behind Judge Dee's chair, his arms folded in his wide sleeves.

Leisurely tasting the fragrant tea, Judge Dee noticed how quiet it was; all noise was kept out by the embroidered curtains and wall-hangings of heavy brocade. The faint scent of rare and very expensive incense floated in the air. All very high class indeed. He set down his cup and began, 'I disapprove of your trade, Mrs Kwang. I recognize, however, that it is a necessary evil. As long as you keep everything orderly and treat the girls well, I won't make any trouble for you. Tell me, how many girls have you working here?'

'Eight, Your Honour. All purchased in the regular manner, of course, mostly directly from their parents. Every three months the ledgers with their earnings are sent to the tribunal, for the assessment of my taxes. I trust that . . .'

'No, I have no complaints about that. But I am informed that one of the girls was bought out recently by a wealthy patron. Who is the fortunate girl?'

Mrs Kwang looked politely astonished. 'There must be some misunderstanding, Your Honour. All my girls here are still very young—the eldest is just nineteen—and haven't yet completed their training in music and dancing. They try hard to please, of course, but none of them has yet succeeded in captivating the favour of a wealthy patron so as to establish an ah . . . more permanent relationship.' She paused, then added primly, 'Although such a transaction means, of course, a very substantial monetary gain for me, I don't encourage it until a courtesan is well into her twenties, and in every respect worthy of attaining the crowning success of her career.'

'I see,' Judge Dee said. He thought ruefully that this information disposed effectively of his attractive theory. Now that his hunch had proved wrong, this case would necessitate a long investigation, beginning with the goldsmith in the capital who had introduced Wang to Guildmaster Ling. Suddenly another possibility flashed through his mind. Yes, he thought he could take the chance. Giving Mrs Kwang a stern look he said coldly:

'Don't prevaricate, Mrs Kwang! Besides the eight girls who are living here, you have established another in a house of her own. That's a serious offence, for your licence covers this house only.'

Mrs Kwang put a lock straight in her elaborate coiffure. The gesture made her long sleeve slip back, revealing her white, rounded forearm. Then she replied calmly:

'That information is only partly correct, Your Honour. I suppose it refers to Miss Liang, who lives in the next street. She is an accomplished courtesan from the capital, about thirty years old—her professional name is Rosedew. Since she was very popular in elegant circles in the capital, she saved a great deal of money and bought herself free, without, however, handing in her licence. She wanted to settle down, and came here to Poo-yang for a period of rest, and to have a leisurely look around for a suitable marriage partner. She's a very intelligent woman, sir; she knows that all those elegant, flighty young men in the capital don't go for permanent arrangements, so she wanted a steady, elderly man of some means and position. Only occasionally did she receive such selected clients here in my house. Your Honour will find the pertaining entries in a separate ledger, also duly submitted regularly for inspection. Since Miss Liang has kept her licence, and since the taxes on her earnings are paid . . .'

She let her voice trail off. Judge Dee was secretly very pleased, for he knew now that he had been on the right track after all. But he assumed an angry mien, hit his fist on the table and barked, 'So the man who is buying Rosedew out to marry her is being meanly deceived! For there is no redemption fee to be paid! Not one copper, neither to you nor to her former owner in the capital! Speak up! Weren't you and she going to share that fee, obtained from the unsuspecting patron under false pretences?'

At this Mrs Kwang lost her composure at last. She knelt down in front of Judge Dee's chair and repeatedly knocked her forehead on the floor. Looking up, she wailed, 'Please forgive this ignorant person, Excellency! The money has not yet been handed over. Her patron is an exalted person, Excellency, a colleague of Your Excellency, in fact, the magistrate of a district in this same region. If he should hear about this, he . . .'

She burst into tears.

Judge Dee turned round and gave Sergeant Hoong a significant look. That could be no one else but his amorous colleague of Chin-hwa, Magistrate Lo! He barked at Mrs Kwang: 'It was indeed Magistrate Lo who asked me to investigate. Tell me where Miss Liang lives; I shall interrogate her personally about this disgraceful affair!'

A short walk brought the judge and his men to the address in the next street that the tearful Mrs Kwang had given him.

Before knocking on the gate, the headman quickly looked up and down the street, then said, 'If I am not greatly mistaken, sir, the drain that beggar fell into is located right at the back of this house.'

'Good!' Judge Dee exclaimed. 'Here, I'll knock myself. You and your two men keep close to the wall while I go inside with the sergeant. Wait here till I call you!'

After repeated knocking the peephole grate in the gate opened and a woman's voice asked, 'Who is there?'

'I have a message from Magistrate Lo, for a Miss Rosedew,' Judge Dee said politely.

The door opened at once. A small woman dressed in a thin houserobe of white silk asked the two men to enter. As she preceded them to the open hall in the front court, the judge noticed that despite her frail build she had an excellent figure.

When they were inside she gave her two visitors a curious look, then bade them seat themselves on the couch of carved rosewood. She said somewhat diffidently: 'I am indeed Rosedew. Who do I have the honour of . . .'

'We shan't take much of your time, Miss Liang,' the judge interrupted quickly. He looked her over. She had a finely chiselled mobile face, with expressive, almond-shaped eyes and a delicate small mouth—a woman of considerable intelligence and charm. Yet something didn't fit with his theory.

He surveyed the elegantly furnished hall. His eye fell on a high rack of polished bamboo in front of the side window. Each of its three superimposed shelves bore a row of orchid plants, potted in beautiful porcelain bowls. Their delicate fragrance pervaded the air. Pointing at the rack, he said: 'Magistrate Lo told me about your fine collection of orchids, Miss Liang. I am a great lover of them myself. Look, what a pity! The second one on the top shelf has wilted, it needs special treatment, I think. Could you get it down and show it to me?'

She gave him a doubtful look, but apparently decided that it was better to humour this queer friend of Magistrate Lo. She took a bamboo step-ladder from the corner, placed it in front of the rack, and nimbly climbed up, modestly gathering the thin robe round her shapely legs. When she was about to take the pot, Judge Dee suddenly stepped up close to the ladder and remarked casually:

'Mr Wang used to call you Orchid, didn't he, Miss Liang? So much more apposite than Rosedew, surely!' When Miss Liang stood motionless, looking down at the judge with eyes that were suddenly wide with fear, he added sharply: 'Mr Wang was standing exactly where I am standing now when you smashed the flower pot down on his head, wasn't he?'

She started to sway. Uttering a cry, she wildly groped for support. Judge Dee quickly steadied the ladder. Reaching up, he caught her round her waist and set her down on the floor. She clasped her hands to her heaving bosom and gasped: 'I don't . . Who are you?'

'I am the magistrate of Poo-yang,' the judge replied coldly. 'After you murdered Wang, you replaced the broken flower pot by a new one, and transplanted the orchid. That's why it's wilted, isn't it?'

'It's a lie!' she cried out. 'Wicked slander. I shall . . .'

'I have proof!' Judge Dee cut her short. 'A servant of the neighbours saw you dragging the dead body to the drain behind your house here. And I found in Wang's room a note of his, stating that he feared you would harm him, now that you had a wealthy patron who wanted to marry you.'

'The treacherous dog!' she shouted. 'He swore he didn't keep one scrap of paper relating to . . .' She suddenly stopped and angrily bit her red lips.

'I know everything,' the judge said evenly. 'Wang wanted more than his weekly visits. Thus he endangered your affair with Magistrate Lo, an affair that would not only bring in a lump sum of money for you and Mrs Kwang, but also set you up for life. Therefore you had to kill your lover.'

'Lover?' she screamed. 'Do you think I allowed that disgusting cripple ever to touch me here? It was bad enough to have to submit to his odious embraces before, when we were still in the capital!'

'Yet you allowed him to share your bed here,' Judge Dee remarked with disdain.

'You know where he slept? In the kitchen! I wouldn't have allowed him to come at all, but he made himself useful by answering my love letters for me, and he paid for and tended those orchids there, so that I would have flowers to wear in my hair. He also acted as doorman and brought tea and refreshments when one of my lovers was here. What else do you think I allowed him to come here for?'

'Since he had spent his entire fortune on you I thought perhaps . . .' Judge Dee said dryly.

'The damnable fool!' she burst out again. 'Even after I had told him that I was through with him, he kept on running after me, saying he couldn't live without seeing my face now and then —the cringing beggar! His ridiculous devotion spoilt my reputation. It was because of him that I had to leave the capital and bury myself in this dreary place. And I, fool that I was, trusted that simpering wretch! Leaving a note accusing me! He's ruined me, the dirty traitor!'

Her beautiful face had changed into an evil mask. She stamped her small foot on the floor in impotent rage.

'No,' Judge Dee said in a tired voice, 'Wang didn't accuse you. What I said just now about that note wasn't true. Beyond a few paintings of orchids which he did when thinking of you, there wasn't one clue to you in his room. The poor, misguided man remained loyal to you, to his very end!' He clapped his hands. When the headman and the two constables had come rushing inside, he ordered: 'Put this woman in chains and lock her up in jail. She has confessed to a foul murder.' As the two constables grabbed her arms and the headman started to chain her, the judge said: 'Since there is not a single reason for clemency, you shall be beheaded on the execution ground.'

He turned round and left, followed by Sergeant Hoong. The woman's frantic cries were drowned by the loud shouts and laughter of a happy group of youngsters who came surging through the street, waving brightly coloured lanterns.

When they were back in the tribunal, Judge Dee took Hoong straight to his own residence. While walking with him to the back hall, he said, 'Let's just have one cup of tea before we go and join the dinner in my women's quarters.'

The two men sat down at the round table. The large lantern hanging from the eaves, and those among the shrubs in the garden had been extinguished. But the full moon lit up the hall with its eerie light.

Judge Dee quickly emptied his cup, then he sat back in his chair and began without further preliminaries:

'Before we went to see Guildmaster Ling, I knew only that the beggar was no beggar, and that he had been murdered elsewhere by having the back of his skull bashed in, probably with a flower pot—as suggested by the fine sand and white grit. Then, during our interview with Ling, I suspected for a moment that the guild-master was involved in this crime. He hadn't said a word about Wang's disappearance when he came to visit me, and I thought it strange that later he didn't inquire what exactly had happened to Wang. But I soon realized that Ling is that unpleasant kind of person who doesn't take the slightest interest in his personnel, and that he was cross because I had interrupted his family party. What the steward told me about Wang brought to light a fairly clear pattern. The steward said that Wang's family life had been broken up because he squandered his wealth, and his mentioning Mrs Wang's jealousy pointed to another woman being involved. Thus I deducted that Wang had become deeply infatuated with a famous courtesan.'

'Why not with some decent girl or woman, or even with a common prostitute?' the sergeant objected.

'If it had been a decent woman, Wang would not have needed to spend his fortune on her; he could have divorced his wife and married his lady-love. And if she had been a common prostitute, he could have bought her out at a moderate price, and set her up in a small house of her own—all without sacrificing his wealth and his official position. No, I was certain that Wang's mistress must have been a famous courtesan in the capital, who could afford to squeeze a lover dry, then discard him and go on to the next. But I assumed that Wang refused to let himself be thrown away like a chewed-out piece of sugar cane, and that he made a nuisance of himself. That she fled from the capital and came to Poo-yang in order to start her game all over again. For it's well known that many wealthy merchants are living here in this district. I assumed that Wang had traced her here and had forced her to let him visit her regularly, threatening to expose her callous racket if she refused. Finally, that after she had caught my foolish colleague Lo, Wang began to blackmail her, and that therefore she had killed him.' He sighed, then added: 'We now know that it was quite different. Wang sacrificed everything he had for her, and even the pittance he received as tutor he spent on orchids for her. He was quite content to be allowed to see and talk to her every week, frustrating and humiliating as those few hours were. Sometimes, Hoong, a man's folly is engendered by such a deep and reckless passion that it lends him a kind of pathetic grandeur.'

Sergeant Hoong pensively pulled at his ragged grey moustache. After a while he asked, 'There are a great many courtesans here in Poo-yang. How did Your Honour know that Wang's mistress must belong to the house of Mrs Kwang? And why did it have to be his mistress who murdered him and not, for instance, another jealous lover?'

'Wang used to go there on foot. Since he was a cripple, this proved that she must live near to the guildmaster's house, and that led us to Mrs Kwang's establishment. I asked Mrs Kwang what courtesan had been recently bought out, because such an occurrence supplied the most plausible motive for the murder, namely that the courtesan had to get rid of an embarrassing former lover. Well, we know that Wang was indeed embarrassing her, but not by threatening to blackmail her or by any other wicked scheme. It was just his dog-like devotion that made her hate and despise him. As to the other possibilities you just mentioned, I had of course also reckoned with those. But if the murderer had been a man, he would have carried the body away to some distant spot, and he would also have been more thorough in his attempts at concealing his victim's identity. The fact that the attempt was confined to dressing the victim in a tattered beggar's gown, loosening his top-knot and mussing up his hair, pointed to a woman having done the deed. Women know that a different dress and hair-do can completely alter their own appearance. Miss Liang applied this method to a man—and that was a bad mistake.'

Judge Dee took a sip from the cup the sergeant had refilled for him, then resumed, 'As a matter of course it could also have been an elaborate scheme to inculpate Miss Liang. But I considered that a remote possibility. Miss Liang herself was our best chance. When the headman informed me that the dead beggar had been found at the back of her house, I knew that my theory must be correct. However, when we had gone inside I saw that she was a rather small and frail woman, who could never have bashed in the head of her tall victim. Therefore I at once looked around for some death-trap, and found it in the potted orchids on the high shelf, where the wilted plant supplied the final clue. She must have climbed up the ladder, probably asking Wang to steady it for her. Then she made some remark or other that made him turn his head, and smashed the pot down on his skull. These and other details we'll learn tomorrow when I question Miss Liang in the tribunal. Now as regards the role played by Mrs Kwang, I don't think she did more than help Miss Liang to concoct the scheme of getting the fictitious redemption fee out of Lo. Our charming hostess draws the line at murder; hers is a high-class establishment, remember!'

Sergeant Hoong nodded. 'Your Honour has not only uncovered a cruel murder, but at the same time saved Magistrate Lo from an alliance with a determined and evil woman!'

Judge Dee smiled faintly. 'Next time I meet Lo,' he said, 'I'll tell him about this case—without mentioning, of course, that I know it was he who patronized Miss Liang. My gay friend must have been visiting my district incognito! This case will teach him a lesson—I hope!'

Hoong discreetly refrained from commenting further on one of his master's colleagues. He remarked with a satisfied smile: 'So now all the points of this curious case have been cleared up!'

Judge Dee took a long draught from his tea. As he set the cup down he shook his head and said unhappily: 'No, Hoong. Not all the points.'

He thought he might as well tell the sergeant now about the ghostly apparition of the dead beggar, without which this murder would have been dismissed as an ordinary accident. But just as he was about to speak, his eldest son came rushing inside. Seeing his father's angry look, the boy said with a quick bow: 'Mother said we might take that nice lantern to our bedroom, sir!'

As his father nodded, the small fellow pushed an armchair up to one of the pillars. He climbed on the high backrest, reached up and unhooked the large lantern of painted silk hanging down from the eaves. He jumped down, lit the candle inside with his tinderbox, and held up the lantern for his father to see.

'It took Big Sister and me two days to make this, sir!' he said proudly. 'Therefore we didn't want Ah-kuei to spoil it. We like the Immortal Lee, he is such a pathetic, ugly old fellow!'

Pointing at the figure the children had painted on the lantern, the judge asked: 'Do you know his story?' When the boy shook his head, his father continued: 'Many, many years ago Lee was a very handsome young alchemist who had read all books and mastered all magic arts. He could detach his soul from his body and then float at will in the clouds, leaving his empty body behind, to resume it when he came down to earth again. One day, however, when Lee had carelessly left his body lying in a field, some farmers came upon it. They thought it was an abandoned corpse, and burned it. So when Lee came down, he found his own beautiful body gone. In despair he had to enter the corpse of a poor old crippled beggar which happened to be lying by the roadside, and Lee had to keep that ugly shape for ever. Although later he found the Elixir of Life, he could never undo that one mistake, and it was in that form that he entered the ranks of the Eight Immortals: Lee with the Crutch, the Immortal Beggar.'

The boy put the lantern down. 'I don't like him anymore!' he said with disdain. 'I'll tell Big Sister that Lee was a fool who only got what he deserved!'

He knelt down, wished his father and Hoong good night, and scurried away.

Judge Dee looked after him with an indulgent smile. He took up the lantern to blow out the candle inside. But suddenly he checked himself. He stared at the tall figure of the Immortal Beggar projected on the plaster wall. Then he tentatively turned the lantern round, as it would turn in the draught. He saw the ghostly shadow of the crippled old man move slowly along the wall, then disappear into the garden.

With a deep sigh the judge blew the candle out and put the lantern back on the floor. He said gravely to Sergeant Hoong, 'You were right after all, Hoong! All our doubts are solved—at least those about the mortal beggar. He was a fool. As to the Immortal Beggar—I am not too sure.' He rose and added with a wan smile, 'If we measure our knowledge not by what we know but by what we don't, we are just ignorant fools, Hoong, all of us! Let's go now and join my ladies.'

THE WRONG SWORD

*This case also occurred in Poo-yang. As readers of The
Chinese Bell Murders will remember, Poo-yang was bordered
on one side by the Chin-hwa district, where Magistrate Lo held
sway, and on the other by the district of Woo-yee, administered by the austere Magistrate Pan. The murder described in
the present story happened in Judge Dee's absence; he had
gone to Woo-yee to discuss with his colleague Pan a case
involving both districts. The judge had set out from Poo-yang
three days previously, taking with him Sergeant Hoong and
Tao Gan, and leaving Ma Joong and Chiao Tai in charge of
the tribunal. The three days had passed uneventfully for his
two lieutenants; it was only on the last day, on the very
evening that Judge Dee was expected back, that things suddenly began to happen.*

'You pay for the fourth dozen stuffed crabs!' Ma Joong told Chiao
Tai with satisfaction as he put the dice back into the box.

'They were worth it,' said Chiao Tai, smacking his lips. He took
his wine beaker and emptied it in one draught.

Judge Dee's two burly lieutenants were sitting at a small table
near the window, on the second floor of the Kingfisher Restaurant, one of their favourite haunts. Situated on the water-way
that crosses the city of Poo-yang from north to south, its second-
floor window offered a splendid view of the evening sun, setting
beyond the western city wall.

The sounds of boisterous applause came up from the street below. Ma Joong poked his head out of the window and looked
down at the crowd that had assembled on the river bank.

'It's that troupe of travelling actors which came here four days
ago,' he remarked. 'In the afternoon they perform acrobatics in
the street, at night they stage historical plays.'

'I know,' Chiao Tai said. 'The rice-dealer Lau helped them rent
the yard of the old Taoist temple for setting up their stage. Lau
came to the tribunal the other day for the permit. The leader of

the troupe was with him—decent-looking fellow, Bao his name is. The troupe consists of his wife, his daughter and his son.' He refilled his beaker and added: 'I had thought of strolling over to the temple; I like a good play with lots of sword-fencing. But since our judge is away and we're responsible for everything, I don't like to leave the tribunal for long.'

'Well, here we have a grandstand seat for their acrobatic turns at least,' Ma Joong said contentedly. He turned his chair round to the window and put his folded arms on the sill. Chiao Tai followed his example.

In the street below a square reed mat had been spread out, surrounded by a dense crowd of spectators. A small boy of about eight was turning somersaults there with surprising agility. Two other actors, a tall lean man and a sturdy woman stood on the left and right of the mat with folded arms, and a young girl was squatting by the side of a bamboo box, evidently containing their paraphernalia. On top of the box was a low wooden rack; two long, shining swords were laid across it, one above the other. All four actors wore black jackets and wide trousers; red sashes were wound tightly round their waists, and red scarves round their heads. An old man dressed in a shabby blue gown was sitting on a tabouret close by, lustily beating the drum he held between his bony knees.

'Wish I could see that girl's face,' Ma Joong said wistfully. 'Look, Lau is there too; he seems to be in trouble!'

He pointed down at a neatly dressed, middle-aged man wearing a black gauze cap, who was standing behind the bamboo box. He was quarrelling with a huge ruffian whose unruly hair was bound up with a blue rag. He grabbed Lau's sleeve but Lau pushed him away. The two men paid no attention to the boy who was now walking around the reed mat on his hands, balancing a wine jar on the soles of his feet.

'I have never seen that tall rogue before,' Chiao Tai remarked. 'Must be from outside the city.'

'Now we'll get a good view of the wenches!' Ma Joong said with a grin.

The boy had finished. The leader of the troupe stood in the centre of the mat, legs apart and knees slightly bent. The sturdy

116

woman placed her right foot on his knee, then with one lithe movement climbed up onto his shoulders. At a shout from the man, the girl climbed up too, put one foot on the man's left shoulder, grabbed the woman's arm with one hand, and stretched out her other arm and leg. At almost the same time the boy followed her example and balanced himself on the man's right shoulder. As the human pyramid stood there precariously, the greybeard in the faded gown beat a frantic roll on his drum. The crowd burst out in loud shouts of approval.

The faces of the boy, the woman and the girl were only ten feet or so from Ma Joong and Chiao Tai. The latter whispered with enthusiasm: 'Look at the woman's splendid figure! Nice friendly face too!'

'I prefer the girl!' Ma Joong said eagerly.

'Much too young! The woman is about thirty, just right. Knows what's what!'

The drummer stopped; the woman and her two children jumped down from Bao's shoulders. All four actors made a graceful bow, then the girl went round among the spectators collecting coppers in a wooden bowl. Ma Joong pulled a string of cash from his sleeve and threw it down at her. She caught it expertly and rewarded him with a smile.

'That's literally throwing money away!' Chiao Tai remarked dryly.

'Call it an investment in a promising project!' Ma Joong countered with a smug grin. 'What's next?'

The boy was standing in the centre of the reed mat. He put his hands behind his back and lifted his chin. As the greybeard started to beat his drum, Bao bared his right arm, grabbed the sword lying on top of the rack, and with a movement quick as lightning plunged it deep into the boy's breast. Blood spurted out; the boy staggered backwards as his father pulled the sword out again. There were horrified cries from the crowd.

'I have seen that trick before,' Ma Joong said. 'Heaven knows how they do it! The sword looks genuine enough.' He turned away from the window and took his wine beaker.

The agonized cry of a woman rose above the confused murmur of voices. Chiao Tai, who had been looking down intently, suddenly jumped up. He snapped: 'That was no trick, brother! It was plain murder! Come along!'

The two men rushed down the stairs and ran outside. They elbowed their way through the excited crowd to the edge of the reed mat. The boy was lying on his back, his breast a mass of blood. His mother was kneeling by his side, sobbing convulsively as she stroked the small, still face. Bao and his daughter were standing there stock still, staring down with pale faces at the pitiful dead body. Bao still held the bloodstained sword.

Ma Joong wrenched it from his hand and asked angrily: 'Why did you do that?'

The actor woke from his stupor. Giving Ma Joong a dazed look, he stammered: 'It was the wrong sword!'

'I can explain, Mr Ma!' the rice-dealer Lau spoke up. 'It was an accident!'

A squat man came forward; it was the warden of the west quarter. Chiao Tai ordered him to roll the dead body in the reed mat and have it brought to the tribunal for examination by the coroner. As the warden gently made the mother rise, Chiao Tai said to Ma Joong, 'Let's take these people up to the dining-room, and try to get this straight!'

Ma Joong nodded. Taking the sword under his arm, he said to the rice-dealer, 'You come too, Mr Lau. And let the greybeard bring the box and that other sword along.'

He looked for the tall ruffian who had accosted Lau, but the fellow was nowhere to be seen.

Up on the second floor of the Kingfisher Restaurant Ma Joong told Bao, the two crying women and the old drummer to sit down at a corner table. He poured them wine from the jar he and Chiao Tai had been drinking from. He hoped that the strong liquor would help them get over the shock. Then he turned to the rice-dealer and ordered him to explain. He knew that the theatre was Lau's hobby, that he attended all shows given by travelling actors. His regular face with the short black moustache and goatee was pale and drawn. He adjusted his black gauze cap, then began diffidently:

'As you may know, Mr Ma, this man Bao is the leader of the

troupe, a fine actor and acrobat.' He paused, passed his hand over his face, then took the second sword which the old drummer had laid on the table. 'You may have seen these trick-swords,' he continued. 'The blade is hollow, and filled with pig's blood. It has a false point a couple of inches long, which slides back into the blade if the sword is pushed against something. Thus it appears as if the point penetrates deeply, the illusion being completed by the pig's blood spurting out. When the sword is pulled out, the point resumes its original position, being pushed out again by a rattan spiral hidden inside. You can see it for yourself!'

Ma Joong took the sword from him. He noticed a thin groove round it, a few inches below the blunt point. He turned round and pressed it against the wooden floor. The point slid into the blade, red blood spurted out. Mrs Bao started to scream. Her husband quickly put his arm round her shoulders. The girl remained sitting, still as a stone figure. The greybeard muttered angrily, pulling at his ragged beard.

'That wasn't too clever, brother!' Chiao Tai snapped.

'Had to verify it, didn't I?' Ma Joong said contritely. He took the real sword in his other hand, and balanced the two weapons carefully. 'These two swords are about the same weight,' he muttered. 'And they look exactly alike. Dangerous!'

'The trick-sword ought to have been lying on top of the rack,' Lau said, 'and the real sword below it. After the stabbing trick the boy would get up, and his father would perform a dance with the real sword.'

Bao had risen. Stepping up to Ma Joong, he asked hoarsely: 'Who exchanged the swords?' As Ma Joong only pursed his lips, Bao grabbed his shoulder and shouted: 'Who did it, I ask you?'

Ma Joong gently loosened his grip and made him sit down again. 'That's what we are going to find out,' he said. 'Are you quite sure that you put the trick-sword on top?'

'Of course! Haven't we been through that routine a hundred, a thousand times?'

Ma Joong shouted downstairs for more wine. He motioned Chiao Tai and Lau to follow him to the table in front of the window. When they had sat down he whispered to Lau, 'My mate and I were looking out from this window here. We saw you and a tall ruffian standing close by the bamboo box and the sword rack. Who else was standing near you two?'

'I really couldn't say,' Lau replied with a frown. 'When the boy was doing his somersaults that tall rogue, who had been standing by my side for some time, suddenly asked me for money. When I refused he began to threaten me. I told him to make himself scarce. Then . . . it happened.'

'Who is he?' Chiao Tai asked.

'Never saw him before. Perhaps Bao knows.'

Chiao Tai got up and asked the actors. Bao, his wife and his daughter all shook their heads, but the old drummer said in a wheezing voice, 'I know him all right, sir! He came to our show in the temple yard every night, paid one copper only! He is a vagabond; his name is Hoo Ta-ma.'

'Did you see anyone else come near the sword rack?' Chiao Tai asked.

'How could I, seeing I had to keep my eyes on the performance all the time?' the greybeard replied indignantly. 'I only noticed Mr Lau and Hoo Ta-ma, because I happen to know both of them. But there were lots of others, all packed close. How could I see what was going on there?'

'I suppose you couldn't,' Chiao Tai said resignedly. 'And we couldn't have arrested the whole crowd.' Turning to Bao again, he asked: 'Did you notice anyone you know standing close to the mat?'

'I don't know anyone here,' Bao replied in a toneless voice. 'We have been to Woo-yee and Chin-hwa, but this is our first visit to this city. I only know Mr Lau. He introduced himself to me when I was surveying the temple yard for the setting up of our stage, and he kindly offered his help.'

Chiao Tai nodded. He liked Bao's open, intelligent face. He turned back to the others and said to Lau, 'You'd better take the actors back to their quarters, Mr Lau. Tell them that the magistrate is expected back here later tonight, and he'll investigate this foul murder at once. Tomorrow they'll have to attend the session of the tribunal, for the formalities. Then the boy's body will be handed back to them for burial.'

'Can I come too, Mr Chiao? Bao is a nice fellow; I'd like to do all I can to help him in this awful predicament.'

'You'll have to be there anyway!' Ma Joong said dryly. 'You are an important witness.'

He and Chiao Tai rose and said a few comforting words to the stricken family. When Lau had taken them and the greybeard downstairs, the two friends sat down again at the window table. Silently they emptied their wine beakers. While Ma Joong was refilling them he said, 'Well, I hope that's everything. Tonight we'll put it all before the judge. It'll be a hard nut to crack, I'd say. Even for him!'

He gave his friend a thoughtful look, but Chiao Tai made no comment. He idly watched the waiter who had come upstairs with a large oil lamp. When the waiter had gone, Chiao Tai banged his beaker down and said bitterly, 'What a dirty murder! Tricking a father into killing his own son, and before his mother's eyes! You know what? We've got to get the mean bastard who did it! Here and now!'

'I agree,' Ma Joong said slowly, 'but a murder is no small matter. I am not so sure that our judge would like us meddling in the investigation. One wrong move might spoil everything, you know!'

'If we do only what the judge would have ordered anyway, I don't see that we can do much harm.'

Ma Joong nodded. Then he said briskly: 'All right, I am with you! Here's luck!' Having emptied his cup, he added with a wry smile, 'This is a chance to prove our mettle! When those worthy citizens talk to us here, butter wouldn't melt in their mouths. But behind our backs they say we are just a couple of vulgar bullies, all brawn and no brain!'

'Up to a point,' Chiao Tai said judiciously, 'they are right. We are not men of letters, after all. That's why I wouldn't dream of tackling a case involving the gentry, for instance. But this murder is just the thing for us, for all concerned are the kind of people we are familiar with.'

'Let's plan out the investigation, then!' Ma Joong growled. He refilled their beakers.

'Our judge always starts by talking about motive and opportunity,' Chiao Tai began. 'In this case, the motive is as plain as a pikestaff. Since nobody could have had anything against that poor boy, the murderer must have hated Bao. Like poison.'

'Right. And since Bao is here in Poo-yang for the first time, our suspects are narrowed down to the people who have been in close contact with him and his troupe these last few days.'

'There still is the possibility that Bao met an old enemy here,' Chiao Tai objected.

'In that case Bao would have told us about him at once,' Ma Joong said. He thought hard for a while. 'I am not too sure that nobody could have had anything against the boy, you know. Youngsters like that have a knack of turning up in the most unexpected places; he could have seen or heard something he shouldn't have. Someone wanted to close the boy's mouth, and the sword-trick was a godsend.'

'Yes,' Chiao Tai admitted. 'Heavens, there are too many possibilities!' He sipped his wine, then frowned and put his beaker down. 'This stuff tastes funny!' he remarked astonished.

'It's the same we had before, but it doesn't taste right to me either! Tell you what, brother! Wine is only good when you are happy and carefree! You can't do real drinking with problems weighing on your mind!'

'That's why our judge is always sipping tea then, the poor sap!' Chiao Tai scowled at the wine jar, then grabbed it and put it down on the floor, under the table. Folding his muscular arms in his sleeves, he resumed: 'As to opportunity, both Lau and Hoo were standing close to the rack, so either of them could have exchanged the swords. What about their motives?'

Ma Joong rubbed his chin. After a while he answered, 'As regards Hoo, I can think of only one. Or two, rather. Meaning Mrs Bao and her daughter. Heavens, I wouldn't mind having a go at those wenches myself! Think of the acrobatic tricks they can do! Suppose Hoo wanted either of them or both, and Bao said hands-off, and Hoo took this badly?'

'Possible. If Hoo is a degenerate, mean type of scoundrel, he might take revenge on Bao in a dirty way like this. But what about Lau?'

'Out of the question! Lau is the old-fashioned, prim type. If he engaged in extramural amorous games, he'd sneak off to some discreet brothel. He wouldn't dare start something with an actress.'

'I agree that Hoo is our best chance,' Chiao Tai said. 'I'll go along now and have a talk with him. Then I'll look up Lau too, just for the sake of completeness, so to speak. You had better go to the temple, brother, and get to know more about the general background. Our judge will want to know everything about the Bao family, I expect.'

'All right, I'll pump the two women; that's the smoothest approach, I'd say!' He got up briskly.

'Maybe not as smooth as you think,' Chiao Tai said dryly as he rose also. 'Those two women are acrobats, remember! They know how to use their hands if you annoy them! Well, we'll meet later, in the tribunal.'

Chiao Tai went straight to the small winehouse in the east city where Sheng Pa, the head of the Beggars' Guild, had his headquarters.

The only occupant of the dingy taproom was a man of colossal proportions reclining in an armchair, snoring loudly. His mast-like arms were folded over his large bare belly, which protruded from under his worn-out black jacket.

Chiao Tai shook him roughly. The man woke up with a start. Giving Chiao Tai a baleful look, he said crossly, 'You would give a peaceful old man a fright! But sit down, anyway. Let me profit by your conversation.'

'I am in a hurry. You know a rogue called Hoo Ta-ma?'

Sheng Pa slowly shook his large head. 'No,' he said ponderously, 'I don't know him.'

Chiao Tai caught the crafty look that flashed through the other's eyes. He said impatiently, 'You may not have met him, but you must know about him, you fat crook! He's been seen in the yard of the old Taoist temple.'

'Don't call me names!' Sheng Pa said with a pained look. Then he added wistfully, 'Ah, that temple yard! My old headquarters! Those were the days, brother! Gay and carefree! Look at me

now, master of the guild, burdened with administrative duties!
I . . .'

'The only burden you carry is your belly,' Chiao Tai interrupted. 'Speak up! Where do I find Hoo?'

'Well,' Sheng Pa replied resignedly, 'if you must push matters
to extremes . . . I have heard it said that a man who calls himself by that name can usually be found in a wine stall below the
east city wall—the fifth one north from the East Gate, as a matter
of fact. It's only hearsay, mind you, I . . .'

'Thank you kindly!' Chiao Tai rushed out.

In the street he stuffed his cap into his sleeve, and rumpled
his hair. A brief walk brought him to a shed of old boards put up
against the base of the city wall. He surveyed the dark, deserted
neighbourhood, then pulled aside the door curtain and stepped
inside.

The shed was dimly lit by a smoking oil lamp, and was filled
with a nauseating stench of rancid oil and cheap liquor. An old
man with bleary eyes was serving wine dregs behind a rickety
bamboo counter. Three men in tattered gowns were standing
about in front of it, Hoo Ta-ma's tall frame towering above the
others.

Chiao Tai stood himself next to Hoo. The men eyed him indifferently; evidently they didn't know him for an officer of the
tribunal. He ordered a drink. After he had taken a sip from the
cracked rice-bowl that served as a wine cup, he spat on the floor
and growled at Hoo: 'Filthy stuff! It's bad when you are down
to your last coppers!'

A wry smile lit up Hoo's broad, sun-tanned face. Chiao Tai
thought he looked like a rough-and-ready rascal, but not entirely
unprepossessing. He resumed, 'You wouldn't know a job with
something in it, would you?'

'No, I don't. Besides, I am the last man to ask, brother! I am
having a spell of dirty luck, these days. Week ago I was supposed
to pinch two cartloads of rice on the road, in Woo-yee. Easy job,
only had to knock out the two carters. Affair had been nicely
planned—on a lonely stretch, in the forest. My bad luck spoiled it.'

'You are getting too old, maybe!' Chiao Tai sneered.

'Shut up and listen! Just as I knock the first carter down, a small brat comes running round the corner. He looks me up and down and asks, silly-like: "What are you doing that for?" I hear noises, and jump into the undergrowth. From my hideout I see a tilt cart with travelling actors come round the corner. The second carter tells them the sad story, adding that I took to my heels. They move on together, rice-carts and all!'

'Bad luck!' Chiao Tai agreed. 'And you may be in for more of it too. Yesterday I saw a troupe performing in the street here, there was a boy doing somersaults. If that's the same brat, you'd better be careful. He might spot you.'

'Spotted me already! Caught me in the act again! With his sister, this second time! Can you imagine worse luck? But the brat had bad luck too. He's dead!'

Chiao Tai tightened his belt. This was a simple case, after all. He said affably, 'You certainly have bad luck, Hoo! I am an officer of the tribunal, and you are coming along with me!'

Hoo cursed obscenely, then barked at the two others, 'You heard him, the dirty running-dog of the tribunal! Let's beat the thief-catcher to pulp!'

The two vagabonds slowly shook their heads. The elder said, 'You don't belong here, brother. Settle your accounts yourself!'

'Rot in hell!' And to Chiao Tai: 'Come outside, I'll get you or you'll get me!'

A beggar who was loitering in the dark alley scurried away when he saw the two men come out and take up boxers' stances.

Hoo started with a quick blow at Chiao Tai's jaw, but he parried it expertly and followed up with an elbow thrust in Hoo's face. The other ducked and grabbed Chiao Tai's waist with his long, muscular arms. Chiao Tai realized that in a body-to-body fight Hoo was no mean opponent; he was of the same height, but much heavier, and he tried to throw Chiao Tai by utilizing this advantage. Soon both men were panting heavily. But Chiao Tai knew more about technique, and he succeeded in slipping out of the other's bear-like hug. He stepped back, then placed an accurate blow in Hoo's face that closed his left eye. Hoo shook his head, then came again for him, growling angrily.

Chiao Tai was on his guard for foul tricks, but apparently Hoo didn't go in for them. He made a feint, then gave Chiao Tai a blow in his midriff that would have floored him if he hadn't ducked and caught it on his breastbone. Chiao Tai feigned to be winded and staggered back. Hoo aimed a straight blow at his jaw to finish him off. Chiao Tai caught Hoo's fist in both hands, ducked under his arm and threw him over his back. There was a snapping sound as the rogue's shoulder dislocated and he crashed to the ground, hitting his head on a stone with a sickening thud. He lay quite still.

Chiao Tai went into the shed again and told the greybeard to give him a rope, then to run out and call the warden and his men.

Chiao Tai tied Hoo's legs securely together. Then he squatted down and waited for the warden. Hoo was carried to the tribunal on an improvised stretcher. Chiao Tai ordered the jail keeper to put Hoo in a cell, call the coroner and have him revive the unconscious man, then set his shoulder.

These things having been attended to, Chiao Tai walked over to the chancery deep in thought. There was one point that was worrying him. Perhaps the case was not so simple after all.

In the meantime Ma Joong had walked from the Kingfisher Restaurant back to the tribunal, where he had taken a bath. When he had put on a nice clean robe he strolled to the Taoist temple.

A mixed crowd was standing about below the raised stage of bamboo poles, lighted by two large paper lanterns. The show had started already, for Bao couldn't afford to let the death of his son interfere with the theatrical routine. He, his wife and his daughter, all three dressed in gorgeous stage costumes, stood in front of two superimposed tables representing a throne. Mrs Bao sang to the accompaniment of a strident fiddle.

Ma Joong went to the bamboo cage next to the stage where the greybeard was vigorously scraping his two-stringed violin, at the same time working a brass gong with his right foot. Ma Joong waited till he put the violin aside and changed to a pair of wooden clappers. He nudged him and asked with a meaningful grin:

'Where can I meet the women?'

The old man pointed with his bearded chin at the stepladder behind him, then beat his clappers extra hard.

Ma Joong climbed up to the improvised green-room, separated from the stage by screens of bamboo matting. There was only a cheap dressing-table littered with platters for rouge and powder, and one low tabouret.

Loud shouts of approval from the audience indicated that the actors had reached the end of a scene. The dirty blue curtain was drawn aside and Miss Bao came in.

She was dressed for the part of a princess, in a long green robe glittering with brass-foil ornaments, and wearing an elaborate headdress decorated with garish paper flowers. Two long tresses of glossy black hair hung down from her temples. Although her face was covered with the thick layer of stage make-up, Ma Joong thought that she still looked remarkably attractive. She gave him a quick look, then sat down on the tabouret. Leaning towards the mirror to inspect her painted eyebrows, she asked listlessly:

'Is there any news?'

'Nothing in particular!' Ma Joong replied cheerfully. 'I just came round for a talk with a charming girl!'

She turned her head and gave him a contemptuous look. 'If you think that'll get you anywhere with me,' she snapped, 'you are wrong!'

'I wanted to talk about your parents!' he said, taken aback by this abrupt rebuff.

'Parents? About my mother, you mean! Well, for her you need no intermediary, she's always open to a fair business proposition!'

Suddenly she buried her face in her hands and started to sob. He stepped up to her and patted her on the back. 'Now don't get upset, dear! Of course this terrible affair of your brother has . . .'

'He wasn't my brother!' she interrupted him. 'This life . . . I can't stand it any longer! My mother a whore, my father a stupid fool who dotes on her . . . You know what part I am acting now? I am the daughter of a noble king and his chaste queen! How's that for a joke?' She angrily shook her head, then started to dab her face energetically with a wad of paper. She resumed in a calmer voice, 'Imagine, mother produced that boy half a year ago, out of nothing! Told father she had made a little mistake, eight years ago. The fellow who had got her into trouble

127

had looked after the boy all that time, then decided he couldn't keep him any longer. Father gave in, as always . . .' She bit her lips.

'Have you any idea,' Ma Joong asked, 'who could have played that infernal trick on your father tonight? Has he met an old enemy here, perhaps?'

'Why should those swords have been exchanged intentionally?' she said curtly. 'My father could have made a mistake, couldn't he? The two swords look exactly the same, you know. They have to, else the trick wouldn't look genuine.'

'Your father seemed sure someone had changed them,' Ma Joong remarked.

Suddenly she stamped her foot on the floor and exclaimed: 'What a life! I hate it! Heaven be praised that I'll be making a new start soon. At last I have met a decent fellow who is willing to pay father a handsome dowry, and take me as a concubine.'

'Life as a concubine isn't always so great, you know!'

'I won't be a concubine for long, my friend! His wife is ailing and the doctors don't give her more than a year or so.'

'Who's the lucky fellow, anyway?'

She hesitated a moment before she replied, 'I'll tell you because you are an officer of the tribunal. Keep it quiet for a while, will you? It's the rice-dealer, Lau. He has had bad luck in business lately, and he doesn't want to speak to my father before he can put the money on the table. Lau is a bit older than me, of course, and he's got old-fashioned ideas in his head, but I tell you I am sick and tired of those so-called gay young blades, who just want to sleep with you once, and then on to the next!'

'How did you come to know Lau?'

'Met him the very day we came here to Poo-yang. He offered father help in renting this yard. Lau took a liking to me at once, he . . .'

Her voice was drowned in the deafening applause from outside. She jumped up, put her headdress straight and said hurriedly:

'I must go on now! Good-bye!'

She disappeared through the curtain.

Ma Joong found his friend sitting all alone in the deserted

128

'I AM THE DAUGHTER OF A NOBLE KING AND HIS CHASTE
QUEEN! HOW'S THAT FOR A JOKE?'

chancery. Chiao Tai looked up and said, 'Seems our case is solved, brother! I have a suspect under lock and key here in jail!'

'Good!' Ma Joong pulled up a chair and listened to Chiao Tai's story. Then he told him about his interview with Miss Bao. 'Combining our information,' he concluded, 'it appears that Miss Bao had a fling with Hoo, in between her meetings with the devoted Lau. Just to keep in good form, I suppose. Well, what are you looking so worried for?'

'I forgot to tell you just now,' Chiao Tai replied slowly, 'that Hoo Ta-ma didn't want to come nice and quiet like, I had to go through some fisticuffs with him. The fellow fought cleanly, not one dirty kick or blow. I can imagine Hoo breaking that boy's neck in a fit of rage when he caught him peeping while he was busy with his sister; but to play that mean trick of exchanging the swords . . . No, brother, that isn't in character, I tell you!'

'Some people have all kinds of characters, all at the same time,' Ma Joong said with a shrug. 'Let's go and see how the bastard is getting along.'

They got up and walked to the jail behind the courtroom. Chiao Tai told the keeper to fetch the senior scribe, to act as witness and makes notes of the interrogation.

Hoo was sitting on the couch in his small dark cell, his hands and feet chained to the wall. When Chiao Tai lifted the candle, Hoo looked up at him and said sourly:

'I hate to admit it, dogshead, but that was a nifty throw!'

'Thank you for nothing! Tell me more about this robbery you bungled.'

'Don't see why I shouldn't! Assault and battery, that's all you have on me. Only knocked out one carter, didn't even touch the rice bales.'

'How had you planned to get rid of those two cartloads?' Ma Joong asked curiously. 'You can't sell so much rice without roping in the guild merchants.'

'Sell nothing!' Hoo said with a grin. 'I'd have heaved the bales into the river, the whole lot!' Seeing their astonished expressions he added: 'That rice had gone bad, all of it, you see. Fellow who had sold it wanted it stolen, then the guild would have had to make good. Since I bungled the job, the rice was duly delivered, found bad, and the dealer had to pay back all the money he had received from the buyer. Bad luck all around. However, I still thought the fellow owed me a silver piece for my trouble. But when I spoke to him about it, he refused to cough up!'

'Who is he?' Chiao Tai asked.

'One of your local rice-dealers, fellow called Lau.'

Chiao Tai shot Ma Joong a perplexed look. The latter asked: 'How did you come to know Lau? You are from Woo-yee, aren't you?'

'Old friend of mine! I've known him for years; he regularly visits Woo-yee. He is a smooth customer, Lau is, always ready for a bit of swindling. Sanctimonious rascal had a love-nest in Woo-yee; the woman he kept there was a friend of a wench I used to go around with—that's how I was introduced to Lau. Some people have funny tastes, though. Mine was a strapping wench, but Lau's an elderly hag. Yet he had a boy by her, my girl told me. Perhaps the hag looked good eight years ago. Heaven knows!'

'Talking about wenches,' Ma Joong said, 'how did you get on to Miss Bao?'

'Simple! Happened to see her on the stage the first night they played here, and took a liking to her. Tried that night, and the next, to get better acquainted, but nothing doing! Yesterday night I tried again—had nothing better to do while waiting for Lau to come across with the silver. It was late at night, after the performance, she looked tired; her nerves were all on edge. But when I asked her anyway, she replied, "All right. But you'd better be good, for it's my last fling!" Well, we slipped into an empty street stall in a quiet corner of the yard there, but just after we got started, that boy popped up, looking for his sister. I told him to make himself scarce, which he did. Whether it was that interruption or lack of proper training I don't know, but anyway I was disappointed by what followed. That's how it goes, you know; sometimes it turns out much better than you expected, other times it's worse. But what I got I got gratis, so who am I to complain?'

'I saw you quarrel with Lau in the street,' Chiao Tai said. 'You two were standing close by that sword rack. Did you see anybody fiddle with those swords?'

Hoo wrinkled his corrugated forehead. Then he shook his head and answered, 'I had to divide my attention between that bastard Lau and the two women all the time, you see. The daughter was standing right in front of me before the boy started on his somersaults—I could have pinched her behind. Seeing that she is so standoffish, I pinched her mother's instead when she came to shift the bamboo box a bit to the side. Only reward I got was a dirty look, though. Meanwhile Lau had tried to slip away from me; he nearly stumbled over the box when I dragged him back by the sleeve. Anybody could have switched those two toothpicks on the rack.'

'Including you!' Ma Joong said coldly.

Hoo tried to jump up, the rattling chains tautened. He sank back with a cry of pain. 'So that's what you are after, you bastards!' he shouted. 'Hang that foul murder on me, eh? Of all the mean tricks . . .' He looked at Chiao Tai and burst out, 'You can't do that to me, officer! I swear that I never killed a man. I've knocked some fellows about a bit, but that's all. To kill a youngster in such a . . .'

'Better think it over!' Ma Joong said gruffly. 'We have ways and means to get the truth out of you!'

'Go to hell!' Hoo shouted.

Back in the chancery Ma Joong and Chiao Tai sat down at the large desk against the back wall. The scribe seated himself opposite them, close by the candle. The two friends watched him morosely while he took from the drawer a few sheets of blank paper and moistened his writing-brush to work out his notes of the interrogation. After a long pause Ma Joong said:

'Yes, I agree with you that Hoo probably didn't do it. The bastard did do one thing, though. He messed up the case for us—thoroughly!'

Chiao Tai nodded unhappily. 'Lau is a crook, and a lecher to boot, despite his prim air. First kept a woman in Woo-yee, now tries to get Miss Bao in his clutches. Our miss didn't live like a nun, but she's still a juicy bit. Lau had no earthly reason to kill the boy or to spite Bao, but we'll put him behind bars anyway. Our judge will want to check Hoo's statements with him.'

'Why not let the headman get the three Baos and the old musician here tonight as well? Then our judge will have all the human data before him, so to speak. Tomorrow morning, during the session of the court, he'll be able to get down to business right away and settle this case!'

'That's a good idea.'

When Ma Joong came back, the old scribe had finished his notes. After he had read them out aloud, and Ma Joong and Chiao Tai had approved them, the latter said, 'Since you wield that writing-brush so deftly, grandpa, you'd better take down our reports too!'

The scribe resignedly took a sheaf of new sheets. Ma Joong leaned back into his chair, pushed his cap away from his forehead, and started upon his story, beginning with how they had witnessed the murder from the window of the Kingfisher Restaurant. Then Chiao Tai dictated his report on the arrest of Hoo Ta-ma. It was hard work, for they knew that Judge Dee disliked wordy statements, yet insisted on having all details in full. When they were ready at last their faces were wet with perspiration.

Thus Judge Dee found them when, an hour before midnight, he came in, clad in his brown travelling-robe. He looked tired and worried. As the three men jumped up quickly, the judge asked sharply :

'What is this all about? When I stepped down from my palankeen the headman told me that you had two men locked up in jail as murder suspects, and four witnesses summoned!'

'Well, sir,' Ma Joong began diffidently, 'it's rather a sordid murder, of a young boy. My mate and I did a little investigating; all we did is written down here. It began . . .'

'Come to my private office!' Judge Dee interrupted curtly. 'Bring the papers along!'

He ordered the scribe to bring a large pot of hot tea to his office, then went outside followed by his two lieutenants.

Sitting down in the large armchair behind his desk, Judge Dee said, 'That affair in Woo-yee was settled all right. My colleague Pan is an efficient fellow, nice to work with. Sergeant Hoong and Tao Gan are staying on there for another day, to look after a few details.' He took a sip of hot tea, then settled back into his chair with the sheaf of papers.

Ma Joong and Chiao Tai sat stiffly erect on the tabourets in front of the desk. Their throats were parched, but they didn't notice it. They anxiously watched Judge Dee's face for his reactions.

First the judge creased his bushy eyebrows in a deep frown. But as he read on his face gradually relaxed. When he had finished the last page, he reread some passages, and asked the two men to quote some of their conversations verbatim. Then he threw the papers on the desk. Sitting up, he said with a slow smile:

'Congratulations! Both of you have done very well. You not only carried out the routine work expected from you, but also proved that you are able to take independent action. The two arrests were amply justified.'

His two lieutenants grinned broadly. Ma Joong grabbed the teapot and quickly poured a cup for Chiao Tai and himself.

'Now then,' Judge Dee resumed, 'let's see where we are. In the first place, the facts now before us are insufficient to prove that it was murder. Bao was in a hurry, for after the acrobatics they had to rush back to the temple for the stage performance; besides, it was getting dark. Thus it is quite possible that Bao placed the wrong sword on top, by mistake. It's true that he himself suggested foul play, but perhaps he was afraid of being accused of criminal negligence, and those travelling actors stand in deadly fear of the authorities.' The judge paused and stroked his long beard. 'On the other hand, the facts you learned about the people connected with this occurrence suggest various reasons why some of them might have intentionally switched the swords. Including Bao.'

'Why should Bao want to kill the boy?' Ma Joong exclaimed.

'To take vengeance on his unfaithful wife and her paramour, the rice-dealer Lau.' Silencing his astonished lieutenants with his raised hand, Judge Dee continued: 'You don't doubt that the boy in Lau's love-nest in Woo-yee was Mrs Bao's illegitimate son, do you? Lau is interested in the stage; I suppose he met Mrs Bao when the troupe was performing in Woo-yee. When their son was born, they entrusted the child to an old crone who kept a house of assignation there. Eight years later Mrs Bao decided to take the child, which meant that she had to confess her infidelity to her husband. Miss Bao stated that her father took this very calmly, but Bao's indifference may have been feigned. Today, when Bao saw Lau standing near the sword rack, he realized that this was a splendid opportunity to take vengeance on his unfaithful wife, get rid of the illegitimate child and involve Lau in a murder case—all at the same time. For we can also formulate a strong case against Lau.'

Again Ma Joong and Chiao Tai wanted to speak, but again the judge silenced them and went on : 'Lau had the opportunity, the special knowledge of stage-props required for utilizing the opportunity, and one can imagine more than one motive. Blackmail is the first that comes to mind. When Bao's troupe comes to Pooyang, Lau offers his services, perhaps hoping to renew his affair with Mrs Bao. But Bao and his wife try to blackmail him—the boy is living proof of Lau's extra-marital activities in Woo-yee. By changing the swords, Lau would destroy that proof, and he could close Bao's mouth by threatening to accuse him of having killed, out of jealousy, his wife's illegitimate child.

'Then, we also have Mrs Bao. Her daughter gave Ma Joong to understand that her mother is practically a prostitute, and the emotions of such women are often difficult to gauge. When Mrs Bao realized that Lau, her former lover, was now transferring his affection to her daughter, she may well have taken revenge on him by having his son killed. However, we shouldn't attach too much importance to Miss Bao's statements, for she seems a rather unbalanced girl. She doesn't hesitate to call her mother a whore and her father a fool, but she herself makes no bones about sleeping with a vagabond on the eve of concluding a more permanent arrangement with Lau. We must find out, by the way, whether Miss Bao knew that Lau had been her mother's lover.' He paused, eyed his two lieutenants speculatively, 'I am only surveying all possibilities, mind you. It's no use going further into all this before we know more about the emotional relationships of the persons concerned.'

Judge Dee took the papers up again and leafed through them,

studying a passage here and there. Putting them down, he said pensively, 'We must remember that these travelling actors live in two quite different worlds. On the stage they have to identify themselves completely with the great men and women of our national past. Off-stage they are impoverished outcasts who can barely scrape enough together for their daily needs. Such a double life can distort a person's character.'

The judge fell silent. He took a sip from his tea, then sat for a while deep in thought, slowly caressing his sidewhiskers.

'Does Your Honour agree that Hoo is innocent?' Chiao Tai asked.

'No. At least not for the time being. It is true that Hoo Ta-ma made a favourable impression on you two, and for all I know your estimate of him may be entirely correct. However, those vagrant bullies have sometimes strange sides to their character. Hoo went out of his way to stress that it was Miss Bao's fault that their rendezvous was not a success, and he mentioned the interruption caused by the boy as a possible cause. But it may well have been the other way round, namely that it was Hoo himself who failed. He may have feared that his virility was permanently impaired, and such an obsession could inspire in him a violent hatred of that unfortunate boy. I thought it odd that Hoo spoke at such great length about his amorous exploits to two officers interrogating him in jail. It makes one suspect that he is obsessed by the problem to such a degree that he simply has to talk about it. And since Hoo had several talks with the old drummer, he also had a chance to learn about the trick-sword. On the other hand, however, Hoo's expanding on his love-life may just as well have been an innocent desire to show off.' Judge Dee rose and added briskly, 'I'll now have a look at the people concerned. This office is too small. Tell the headman to bring them all to the reception hall. And let the scribe call two clerks, so that the proceedings can be taken down properly. While you two are attending to this, I'll go and have a quick bath.'

The spacious reception hall was very bright. The wall-candles had all been lit, and on the desk in the centre stood two large candelabras of wrought silver. Bao, his wife and his daughter, and the old musician, were seated on chairs in front of the desk. Hoo stood between two constables on the left; Lau on the opposite side, also flanked by two constables. The senior scribe and his two assistants sat at a smaller table. The actors and the prisoners studiously ignored each other; all were staring straight ahead. The hall was deadly quiet.

Suddenly the double-doors were pushed open by the headman of the constables. Judge Dee entered, followed by Ma Joong and Chiao Tai. The judge was clad in a plain, dark-grey robe, and wore a small black skull-cap on his head. All bowed deeply as he went to the desk and sat down in the large armchair of carved ebony. His two lieutenants stood on either side of him.

Judge Dee first surveyed the two prisoners, the sullen Hoo and the prim, rather fussy Lau. He thought that his two lieutenants had described these two men very accurately. Then he silently studied the three actors. Noticing how wan and tired they looked, he thought of the long and heavy day they had behind them, and he felt some compunction about playing on their emotions, as he intended to do. He sighed, then cleared his throat and spoke in an even tone:

'Before I question the two prisoners, I first want to establish the exact family-relationship that links those present here with the dead boy.' Looking fixedly at Mrs Bao, he went on: 'I am informed, Mrs Bao, that the boy was your illegitimate child. Is that correct?'

'Yes, Your Honour,' she replied in a voice that sounded very tired.

'Why didn't you take the child to you until it was eight years old?'

'Because I hesitated to tell my husband, and because the father had promised to take care of it. At one time I thought I loved the man, sir; because of him I left my husband for more than a year. The man had told me that his wife was mortally ill, and that after her death he would marry me. But after I had found out what a mean person he really was, I broke off relations. I didn't meet him again until, half a year ago, I ran into him when we were performing in the capital. He wanted to renew our relationship, and when I said no, he said in that case there was no

137

reason why he should pay any longer for the boy. Then I told my husband everything.' She gave the actor by her side an affectionate look and went on: 'Understanding man as he is, he didn't scold me. He said that the boy was just what he needed to complete our troupe, and that he would make a good acrobat out of him. And he did indeed! People look down on our profession, sir, but my husband and I take pride in it. My husband loved the boy as if he were his own son, he . . .'

She bit her twitching lips. After a brief pause Judge Dee asked: 'Did you tell your husband who your lover was?'

'No, Your Honour. The man treated me shabbily, but I saw no reason why I should ruin his reputation. Neither do I see a reason for doing so now. And my husband never asked me.'

'I see,' the judge said. The woman's frank statement bore the hallmark of truth. Now he knew who had murdered the boy. And also the motive: the boy had had to be silenced, as Ma Joong had correctly supposed at the very beginning. But thereafter his lieutenant had failed to apply this theory to the facts that had come to light. Tugging at his moustache, the judge reflected ruefully that although he now knew who had exchanged the swords, there wasn't a shred of evidence. If he didn't act quickly, he would never be able to prove who committed the crime. He must make the criminal confess here and now, before he had time to realize the full implications of Mrs Bao's statement. He curtly told the headman: 'Bring the accused Lau before me!'

When the rice-dealer was standing in front of the desk, Judge Dee addressed him harshly: 'Lau, here in Poo-yang you have carefully built up a reputation as an honest rice-dealer and a man of impeccable morals, but I know all about your activities in Woo-yee. You tried to deceive your own guild, and you kept a mistress there. Hoo Ta-ma supplied additional details. I advise you to answer my questions truthfully! Speak up, do you admit that it was you who had a liaison with Mrs Bao, eight years ago?'

'I do,' Lau replied in an unsteady voice. 'I beg Your Honour to . . .'

There was a strangled cry. Miss Bao had risen from her chair. Clenching her hands, she stared at Lau with wide, burning eyes. He stepped back, muttering something. Suddenly she screamed:

138

'You unspeakable cad! May heaven and hell curse me for foolishly believing your string of lies! Played the same trick on my mother, eh? And to think that because I was a credulous fool, was afraid, afraid that the brat would tell you about my meeting Hoo, I put the wrong sword on top! I'll kill you too, you . . .'

She went for the cowering man, raising her hands like claws. The two constables quickly stepped forward and grabbed her arms. On a sign from the judge they led her away, screaming and fighting like a wildcat.

Her parents looked after her with unbelieving eyes. Then her mother burst out in sobs.

Judge Dee rapped his knuckles on the table. 'Tomorrow I shall hear Miss Bao's full confession in court. As to you, Lau, I shall institute a thorough inquiry into all your affairs, and I shall see to it that you get a long prison term. I dislike people of your type, Lau. Hoo Ta-ma, you shall be sentenced to one year compulsory labour with the sappers of our Northern Army. That'll give you a chance to prove what you are worth; in due time you'll perhaps be enlisted as a regular soldier.' Turning to the headman, he added: 'Lead the two prisoners back to jail!'

For a while the judge looked silently at the actor and his wife. She had stopped crying; now she sat very still, her eyes downcast. Bao looked worriedly at her, the lines on his expressive actor's face had deepened. Judge Dee addressed them gently:

'Your daughter could not cope with the hard life fate had allotted to her, and it thoroughly corrupted her character. I must propose the death penalty for her. That means that you lose, on one and the same day, both your daughter and your son. But time shall heal this cruel wound. You two are still in the prime of life, you love each other and your profession, and that twofold devotion shall be a lasting support. Though everything will seem dark to you now, remember that even behind the darkest clouds of night there shines the moon of dawn.'

They rose, made a deep bow and took their leave.

THE COFFINS OF THE EMPEROR

The events described in this story took place when Judge Dee was occupying his fourth post as magistrate, namely of Lan-fang, an isolated district on the western frontier of the mighty T'ang Empire. Here he met with considerable trouble when taking up his duties, as described in the novel The Chinese Maze Murders. *The present story tells about the grave crisis that threatened the Empire two years later, in the winter of the year A.D. 672, and how Judge Dee succeeded in solving, on one and the same night, two difficult problems, one affecting the fate of the nation, the other the fate of two humble people.*

As soon as Judge Dee had entered the dining-room on the restaurant's top floor, he knew that the banquet would be a dismal affair. The light of two large silver candelabras shone on the beautiful antique furniture, but the spacious room was heated by only one small brazier, where two or three pieces of coal were dying in the embers. The padded curtains of embroidered silk could not keep out the cold draught, reminding one of the snowy plains that stretched out for thousands of miles beyond the western frontier of the Chinese Empire.

At the round table sat only one man, the thin, elderly magistrate of Ta-shih-kou, this remote boundary district. The two girls who were standing behind his chair looked listlessly at the tall, bearded newcomer.

Magistrate Kwang rose hastily and came to meet Judge Dee. 'I profoundly apologize for these poor arrangements!' he said with a bleak smile. 'I had invited also two colonels and two guildmasters, but the colonels were suddenly summoned to the Marshal's headquarters, and the guildmasters were wanted by the Quartermaster-General. This emergency . . .' He raised his hands in a helpless gesture.

'The main thing is that I shall now profit from your instructive conversation!' Judge Dee said politely.

His host led him to the table and introduced the very young girl on his left as Tearose, and the other as Jasmine. Both were gaudily dressed and wore cheap finery—they were common prostitutes rather than the refined courtesans one would expect at a dinner party. But Judge Dee knew that all the courtesans of Ta-shih-kou were now reserved for the high-ranking officers of the Marshal's headquarters. When Jasmine had filled Judge Dee's wine beaker, Magistrate Kwang raised his own and said:

'I welcome you, Dee, as my esteemed colleague of the neighbour-district and my honoured guest. Let's drink to the victory of our Imperial Army!'

'To victory!' Judge Dee said and emptied his beaker in one draught.

From the street below came the rumble of iron-studded cart-wheels on the frozen ground.

'That'll be the troops going to the front at last for our counter-offensive,' the judge said with satisfaction.

Kwang listened intently. He sadly shook his head. 'No,' he said curtly, 'they are going too slowly. They are coming back from the battlefield.'

Judge Dee rose, pulled the curtain aside and opened the window, braving the icy wind. In the eerie moonlight he saw down below a long file of carts, drawn by emaciated horses. They were packed with wounded soldiers and long shapes covered with canvas. He quickly closed the window.

'Let's eat!' Kwang said, pointing with his chopsticks at the silver bowls and platters on the table. Each contained only a small quantity of salted vegetables, a few dried-out slices of ham and cooked beans.

'Coolie fare in silver vessels—that sums up the situation!' Kwang spoke bitterly. 'Before the war my district had plenty of everything. Now all food is getting scarce. If this doesn't change soon we'll have a famine on our hands.'

Judge Dee wanted to console him, but he quickly put his hand to his mouth. A racking cough shook his powerful frame. His colleague gave him a worried look and asked, 'Has the lung epidemic spread to your district too?'

The judge waited till the attack had passed, then he quickly

141

emptied his beaker and replied hoarsely, 'Only a few isolated cases, and none really bad. In a milder form, like mine.'

'You are lucky,' Kwang said dryly. 'Here most of those who get it start spitting blood in a day or two. They are dying like rats. I hope your quarters are comfortable,' he added anxiously.

'Oh yes, I have a good room at one of the larger inns,' Judge Dee replied. In fact he had to share a draughty attic with three officers, but he didn't like to distress his host further. Kwang hadn't been able to accommodate him in his official residence because it had been requisitioned by the army, and the magistrate had been obliged to move with his entire family into a small ramshackle house. It was a strange situation; in normal times a magistrate was well-nigh all-powerful, the highest authority in his district. But now the army had taken over. 'I'll go back to Lan-fang tomorrow morning,' the judge resumed. 'There are many things to be attended to, for in my district also food is getting scarce.'

Kwang nodded gloomily. Then he asked : 'Why did the Marshal summon you? It's a good two days' journey from Lan-fang to here, and the roads are bad.'

'The Uigurs have their tents on the other side of the river that borders my district,' Judge Dee replied. 'The Marshal wanted to know whether they were likely to join the Tartar armies. I told him that . . .' He broke off and looked dubiously at the two girls. The Tartar spies were everywhere.

'They are all right,' Kwang said quickly.

'Well, I informed the Marshal that the Uigurs can only bring two thousand men in the field, and that their Khan went on a prolonged hunting trip to Central Asia, just before the Tartar emissaries arrived at his camp to ask him to join forces with them. The Uigur Khan is a wise man. We have his favourite son as hostage, you see, in the capital.'

'Two thousand men won't make any difference either way,' Kwang remarked. 'Those accursed Tartars have three hundred thousand men standing at our frontier, ready to strike. Our front is crumbling under their probing attacks, and the Marshal keeps his two hundred thousand men idle here, instead of starting the promised counteroffensive.'

142

For a while the two men ate in silence, while the girls kept their cups filled. When they had finished the beans and salted vegetables, Magistrate Kwang looked up and asked Tearose impatiently, 'Where is the rice?'

'The waiter said they don't have any, sir,' the girl replied.

'Nonsense!' the magistrate exclaimed angrily. He rose and said to Judge Dee: 'Excuse me a moment, will you? I'll see to this myself!'

When he had gone downstairs with Tearose, the other girl said softly to Judge Dee, 'Would you do me a great favour, sir?'

The judge looked up at her. She was a not unattractive woman of about twenty. But the thick layer of rouge on her face could not mask her sallow complexion and hollow cheeks. Her eyes were unnaturally wide and had a feverish glow.

'What is it?' he asked.

'I am feeling ill, sir. If you could leave early and take me with you, I would gladly receive you after I have rested awhile.'

He noticed that her legs were trembling with fatigue. 'I'll be glad to,' he replied. 'But after I've seen you home, I shall go on to my own lodging.' He added with a thin smile: 'I am not feeling too well myself, you know.'

She gave him a grateful look.

When Magistrate Kwang and Tearose came back, Kwang said contritely, 'I am very sorry, Dee, but it's true. There is no rice left.'

'Well,' Judge Dee said, 'I enjoyed our meeting very much. I also think that Jasmine here is quite attractive. Would you think it very rude if I asked to be excused now?'

Kwang protested that it was far too early to part, but it was clear that he too thought this the best solution. He conducted Judge Dee downstairs and took leave of him in the hall. Jasmine helped the judge don his heavy fur coat, then they went out into the cold street. Sedan-chairs were not to be had for love or money; all the bearers had been enlisted for the army transports.

The carts with the dead and wounded were still filing through the streets. Often the judge and his companion had to press them-

143

selves against the wall of a house to let dispatch-riders pass, driving their weary horses on with obscene curses.

Jasmine led the judge down a narrow side street to a small hovel, leaning against a high, dark godown. Two struggling pine trees flanked the cracked door, their branches bent low under the load of frozen snow.

Judge Dee took a silver piece from his sleeve. Handing it to her, he said, 'Well, I'll be going on now, my inn . . .' A violent attack of coughing seized him.

'You'll come inside and at least drink something hot,' she said firmly. 'You aren't fit to walk about as you are.' She opened the door and dragged the judge inside, still coughing.

The attack subsided only after she had taken his fur coat and made him sit down in the bamboo chair at the rickety tea-table. It was very warm in the small dark room; the copper brazier in the corner was heaped with glowing coals. Noticing his astonished glance, she said with a sneer; 'That's the advantage of being a prostitute nowadays. We get plenty of coal, army issue. Serve our gallant soldiers !'

She took the candle, lit it at the brazier, then put it back on the table. She disappeared through the door curtain in the back wall. Judge Dee surveyed the room in the flickering light of the candle. Against the wall opposite him stood a large bedstead; its curtains were drawn, revealing rumpled quilts and a soiled double-pillow.

Suddenly he heard a queer sound. He looked round. It came from behind a faded blue curtain, which was covering something close to the wall. It flashed through his mind that this could well be a trap. The military police flogged thieves on the street corners till their bones lay bare, yet robbery and assault were rampant in the city. He rose quickly, stepped up to the curtain and ripped it aside.

He blushed despite himself. A wooden crib stood against the wall. The small round head of a baby emerged from under a thick, patched quilt. It stared up at him with its large wise eyes. The judge hurriedly pulled the curtain close, and resumed his seat.

The woman came in carrying a large teapot. Pouring him a

cup, she said, 'Here, drink this. It's a special kind of tea; they say it cures a cough.'

She went behind the curtain and came back with the child in her arms. She carried it to the bed, pulled the quilts straight with one hand and turned the pillow over.

'Excuse this mess,' she said as she laid the child on the bed. 'I had a customer here just before the magistrate had me called to attend our dinner.' With the unconcern marking women of her profession, she took off her robe. Clad only in her wide trousers, she sat on the bed and leaned back against the pillow with a sigh of relief. Then she took up the child and laid it against her left breast. It started drinking contentedly.

Judge Dee sipped the medicinal tea; it had an agreeable bitter taste. After a while he asked her: 'How old is your child?'

'Two months,' the woman replied listlessly. 'It's a boy.'

His eye fell on the long white scars on her shoulders; one broad weal sorely mutilated her right breast. She looked up and saw his glance. She said indifferently, 'Oh, they didn't mean to do that, it was my own fault. When they were flogging me, I tried to wrench myself loose, and one tongue of the scourge curled over my shoulder and tore my breast.'

'Why were you flogged?' the judge asked.

'Too long a story to tell!' she said curtly. She concentrated her attention on the child.

Judge Dee finished his tea in silence. His breathing came easier now, but his head was still throbbing with a dull ache. When he had drunk a second cup, Jasmine carried the baby back to the crib and pulled the curtain shut. She came to the table, stretched herself and yawned. Pointing at the bedstead, she asked, 'What about it? I have rested a bit now, and the tea hardly covers what you paid me.'

'Your tea is excellent,' the judge said wearily; 'it more than covers what I gave you.' In order not to offend her he added quickly, 'I wouldn't risk infecting you with this accursed lung trouble. I'll have one more cup, then I'll be on my way.'

'As you like!' Sitting down opposite him, she added, 'I'll have a cup myself, my throat is parched.'

In the street footsteps crunched in the frozen snow. It was the men of the night watch. They beat midnight on their wooden clappers. Jasmine shrank in her seat. Putting her hand to her throat, she gasped, 'Midnight already?'

'Yes,' Judge Dee said worriedly, 'if we don't start our counter-offensive very soon, I fear the Tartar hordes will break through and overrun this area. We'll drive them back again, of course, but since you have that nice child, wouldn't it be wiser if you packed up and went east tomorrow morning?'

She was looking straight ahead, agony in her feverish eyes. Then she spoke, half to herself, 'Six hours to go!' Looking at the judge, she added: 'My child? At dawn his father will be beheaded.'

Judge Dee set his cup down. 'Beheaded?' he exclaimed. 'I am sorry. Who is he?'

'A captain, name of Woo.'

'What did he do?'

'Nothing.'

'You aren't beheaded for nothing!' the judge remarked crossly.

'He was falsely accused. They said he strangled the wife of a fellow officer. He was court-martialled and condemned to death. He has been in the military jail now for about a year, waiting for the confirmation. It came today.'

Judge Dee tugged at his moustache. 'I have often worked together with the military police,' he said. 'Their judicial system is cruder than our civilian procedure, but I have always found them efficient, and very conscientious. They don't make many mistakes.'

'They did in this case,' Jasmine said. She added resignedly: 'Nothing can be done; it's too late.'

'Yes, since he is to be executed at dawn, there isn't much we can do about it,' the judge agreed. He thought for a while, then resumed, 'But why not tell me about it? You would get my mind off my own worries and perhaps it might help you to pass the time.'

'Well,' she said with a shrug, 'I am feeling too miserable to sleep anyway. Here it is. About a year and a half ago, two captains of the garrison here in Ta-shih-kou used to frequent the licensed quarters. One was called Pan, the other Woo. They had to work together because they belonged to the same branch of the service, but they didn't get along at all; they were as different as can be. Pan was a milksop with a smooth face, a dandy who looked more like a student than an officer. With all his fine talk he was a nasty piece, and the girls didn't like him. Woo was just the opposite, a rough-and-ready boy, a good boxer and swordsman, quick with his hands and quick with a joke. They used to say that the soldiers would go through fire and water for him. He wasn't what you'd call handsome, but I loved him. And he would have no one but me. He paid the owner of the brothel I belong to at regular times so that I didn't have to sleep with the first comer. He promised to buy and marry me as soon as he got his promotion, that's why I didn't mind having his child. Usually we get rid of them when we are pregnant or sell them. But I wanted mine.' She emptied her cup, pushed a lock away from her forehead, and went on, 'So far so good. Then, one night about ten months ago, Pan came home and found his wife lying there strangled to death, and Woo standing by her bed, looking dazed. Pan called in a passing patrol of the military police, and accused Woo of having murdered his wife. Both were brought before the military tribunal. Pan said that Woo kept bothering his wife, who wouldn't have him. The slimy bastard said he warned Woo many times to leave her alone; he hadn't wanted to report him to the colonel because Woo was his fellow-officer! Well, Pan added that Woo knew that Pan was on night duty in the armoury that evening, so he had gone to Pan's house and again tried to bed with his wife. She had refused, and Woo had flown into a rage and strangled her. That was all.'

'What did Woo have to say to that?' Judge Dee asked.

'Woo said that Pan was a dirty liar. That he knew that Pan hated him, and that Pan himself had strangled his wife in order to ruin him.'

'Not a very clever fellow, that captain of yours,' the judge remarked dryly.

'Listen, will you? Woo said that when he passed by the armoury that night, Pan hailed him and asked him to go round to his house and see whether his wife needed anything, for she had felt indisposed that afternoon. When Woo got there, the front door was open, the servants gone. No one answered his calls, so he went into the bedroom where he found her dead body. Then Pan came rushing inside and started hollering for the military police.'

'A queer story,' Judge Dee said. 'How did the military judge formulate his verdict? But no, you wouldn't know that, of course.'

'I do. I was there myself, sneaked in with the others. Wet all over with fright, I tell you, for if they catch a whore in a military establishment she gets scourged. Well, the colonel said that Woo was guilty of adultery with the wife of a fellow-officer, and sentenced him to have his head chopped off. He said he wouldn't say too much about murder, for his men had found out that Pan himself had sent his servants away after dinner that night, and as soon as he had gone on duty at the armoury, he had told the military police that he had been warned about thieves in his neighbourhood, and asked them to keep an eye on his house. The colonel said that it was possible Pan had discovered that his wife was carrying on with Woo, and that he had therefore strangled her. That was his right; according to the law, he could have killed Woo too, if he had caught them in the act, as they call it. But maybe Pan had been afraid to tackle Woo, and had chosen this roundabout way of getting at him. Anyway that was neither here nor there, the colonel said. The fact was that Woo had played games with the wife of a fellow-officer, and that was bad for the morale of the army. Therefore he had to be beheaded.'

She fell silent. Judge Dee caressed his sidewhiskers. After a while he said, 'On the face of it I would say that the colonel was perfectly right. His verdict agrees with the brief character sketch you gave me of the two men concerned. Why are you so sure that Woo didn't have an affair with Pan's wife?'

'Because Woo loved me, and wouldn't even look at another woman,' she replied promptly.

Judge Dee thought that this was a typical woman's argument. To change the subject, he asked: 'Who flogged you, and why?'

'It's all such a stupid story!' she said in a forlorn voice. 'After the session I was furious with Woo. I had discovered that I was pregnant, and the mean skunk had been carrying on with the

Pan woman all the time, behind my back! So I rushed to the jail and got inside by telling the guards I was Woo's sister. When I saw him I spat in his face, called him a treacherous lecher, and ran off again. But when I was so far gone I couldn't work any more, I got to thinking things over, and I knew I had been a silly fool, and that Woo loved me. So eight weeks ago, after our child had been born and I was a little better, I again went to the military prison to tell Woo I was sorry. But Woo must have told the guards how I fooled them the time before—and he was right, too, the way I had shouted at him! As soon as I was inside they lashed me to the rack and gave me a flogging. I was in luck, I knew the soldier who handled the scourge; he didn't hit too hard, else the army would have had to supply a coffin then and there. As it was, my back and shoulders were cut to ribbons and I was bleeding like a pig, but I am no weakling and I made it. As strong as a farmhand, father used to say of me before he had to sell me to pay the rent for our field. Then there came rumours about the Tartars planning an attack. The garrison commander was called to the capital, and the war started. What with one thing and another Woo's case dragged on. This morning the decision came, and at dawn they'll chop his head off.'

Suddenly she buried her face in her hands and started to sob. The judge slowly stroked his long black beard, waiting till she had calmed down. Then he asked:

'Was the Pans' marriage a happy one?'

'How do I know? Think I slept under their bed?'

'Did they have children?'

'No.'

'How long had they been married?'

'Let me see. About a year and a half—I know that. When I first met the two captains, Woo told me that Pan had just been called home by his father to marry the woman his parents had got for him.'

'Do you happen to know his father's name?'

'No. Pan only used to brag that his father was a big noise in Soochow.'

'That must be Pan Wei-liang, the Prefect,' Judge Dee said at once. 'He is a famous man, a great student of ancient history. I have never met him, but I have read many of his books. Quite good. Is his son still here?'

'Yes, attached to headquarters. If you admire those Pans so much, you'd better go there and make friends with the mean bastard!' she added contemptuously.

Judge Dee rose. 'I'll do that,' he said, half to himself.

She mouthed an obscene word. 'You are all the same, all of you!' she snapped. 'Am I glad I am just an honest whore! The gentleman is choosy, doesn't want to sleep with a woman with half a breast gone, eh? Want your money back?'

'Keep it!' Judge Dee said calmly.

'Go to hell!' she said. She spat on the floor and turned her back on him.

Judge Dee silently put on his fur coat and left.

While he was walking through the main street, still crowded with soldiers, he reflected that things didn't look too good. Even if he found Captain Pan, and even if he succeeded in extracting from him the fact he needed for the testing of his theory, he would then have to try to obtain an audience with the Marshal, for only he could, at this stage, order a stay of execution. And the Marshal was fully occupied by weighty issues, the fate of the Empire was in the balance. Moreover, that fierce soldier was not notorious for his gentle manner. Judge Dee set his teeth. If the Empire had come to such a pass that a judge couldn't prevent an innocent man from being beheaded . . .

The Marshal's headquarters were located in the so-called Hunting Palace, an immense compound that the present Emperor had built for his beloved eldest son, who had died young. The Crown Prince had been fond of hunting on the western frontier. He had died on a hunting expedition there, and it had been his wish to be buried in Ta-shih-kou. His sarcophagus had been placed in a vault there, and later that of his Princess beside it.

Judge Dee had some trouble in getting admitted by the guards, who looked with suspicion on every civilian. But at last he was led to a small, draughty waiting-room, and an orderly took his red visiting-card to Captain Pan. After a long wait a young officer came in. The tight-fitting mail jacket and the broad swordbelt accentuated his slender figure, and the iron helmet set off his handsome but cold face, smooth but for a small black moustache. He saluted stiffly, then stood waiting in haughty silence till the judge addressed him. A district magistrate ranked much higher, of course, than an army captain, but Pan's attitude suggested that in wartime things were different.

'Sit down, sit down!' Judge Dee said jovially. 'A promise is a promise, I always say! And better late than never!'

Captain Pan sat down on the other side of the tea-table, looking politely astonished.

'Half a year ago,' the judge continued, 'while passing through Soochow on my way to Lan-fang, I had a long conversation with your father. I also am a student of history, you know, in my spare time! When I was taking my leave, he said: "My eldest son is serving in Ta-shih-kou, your neighbour-district. If you should happen to pass by there, do me a favour and have a look how he's doing. The boy had awfully bad luck." Well, yesterday the Marshal summoned me, and before returning to Lan-fang I wanted to keep my promise.'

'That's most kind of you, sir!' Pan muttered, confused. 'Please excuse my rudeness just now. I didn't know . . . and I am in a terrible state. The bad situation at the front, you see . . .' He shouted an order. A soldier brought a pot of tea. 'Did . . . did my father tell you about the tragedy, sir?'

'Only that your young wife was murdered here last year. Accept my sincere . . .'

'He shouldn't have forced me to marry, sir!' the captain burst out. 'I told him . . . tried to tell him . . . but he was always too busy, never had time . . .' With an effort Pan took a hold of himself, and continued, 'I thought I was too young to marry, you see. Wanted my father to postpone it. For a few years, till I would've been stationed in a large city, for instance. Give me time to . . . to sort things out.'

'Were you in love with another girl?'

'Heaven forbid!' the young officer exclaimed. 'No sir, it was simply that I felt I was not the marrying kind. Not yet.'

'Was she murdered by robbers?'

Captain Pan sombrely shook his head. His face had gone

a deadly pale. 'The murderer was a fellow-officer of mine, sir. One of those disgusting woman-chasers; you could never have a decent, clean conversation with him. Always talking about women, women, always letting himself be caught in their filthy little games . . .' The young man spat out those last words. He quickly gulped down the tea, then added in a dull voice, 'He tried to seduce my wife, and strangled her when she refused. He'll be beheaded at dawn.' Suddenly he buried his face in his hands.

Judge Dee silently observed the stricken youngster for a while. Then he said softly : 'Yes, you had very bad luck indeed.' He rose and resumed in a businesslike manner, 'I must see the Marshal again. Please take me there.'

Captain Pan got up quickly. As he conducted the judge down a long corridor where orderlies were rushing to and fro, he said : 'I can take you only as far as the anteroom, sir. Only members of the High Command are allowed beyond.'

'That'll do,' Judge Dee said.

Captain Pan showed the judge into a hall, crowded with officers, then said he would wait outside to lead the judge back to the main gate. As soon as the judge had entered, the hubbub of voices ceased abruptly. A colonel stepped up to him. After a cursory glance at Judge Dee's cap he asked coldly : 'What can I do for you, Magistrate?'

'I have to see the Marshal on urgent business.'

'Impossible !' the colonel said abruptly. 'The Marshal is in conference. I have strict orders to admit nobody.'

'A human life is at stake,' the judge said gravely.

'A human life, you say !' the colonel exclaimed with a sneer. 'The Marshal is deliberating on two hundred thousand human lives that are at stake, Magistrate ! May I lead the way?'

Judge Dee grew pale. He had failed. Piloting the judge politely but firmly to the exit, the colonel said : 'I trust that you'll understand, Magistrate. . . .'

'Magistrate !' shouted another colonel who came rushing inside. Despite the cold his face was covered with sweat. 'Do you happen to know where a colleague of yours is, called Dee?'

'I am Magistrate Dee,' the judge replied.

'Heaven be praised! I have been looking for you for hours! The Marshal wants you!'

He dragged the judge by his sleeve through a door at the back of the anteroom into a semi-dark passage. Thick felt hangings dampened all sound. He opened the heavy door at the end, and let the judge go inside.

It was curiously still in the enormous palace hall. A group of high-ranking officers in resplendent armour stood round a monumental desk, piled with maps and papers. All were looking silently at the giant who was pacing the floor in front of it, his hands clasped behind his back.

He wore an ordinary mail jacket with battered, iron shoulder-plates and the baggy leather trousers of a cavalry man. But on top of his high helmet the golden marshal's dragon raised its horned head. As the Marshal walked to and fro with heavy tread, he let the point of the broad sword that was dangling from his belt clatter carelessly on the delicately carved, marble floor-tiles.

Judge Dee knelt down. The colonel approached the Marshal. Standing stiffly at attention, he said something in a clipped voice.

'Dee?' the Marshal barked. 'Don't need the fellow anymore, send him away! No, wait! I still have a couple of hours before I order the retreat.' Then he shouted at the judge: 'Hey there, stop crawling on the floor! Come here!'

Judge Dee rose hurriedly, went up to the Marshal and made a deep bow. Then he righted himself. The judge was a tall man, but the Marshal topped him by at least two inches. Hooking his thumbs in his swordbelt, the giant glared at the judge with his fierce right eye. His left eye was covered by a black band—it had been pierced by a barbarian arrow during the northern campaign.

'You are good at riddles, they say, eh, Dee? Well, I'll show you a riddle!' Turning to the desk, he shouted: 'Lew! Mao!'

Two men wearing generals' armour hurriedly detached themselves from the group round the table. Judge Dee recognized the lean general in the shining golden armour as Lew, commander of the left wing. The broad-shouldered, squat man wearing a golden cuirass and a silver helmet was Mao, commanding general of the military police. Only Sang, the commander of the right wing, was missing. With the Marshal these three were the highest military leaders; in this national crisis the Emperor had placed the fate of the Chinese people and the dynasty in their hands. The judge made a low bow. The two generals gave him a stony look.

The Marshal strode through the hall and kicked a door open. They silently passed through a number of broad, empty corridors, the iron boots of the three officers resounding hollowly on the marble floor. Then they descended a broad staircase. At the bottom two palace guards sprang to attention. At a sign of the Marshal they slowly pushed open a heavy double-gate.

They entered a colossal vault, dimly lit by tall silver oil lamps, placed at regular intervals in recesses in the high, windowless walls. In the centre of the vault stood two enormous coffins, lacquered a bright red, the colour of resurrection. They were of identical size, each measuring about ten by thirty foot, and over fifteen foot high.

The Marshal bowed, and the three others followed his example. Then the Marshal turned to Judge Dee and said, pointing at the coffins, 'Here is your riddle, Dee! This afternoon, just when I was about to order the offensive, General Sang came and accused Lew here of high treason. Said that Lew had contacted the Tartar Khan and agreed that as soon as we would attack, Lew would join the Tartar dogs with his troops. Later Lew would get the southern half of the Empire as a reward. The proof? Sang said that Lew had concealed in the coffin of the Crown Prince two hundred suits of armour complete with helmets and swords, and marked with the special sign of the traitors. At the right moment Lew's confederates in the High Command would break the coffin open, don those marked suits of armour and massacre all the staff officers here who aren't in the plot.'

Judge Dee started and looked quickly at General Lew. The lean man stood there stiffly erect, staring ahead with a white, taut face.

'I trust Lew as I trust myself,' the Marshal went on, aggressively thrusting his bearded chin forward, 'but Sang has a long and honourable career behind him, and I can't take any chances. I must verify the accusation, and quick. The plans for our counter-offensive are ready. Lew will head a vanguard of fifteen thousand

'YOU ARE GOOD AT RIDDLES, THEY SAY, EH, DEE?' THE
MARSHAL GROWLED

men and drive a wedge into the Tartar hordes. Then I'll follow up with a hundred and fifty thousand men and drive the dogs back into their own steppes. But there are signs that the wind is going to shift; if I wait too long we'll have to fight with snow and hail blowing right into our faces.

'I have examined the coffin of the Crown Prince for hours, together with Mao's best men, but we can find no sign that it has been tampered with. Sang maintains they excised a large section of the lacquer coating, made a hole, pushed the stuff inside and replaced the section of coating. According to him, there are experts who can do this without leaving a trace. Maybe there are, but I must have positive proof. But I can't desecrate the coffin of the Emperor's beloved son by breaking it open—I may not even scratch it without the special permission of His Majesty—and it'll take at least six days before I can get word from the capital. On the other hand I can't open the offensive before I have made sure that Sang's accusation is false. If I can't do that in two hours, I shall have to order a general retreat. Set to work, Dee!'

The judge walked around the coffin of the Crown Prince, then he also examined cursorily that of the Princess. Pointing at a few long poles that were lying on the floor, he asked, 'What are these for?'

'I had the coffin tilted,' General Mao said coldly, 'in order to verify whether the bottom hadn't been tampered with. All that was humanly possible has been done.'

Judge Dee nodded. He said pensively, 'I once read a description of this palace. I remember that it said that the August Body was first placed in a box of solid gold, which was then placed in one of silver, and that in turn in a case of lead. The empty space around it was filled up with the articles of adornment and court costumes of the Crown Prince. The sarcophagus itself consists of thick logs of cedarwood, covered on the outside with a coat of lacquer. The same procedure was followed two years later, when the Princess died. Since the Princess had been fond of boating, behind the palace a large artificial lake was made, with models of the boats used by the Princess and her court ladies. Is that correct?'

'Of course,' the Marshal growled. 'It's common knowledge. Don't stand there talking twaddle, Dee! Come to the point!'

'Could you get me a hundred sappers, sir?'

'What for? Didn't I tell you we can't tamper with that coffin?'

'I fear the Tartars also know all about these coffins, sir. Should they temporarily occupy the city, they'll break the coffins open to loot them. In order to prevent the coffins from being desecrated by the barbarians, I propose to sink them to the bottom of the lake.'

The Marshal looked at him dumbfounded. Then he roared: 'You accursed fool! Don't you know the coffins are hollow? They'll never sink. You . . .'

'They aren't meant to, sir!' Judge Dee said quickly. 'But the plan to sink them provides us with a valid reason for deplacing them.'

The Marshal glared at him with his one fierce eye. Suddenly he shouted: 'By heaven, I think you've got it, Dee!' Turning to General Mao, he barked: 'Get me a hundred sappers here, with cables and rollers! At once!'

After Mao had rushed to the staircase, the Marshal started pacing the floor, muttering to himself. General Lew covertly observed the judge. Judge Dee remained standing there in front of the coffin of the Crown Prince, staring at it silently, his arms folded in his long sleeves.

Soon General Mao came back. Scores of small, squat men swarmed inside behind him. They wore jackets and trousers of brown leather and peaked caps of the same material, with long neck- and ear-flaps. Some carried long round poles, others rolls of thick cable. It was the sappers corps, expert at digging tunnels, rigging machines for scaling city walls, blocking rivers and harbours with underwater barriers, and all the other special skills used in warfare.

When the Marshal had given their commander his instructions, a dozen sappers rushed to the high gate at the back of the vault, and opened it. The bleak moonlight shone on a broad marble terrace. Three stairs descended into the water of the lake beyond, which was covered by a thin layer of ice.

The other sappers crowded round and over the coffin of the

Crown Prince like so many busy ants. One heard hardly a sound, for the sappers transmit orders by finger-talk only. They are so quiet they can dig a tunnel right under a building, the occupants becoming aware of what is happening only when the walls and the floor suddenly cave in. Thirty sappers tilted the coffin of the Crown Prince, using long poles as levers; one team placed rollers under it, another slung thick cables round the huge sarcophagus.

The Marshal watched them for a while, then he went outside and on to the terrace, followed by Dee and the generals. Silently they remained standing at the water's edge, looking out over the frozen lake.

Suddenly they heard a low rumbling sound behind them. Slowly the enormous coffin came rolling out of the gate. Dozens of sappers pulled it along by thick cables, while others kept placing new rollers underneath it. The coffin was drawn across the terrace, then let down into the water as if it was the hulk of a ship being launched. The ice cracked, the coffin rocked up and down for a while, then settled with about two-thirds of it under water. A cold wind blew over the frozen lake, and Judge Dee started to cough violently. He pulled his neckcloth up over the lower part of his face, beckoned the commander of the sappers and pointed at the coffin of the Princess in the vault behind them.

Again there was a rumbling sound. The second coffin came rolling across the terrace. The sappers let it down into the water where it remained floating next to that of the Crown Prince. The Marshal stooped and peered at the two coffins, comparing the waterlines. There was hardly any difference, if anything the coffin of the Princess was slightly heavier than that of the Crown Prince.

The Marshal righted himself. He hit General Lew a resounding clap on his shoulder. 'I knew I could trust you, Lew!' he shouted. 'What are you waiting for, man? Give the signal, go ahead with your troops! I'll follow in six hours. Good luck!'

A slow smile lit up the general's stern features. He saluted, then turned round and strode off. The commander of the sappers came and said respectfully to the Marshal: 'We shall now weigh the coffins with heavy chains and rocks, sir, then we . . .'

'I have made a mistake,' the Marshal interrupted him curtly.

'Have them drawn on land again, and replace them in their original position.' He barked at General Mao: 'Go with a hundred men to Sang's camp outside the West Gate. Arrest him on the charge of high treason, and convey him in chains to the capital. General Kao shall take over his troops.' Then he turned to Judge Dee, who was still coughing. 'You get it, don't you? Sang is older than Lew, he couldn't swallow Lew's appointment to the same rank. It was Sang, that son of a dog, who conspired with the Khan, don't you see? His fantastic accusation was meant only to stop our counteroffensive. He would have attacked us together with the Tartars as soon as we started the retreat. Stop that blasted coughing, Dee! It annoys me. We are through here, come along!'

The council room was now seething with activity. Large maps had been spread out on the floor. The staff officers were checking all details of the planned counteroffensive. A general said excitedly to the Marshal: 'What about adding five thousand men to the force behind these hills here, sir?'

The Marshal stooped over the map. Soon they were deep in a complicated technical discussion. Judge Dee looked anxiously at the large water-clock in the corner. The floater indicated that it would be dawn in one hour. He stepped up to the Marshal and asked diffidently: 'May I take the liberty of asking you a favour, sir?'

The Marshal righted himself. He asked peevishly: 'Eh? What is it now?'

'I would like you to review a case against a captain, sir. He's going to be beheaded at dawn, but he is innocent.'

The Marshal grew purple in his face. He roared: 'With the fate of our Empire in the balance, you dare to bother me, the Marshal, with the life of one wretched man?'

Judge Dee looked steadily into the one rolling eye. He said quietly: 'A thousand men must be sacrificed if military necessity dictates it, sir. But not even one man must be lost if it's not strictly necessary.'

The Marshal burst out in obscene curses, but he suddenly checked himself. With a wry smile he said: 'If ever you get sick of that tawdry civilian paperwork, Dee, you come and see me. By God, I'll make a general officer out of you! Review the case, you say? Nonsense, I'll settle it, here and now! Give your orders!'

Judge Dee turned to the colonel who had rushed towards them when he heard the Marshal cursing. The judge said, 'At the door of the anteroom a captain called Pan is waiting for me. He falsely accused another captain of murder. Could you bring him here?'

'Bring also his immediate superior!' the Marshal added. 'At once!'

As the colonel hastened to the door, a low, wailing blast came from outside. It swelled in volume, penetrating the thick walls of the palace. It was the long brass trumpets, blowing the signal to assemble for the attack.

The Marshal squared his wide shoulders. He said with a broad smile: 'Listen, Dee! That's the finest music that ever was!' Then he turned again to the maps on the floor.

Judge Dee looked fixedly at the entrance. The colonel was back in a remarkably short time. An elderly officer and Captain Pan followed him. The judge said to the Marshal, 'They are here, sir.'

The Marshal swung round, put his thumbs in his swordbelt and scowled at the two men. They stood stiffly at attention, with rapt eyes. It was the first time they had ever seen the greatest solder of the Empire face to face. The giant growled at the elderly officer: 'Report on this captain!'

'Excellent administrator, good disciplinarian. Can't get along with the men, no battle experience . . .' The officer rattled it off.

'Your case?' the Marshal asked Judge Dee.

The judge addressed the young captain coldly: 'Captain Pan, you weren't fit to marry. You don't like women. You liked your colleague Captain Woo, but he spurned you. Then you strangled your wife, and falsely accused Woo of the crime.'

'Is that true?' the Marshal barked at Pan.

'Yes, sir!' the captain replied as if in a trance.

'Take him outside,' the Marshal ordered the colonel, 'and have him flogged to death slowly, with the thin rattan.'

'I plead clemency, sir!' Judge Dee interposed quickly. 'This captain had to marry at his father's command. Nature directed him differently, and he couldn't cope with the resulting problems. I propose the simple death penalty.'

'Granted!' And to Pan: 'Can you die as an officer?'

'Yes, sir!' Pan said again.

'Assist the captain!' the Marshal rasped at the elder officer.

Captain Pan loosened his purple neckcloth and handed it to his immediate superior. Then he drew his sword. Kneeling in front of the Marshal, Pan took the hilt of the sword in his right hand, and grabbed the point with his left. The sharp edge cut deeply into his fingers, but he didn't seem to notice it. The elder officer stepped up close to the kneeling man, holding the neckcloth spread out in his hands. Raising his head, Pan looked up at the towering figure of the Marshal. He called out :

'Long live the Emperor!'

Then, with one savage gesture, he cut his throat. The elder officer quickly tied the neckcloth tightly round the neck of the sagging man, staunching the blood. The Marshal nodded. He said to Pan's superior, 'Captain Pan died as an officer. See to it that he is buried as one!' And to the judge: 'You look after that other fellow. Freed, reinstated to his former rank, and so on.' Then he bent over the map again and barked at the general: 'Put an extra five thousand at the entrance of this valley here!'

As the four orderlies carried the dead body of Pan outside, Judge Dee went to the large desk, grabbed a writing-brush and quickly jotted down a few lines on a sheet of official paper of the High Command. A colonel impressed on it the large square seal of the Marshal, then countersigned it. Before running outside Judge Dee cast a quick look at the water-clock. He still had half an hour.

It took him a long time to cover the short distance between the Palace and the Military Jail. The streets were crowded with mounted soldiers; they rode in rows six abreast, holding high their long halberds, so greatly feared by the Tartars. Their horses were well fed and their armour shone in the red rays of dawn. It was General Lew's vanguard, the pick of the Imperial army. Then there came the deep sound of rolling drums, calling up the Mar-

161

shal's own men to join their colours. The great counteroffensive had begun.

The paper with the Marshal's seal caused Judge Dee to be admitted at once to the prison commandant. A sturdily built youngster was brought in by four guards; his thick wrestler's neck had been bared already for the sword of the executioner. The commandant read out the document to him, then he ordered an adjutant to assist Captain Woo in donning his armour. When Woo had put on his helmet, the commandant himself handed him back his sword. Judge Dee saw that although Woo didn't look too clever, he had a pleasant, open face. 'Come along!' he said to him.

Captain Woo stared dumbfounded at his black judge's cap, then asked: 'How did you get involved in this case, Magistrate?'

'Oh,' Judge Dee replied vaguely, 'I happened to be at Headquarters when your case was reviewed. Since they are all very busy there now, they told me to take care of the formalities.'

When they stepped out into the street Captain Woo muttered: 'I was in this accursed jain almost a year. I have no place to go.'

'You can come along with me,' Judge Dee said.

As they were walking along the captain listened to the rolling of the drums. 'So we are attacking at last, eh?' he said morosely. 'Well, I am just in time to join my company. At least I'll die an honourable death.'

'Why should you deliberately seek death?' the judge asked.

'Why? Because I am a stupid fool, that's why! I never touched that Mrs Pan, but I betrayed a fine woman who came to see me in jail. The military police flogged her to death.'

Judge Dee remained silent. Now they were passing through a quiet back street. He halted in front of a small hovel, built against an empty godown.

'Where are we?' Captain Woo asked, astonished.

'A plucky woman, and the son she bore you are living here,' the judge answered curtly. 'This is your home, Captain. Good-bye.'

He quickly walked on.

As Judge Dee rounded the street corner, a cold blast blew full into his face. He pulled his neckcloth up over his nose and mouth, stifling a cough. He hoped that the servants would be on hand already in his inn. He longed for a large cup of hot tea.

162

MURDER ON NEW YEAR'S EVE

The scene of this story is also laid in Lan-fang. As a rule a magistrate's term of office was three years. But at the end of the year A.D. 674, when Judge Dee had been serving four years in Lan-fang, there was still no news from the capital. This is the story of what happened on the last evening of that dreary year. In the criminal cases previously solved by Judge Dee his theories always proved right in the end. However, the reader will see that in this particular case Judge Dee made two big mistakes. But, contrary to the rule, this time two wrongs made a right!

When Judge Dee had put away the last file and locked the drawer of his desk he suddenly shivered. He rose and, pulling his padded house-robe closer round his tall frame, he walked across his cold, empty private office to the window. He pushed it open, but after a brief glance at the dark courtyard of the tribunal outside, he quickly pulled it shut. The snow had stopped but a gust of icy wind had nearly blown out the candle on his desk.

The judge went to the couch against the back wall. With a sigh he started to fold back the quilts. That night, the last of the weary year that had passed, the fourth of his stay in Lan-fang, he would sleep in his office. For his own house at the back of the tribunal compound was deserted except for a few servants. Two months before, his First Lady had set out to visit her aged mother in her home town, and his two other wives and his children had accompanied her, together with his faithful old adviser Sergeant Hoong. They would be back early in spring—but spring seemed very far away on this cold and dreary night.

Judge Dee took up the teapot to pour himself a last cup of tea. He found to his dismay that it had grown cold. He was about to clap his hands to summon a clerk, then remembered that he had given the personnel of the tribunal the night off, including his three personal assistants. The only men about would be the constables on guard duty at the main gate.

Pulling his house-bonnet over his ears, he took up the candle and walked through the dark, deserted chancery to the guard-house.

The four constables squatting round the blazing log fire in the centre of the stone floor jumped up when they saw Judge Dee enter and hastily set their helmets straight. The judge could see only the broad back of their headman. He was leaning out of the window cursing violently at someone outside.

'Hey there!' Judge Dee barked at him. When the headman turned round and bowed deeply, he said curtly, 'Better mind your language on the last day of the year!'

The headman muttered something about an insolent ragamuffin who dared to bother the tribunal so late at night. 'The small monkey wants me to find his mother for him!' he added disgustedly. 'Do they take me for a nursemaid?'

'Hardly that!' Judge Dee said dryly. 'But what is it all about?' He stepped up to the window and looked out.

In the street below the tiny boy was cowering against the wall for shelter against the icy wind. The moonlight shone on his tear-stained face. He cried: 'It is all . . . all over the floor! I slipped and fell in it . . . And Mother is gone!'

He stared at his small hands, then tried to rub them clean on his thin, patched jacket. Judge Dee saw the red smears. Quickly turning round, he ordered the headman, 'Get my horse and follow me with two men!'

As soon as he was outside, the judge lifted the boy up and placed him on his saddle. Then he put his foot in the stirrup and slowly mounted behind him. Wincing, he remembered how not so long ago he could still jump on his horse. But a touch of rheumatism had been bothering him of late. He suddenly felt tired, and old. Four years in Lan-fang . . . With an effort he took hold of himself. He said in a cheerful voice to the sobbing boy, 'Now we'll go together and find your mother for you! Who is your father, and where do you live?'

'My father is pedlar Wang,' said the boy, swallowing his tears. 'We live in the second alley to the west of the Temple of Confucius, not far from the watergate.'

'That's easy!' Judge Dee said. He carefully guided his horse along the snow-covered street. The headman and two constables rode silently behind him. A strong gust of wind blew the snow from the roofs, the fine particles striking their faces like so many needles. Wiping his eyes, the judge asked again, 'What is your name, small boy?'

'I am called Hsiao-pao, sir,' he answered in a trembling voice.

'Hsiao-pao, that means Small Treasure,' Judge Dee said. 'What a nice name! Now where is your father?'

'I don't know, sir!' the boy cried out unhappily. 'When father came home, he had such a big quarrel with mother. Mother didn't have any food ready, she said there weren't even any noodles in the house. Then . . . then father began to scold her, he shouted that she had passed the afternoon with Mr Shen, the old pawnbroker. Mother started to cry, and I ran out. I thought I could perhaps borrow a package of noodles from the grocer, to make father happy again. But there was such a crowd at the grocer's that I could not get through, and I went back. But then father and mother were not there anymore, there was all that blood, all over the floor. I slipped, and I . . .'

He burst out in sobs that shook his small back. The judge drew the boy closer to him in the fold of his fur coat. They rode on in silence.

When Judge Dee saw the large gate of the Temple of Confucius looming ahead against the winter sky, he descended from his horse. Putting the boy down too, he said to the headman, 'We are nearly there. We shall leave our horses here at the gate. We'd better not give warning that we have come.'

They entered a narrow alley, lined on both sides by a row of ramshackle wooden houses. The boy pointed at a street door that stood ajar. A dim light shone behind the paper window, but the second floor was brightly lit and a confused noise of singing and shouting came from there.

'Who lives above?' Judge Dee asked, pausing in front of the door.

'That's Tailor Liu,' the boy said. 'They are having some friends in for the feast tonight.'

'You show the headman the way up there, Hsiao-pao,' the judge said. To the headman he added in a low voice: 'Leave the boy with the people upstairs, but bring that fellow Liu down here for questioning.'

Then he entered the house, followed by his two constables.

The cold, bare room was lit only by a spluttering oil lamp on a rickety corner stand. In the centre, on a large, coarsely made table, stood three bowls of cracked earthenware, and a large kitchen chopper lay at one end, spattered with blood. On the stone-flagged floor there was more blood, in a large pool.

Pointing at the chopper, the elder constable remarked, 'Someone neatly cut someone's throat with that, sir!'

Judge Dee nodded. He felt the bloodstain on the chopper with his forefinger and found that it was still wet. Looking round, he quickly surveyed the rest of the dim room. Against the back wall stood a large couch with faded blue curtains, and a small un-curtained bed was placed against the wall on the left, evidently the boy's. The plaster walls were bare, and had here and there been clumsily patched. Judge Dee went to the closed door by the side of the bedstead. It led into a small kitchen. The ashes in the stove were cold.

When the judge stepped back into the room the younger con-stable remarked with a sneer, 'Not a place for robbers to visit, Your Honour! I have heard about that pedlar Wang, he is as poor as a rat!'

'The motive was passion,' the judge said curtly. He pointed at a silk handkerchief that was lying on the floor, near the bed. The flickering light of the oil lamp shone on the large character 'Shen' embroidered on it in gold thread. 'After the boy had left to borrow the noodles,' Judge Dee went on, 'the pedlar found the handkerchief, left by his wife's paramour. Heated as he was by the quarrel, it was too much for him. He took the chopper and killed her. The old, old story.' He shrugged his shoulders. 'He must have gone to hide her body. Is the pedlar a strong fellow?'

'Strong as an ox, Your Honour!' the elder constable replied. 'I have often seen him about, he walks the street from morning till night carrying that heavy box on his back.'

Judge Dee glanced at the large square box covered with oil cloth standing next to the door. He nodded slowly.

The headman came in, pushing in front of him a tall, lean man. He seemed very drunk. Tottering on his feet, he gave the judge a bleary look from his small, shifty eyes. The headman grabbed his collar and forced him down on his knees. Judge Dee folded his arms in his wide sleeves and said curtly, 'A murder was committed here. State exactly what you heard and saw!'

'It must have been that woman's fault!' the tailor muttered with a thick tongue. 'Always gadding about, but not even looking at a fine upstanding fellow like me!' He hiccoughed. 'I am too poor for her, just like her husband! It's the money of the pawn-broker she's after, the slut!'

'Keep a civil tongue in your mouth!' Judge Dee ordered angrily. 'And answer my question! The ceiling here consists only of thin boards; you must have heard them quarrel!'

The headman gave him a kick in the ribs, and barked: 'Speak up!'

'I didn't hear a thing, Your Excellency!' the frightened tailor whined. 'Those bastards upstairs are all drunk, they are shouting and singing all the time! And that stupid woman of mine over-turned the bowl, and she was too drunk to wipe the stuff up. I had to shake her quite some time before I could make her set to work.'

'Nobody left the room?' Judge Dee asked.

'Not them!' the tailor muttered. 'They are all too busy gloat-ing over the pig Butcher Li slaughtered for us! And who has to do the roasting? I do! Those fellows only swill my wine, they are too lazy even to keep the coal fire burning right! The room got full of smoke, I had to open the window. Then I saw that slut run off!'

Judge Dee raised his eyebrows. He thought for a while, then asked: 'Was her husband with her?'

'Would she want him?' the tailor sneered. 'She does better alone!'

The judge quickly turned round. He stooped and scrutinized the floor. He noticed among the confused, bloody footprints those

167

of small pointed shoes leading to the door. He asked the tailor in a tense voice: 'What direction did she go?'

'To the watergate!' the man answered sullenly.

Judge Dee pulled his fur coat round him. 'Take that rascal upstairs!' he ordered the constables. Going to the door, he whispered hurriedly to the headman, 'You wait for me inside here. When Wang returns, arrest him! The pawnbroker must have looked in here to get his handkerchief just when Wang, quarrelling with his wife, discovered it. Wang killed him, and his wife fled.'

The judge went out and tramped through the snow to the next street. He mounted his horse and rode to the watergate as fast as he could. One death was enough, he reflected.

Arriving at the bottom of the stone steps leading up the gate tower, he jumped down and went hurriedly to the steep stairs, slippery with the frozen snow. On top of the tower he saw a woman, standing on the farthest parapet. She had gathered her robe round her, and with bent body looked down at the water of the city moat far below.

Judge Dee ran up to her, and laid his hand on her arm. 'You shouldn't do that, Mrs Wang!' he said gravely. 'Killing yourself won't bring the dead back to life!'

The woman shrank back against the battlement and looked at the judge with startled eyes, her lips parted in fright. He saw that although her face was drawn and haggard, she was still handsome in a common sort of way.

'You must be from the tribunal!' she faltered. 'That means they have discovered that my poor husband murdered him! And it's all my fault!' She burst out in heart-breaking sobs.

'Was it the pawnbroker Shen he murdered?' Judge Dee asked.

She nodded her head forlornly. Then she cried out: 'I am such a fool! I swear there was nothing between Shen and me; I only wanted to tease my husband a little. . . .' She pushed a wet lock back from her forehead. 'Shen had ordered a set of embroidered handkerchiefs from me, to give to his concubine as a New Year's present. I had not told my husband, I wanted to surprise him with the money. Tonight, when Wang found the last handker-

168

chief I was working on, he went to get the kitchen knife, shouting that he would kill Shen and me. I fled outside; I tried to get to my sister in the next street, but the house was closed. And when I came back to our place, my husband was gone and . . . there was all that blood.' She covered her face with her hands, then added sobbing: 'Shen . . . he must have come for the handkerchief and . . . Wang killed him. It's all my fault, how can I go on living when my husband . . . ?'

'Remember that you have your son to look after,' Judge Dee interrupted her. He gripped her arm firmly and led her to the stairs.

Back at the house he told the headman to take the woman upstairs. When the headman had done so, the judge said, 'We shall stand close to the door, against the wall. We have only to wait for the murderer's return. Wang killed Shen here, then went out to hide his victim's body. He planned to come back here to clean up that blood, but his son brought us here, and his plan has fallen through.' After a while he added with a sigh, 'I am sorry for that boy, he's a likable little fellow!'

The four men stood against the wall, two on either side of the door, Judge Dee next to the pedlar's box. Upstairs, some coarse voices were shouting in argument.

Suddenly the door opened and a big, broad-shouldered man came in. The constables jumped on him. Taken by surprise, before he knew what was happening they had chained Wang's arms behind his back, and pressed him down on his knees. A package wrapped in oil paper fell from his sleeve, noodles spilled on the floor. One of the constables kicked the package into a corner.

Upstairs some people were dancing. The thin boards of the ceiling bent and creaked.

'Don't throw away good food!' Judge Dee barked, irritated at the constable. 'Pick that up!'

Thus rebuked, the constable made haste to scoop up the noodles. When placing them on the table, he muttered, 'They aren't much good any more, the dirt that came down from the ceiling has spoiled them.'

'The rascal has blood on his right hand, Your Honour!' the

headman who had been inspecting Wang's chains exclaimed excitedly.

Wang had been staring with wide eyes at the blood on the floor in front of him. His lips were moving but no sound came. Now he lifted his face up to the judge and brought out: 'Where is my wife? What has happened to her?'

Judge Dee sat down on the box and folded his hands in his wide sleeves. He said coldly: 'It is I, the magistrate, who asks questions here! Tell me . . .'

'Where is my wife?' Wang shouted frantically. He wanted to scramble up but the headman hit him over the head with the heavy handle of his whip. Wang dazedly shook his head, and stammered: 'My wife . . . and my son . . .'

'Speak up! What happened here tonight?' the judge asked.

'Tonight . . .' Wang said in a toneless voice, then hesitated. The headman gave him a kick. 'Answer and speak the truth!' he growled.

Wang frowned. He again looked at the blood on the floor. At last he began, 'Tonight, when I was walking home, the grocer told me that the pawnbroker Shen had been here. And when I came in, there was nothing to eat, not even our New Year's noodles. I told my wife I did not want her any more, that she could go to that fellow Shen, and stay there. I said that the entire neighbourhood knew that he visited her when I was out. She would not say yes or no. Then I found that handkerchief there by the bed. I went for the chopper. I would first kill her and then go and finish off that fellow Shen. But when I came back from the kitchen with the chopper, my wife had run away. I grabbed the handkerchief, I wanted to throw that in Shen's face before I cut his throat. But I scratched my hand on the needle stuck in it.'

Wang paused. He bit his lips and swallowed. 'I knew then what an utter fool I had been. Shen had not dropped the handkerchief there; it was one he had ordered from her, and on which she was still working. . . . I went out to look for my wife. I went to her sister's home, but nobody was there. Then I walked to Shen's shop; I wanted to pawn my jacket and buy something nice for my wife. But Shen said he owed me a string of coppers for a set of twenty handkerchiefs he had ordered from her. The last one had not been quite finished when he had looked in at our house in the afternoon, but his concubine had been very pleased with the ones he had given her. And since it was New Year's eve, he said, he would pay me anyway. I bought a package of noodles, and a paper flower for my wife, and came here.' Gazing at the judge, he burst out: 'Tell me, what has happened to her? Where is she?'

The headman guffawed. He shouted: 'What a string of stupid lies the dog is telling! The bastard hopes to gain time!' Lifting the handle of his whip, he asked the judge: 'Shall I knock his teeth in, Your Honour, to make the truth come out a bit easier?'

Judge Dee shook his head. Slowly stroking his long sidewhiskers, he looked fixedly at the drawn face of the pedlar kneeling before him. Then he ordered the headman: 'See whether he has a paper flower on him!'

The headman put his hand in the pedlar's bosom, and brought out a red paper flower. He held it up for the judge to see, then threw it disdainfully on the floor and put his foot on it.

Judge Dee rose. He walked over to the bedstead, picked up the handkerchief and looked it over carefully. Then he went to the table and stood there for a while, staring down at the dirty noodles on the piece of oil paper. The only sound heard was the heavy breathing of the kneeling man.

Suddenly the uproar of voices on the floor above burst out again. Judge Dee looked up at the ceiling. Then he turned to the headman and ordered: 'Bring those two down here!'

As soon as the pedlar saw his wife and his son, his mouth opened in astonished delight. He cried out: 'Heaven be praised, you are safe!' He would have jumped up, but the constables roughly pressed him down again.

His wife threw herself down on the floor in front of the kneeling man. She moaned, 'Forgive me, forgive me! I was such a fool, I only wanted to tease you! What have I done, what have I done! Now you have . . . They will take you away and . . .'

'Rise, you two!' the stern voice of the judge interrupted her. At his peremptory gesture the two constables let go of Wang's shoulders.

'Take the chains off him!' Judge Dee ordered. As the dumb-

AS SOON AS THE PEDLAR SAW HIS WIFE AND SON . . .

*The Two Beggars	Murder solved by Judge Dee, with Sergeant Hoong. Magistrate Lo referred to again.
*The Wrong Sword	Murder of a young acrobat, solved by Judge Dee, with Ma Joong and Chiao Tai. Sheng Pa reappears.
The Red Pavilion (London 1964). The Callous Courtesan, The Amorous Academician, The Unlucky Lovers.	Scene is laid in the amusement resort of Paradise Island where Judge Dee stays two days with Ma Joong. Magistrate Lo reappears in Chapters II and XX.
The Emperor's Pearl (London 1963). The Dead Drummer, The Murdered Slavemaid, The Emperor's Pearl.	Murders during the annual boat races, solved by Judge Dee, assisted by Sergeant Hoong, Sheng Pa reappears in Chapter VIII; his romance with Miss Violet Liang.
The Chinese Maze Murders (London 1952). The Murder in the Sealed Room, The Hidden Testament, The Girl with the Severed Head.	On p. 22 are given the reasons for Judge Dee's abrupt transfer to this remote border district. The overthrow of a local tyrant and several mysterious murders, solved by Judge Dee, with Hoong, Ma Joong, Chiao Tai and Tao Gan. The Uigur girl Tulbee becomes Ma Joong's sweetheart (p. 173). Headman Fang's story (p. 35); Fang's son appointed constable (p. 289).
670 Magistrate of Lan-fang, a district on the extreme western frontier.	
The Phantom of the Temple (London 1966).	Three crimes that turn out to be one, solved by Judge Dee with Sergeant Hoong and Ma Joong. Description of Judge Dee's three wives on p. 40; more details about his Third Lady (the former Miss Tsao) on p. 104. The Uigur girl Tulbee reappears (p. 56). References to Headman Fang and his son (pp. 11 and 136).
*The Coffins of the Emperor	Two difficult cases solved by Judge Dee alone, when summoned to the border district Ta-shih-kou during the Tartar war.
*Murder on New Year's Eve	A most unusual case, solved by Judge Dee alone, after he had been four years in Lan-fang.

JUDGE DEE CHRONOLOGY (cont.)

Time, place and Judge Dee's office	Titles (the short stories of the present volume are marked by an asterisk)	Information on Judge Dee, his family, his lieutenants, and persons who appear in more than one story (page numbers refer to the first London editions)
676 Magistrate of Pei-chow, a desolate district up in the barren north.	The Chinese Nail Murders (London 1961). The Headless Corpse, The Paper Cat, The Murdered Merchant.	After only a few months in this new post, Judge Dee was appointed Lord Chief Justice, in the capital. In Pei-chow he solves several particularly cruel murders, with Hoong, Ma Joong, Chiao Tai and Tao Gan; but Sergeant Hoong is killed while working on a case. The antecedents of Judge Dee's three wives are given on p. 116. Introduction of Mrs Kuo, the Lady of the Medicine Hill (p. 38).
	The Night of the Tiger (in The Monkey and the Tiger [London 1965]).	Murder of a young girl solved by Judge Dee alone when, on his way from Pei-chow to the capital, he has to stay overnight in a lonely country house. References to Mrs Kuo and Sergeant Hoong's death, on p. 91.
677 Lord Chief Justice, in the imperial capital.	The Willow Pattern (London 1965). The Willow Pattern, The Steep Staircase, The Murdered Bondmaid.	Judge Dee has taken up his new office of Lord Chief Justice, Ma Joong and Chiao Tai have been appointed Colonels of the Guard, Tao Gan chief secretary of the Metropolitan Court. Ma Joong marries the Yuan twin sisters.
681 Lord Chief Justice.	Murder in Canton (London 1966). The Vanished Censor, The Smaragdine Dancer, The Golden Bell.	Scene is laid in Canton, where Judge Dee has been sent on a special mission. Murders solved by Judge Dee, with the assistance of Chiao Tai and Tao Gan. Chiao Tai is killed by the sword Rain Dragon, Tao Gan decides to marry Miss Liang. Reference to Mrs Kuo and the tragedy on Medicine Hill on p. 160.

Historical Note. Judge Dee died in A.D. 700, at the age of seventy. He was survived by two sons, Dee Guang-se and Dee Djing-hui, who had an honourable official career without, however, particularly distinguishing themselves. It was his grandson Dee Djien-mo who inherited his grandfather's remarkable personality and great wisdom; he died as governor of the Imperial Capital.

founded headman carried out this order, the judge continued to Wang, 'Tonight your foolish jealousy nearly made you lose your wife. It is your son who averted a terrible tragedy, he came to warn me just in time. Let tonight be a lesson to you—to both of you, man and wife. New Year's eve is a time to remember. To remember the blessings Heaven has bestowed on you, the gifts we are wont to take too much for granted and forget too soon. You love each other, you are in good health, and you have a fine son. That is more than many can say! Make the resolution that henceforward you shall try to prove yourselves worthy of those blessings!' Turning to the small boy, he patted him on his head and added: 'Lest you forget, I order you to change this boy's name into Ta-pao. That means "Big Treasure"!'

He signalled to his three men and went to the door.

'But . . . Your Honour, that murder . . .' the woman faltered.

Pausing in the open doorway, the judge said with a bleak smile: 'There was no murder. When the people upstairs had killed a pig, the tailor's wife overturned the bowl in which they had poured the blood, and she was too drunk to wipe it up at once. It leaked through the cracks in the ceiling on to the table and the floor in this room. Good-bye!'

The woman put her hand over her mouth to suppress a cry of joy. Her husband smiled a little foolishly at her, then stooped and picked up the paper flower. Having clumsily smoothed out its petals, he stepped up to her, and stuck the flower in her hair. The boy looked up at his parents, a broad smile on his small round face.

The headman had led Judge Dee's horse in front of the door. Only after the judge had jumped into the saddle did he suddenly realize that his rheumatism was gone.

The gong of the nightwatch announced midnight. Firecrackers started an uproar in the market place. As the judge urged on his horse he turned round in his saddle and called out:

'Happy New Year!'

He doubted whether the three people in the doorway had heard him. It didn't really matter.

COLOPHON

JUDGE DEE was a historical person. His full name was Dee Jen-djieh and he lived from A.D. 630 to 700. In the latter half of his career he became a Minister of State, and through his wise counsels exercised a beneficial influence on the internal and external affairs of the T'ang empire.

However, it is chiefly because of his reputation as a detector of crimes, acquired while serving as district magistrate, that his name lives on among the Chinese people. Today the Chinese still consider him their master-detective, and his name is as popular with them as that of Sherlock Holmes with us.

Although the stories told in the present volume are entirely fictional, I utilized some data from old Chinese crime literature, especially a thirteenth-century manual of jurisprudence and detection which I published ten years ago in an English translation (T'ang-yin-pi-shih, Sinica Leidensia vol. X, E. J. Brill, Leiden 1956). The final passage of 'The Murder on the Lotus Pond' was suggested by Cases 33A and B recorded in that book, and the weighing of the sarcophagus described in 'The Coffins of the Emperor' by a note added to Case 35B.

The design of the incense-clock utilized in 'Five Auspicious Clouds' I copied from the Hsiang-yin-t'u-k'ao, a collection of such patterns published in 1878; I used the same source for the pattern of the maze in The Chinese Maze Murders.

Note that in China the surname precedes the personal name. Also that in Judge Dee's time the Chinese wore no pig-tails; that custom was imposed upon them in A.D. 1644 by the Manchu conquerors. Men did their long hair up in a top-knot, they wore caps both inside and outside the house. They didn't smoke, tobacco and opium were introduced into China only many centuries later.

Tokyo: 1967   Robert van Gulik

JUDGE DEE CHRONOLOGY
(Fictitious, except for his birthdate, and the historical note at the end)
covering 15 novels and 8 short stories.

Time, place and Judge Dee's office	Titles (the short stories of the present volume are marked by an asterisk)	Information on Judge Dee, his family, his lieutenants, and persons who appear in more than one story (page numbers refer to the first London editions)
A.D. 630 Tai-yuan, capital of Shansi Province.		Judge Dee born. Receives elementary education at home. Passes the provincial literary examinations.
650 The capital.		Judge Dee's father appointed Imperial Councillor in the capital. Judge Dee acts as his father's private secretary, marries his First and Second Ladies. Passes metropolitan literary examination, and is appointed secretary in the Imperial Archives
663 Magistrate of Peng-lai, a district on the north-east coast of the Chinese Empire.	The Chinese Gold Murders (London 1959). The Murdered Magistrate, The Bolting Bride, The Butchered Bully.	Judge Dee's first independent official post. Proceeds there accompanied by Sergeant Hoong. Meets on the way Ma Joong and Chiao Tai. First mention of the sword Rain Dragon; Chiao Tai foresees he will be killed by that sword (p. 31). Ch. XV describes adventures of Miss Tsao.
	*Five Auspicious Clouds	One week after Judge Dee's arrival in Peng-lai. Mrs Ho: suicide or murder? Solved by Judge Dee alone.
	*The Red Tape Murder	One month later. A military murder, solved by Judge Dee, assisted by Ma Joong and Chiao Tai. Colonel Meng appears.
	*He Came with the Rain	Six months later. Murder of a pawnbroker, solved by Judge Dee alone. Colonel Meng is again referred to. Judge Dee decides to marry Miss Tsao as his Third Lady.

JUDGE DEE CHRONOLOGY (cont.)

Time, place and Judge Dee's office	Titles (the short stories of the present volume are marked by an asterisk)	Information on Judge Dee, his family, his lieutenants, and persons who appear in more than one story (page numbers refer to the first London editions)
663	*The Lacquer Screen* (London 1962). The Lacquer Screen, The Credulous Merchant, The Faked Accounts.	Solved by Judge Dee, assisted by Chiao Tai, during a brief sojourn in the district Wei-ping. Second reference to Chiao Tai dying by the sword (p. 140).
666 Magistrate of Han-yuan, a district on the bank of a lake, near the capital.	*The Chinese Lake Murders* (London 1960). The Drowned Courtesan, The Vanished Bride, The Spendthrift Councillor.	Solved by Judge Dee, Hoong, Ma Joong and Chiao Tai. His future fourth lieutenant Tao Gan here makes his first appearance (p. 153). The rich landowner Han Yung-han appears (*passim*). Description of the King of the Beggars of Han-yuan (p. 118).
	The Morning of the Monkey (in *The Monkey and the Tiger* [London 1965]).	Murder of a tramp, solved by Judge Dee and Tao Gan; Tao Gan is definitively taken into Judge Dee's service. The King of the Beggars reappears (p. 31). Han Yung-han mentioned (p. 59).
	The Haunted Monastery (London 1961). The Embalmed Abbot, The Pious Maid, The Morose Monk.	Scene is laid in an old Taoist temple, in the mountains of Han-yuan. Murders solved by Judge Dee, with Tao Gan. Judge Dee's attitude to his wives described on p. 12.
	*The Murder on the Lotus Pond	The murder of an old poet, solved by Judge Dee, with Ma Joong.
668 Magistrate of Poo-yang, a large, flourishing district in Kiangsu Province, on the Grand Canal.	*The Chinese Bell Murders* (London 1958). The Rape Murder in Half Moon Street, The Secret of the Buddhist Temple, The Mysterious Skeleton.	Solved by Judge Dee, with his four lieutenants Sergeant Hoong, Ma Joong, Chiao Tai and Tao Gan. Introduction of Sheng Pa, Head of the Beggars (*passim*). Introduction of Magistrate Lo, of the neighbouring district (Ch. IX).

"HOW ABOUT HAWAII FOR OUR HONEYMOON?"

Brock spoke in a cheerful tone as he deftly uncorked the wine. "Sound good?"

Charlotte didn't look up from her dinner preparations, but her hands trembled. "Uh, great..."

What was wrong, he wondered. Aloud, he said, "Okay, I'll look into it. Will you have any difficulty taking time off from work?"

Without warning, she asked, "Do you think you could face honeymooning with a grandmother?" When he didn't reply, she finally looked up. Her cheeks were flushed and she appeared near to tears. "Tell me straight, Brock, and don't try to be tactful. How would you *really* feel knowing you were making love to a grandmother?"

Apprehension ran through his body. "Very, very old," he said with an attempt at humor.

But Charlotte wasn't laughing.

ABOUT THE AUTHOR

"There was never any question but that I would be a writer," Virginia Nielsen once said. Looking back over her long and prolific career, we're aware of the truth of those words. She's written more than 250 short stories and over thirty books. Some years ago she received the Golden Treasure Award from the Romance Writers of America to mark her contribution to the field of romance fiction. Virginia lives in Sacramento with her husband and travels extensively when she's not writing.

Books by Virginia Nielsen

HARLEQUIN SUPERROMANCE

Virginia Nielsen

ROOM FOR ONE MORE

Harlequin Books

TORONTO • NEW YORK • LONDON
AMSTERDAM • PARIS • SYDNEY • HAMBURG
STOCKHOLM • ATHENS • TOKYO • MILAN

Published October 1987

First printing August 1987

ISBN 0-373-70279-5

CHAPTER ONE

CHARLOTTE EMLYN PAUSED in the open doorway of the echocardiogram room and watched Brock Morley, the support technician from Echo, Ltd. He was sitting in the chair she normally used and working on the machine she operated to take pictures and calculate measurements of the hearts of patients who were sent by their physicians to the cardiology clinic.

As usual, Brock's concentration was so intense that he had not heard her stop by. His briefcase was open on the examining table and his coat and tie were lying beside it. Someone—probably one of the impressionable young women from reception—had brought him a cup of coffee and it stood on the floor beside his feet.

Charlotte worried about Brock Morley. He was lean, almost thin, and she suspected he didn't eat enough. She had never known anyone who could become so absorbed in a technical problem that he forgot to eat.

"It's still down?" she commented dryly.

Brock glanced up, the look of preoccupation in his eyes swiftly melting into the warmth of his smile, and she caught her breath at its impact. "This is a very complex machine, lady."

His intense concentration of a moment ago and his casual ease when he relaxed both seemed marks of youth to her, but his observant gaze was frankly masculine in its appraisal. She guessed that he was about ten years her junior, and was embarrassed to feel a feminine, even sensuous awareness of the profusion of dark hairs on his forearms below the rolled-up sleeves of his white shirt.

"Can you have it in operation by tomorrow?" she asked. "The front office wants to know if they have to reschedule tomorrow's tests for me."

"Can't promise yet. Is there any more coffee?"

Her reaction was automatic and chilly. "I'll ask the receptionist to bring you a refill."

"Sorry," he said, but he looked amused. "You're the cardiac technician, right?"

"Right."

"Who brings you coffee?"

She shrugged. "We get our own."

"Then why don't you bring some for both of us? I'd like to ask you a few questions."

She hesitated in the doorway, and Brock waited for her answer, giving his full attention to the picture she made. She was a tall woman, almost as tall as he was, with an individuality that had intrigued him from the first time he had come to the clinic. Slender, she wore a long white starched uniform jacket that was a little too large for her over a loose-fitting silky skirt, making him speculate pleasantly about the curves she was hiding; and she had pulled her flowing hair into a frank topknot on the crown of her head so that there was fullness above her forehead and her surprisingly pretty ears. A pencil was stuck into the flow of hair above her right ear—a habit, he guessed, because a few shiny strands fell down beside each cheek. The effect was that of a deliberate untidiness that was somehow elegant.

Charlotte recognized the gleam in his eyes. Had he sensed her response to him? She wondered why she had made an issue of the coffee. After all, she couldn't expect him to know where they made the coffee.

"Cream and sugar?" Suddenly realizing that the way she was leaning against the door frame with one hip jutting out could be construed as provocative, she straightened.

Brock noted the movement with interest. Married, he guessed, scrapping a vague impulse he'd felt before, on other maintenance calls, to ask her to go out with him. He handed her the mug. "Black."

"Be right back," she said, and left.

He watched her go with wry regret. Most women his age who attracted him were already married. Anyway, it was against his policy to make a pass on the job.

When Charlotte returned with two steaming mugs, he was once more totally engrossed in testing the components of the program that ran the machine's complicated computations, trying to locate the source of error. She watched him for a moment, analyzing what it was that made him different. It occurred to her that there was no trace of anxiety in his absorption; it seemed to reflect, rather, a deep pleasure in his work and a secure sense of its worth. She admired that.

The aromatic steam from the coffee roused him from his intent study. He swiveled his chair toward her and took the mug she offered. She sat at the small desk at the foot of the examining table with her legs crossed, one smartly clad foot gently waving at him below her concealing skirt, and they sipped the hot drink while they discussed the problems she had had with the machine.

When Brock's mug was empty, he set it down and rolled up his pant legs. She watched in unself-conscious fascination while he fastened the monitor suction cups above his ankles. He then unbuttoned his shirt. Like Wade, her teenage son, he wore no undershirt and she felt an unwar-

ranted embarrassment because she noticed the dark hairs
covering his chest curled slightly.

"Help me get these monitors on right?"

It was something she did daily, to both male and female
patients, yet she felt reluctant to touch him. "You can't take
the test sitting at the machine," she protested.

"Do you want to play patient for me? I have to work the
dials."

"No." Flushing slightly, she placed the monitors on the
left side of his chest and fastened the blood-pressure cuffs
around his arms. Together they watched the screen while
Brock worked the controls. For an instant an outline of his
beating heart flashed on the screen, contracting and expanding—the sensation it gave her was curiously intimate—then the image disappeared.

"Uh-hmm," he said absently, twirling dials. He finally
turned off the machine and removed his monitors.

The light flashed on the telephone on the small desk at
the end of the examining table. Charlotte punched her
button and took up the receiver. Joy, in the front office,
said, "Your son's on the line, Charlotte."

"Put him on, please."

Wade's voice said, "Hi, Mom."

"Hi, honey, how did the exam go?"

"I passed." He was laconic, just as if he hadn't stayed up
studying half the night. He was finding the adjustment
from high-school senior to college freshman difficult but
not unsettling.

"Good for you," she said warmly.

"Listen, Mom, I'm taking your car. The van's being
lubed and I have to run by Kate's. She says it's important.
I'll pick you up at five, okay?"

"Okay." He was a good son, reliable and caring. She put the receiver down with a glow of thankfulness that he was not like some teenagers she knew.

Watching her expression as he buttoned his shirt, Brock thought regretfully that he had been right. She was married.

Charlotte glanced at her watch. It was noon. On an impulse she said, "Are you going to break for lunch? There's a snack bar downstairs that serves great hamburgers."

He shook his head. Once more preoccupation was beginning to spread a mask over his face. "I seldom eat lunch."

"You can't live on coffee," she chided.

"I know, but I do." He flashed her a brief grin. "What about the audio on this thing?"

"It sounds like an ancient Maytag washer."

He laughed. "I'll check it out while I'm here." He started fiddling with the dials again. "I may have to bring in another board."

No WONDER HE WAS THIN, Charlotte thought, as she ordered a hamburger and fries at the small counter on the ground floor of the modern medical and professional building that housed the clinic. It wasn't healthy for a young man to subsist on black coffee. She compared Brock's diet with Wade's hearty appetite, placing him vaguely in Wade's generation, even though he must be ten years older than her son.

On an impulse she ordered another hamburger to go, with shoestring potatoes, and when she had finished eating, took the bag back to the cardiologists' suite with her.

Brock took the package with a look of surprise. "Gee, thanks!" He opened it, sniffed the rich aroma of browned beef, and grinned at Charlotte. "I'll need more coffee."

She bit back a retort. He was outrageous, but charming.

But when she brought the coffee, he was completely absorbed in the innards of the machine again, and the hamburger was congealing in its basket. She sat at her desk with her back to him, feeling like a fool, and plunged into her paperwork.

She envied Brock his preoccupation. She couldn't seem to concentrate on her own work because she was so sharply aware of his movements. She knew exactly which knob he twirled because she was so familiar with the subtle sounds of the machine. Sometimes he muttered a single word under his breath, and she realized she was waiting for the sound of his voice.

Finally she got up in disgust with herself, and with a purposeful stride headed down the hall for the file library. Brock Morley was still working on the machine at five o'clock when she was ready to leave the clinic. He was also drinking more coffee. "When do you eat?" she asked him rather tartly.

He looked up, taking in her topcoat and scarf and the purse slung from her shoulder. "Oh, is it time to close up shop?"

"Dr. Ferdinand and the nurse will be around until he finishes with his last patient—maybe twenty minutes."

"Then I'd better pack up," he said reluctantly. "Too bad. I think I've almost got it."

She felt exasperated with him. "You know, you're too thin," she said severely.

"I'm going to pick up some dinner at the first place I see," he promised. "Care to join me?" he asked lightly.

She looked surprised, then colored, and Brock thought it made her appear charmingly younger. "Thanks, but I have a ride home waiting for me."

Her husband, of course. He grinned at her. "Thanks for worrying about me."

"Sorry, must be my nurturing instinct," she said incautiously.

With a bemused smile, Brock glanced fleetingly at the gentle swell beneath her topcoat. Charlotte realized he was not even conscious of where he was looking and that made it even more embarrassing. She turned and left the room, taking the peculiar sweetness of his smile with her and berating herself for fussing about his eating habits. She probably reminded him of his mother!

Thanks for worrying . . . ?

Right. Why should she?

She left the building and found Wade waiting at the back entrance with her car. Taking in the bulk blocking the driver's side of the sedan, she was struck anew by how much his silhouette reminded her of his father, who had been a large, square man—an entirely different type, physically, from Brock Morley.

Wade was unusually quiet as he pulled out of the parking lot. "Tired, hon?" she asked. He had a heavy schedule for a student not yet out of his teens.

"Sleepy," he said carelessly. "Didn't get my eight hours last night."

"How's Kate?"

She thought he hesitated for a second. "Fine. She sent love."

Perhaps that twosome was dissolving, Charlotte thought fleetingly. She had been expecting it for some time. Kate was a nice girl, but hardly the type to interest Wade in a long-term relationship.

The clinic was on the south side of Seattle on a small rise people in the neighborhood called Pill Hill because of its profusion of hospitals and related medical facilities. The slight eminence gave them a view of Puget Sound and the mountains of the Olympic peninsula. The days were getting shorter, but the sun was out—high enough to add sparkles to the water and to flash an occasional reflection from windows on the ferries moving between the mainland and the islands in the Sound. Wade turned the car inland and they began climbing toward the house that they shared.

"Can you stop at the supermarket?" Charlotte asked. "I want to pick up some chops."

"I'm not very hungry tonight, Mom."

She looked at him in surprise. "Are you feeling okay, Wade?"

"I'd rather sleep than eat, that's all."

She remembered the congealing hamburger and wondered if Brock Morley would remember to eat some dinner. "Okay, sweetie," she said, patting Wade's arm, "but we'll still need to make a quick stop at the store." He had just reinforced her impression of Brock Morley's youth. But why should she be thinking about the maintenance technician?

When they pulled into the driveway later, Wade unloaded the groceries and carried them in through the back porch of the house. Her son was taller than she was, Charlotte thought, and built solidly like his father, who had died of encephalitis when Wade was seven. Wade was paying his own way through college with the sound equipment he had purchased piece by piece while he was in high school carrying a large paper route. Now he had a three-nights-a-week late-hour disc-jockey job at a local radio station besides his gigs playing recorded music for private parties. He and his mother seldom saw each other for more than a meal together.

Wade retired to his room while she prepared dinner. At the table he had little to say but did eat his chop. Charlotte endured his silence as long as she could. "Have you and Kate quarreled?" she finally asked.

He looked startled. "No, why?"

"You seem so preoccupied tonight. I thought maybe you two were breaking up."

He grinned. "On the contrary."

"Really?"

"What's the matter, Mom? You sound surprised."

"Frankly, I didn't expect your interest in Kate to last this long."

"Why? Don't you like her?"

"Of course I like her! She's a darling girl. But she's—she's—so different from other girls you've gone out with."

"Yeah." Momentarily, Wade's sober face lit with pleasure. "Mom, have you ever noticed how Kate never just walks? It's always like she's dancing."

Charlotte looked at her son with a deep love. Slowly she nodded her head. She could understand how a steady, reliable young man like Wade could fall under the spell of a lovely, mercurial girl like Kate. But she hoped he was not getting too serious about her. Kate Parsons still had a lot of growing up to do.

She said no more, and Wade went to his room, threatening to sleep for twelve hours. As Charlotte washed dishes alone, she worried briefly about Wade and Kate but almost at once her thoughts returned to Brock Morley. When she found herself wondering how his system could possibly stand all those cups of black coffee, she slapped the dishcloth angrily against the sink.

Brock Morley was already at the cardiology clinic when Charlotte arrived the next morning. His expression as he greeted her was amiable, even admiring, but there was nothing in it to justify the tinge of eroticism in the dream that she found embarrassing to remember. Her sleep the

night before had been broken by a crazy mixed-up sequence of adventures involving Wade and his friends, and
Brock Morley had been a disturbing participant, apparently one of Wade's crowd.

She studied him swiftly and secretly to see if he matched
the image in her dreams. He was closing her machine, still
wearing his coat and tie, and he looked wonderful and—she
had to admit—older than her sleeping mind had pictured
him.

He twisted several dials, watching the results. "I put in
a new board this morning," he told her. "I don't think
you'll have any more problems."

He was all business today and her vague feeling of disappointment irritated her. *You're thirty-eight years old!* she
reminded herself vehemently. Aloud she asked, "How late
did you work last night?"

"Until the receptionist ran me out," he answered with a
grin. "When I get on the trail of a bug I stay on it." He gave
the knot of his tie a tug, picked up his briefcase and said,
"If you have any more trouble, let me know." Then he was
gone, and Charlotte heard his teasing voice as he kidded
with the receptionists on his way out of the clinic. She
picked up the phone to tell Joy she could begin scheduling
tests.

The following week, the echocardiogram unit was down
again, and Charlotte was shocked to feel a secret pleasure.

When she told Dr. Ferdinand the machine was inoper-
able, he took off his glasses and pinched the bridge of his
nose. "Call the hospital and see if we can send some of our
patients over there for tests. Then get on the phone to Echo
and give 'em hell."

With a little glow of anticipation, Charlotte called the
firm and asked the woman who answered for Brock Morley.

"He may already have left on a maintenance call. Hold, please, and I'll see."

A few minutes later she heard his voice with a flutter of recognition. "Morley here."

"This is Charlotte Emlyn at the cardiology clinic."

"Hello, Charlotte!" he said, as if he were genuinely pleased to hear from her.

She replied more tartly than necessary, "I was instructed to give you hell."

He chuckled. "You're still having a problem." He didn't sound displeased.

"You've got it."

"I have another call to make today, but I'll try to work you in. In fact," he said pleasantly, "I'll work you in first."

"Thanks, Brock. Dr. Ferdinand will appreciate it."

"How about you?"

"What?" she said blankly.

"Will you appreciate it?" he asked with a touch of amusement in his voice.

"What do you want? Another hamburger?"

"You might bring me a doughnut. I won't have time for breakfast if I come to the clinic now."

He was teasing her about mothering him! She felt warmth rise to her cheeks. "A doughnut, right. Rich and greasy and loaded with sugar."

"Right," he repeated, "with coffee." She groaned.

He came in a half hour later, with his familiar air of casual competence and his easy way with her. He lacked any self-consciousness. Soon he was wholly involved in his investigation of the computer problem. Charlotte had such a strong inclination to become just as absorbed in watching him work that she got up from her chair and started to leave.

"You're going after doughnuts," Brock said without turning around.

"Not a chance."

She heard him laugh as she went down the hall. But she was hugging her secret knowledge that he had not been as absorbed in his work as he had appeared.

As she approached Dr. Ferdinand's office, the door opened and he ushered out a plump white-haired woman in a pea-green pantsuit.

"Oh, Charlotte, can you come in here for a moment?" he requested over his patient's shoulder as he clasped the woman's hand in a reassuring goodbye.

"Certainly, Doctor." Charlotte followed him back into the room and closed the door.

He walked around his desk, looking somewhat lost in thought as he sat down. "When will you be able to use the echocardiogram?" he asked. "Tomorrow?"

She shrugged. "Possibly."

"I'm wondering if we shouldn't replace it with a later model. IBM and Hewlett-Packard and some other manufacturers will be displaying medical computers at a weekend seminar I'm attending in Denver after the holidays. Could you get away if the clinic pays your expenses?" He picked up the gold-framed picture of his wife and put it down again, aligning it with the telephone, but not appearing to be conscious of what he was doing.

"I don't know any reason why not. Is Mrs. Ferdinand going with you?"

A shadow crossed his face. "I hope so."

"What's the date?"

He checked his calendar. "We'll leave on Friday, the thirteenth. You're not superstitious, are you?" he asked, with a slight smile.

"I'll risk it," she said, grinning back at him.

"Good. I'll arrange for your plane ticket, then." He left the office, headed for another examining room where his nurse had the next patient waiting, and Charlotte went on to the library, wondering why Dr. Ferdie, as she fondly thought of him, was worried about his attractive wife.

As she passed the small lounge where she had hung her coat, she met Joy coming out with a steaming mug and a doughnut. A suspicion made her comment, "Your second breakfast?"

"I'm sharing it." The young receptionist winked. "He's a love, isn't he?"

A memory of her dream about Brock Morley made Charlotte blush.

Joy laughed.

CHAPTER TWO

THE HOLIDAYS HAD COME AND GONE before Charlotte saw Brock Morley again. It was February and she had flown to Denver with Dr. Ferdinand and his wife Ellin to attend the cardiologists' symposium at the Marriott Hotel. While Dr. Ferdie attended lectures and Ellin went shopping, Charlotte critically inspected the array of monitoring equipment set up in a large ballroom.

Almost at once she saw Brock Morley. He was seated before a competitor's machine in his shirtsleeves with his jacket hung carelessly over his chair, utterly engrossed in checking out the monitor. He didn't even raise his head when she walked by, and she decided not to humiliate herself by trying to break into his concentration. It was a challenge to one's femininity, that ability of his to become so totally absorbed. She wondered if a woman had ever been able to dent it. Some dewy young thing like Joy, maybe, but no one her age, she would bet.

So it was a surprise when later in the afternoon, their gazes met across the big room and she saw his face brighten. He had been slouched against the far wall near the Echo display, looking bored. The moment he saw her, however, he straightened and smiled and her heart gave a little flutter of pleasure. He buttoned his jacket and began casually strolling toward her and she walked to meet him. They met in the center of the room, almost eye-to-eye, thanks to her high heels.

"I thought I might see you here," he greeted her casually as if they had been together only a few days ago.

"Well, I didn't expect you," she retorted. "Or do your display machines break down, too?"

"I'm here to see that it doesn't happen. Right now, I'd like to sit down with a cold beer. Join me?"

"Love to," she said.

"Your husband isn't with you?"

"I'm a widow, Brock."

"With children?"

"A son."

He had wondered about that "Hi, honey!" he'd overheard. "Then my conscience is clear. Watch yourself, Charlotte Emlyn," he said lightly, taking her arm. "I'm a likable mutt, but don't let that deceive you. Basically, I'm a predatory single."

She laughed, flattered. "You remembered my name?"

"It's on your name tag." He touched it lightly and her breast tingled beneath the tag. Then he said, "You remembered mine."

He was not wearing a tag.

She flushed, and he thought how pretty she looked with her cheeks rosy and her eyes bright with laughter. "I'm teasing you," he confessed. "Of course I remembered you! Why wouldn't I?"

Because I'm an older woman, she thought, her flush deepening.

His gaze swept over her. In the clinic she always wore a uniform, but now she had on a dress that was as distinctive as everything else about her. It was composed of a rather long loose jacket over a longish slender skirt. He wondered if she had a thing about wearing tight-fitting clothing. Or was this a new style? Whatever, he found the way she moved inside her clothes provocatively sexy. He didn't know much about fashion, but this woman had a way of wearing ordinary clothes that made them extraordinary. In fact, she was extraordinary. And she was not somebody's wife, after all! With his hand on her arm, he directed their steps toward the bar.

Charlotte was losing her awkward feeling in an exhilaration that was rare enough to be delightful. She had persuaded herself that it was primarily her maternal instincts that were responding to Brock, but in this environment he was revealing a maturity and sophistication that aroused another kind of interest. At the same time, it was flattering that anyone his age would think her desirable—and it was obvious that he did. She was remembering how Brock had invaded her dreams when he was servicing her machine at the clinic, and the memory was coloring her reaction. She had not responded in this way to a man for a long time, and the circumstances were conspiring to make her feel adventurous.

They had chosen one of the minuscule tables in the lounge and were sitting on the banquette with their knees occasionally touching. His eyes, a golden brown with little flickers of light in them, were focusing his awesome powers of concentration directly on her.

"Smile again," he ordered softly and when she obeyed, he said in triumph, "I was right. You've got dimples."

She felt ridiculously young. No one had called them dimples in a long time.

A waitress approached them, and Brock questioned Charlotte with a raised eyebrow. "You invited me for a beer," she reminded him.

"Is that what you want?"

He looked hopeful, so she said, "Make mine dark."

"Incredible!" he said admiringly, and ordered two bock beers.

"Where is everyone?" Charlotte asked the waitress. The lounge was almost empty.

"Changing for the banquet, I expect," the girl answered. "You're not with the doctors?"

"Not now," Charlotte murmured with a sidelong glance at Brock.

The waitress laughed and gave her an okay signal.

A young man at the piano was providing cocktail music seemingly just for them since there were only the bartender and waitress and a couple of solitary drinkers on stools at the bar to hear him. They listened and talked and sipped the beers.

"Why haven't you remarried, Charlotte?" he asked at one point.

"I never really wanted to." When his speculative gaze settled on her, she elaborated. "Oh, I considered it more than once. In fact, a couple of times I thought I was falling in love, but I had a child to think of...." Her voice trailed off.

He realized he had forgotten the son. He blinked, adjusting to the thought of her as a mother. That could explain her concern about his diet. He rather liked that in her. He had experienced very little of that kind of caring.

"I've had to raise my son alone. I was an old-fashioned wife. We married so young that I didn't know anything but keeping house. It was luck that I got on as a file clerk at the hospital after my husband died. I didn't make much money, but Dr. Ferdinand took notice of me—"

"Was he one of the men you considered marrying?"

"Oh, no! But he's been a good friend. My first day he was sharp with me for being so slow in finding a file he urgently needed. It was not long after my husband died and I was still in such a state that I took his reprimand hard. Later he came to apologize for his short temper—he'd learned a little more about me and the stress I'd been through from the doctor who treated my husband. He explained he was all out of sorts because the hospital was out of some form he needed and the duplicating machine was down, and I—well, it was a stroke of luck, but I fixed it.''

''You fixed it? Why does the clinic need me?''

She laughed. ''So he decided I had what he called 'an affinity for machines,' and when he needed a technician for the echocardiogram equipment he was installing in his new clinic, he loaned me some money to go to Spokane Community College and get my training.''

''Who took care of your son?'' Brock asked, thinking of his own lonely childhood at various military posts around the world.

''Oh, I took him with me. I got a part-time job over there and I was able to hire a baby-sitter to pick him up every day after school.'' My, how she was nattering on! ''It was so good of Dr. Ferdinand,'' she finished. ''I don't know why he did it, but it made all the difference.''

He wondered how much Ferdinand meant to her now. He realized that life must have been difficult for her, and her technician's salary at the clinic would have made quite a difference. ''I know why he did it. I just wish I could have helped you.''

She laughed again, this time a little laugh of pleased surprise.

An hour passed very pleasantly. Several doctors and their beautifully gowned wives walked by the entrance to the lounge on their way to the banquet hall. ''You don't have to show at the banquet, I hope?'' Brock asked.

''I won't be missed,'' Charlotte assured him recklessly, hoping it was true. ''How about you?''

He grinned at her. ''This is more fun.''

A few other guests wandered into the lounge. The music had picked up in tempo and when Brock noticed that she was tapping her foot in time with the piano notes, he suggested, "Dance?"

It was completely crazy—she hadn't danced in years, but she wanted to dance with him. He followed her to the tiny circle of waxed oak flooring and she put her hand on his shoulder with a feeling of moving back in time. At first she felt stiff and awkward, acutely conscious that by accepting his invitation she was acting out a lie. He thought she was a "single," as he had described himself, like the women he dated, perhaps: young people somewhere in between Wade's nineteen years and her thirty-eight, unattached and continually moving from one "relationship" to another.

Then the pleasure of once again sharing the music and the rhythm with an accomplished dancer took over and Charlotte gave herself up to enjoying the delightful exercise. Gradually the intimacy of the dance began to work its magic on her. That physical awareness, that elusive attraction she had experienced every time he came to the clinic, was powerfully enhanced here. She was conscious of the play of his muscles as he subtly directed her body in the movements they shared. His voice, occasionally murmuring in her ear, had an almost narcotic effect on her, and the music permeating the atmosphere in which they moved was magically seductive.

It was a wonderful sensation, and it had been so long, so long. . . .

The music was attracting others and the lounge began filling up with strangers who were asking for songs she didn't know. "It's getting a bit crowded," Brock murmured. "Shall we switch to champagne . . . in my room?"

He had warned her, she thought. A likable mutt—and he was that—but also a predatory single male. First he gained her confidence by listening to the story of her life and then he danced with her.... *But I'm a single female and I have needs, too.* Needs she had denied in the years she had been struggling to give Wade a secure home and an education.

Oh, if she could only forget her scruples, her responsibilities, her innate good sense! Just this once! She wanted Brock Morley—as she had not wanted another man since she fell in love with Wade's father those countless years ago, the years she was denying in this foolish flirtation. Even those times when she had considered remarrying, she had not felt as powerfully attracted as she was right now. Even if Brock was too young, she wanted him.

Her hesitation had given Brock the signal he wanted, and the swift certainty with which he moved told her that he was indeed an experienced predator. He danced her by the bartender, murmured a few words, and a bill changed hands. Then, holding her firmly by the elbow, he took her to the elevators.

She could have stopped him at any time but she made no protest. Her whole body tingled from his closeness during the dance. He pressed the button to summon the elevator and while they waited she studied his face, her growing hunger matching the desire she read in the tense shape of his lips and the deep glow darkening his eyes.

The elevator was empty and as it sped them upward, he reached out and tenderly touched her cheek, and the excitement built in her until she was trembling.

He unlocked his door and she stepped into a room much like her own. Beyond the wide bed, the drapes were open, and visible through the glass was a white city of lights. There was a moon somewhere overhead, its reflection faintly picking out the snowy peaks beyond the city. It was a fairyland out there—and what was happening inside was unreal, too. What was she—Charlotte Emlyn, mother of

Wade Emlyn, cardiology technician to Dr. Saul Ferdinand—doing here?

Brock put his arms around her and felt the tremor. "Are you cold?"

"No... I mean, yes..."

Brock saw with surprise that she was nervous. He had moved too fast, he thought, and it made him feel insensitive. He brushed his lips down her cheek to the corner of her mouth and made them linger there, withholding the kiss that he sensed she wanted as intensely as he did.

"Brock, I'm not—I don't usually—" Her lips quivered, but her eyes were confessing her need for him even while she was saying, "I don't recognize myself...."

His desire was shot through with tenderness. "Shall I tell you who you are? You're a woman who wants to be loved... a very exciting woman."

There was a knock at the door and Brock said, "Our champagne."

As he turned away, Charlotte gulped air to slow her quickened breathing. Oh, she could recognize a master of the art of seduction, and he was a master, even if he was only a decade older than her son! She was completely under his spell. But she had come to this point by her own choice, and there was no turning back now.

He left her standing there while he opened the door for the waiter who carried a tray to the round table beneath the window and set down champagne in a bucket of ice and two flute glasses. Deftly he uncorked the bottle with a muffled pop and filled the glasses, then left with Brock's tip in his pocket.

Brock offered Charlotte a glass and held his up in a silent toast with a warmth in his eyes that made her feel beautiful and desirable. They sipped and then at last he kissed her, his lips tasting of the bubbly wine.

It was a kiss that, once started, they could not end. It took off like a soaring bird spiraling up and up on a rising current until Brock set down his glass and, without breaking the thrilling contact, took hers gently from her hand and set it down beside his own. He folded his arms around her then, with his right hand splayed on her buttocks, pressing her body firmly against his.

The revealing touch lit a fuse to her mounting desire. She pressed even closer to him, letting her hands wander inside his jacket to feel the muscles of his shoulders, his hard chest, his flat stomach, all the while thinking, *This can't be me.... This isn't happening.... I'm dreaming....*

At last Brock let her go and went to close the draperies over the map of the city spread in light below their window. He came back to her and ran his hands over her body, from her shoulders down over her breasts and then her hips, exploring all her curves through the layers of fabric that concealed them. "Ah, delicious," he murmured. Slowly, lingeringly, he began to undress her.

She wondered that it should surprise her to find him so at ease with his sensuality when he was relaxed in all that he did, except for his intense concentration on his work. It put her at ease, too, and she caressed him with a natural unself-consciousness that made every touch pure joy. Then she put all wondering out of her mind and gave herself up to her feelings. She helped him shed his clothes and took pleasure in the long, lean shape of his body, the smooth way his shoulder muscles moved under his skin, the wedge of fine dark hair that covered his chest and the easy coordination with which he moved.

On the bed Brock began his own slow, agonizingly sweet exploration, marveling aloud at the beauty she had hidden beneath her loose clothing. "Exquisite," he muttered between nibbling kisses that were driving her crazy. "I knew you would be beautiful. God, you're exciting, Charlotte. You excite me out of my mind."

She was letting her fingers move, too, memorizing the planes and angles of his muscles and the male shape of him, familiar and yet new in his differences from her memories of Garth Emlyn. Her desire was almost more than she could contain. "Please, Brock, love me, love me...."

With an incoherent sound he thrust inside her and in moments something beyond them both was taking over—something far beyond physical excitement. As they moved together, she felt his great gulps of pleasure as keenly as her own. It was as if when he entered her, she entered his mind and shared with him the sensations they were feeling...as if they were merging into each other, a man and woman becoming one in a closeness she could not remember experiencing before nor even dreamed was possible. Their sharing of pleasure was so unexpectedly complete that when they calmed and sank into a sweet lethargy, it left her shaken and disbelieving.

She was quiet in Brock's embrace and he lay unmoving for long minutes. Then he turned and, holding her chin in his hand, deliberately kissed her again, long and tenderly. When the kiss ended he began without a word to caress her. This time they went slowly, with infinite enjoyment, discovering each other's sensitive spots, both giving pleasure as much as receiving it. When they reached a shattering climax, it was a long time before either could speak.

"Did you enjoy that as much as I did, Charlotte Emlyn?" Brock asked softly.

"It was wonderful," she said honestly, thinking how extraordinarily *intimate* their lovemaking had been—and how close in spirit she felt to this man about whom she knew very little except how his eyes darkened in passion and emotion could make his face glow as from an inner light.

How had Brock Morley ensnared her in such magic, when she knew so little about him?

Holding her close, Brock was overtaken by the lassitude of complete relaxation, and for a few seconds he dozed, waking almost immediately to an awareness of Charlotte's exquisite, long-limbed body lying warm and inviting along his full length. It gave him a surprising pleasure, still. He opened his eyes and studied her face, a long oval with the dark gold lashes of her closed eyes lying on her cheeks.

It was an attractive face. She did not call attention to it with the billboard cosmetics many women used—she did not outline her eyes with black crayon or paint her lids with indigo—but here on his shoulder, framed by her golden brown hair, it had a haunting beauty that another man might never see by day. He liked that.

He raised himself on one elbow, and she opened her eyes. Looking into them was like looking down into a clear stream of running water. Emotions rippled there, surfacing and then disappearing. He felt an intense curiosity about her. What was she thinking? What did she think of him? How did she feel about what had just happened between them? They were questions that did not ordinarily occur to him in such a situation.

"It's been a long time for you, hasn't it?"

"Yes." Her eyes were clear and honest. "I don't play the singles game."

"It can be lonely at times," he admitted. "Lately, I find I'm working overtime just to avoid it."

The familiar steps of the chase, he thought, with a flicker of distaste. The calculated approach, the practised moves leading to "Your place or mine?" followed by the staleness of so many mornings-after when he realized the woman with whom he had made love was still a stranger.

This had been so different, so spontaneous and wonderful. This was a very special woman.

He smoothed one of her eyebrows with a tender finger. "Thank you, Charlotte."

"Whatever for?"

"For choosing me to help you end your fast."

It had been a long fast, Charlotte reflected. Too long. "How could you tell?"

"Your pleasure was so intense. It was a very moving experience for me." He had seen the shadows rise to the surface of her eyes. "How long has it been since there was someone special in your life, Charlotte?"

"My husband died twelve years ago. Since then my son has been the special person in my life."

"You said you'd considered remarrying," he reminded her.

"Briefly." Again an emotion rippled through her clear eyes. "Those experiences were . . . not like this."

Brock trailed his fingers down her cheek. What an extraordinary woman she was! A woman not afraid to express her feelings honestly and without guile. He knew he wanted to see her again.

"Did you know I'd been wanting to ask you out for months, but I thought you had a husband?"

A great wave of pleasure engulfed her. "I'm glad you, uh, finally made a move."

He laughed with delight. "Can we do this again when we're back in Seattle?"

Charlotte caught her breath. She wanted more than anything to see him again, but would it be wise? She thought of Wade—and with a little shock she remembered the difference in their ages.

"Are you suggesting a . . . a relationship?" The catch in her breathing belied the lightness of her tone.

Amused, he said, "We already have a relationship, my sweet."

"We have a strong physical attraction," she agreed. "You're a very sexy man."

"And you're a fantastic woman. But we have more than sex going. I like you, Charlotte."

"I like you, too, Brock, but—"

"But what, sweet?"

She could not lie about the closeness she felt with him, but neither could she quite believe the evidence of her senses. The talk of a relationship frightened her. She was not sure she should see him again. "We've only just met, really," she tried to explain. "It was like fireworks—fantastic while it lasts but—"

"Look, Charlotte," he said in that relaxed way he had, "you may not know it yet, but you're already in over your head. Trust a confirmed bachelor like me to know the difference."

"But there are things you don't know—"

"What don't I know about you?" he asked tenderly.

"That I'm thirty-eight years old!" she blurted. "With a teenage son!"

For an agonizing second he didn't speak. Then he said thoughtfully. "You look about twenty-eight, do you know that?" He smiled down at her. "How old do you think I am?"

"Twenty-nine?" she ventured painfully.

"I was thirty-three on my last birthday."

She stared at him, only half believing him.

"What's five years?" he said, and kissed her.

His kiss was ambrosia, but even while she was savoring the softness and sweetness of his lips, she was thinking that thirty-three was just over thirty, really, while thirty-eight was only a step from forty.

CHAPTER THREE

CHARLOTTE FLEW BACK TO SEATTLE the next afternoon in
a glow of shimmering happiness. Brock was staying over to
see that the Echo display was properly crated and shipped.
Dr. and Mrs. Ferdinand were also taking a later plane. But
Charlotte was not alone. She flew in an iridescent bubble
that was as insubstantial as a dream, and she shared it with
Brock. They had talked the night away, yet she did not feel
sleepy.

It was raining when the plane descended toward the city
on the Sound. The group of skyscrapers marking the city's
core and the Space Needle thrusting its bulbous restaurant
up into the sky were shrouded in the drizzle that was half
mist. Charlotte did not find this familiar weather pattern
at all depressing. Her thoughts were all inward. *This can't
be happening to me. I'll wake up and find the bubble burst.*

The feelings Brock had aroused in her were so new that
she was thrown off balance, and so tender that she felt
young and vulnerable. "You have entered into a relationship," she told herself, still disbelieving. It was unrealistic
to expect it to last, yet there was something more than
physical attraction in the swift and unexpectedly passionate response to each other that she and Brock had experienced.

She had left her car in the airport's long-term parking lot,
and when she drove up to the modest bungalow south of
Seattle with its view of the Sound, Wade was in the drive-

way, with his audio equipment in his van, just about ready to leave for his party job that evening. Getting out of the car, she found herself having to lift her head to look her son in the eye and was reminded again how tall he was. Already the roots of a heavy beard showed in a faint shadow on his clean-shaven cheeks—only the texture of his skin revealed how very young he was.

"Hi, Mom," he said as laconically as if she had just been to the supermarket. But his quick glance was fondly observant. "Had a good time, huh?"

She was shaken. Did it show? It came to her forcibly that Wade was no longer a child but another person with whom she shared a home, in the house his father had bought and whose life insurance had paid off the mortgage, making it possible for them to go on living in it. She was struck again how very like his father Wade was. How was a lover going to fit into their lives?

It shouldn't make any difference, she told herself. She and Wade were both so busy that their life together consisted mostly of notes left on the refrigerator door. Because he worked most nights, Wade seldom had an early class and he was still asleep most mornings when she left for the clinic. Sometimes she prepared their evening meal, but when he didn't have much time between his class and his disc-jockey hours at the radio station, he often joined his friends at the burger stand where they hung out.

"Only time I get to see them," he told her, and because he was working so hard she did not object.

So they left their little notes—"Kiwanis gig tonight," "Home late," or "Buy milk!"—and snatched a few moments to talk now and then between their comings and goings. When Wade was still a child, Charlotte had built her life around him. At times friendships had not developed into affairs simply because her son's needs always took priority. Since Wade had become virtually an adult, she had been lonelier.

No, Wade and Brock probably wouldn't be stumbling over each other. Come to think of it, how was Brock going to find time for her when his work so absorbed him that he forgot to eat?

Could she be comfortable with a relationship after all these years, especially one with a man five years her junior?

"What's five years?" he'd said. Logically she agreed, but her first impressions of him at the clinic had been of the quintessential young bachelor. Worse, that impression had somehow become entangled with her dream about Brock with Wade and his young friends. Even though it was just a dream, they seemed alike in their ability to wipe out everything else in their concentration on what immediately interested them, their indifferences to good food and to their health.... The young always assumed they were indestructible!

Granted, she'd been wrong about Brock. He had certainly proved that in some matters he was more mature than she had expected. But she was still afraid to trust this new and special relationship. It was just a weekend, she told herself. One that she considered a gift from the gods.

She was awake, trying to read in bed, when Brock called. "Charlotte?" he said. "Sweetheart?"

His voice sent a little shiver of pleasure rippling down her spine, and her throat tightened, surprising her when his name came out in a breathless gasp.

"Charlotte! Are you in bed?"

"Uh-hmm."

He made a low purr of sound. "Wish I were with you."

She got control of her voice and said softly, "You are, Brock. You're very much with me."

"Yeah, your head's on my shoulder, isn't it?" he murmured. "Umm, you're lying very close, darling, and my hand's on your breast. Do you feel it . . . ? Now I'm kissing you. Can you hear how my heart's thumping?" He must have put the telephone to his chest, because she heard the familiar *ker-thump, ker-thump*. . . .

Her breath caught in her throat as intimate memories flooded her senses. "Have you seen your cardiac technician lately?" she asked in a husky murmur. "Perhaps you'd better make an appointment. . . ."

"Tomorrow," he said urgently. "Tomorrow night. I'm getting an early plane. I'll call you at the clinic."

She pictured the light flashing madly on her telephone while she was in the middle of giving one of Dr. Ferdie's patients an echocardiogram. "You'd better leave a message at the desk," she said ruefully. "Just tell Joy what time you're coming."

"Okay. Have I told you that you're a very special woman? Good night, my love. I'll be knocking at your door."

She went to sleep smiling and wakened with a happy feeling of anticipation. She would see Brock tonight!

She hadn't heard Wade come in last night and on her way to the kitchen she quietly opened his door to assure herself that he was there. His head was burrowed under his pillow in a way that used to worry her for fear he would suffocate. She closed his door again and went down the hall, trying to imagine how her rooms would look to Brock. She knew so little about him! How strange that she should feel so close to him!

She prepared her breakfast, dressed for work and left Wade sleeping.

Her step was springy when she entered the clinic. Joy looked up from her appointment book as Charlotte passed. "Had a good time in Denver, huh?"

Good Lord, was it that obvious? "I'm glad to be home," Charlotte said aggressively.

Joy winked.

And she had told Brock to leave a message with Joy!

Well, what of it? Charlotte asked herself as she took off her sweater, put on the freshly starched white jacket and went to check the appointment book with Joy for her morning's schedule.

"It must have been a good conference," Joy observed, "because Dr. Ferdinand hasn't called in yet. How was the banquet Mrs. F. bought a new dress for?"

"Boring," Charlotte lied.

Joy laughed, and Charlotte left before the girl could ask any more questions.

Her morning was full, but after lunch she began expecting to hear from Brock, wishing he'd told her what time his plane was arriving. She tried not to think about him, but without much success. She wished she had his ability to ignore distractions. At last she could stand the uncertainty no longer and after she dismissed a patient, called Joy. "Are you holding a message for me, by any chance?"

"No, are you expecting one?"

"Why else would I ask?"

"Don't bite," Joy said mildly. "If a call comes, I'll put it through."

"I'm sorry. Just take a message for me."

She managed to make it through the rest of the day, but by five o'clock Brock still had not phoned. Now he would have to call her at home, and Wade was going to be there. Wade did a lot of telephoning on the nights he was home. It was the only time he had to return the calls left for him

on the answering machine and fill his calendar with playing dates. Then he usually spent an hour talking to Kate
before he did his homework. Perhaps tonight he would go
to see her instead. If he didn't, it was going to be awkward
if Brock wanted to come over. Immediately Charlotte began reproaching herself for the thought. She had Wade at
home so seldom!

All evening while she cooked beef stroganoff and noodles and made Wade's favorite chocolate cake, she listened
for the telephone. It was always for Wade. In between answering, he made calls. When his voice dropped to a low
murmur of *umm*, Charlotte realized he was talking to Kate,
and quite involuntarily began timing him. They talked for
forty-five minutes.

She hoped her nervousness wasn't showing, and then told
herself that Wade was probably too engrossed in what he
and Kate were saying to notice her. Brock would eventually get through to her, she assured herself, but she began
to think seriously about asking Wade to get his own telephone.

At ten Wade went to his room to study for the next day's
classes, and Charlotte's hopes rose. Brock must be working late. There were bound to be problems waiting for him
to solve on his return. She tried to banish the image of him
sitting before a machine so totally absorbed that he completely forgot about her.

It could happen.

She settled herself in bed, with her extension within reach
and a book on her lap. By eleven-thirty she knew he was not
going to call, and the part of her mind that kept reminding
her she was thirty-eight years old was saying, "I told you
so."

But when she entered the clinic at eight-fifteen the next
morning, Joy sang out through the pane of the glass that

separated her from the public, "I have a message for you! Brock Morley just called."

Charlotte stopped, her heart doing a little skip. "Well?"

"Seven-thirty."

"Seven-thirty what? I mean where?"

"You tell me." Joy's eyes were dancing. Charlotte knew her date would be a topic of conversation all over the clinic. Everybody knew who Brock Morley was. And Joy had called him a love.

"Eat your heart out," she said, and Joy laughed.

Charlotte grinned. All at once she felt relaxed and at peace with the world. Wade had a gig at a private party tonight. Brock would come to the house, and they would be alone. She hummed as she began planning a really special dinner.

When she passed the open door of Dr. Ferdinand's office, he was already behind his desk. A distinguished-looking man about fifteen years her senior, graying at the temples, wearing steel-rimmed glasses, he looked up and smiled as if he saw something pleasurable in the way she moved. "The conference was stimulating, wasn't it?"

"I thought so," Charlotte said airily, going on.

"If we have a spare minute—" his voice stopped her "—let's talk about Poston's recommendations. He's given me some thoughts about our procedures here."

Charlotte's mind went blank. The banquet she had not attended! A Dr. Poston had made the keynote speech. "Okay," she said, "but I couldn't hear him very well."

Dr. Ferdinand looked puzzled. "Where were you sitting, Charlotte? I thought the sound system was excellent."

She said the first thing that popped into her mind: "I was getting an echo…." Flushing, she finished hastily, "I must

have been too close to a speaker.'' She waggled her fingers
at him and went on to her own examination room.

I must be losing my mind! she thought. Trying to cover
up with Dr. Ferdie who had been such a good friend to her,
and all the while bubbling inside with the prospect of being
in Brock's arms again tonight! Who would have thought,
at her age . . . !

The day dragged interminably. She stopped at the supermarket on the way home and bought three extravagant
steaks and some Idaho baking potatoes and watercress and
fresh mushrooms for the salad. When she came in carrying a large brown paper sack, Wade eyed it apprehensively.

''I've got to leave in time to set up by seven, Mom. I
thought I'd stop at the hamburger stand.''

''No problem,'' she said, feeling guilty because she was
relieved. She wasn't ready to face introducing a lover to her
son just yet. ''I may have a dinner guest this evening.''

He looked curious, but didn't ask. ''I'll probably be
late,'' he warned her and went out to his loaded van.

Alone in the house, Charlotte took a long luxurious bath,
then brushed her hair and pinned it up on top of her head
before she began to dress. She put on a longish white sheath
that let her body move inside it with the freedom she liked.
Donning an apron, she went into the kitchen to scrub the
potatoes and prepare the salad.

Seven-thirty came, and then eight. She took off the apron
and redid her hair. The table was set, the wine was cooled,
the steaks were in the broiler ready to go and the potatoes
were done. No Brock.

Charlotte was beginning to feel as if she were in an elevator that was descending too fast, when a car drove up and
parked across the street. She ran to open the front door just

as Brock stepped up on her entry porch with an armload of yellow roses.

The light from behind her shone on his slightly windblown hair and heightened the glow that sprang to his eyes when he saw her. His gaze went swiftly over her, brightening as it traveled down the narrow length of her simple but sinuous dress. He stepped over the threshold, thrust the roses into her hands and embraced her. The fragrance of crushed flowers rose between them as they kissed, mingling with the remembered taste of his lips and with the lemony tang of the light perfume she had dabbed in the V of her throat.

"It seems forever since I held you," he murmured when he finally raised his head.

"Well, it *was* a thousand miles away," she said with a smile, adding teasingly, "It's a good thing I didn't prepare dinner for you last night. As it is, I've only had to hold it one hour."

He kissed her again and murmured, "Who wants dinner?"

Charlotte laughed shakily. The magic was still there between them, dazzlingly strong. "I do." She drew away from him, and one decapitated rose fell at her feet. "Now I know why I keep thinking you're so young."

He was not sure how he should take that remark. "I wanted to come last night," he explained with remorse. "But when I took the display equipment back to the main office, they had a problem that they threw at me and—"

"You couldn't resist it," she said dryly. "And you didn't eat."

He grinned. "When I found the bug, it was nearly midnight, and I knew you'd be sleeping. And yes, I ate some cheese and bread before I went to bed."

"Well, you'll have dinner tonight," she promised, "as soon as I broil the steaks. And you'd better eat this time," she warned, remembering the hamburger that had congealed in its own fat.

He laughed. "How did I get so lucky?"

She looked so good to him that he could hardly keep his hands off her. He restrained himself from reaching for her again and glanced around her living room with eager interest, seeing her individual touch in its simplicity and the clean uncluttered lines of the furniture. It was a very personal room, he saw at once. There was nothing in it that smacked of "decor."

A piano stood in one corner, with sheet music open on its rack. The walls were painted off-white with white drapes at the windows, and few pictures cluttered their starkness. One was a round gold-framed portrait of a young woman with an upswept Gibson girl look that reminded him vaguely of the way Charlotte pinned up her hair. Her grandmother?

The largest picture in the room was not a poster or a painting but a color photograph of a white Victorian farmhouse with a windmill silhouetted against blue-black storm clouds.

She saw him looking at it and said, "That's my grandfather's farm in Kansas."

"Who took the picture?"

"I did."

It was almost professional. On the piano, beside a delicate terra-cotta head of a young girl, was a photograph of a clean-cut boy who looked about thirteen. Brock studied it with undisguised curiosity. "Is that your son?"

She was walking ahead of him toward the kitchen. "Yes. His name is Wade."

He followed her and looked around at a kitchen as un-cluttered as the living room except for the refrigerator door, which was plastered with little notes held by magnetic colored stars. The only one he could read from where he stood shouted, in block letters: "A glass of orange juice every morning!"

"Do you write notes to yourself about orange juice?"

"That's for Wade. He makes his own breakfast before he goes to school because I leave pretty early to avoid the rush-hour traffic."

He thought about the young teenager who belonged to this woman he found so attractive. He hadn't been around children much. The only family he had was his father, who was seventy and living alone in Portland.

"Would you like a drink before dinner?" Charlotte asked. "I've got wine cooling."

"Wine's fine. What can I do?"

"Light the candles."

He went into the dining room. A small round mahogany table was set with dishes that had roses on them and silver that gleamed softly. There were only two place settings, with linen napkins. The candles were pale blue. As he lit them, Brock thought of his own studio apartment, its walls decorated mostly with posters. He had left his pull-down bed unmade this morning and his breakfast dishes in the sink, and wondered what Charlotte would think of it. "Where is he?" he asked, going back to the kitchen.

She was standing in front of the built-in oven holding two hot plates with mitts on her hands, looking flushed and happy. When she glanced questioningly at him, he said, "Your son. Isn't he eating with us?"

"Oh, he has a party tonight. Will you open the wine? It's in the fridge."

A few minutes later they sat down to dinner. He pulled her chair out with a flourish and then bent over to kiss her. The kiss threatened to take wing and he had a wild urge to scoop her up and carry her down the hall to the bedroom. But when he drew back and looked at her warm face and the little strands of hair that had worked loose while she cooked, he felt choked by tenderness, and he went around the table and lifted his wineglass to her in silent toast before he sat down.

They gazed at each other through the candlelight as they ate. Her eyes were full of questions and at the same time were communicating excitingly intimate thoughts that seemed too profound for words. He must have eaten something because his plate was almost clean when he looked at it again, but he was aware of nothing but his more pressing hunger—and the desire he read in the revealing little glances Charlotte gave him.

When she got up to take their plates to the kitchen, he stood up and took them from her. He set them down again and pulled her into his arms. With a sigh of pleasure she fitted herself against him and tilted her face for his kiss.

His arms tightened around her and his fingers slipped through the wide short sleeve of her dress and touched the curve of her breast. Just a touch, and yet it brought a host of the most intimate sensual memories flooding back: the silken feel of her hot flesh in all the secret places he had explored... She shivered with obvious pleasure and he felt his immediate physical response with an acute emotion that was almost pain.

It was the thought of the boy that stiffened the control he was in danger of losing. But when he tried to disengage from her, she took him by the hand and led him to her bedroom.

A COUPLE OF HOURS LATER they decided to clean up the kitchen. She handed him a filled plastic garbage sack. "Sorry, Brock, this simply must go out tonight."

He slanted a grin at her. "So this is the way I pay for my dinner?"

"You have to take the lumps with the gravy." Her dimples flashed.

He reached out and pulled a fine strand of her hair down in front of one ear.

"I just put up my hair," she protested.

"I know." He had watched her, bemused, as her clever fingers rolled and twisted the golden brown strands. "That's why it was too neat. Where's the garbage can?"

"It's out by the garage. You'll see it as soon as you step out the back door."

The moon was hidden behind some clouds so it was as dark as a cave once Brock stepped off the back porch. A dog was barking in a nearby yard. He made out the rear of the detached garage, with its peaked roof silhouetted against a starless sky. A moment later he saw the gleam of metal marking a garbage container and started across the yard toward it, his steps muffled on the thick grass.

A shadow moved against the garage wall. Someone was in the yard. Brock stopped. The shadow was that of a tall man with wide, hulking shoulders.

Brock's muscles tightened. He had no weapon but his fists and the plastic bag of garbage in his hand.

"Who's there?" he challenged.

"Who the hell are you?" The man had come into view. He was not quite as large as his shadow, but his voice was deep with suspicion and he kept one hand in his pocket.

Brock said quietly, "I might ask you the same question."

"I live here, man. What are you doing here?"

"Taking out the garbage." Brock was struggling out of his confusion. "You wouldn't be Charlotte's son?" he asked, incredulous.

"Yeah, I'm Wade Emlyn. Hey, you must be Mom's dinner guest. Is that garbage you're carrying? Got it tied up? Toss it here."

This hulk was the teenager Charlotte had to remind to drink his milk and orange juice? Brock tossed the plastic sack at him. Wade caught it expertly and with a clatter of the lid, deposited it in the can.

Inside, Charlotte heard the noise and thought with remorse of her sleeping neighbors. Formerly sleeping, she amended. When Brock and Wade came in together into the bright light of the kitchen, she caught their quick curious looks at each other and the blankness that instantly masked Brock's gaze.

Please, let them like each other! she thought.

"Got any milk?" Wade asked.

"I think there's some left. I didn't hear you drive in, Wade. This is Brock Morley."

Brock offered his hand, and Wade grasped it. His grip was as strong as an athlete's.

Charlotte sensed some strain and looked anxiously from one to the other. Wade turned casually toward the refrigerator and took out a carton of milk, but Brock was staring at him with a strange expression. Charlotte wondered why and could think of nothing that could be a satisfactory explanation. But she had noticed without surprise that Wade was a good inch and a half taller than Brock and at least thirty-five pounds heavier.

"How was the party?" Brock asked.

Wade grimaced. "They wanted nothing but country music. Not my bag." He shrugged. "But I give 'em what they pay for."

Brock felt as if he had been left behind. He had visualized the after-game parties he remembered from his high-school days. "You're a musician?" he ventured.

Wade grinned. "An electronic musician. I'm a disc jockey at KQRD three nights a week—Wednesday, Thursday and Friday—and I haul my sound equipment around and play records for private parties on the other nights."

"And go to school?" Brock asked, somewhat bowled over by the kid's schedule.

"Yeah. I'm a first-year student at the U."

"What do you do in your spare time?"

Wade chuckled. "What spare time? Nice meeting you. I'll hold my fire next time I meet you carrying out the garbage. 'Night, Mom, I'm off to bed." He kissed Charlotte's cheek and left the kitchen.

When she glanced at Brock, he said, "You should have warned me. I might have attacked him, and he would have creamed me."

"Why on earth should you attack him?"

"I didn't recognize him from his picture."

She looked at him blankly for a second, then realized what picture he was talking about. "Oh! On the piano? He was thirteen when that was taken. Do you know, I walk by it now without even seeing it."

"There's been quite a change. He's bigger than I am." Brock picked up a tea towel and began drying the dishes she was putting in the draining rack beside the sink.

"Does that bother you?"

"Of course not." But he was not sure how he felt about it.

She heard the uncertain note in his voice. "Well," she said, "it bothers me that he's taller than I am."

When Brock said nothing, she went on, "He's always been large for his age, and . . . and mature. He's really a sweet guy."

"He's a hustler," Brock said.

"Oh, he is! He's been earning his own spending money since he was fifteen."

"And how old is he now?"

"Just turned nineteen." She was watching Brock closely, and her heart sank. He didn't like Wade!

Brock did not look at her. Her throat tightened and her manner became a little strained.

He carefully finished wiping the silverware and hung up the tea towel. "I'd better go and let you get your rest."

She dried her hands and walked to the door with him. His kiss was warm and lingering, and brought back echoes of the closeness they had forged.

"I'll call you," he said before he let her go. Then he tightened his grasp and kissed her again. "Umm," he murmured.

She closed her mind to her misgivings.

CHAPTER FOUR

AS HE DROVE ACROSS TOWN to his apartment, Brock was filled with wonder at what was happening to him. Charlotte Emlyn delighted him in every way. When he recalled the look on her face as she took his hand and without a word led him to her bedroom, he felt as if he were in a dream.

He had not wanted to return to the singles scene after Jenny Clay moved out of his apartment. Theirs had been a stormy relationship, but it had spoiled him for the succession of promising but ultimately disappointing encounters that left him feeling somehow diminished. Empty sex, he thought with a grimace. That's all it had been.

Lately, it had occurred to him that he was becoming a loner like his father, and the prospect was not attractive. But now there was this wonderful woman.... His memories drifted back to the passion of her response, and he smelled the fragrance of her hair and felt the silken touch of her skin. She came back to him so strongly that he could feel her presence beside him in the car.

The difference in their ages that had seemed to bother her was negligible—he hadn't given it a thought. But he was more shaken by his encounter with her son than he wanted to admit. Until that jolting moment on her back lawn when the hulking shadow that had towered over him calmly identified himself as Charlotte's son, Brock had still thought of himself as a young man.

Looking at Wade Emlyn under the kitchen lights moments later, it had struck him that this was another generation, and that he could not go on believing that most of his life lay ahead of him.

He did not want to think of Charlotte as Wade Emlyn's mother. The images that danced through his head were of her golden brown hair flowing over his shoulder and across his lips, and of sitting across the table from her, bemused by the rise and fall of her breasts as she talked and laughed. What a woman she was!

She fit into his fantasies of the perfect relationship as if she had been tailored for the role. He could not believe his good fortune. But where did that hulking son of hers fit in?

Better slow down, Morley, he warned himself. *You're getting in deep.*

He remembered how Charlotte had wailed that night in Denver, "I don't recognize myself!" and knew that she had not given herself to him lightly. She had been swept away by a deep need for him. His instinct told him she was looking for a commitment—something he wasn't quite ready to make.

Brock imagined his father's reaction to the whole situation, and laughed dryly. That cynical old warrior would ask him if he had lost his marbles!

But when he unlocked the door of his apartment, its sterile masculinity and the staleness of living alone were depressing.

He did not sleep well that night.

It was something of a relief when he arrived at work the next morning to discover that he would have to spend a couple of days at a hospital in Tacoma working out a problem with one of their monitoring machines. Although the hospital was only a little over an hour's drive from his apartment, he made a reservation at a Tacoma hotel. It was

most likely he would be working late. He looked forward
to losing himself in concentration on a new problem. He
needed some time to mull over this incredible thing that was
happening and to try to sort out his feelings about Charlotte Emlyn and the son whom he had visualized as a kid he
could play ball with, but who had turned into a jock bigger then he was.

WHILE BROCK WAS DRIVING SOUTH along the freeway to
Tacoma, Charlotte was waiting in some trepidation for
Wade to say something about her dinner guest of the evening before. Wade had surprised her by coming into the
kitchen while she was preparing her solitary breakfast of
fruit and toast and asking if there was any coffee.

While she poured it, she asked, "Shall I scramble eggs
for you, Wade?"

"Nah, Mom, I'll get some cereal."

It was so unusual for Wade to appear at the breakfast
table on a morning after a late party date that she thought
she knew why he was up, and she waited apprehensively for
his questions.

But Wade was preoccupied, eating his cereal with absorption but an air of not really tasting it. He seemed to
find it as difficult to approach the subject of Brock as she
did. Charlotte resisted a strong urge to say, "Well, what do
you think?"

Instead she recalled the expression on Brock's face when
he got his first good look at Wade's height and brawny
arms and shoulders, and his remark that Wade could have
"creamed him." What had Wade thought of the encounter?

"You're up early this morning."

"Yeah."

"An eight o'clock class?" She knew he didn't have one. He had worked out his schedule with care to avoid an early class.

"I'm gonna pick up Kate."

When Charlotte looked at him in surprise, he said, "Uh, I can drop her off on my way to the U."

"Oh, yes. Right." She should have thought of that.

But why should she? It was out of his way to drop Kate off at the high school now that he was in college.

Wade continued eating in silence. Maybe it was Kate he was thinking about and not his mother's caller. Charlotte was keeping an eye on the clock. If she didn't leave at her usual time, she could become snarled in traffic and be late to the clinic instead of a little early.

Wade ate in silence except to ask for some toast. Finally Charlotte could take it no longer and she asked, "Did you like Mr. Morley, Wade?"

"Who?"

"My dinner guest."

"Oh, him. He's okay."

Charlotte ground her teeth in frustration. How strangely she and Wade were behaving this morning! As if they were two people who had just met. Was this the way it was going to be if she continued to see Brock? *Oh, Wade, please understand!* she begged silently. *I've been so lonely.*

She wanted to press Wade further, but she didn't know yet how large a part Brock Morley was going to play in her future. Right now, she didn't even know if he would be back, she thought ruefully.

Before she could say anything more, Wade went to his room. He came back carrying his books. "See ya," he said absently, and went out to start his van. She backed her car out ten minutes later.

They were busy at the clinic that morning, and Charlotte was glad for more than one reason. Dr. Ferdinand mentioned Dr. Poston's recommended procedures again, and again she evaded revealing that she had no idea what he was talking about. She didn't have much time to think about how a love affair would affect her relationship with her son, and that was a relief because Wade's behavior at breakfast had raised doubts in her mind.

But at odd moments she was assailed by memories of the previous evening—the warmth in Brock's eyes shining at her across the flowers on her dinner table, the unforgettable look of surprise and pleasure on his face when she took his hand and led him to her bedroom. What transpired there had been so wonderful, so moving, that she dare not let her thoughts dwell on it for fear she would make a dreadful mistake in the diagnostic test she was giving.

The busy day was made long by her expectations. She drove home in a state of anxiety that was new to her, eager to reach her telephone. Wade was not at home, and when the phone rang, it was not Brock, but her son.

"Hi, Mom. Thought I'd better let you know I'm having dinner at Kate's," he said. "See you later."

"I'm glad you called, dear. Give Kate my love."

They were spending a lot of time together lately, she thought, frowning. Even though Wade was mature for his age, he still had three more years of college before he could afford to get serious about a girl. As for Kate, she was definitely not the daughter-in-law of Charlotte's choice.

But she wouldn't dream of telling Wade how unsuitable she considered the pretty but immature girl who was still in her junior year at the high school Wade had attended. There was no need, she assured herself uneasily. There had been someone else last year; there would be another next year. Wade would have a dozen more girlfriends before he chose a wife.

Only a few short days ago Charlotte would have welcomed a quiet evening alone in which to take care of such personal chores as laundering her lingerie and doing her nails, but that night she felt lonely in the empty house. At last she picked up the telephone and dialed Brock's number. It did not help her spirits to hear the telephone ring and ring in an apparently empty apartment.

Charlotte couldn't help wondering about the women Brock had dated before her. Was there an entanglement that he needed to free himself from? That thought led her to an empathy with the woman he was discarding, envisioning a time when his interest in *her* would fade, and she went to bed feeling quite morose.

IN HIS TACOMA HOTEL ROOM, Brock was lonely, too. The desire to hear Charlotte's light, wry voice was a nagging hunger. He picked up his telephone and punched the outside line. But when he heard the dial tone, the possibility of Charlotte's husky son answering his ring made him hesitate. He still had some thinking to do before he called Charlotte again.

Instead of punching her number, his fingers automatically moved over a familiar sequence. Precisely after the second ring, Major Henry Morley, U.S. Army retired, barked, "Yes!" It was always a statement, never a question.

"Hello, sir," Brock said.

"I'm glad you called," his father's clipped voice, slightly hoarse now with age, said. "That woman's been around again."

"What woman is that?" Brock asked, smiling lightly.

"You know damn well what woman! That cat woman. My landlady."

"She likes you, huh?" Brock teased. "Still a ladies' man, aren't you?"

"The hell she does! She comes complaining because Quarters has been chasing her cat. That miserable castrated tom is a skulking coward. If he didn't run every time Quarters sneezes, it wouldn't be any fun to chase him."

Quarters, the Major's inseparable companion, was a standard black poodle with an unconquerable joie de vivre. He had never been professionally groomed, because the Major, as Brock more often than not thought of his father, refused to "make a sissy of him." Consequently the dog loped around with his ragged dusty-black curls looking quite ruffianly, an intriguing contrast to the knife-edge trouser creases, neatly trimmed beard and polished boots of his master.

"We had a row," his father was saying with a tinge of satisfaction. "She made threats."

Carefully Brock asked, "What kind of threats?"

"Calling the police. Evicting Quarters. But she can't do that."

"I'm not sure. Try to cool it, will you, Major?"

"I never run from a fight." Brock could hear unmistakable signs of enjoyment in his father's age-roughened voice. "Cat women are just like their cats, you know. I'll have that woman running from me the way that miserable alley cat runs from Quarters. Her and her lawyers!"

"Lawyers?" Brock said with a sinking feeling. *Not again.* "Listen, Dad, I'm calling from a job in Tacoma. I thought I'd run down to see you before I go back to Seattle."

"Fine! Good to see you."

"Take it easy until I get there," Brock begged before he hung up.

THREE DAYS HAD GONE BY and Charlotte had not heard from Brock. Wade still had not mentioned him. Her worst fears seemed realized. They had taken an instant dislike to each other! Or Brock could not face the fact that she was a widow with a grown son, in spite of his protests that her age made no difference. As for Wade, he seemed to be refusing even to acknowledge the possibility that his mother might be interested in a man at her age.

Another day went by, and she began to doubt her memories of the weekend in Denver. Had she been reading more into that whirlwind of emotion than was really there? Was it nothing but a weekend fling, after all?

She thought that nothing could make her feel any worse until she arrived at the clinic and Joy said, "Dr. Ferdinand wants to see you in his office."

Uh-oh! Now she was going to have to confess that she had skipped that banquet in Denver—in order to make an utter fool of herself!

She walked down the hall and paused at Dr. Ferdinand's open door. He was sitting behind his desk holding his telephone to his ear, a mild-looking man distinguished in medical circles, particularly among those interested in heart research, but to Charlotte a dear and respected friend. If he had been a woman, she had told him once, she would call him her fairy godmother. He had laughed and said he would look dumb with a tiara and a sparkling wand.

When she thought of his many kindnesses to her and how he had arranged for the clinic to send her to the conference in Denver, Charlotte felt even guiltier.

He looked up and saw her and murmured into the phone, "I'll talk to you later," before he put it down. While

Charlotte cast around in her mind for what she was going to tell him, she noted something out of place on his usually orderly desk. It was the picture of his beautiful wife, Ellin, whose hair was still golden and who looked sidewise out of the silver frame with a lazy, challenging smile and mischief in her eyes. The photograph was turned awkwardly as though he had been holding it in his hand and had hastily put it down when he heard her coming.

What an odd thought!

He smiled at her, but when she looked closely into his steel-rimmed glasses his gray eyes revealed a worry beneath their warmth. "We should talk, Charlotte. How's your schedule? Can you lunch with me today?"

She visualized her calendar. "I think my first test after twelve is at two, Dr. Ferdie." She was the only employee in the clinic privileged to call him that to his face.

"Fine. Come by here at twelve-thirty and we'll find a salad bar, okay?"

"Okay." She went along the hall to the echocardiogram room, with the weight of that promised "talk" hanging over her. She might as well tell Dr. Ferdie the truth: she had skipped the banquet he paid for to make a fool of herself over a young man who worried her because he forgot to eat!

There's no fool like a woman approaching forty, he'd think but be too kind to say.

He was so good. Had he never had a mid-life crisis? No, he had a beautiful wife who went with him to conferences, worrying only about what she should wear. But because Charlotte was already a little rebellious about the scolding she expected, she wondered to whom Dr. Ferdie was talking when he picked up the photograph of his wife. Surely it had not been Mrs. F. herself?

Noon came and when she had finished with her last patient, Charlotte slipped out of her uniform jacket and into a Chanel-type cardigan. Dr. Ferdinand came out of his office as she walked down the hall toward it. He gave Joy the name of the natural food restaurant where he could be reached, and he and Charlotte left by the suite's private door.

Dr. Ferdie was silent as they walked through the parking lot between the clinic and the hospital toward his car, a trim gray Mercedes. He moved with the speed and precision of a man who has to make every minute count. But he looked worried, and Charlotte began to speculate uneasily on what he planned to say to her. Did he know exactly where she had been during the banquet? Or was there a more serious problem in the clinic than just the office procedures he wanted to improve?

When they were in the Mercedes, driving toward the natural-food restaurant that was a favorite of the cardiologists because it served the special diet they recommended for preventing heart attacks, he relieved some of Charlotte's anxiety by asking friendly questions about Wade's school activities and his job.

They chatted easily until they arrived at the restaurant and were seated in the center of an airy dining room at an oak table shielded by a sizable potted Japanese maple. The entire room was leafy with miniature trees and many hanging plants. When they had ordered, selecting dishes consisting mainly of vegetables and nuts and marked by the small red heart that signaled that they were free of cholesterol, Charlotte drew a deep breath and braced herself.

"I've always thought you were a very levelheaded woman," Dr. Ferdie began.

She swallowed hard, still wondering whether she was going to defend herself or tell him everything.

"I'm going to ask a very great favor of you. It's a personal thing, and I won't blame you if you refuse me. But I don't know of anyone else who might be able to help."

Charlotte's eyes widened in surprise. "Dr. Ferdie, if there is anything I can do for you, you have only to ask. You know that. After all you have done to help me—"

He swept that remark away with one hand. "You owe me nothing, Charlotte. But it seems to me that you of all my friends are in a unique position to help me now."

More and more mystified, Charlotte said, "Just tell me what you want."

"I'm hoping you can interest my wife in doing some kind of volunteer work at the clinic."

She stared at him in surprise. If Ellin Ferdinand had wanted to do volunteer work at the clinic, she could have done it anytime. "Why now?" Charlotte blurted. "And why me? Why don't *you* ask her, Dr. Ferdie?"

"She's got a bee in her bonnet about my retirement. Hell, I'm not ready to retire yet! I thought if you talked to her, you could make her understand the importance of what I'm doing."

Charlotte was appalled. "Oh, Dr. Ferdie, I just don't know!" she exclaimed. "What can I say to your wife? She'll tell me to mind my own business!"

Although she saw Dr. Ferdinand almost daily and was very fond of him, she knew Ellin Ferdinand only slightly, and they had little in common. The very thought of talking to the woman about her husband's work made Charlotte flinch. She knew instinctively that the doctor's wife would consider it an insufferable intrusion into their private affairs.

The waitress came with their orders, and Charlotte picked up her fork and tasted her chicken cashew casserole. It was wonderful, and she wished she were more comfortable so she could enjoy it.

Ignoring his plate of Mongolian beef with vegetables, Dr. Ferdie said, "You're a resourceful woman. You'll think of some tactful way—"

"Mrs. Ferdinand and I don't even speak the same language," Charlotte answered miserably.

"That may be true." He sounded disappointed and was silent for a moment, watching her with unhappy eyes.

"Ellin says she's tired of being alone so much," he said at length. "Now that the children are grown and gone, she's lonely for the kind of daily companionship I can't give her. She says I've made enough money—which is true. She wants to travel and I don't. We love each other very much, Charlotte, and she says now she wants more of my time. What can I do?"

When he saw her expression, he smiled tiredly. "Okay, she has a point. When have I taken a real vacation? She claims that we have no social life. The trip to Denver was scarcely that. Ellin was frankly bored."

"Then take a vacation!" Charlotte urged. "Take her to some wonderful place like Paris or Tahiti or—"

"We went to Europe last year, remember? But it wasn't a success. I was so concerned about the threatened nurses' strike and my two patients in intensive care at the hospital that I phoned here at every stop. She knew I wasn't enjoying it, and we finally left the tour and flew home. She says retirement is the only answer, because I can't stop caring—"

"But you're too young to retire! You love your work. And what about the patients who depend on you? All the years you spent in study and specialization? How can any woman ask you to give that up?"

He held up a hand to stop her. "I love her, Charlotte . . . but I'm afraid I can't change."

"You wouldn't be happy!" she burst out. "You know
you wouldn't!

"Ellin's happiness is very important to me."

"You care about your patients, too, and they need you.
You're a good doctor—the best! Doesn't she know that?"

He picked up his fork and smiled at her. "I knew you
would make a good advocate. Maybe you can make her see
what she's asking of me."

She had put her foot right in her mouth by jumping to his
defense. She would have to think of some reason for approaching Ellin Ferdinand. Any reason but the real one.
She could never let Ellin Ferdinand know her husband had
discussed their problem with her. "I'll try," she promised.
What else could she say?

She chewed thoughtfully. "Maybe we can think of some
way to get her involved in the heart-research volunteer
support group. It's very active and Mrs. Ferdinand needs
more activity now that your last chick has left the nest."

He nodded. "The suggestion would come better from
you than from me."

They finished their lunch, and Dr. Ferdie called for the
check. Charlotte was so engrossed in his dilemma that she
didn't even miss the scolding she had expected for skip-
ping out on the banquet in Denver until he had pulled into
the parking lot of the clinic. He looked over at her then
with a twinkle in his gray eyes and asked, "Did that young
technician from Echo show you a good time?"

When her eyes opened wide in surprise, he teased her, "I
have my spies, you know."

She gave him a reproachful look. "You've been having
a lot of fun with me, haven't you, Dr. Ferdie?"

He chuckled, and she wondered how much he had guessed.

"We didn't talk about the conference," he said. "What did you think of the new monitors? Do you think I should order a new one?"

"If you do," she said airily, "I won't have any reason to call 'my' technician."

The doctor laughed. "Maybe I'd better hold off, then, and give you your chance at him."

She laughed with him, but thinking of Brock darkened the already clouded day. He had not called her for three days now. She was convinced in her heart that her little fling in Denver had been just that.

A bit tartly she said, "Maybe *you* should have skipped the banquet and taken your wife dancing."

Dr. Ferdie winced. "Touché!"

She opened the passenger door of the car and followed him into the clinic, trying not to wonder why Brock had not called.

CHAPTER FIVE

WHEN BROCK ARRIVED in Portland a little before eleven on Sunday morning, the sun was peering out between scattered clouds and the streets were almost dry, but the air was still moist and rain-scented. Snow softened the blown-out crater of Mount Saint Helens, visible on his right as he crossed the Willamette River. He drove directly to the narrow red-brick-and-concrete building where his father had a one-bedroom apartment on the third floor.

There was no elevator; the Major claimed the stairs kept him fit. Climbing swiftly, Brock hoped the trouble with the landlady had not escalated to the point where the Major would have to look for another apartment. He had been here for three months now. On a recent visit, Brock had seen with concern how age was exaggerating those traits that had made his father a successful officer but a difficult man to know and love. He was a proud man and a perfectionist, and the older he became, the less easily he tolerated fools.

At the top of the stairs, Brock paused at the right-hand door and immediately a noisy barking erupted.

"Quiet, sir!" Behind the door his father's command was instantly obeyed.

Brock rapped, and the door was opened by his father, his white hair and beard clipped short, his posture and stern expression giving the impression of a military uniform although he was wearing an open-collared shirt with his navy sport coat and white trousers. Brock fought back an impulse to salute, the way he'd been taught as a boy. He didn't think his father would be amused.

"Hello, Major."

The fierce blue gaze was paler than it had once been but still piercing. It had always intimidated, never invited intimacies such as a hug. "Come in, Son," he said, holding Quarters firmly by the collar.

Quarters was literally quivering with the frustrated desire to jump up and lick Brock's face in frenzied welcome. Brock knelt and put his arms around the dog, offering his cheek, which was passed over in favor of an ecstatic swipe as near his lips as Quarters's tongue could get.

"You ugly beast," Brock said, giving him one last affectionate slap before standing and looking around him. Everything was in its place in the spotless apartment. Everywhere he looked he saw pictures of himself: standing in front of Heidelberg castle when he was twelve; a year later at the Acropolis when he and the Major vacationed in Greece; in his high-school football uniform the year they were in Texas; carrying a hand of small bananas with a big grin in front of their quarters in Manila.

Through the bedroom doorway he could see sitting on a cherry chest the trophy he had won in a high-school tennis tournament. The way his father hung on to it, one would think it was an Olympic medal. He knew that if he opened a drawer in the chest he would find rolled shorts and undershirts in perfect rows, paired socks and folded shirts still banded from the laundry.

"How are you, Dad?"

"As well as can be expected, trapped here with Neanderthals who can't distinguish music from noise."

Brock chuckled. "You must have been playing your Bach too loudly again."

"Music, real music, wasn't written to be whispered."

"Are you hungry?" Brock asked, mainly to change the subject, which they had covered many times before. "Shall we find a place that serves a Sunday brunch?"

"You mean one of those places where you walk around in a forest of ferns filling your own plate?" The Major snorted. "I'd prefer a *hofbrau* where there's some good imported beer."

Brock felt a twist of almost painful love. His father was selecting what he knew Brock would most enjoy. "Okay," he said, knowing the Major would hate it if he acknowledged the gesture. "Let's go, then."

His father clipped a leash to Quarters's collar and opened the door. The dog dashed for the stairs, jerking the Major after him. Brock closed the door, locking it, and followed them.

Quarters dragged them down the two flights and through the lobby at a breakneck speed, their feet pounding on the thinly carpeted stair. Brock imagined muttered curses behind each door they passed. Once outside, Quarters gave a leap that tore his leash out of the Major's hand. A long-haired black Persian cat on the front walk hissed once, then turned and fled, and Quarters took off after it, barking furiously.

Brock glanced over his shoulder at the window to his right. Mrs. Carnady, the Major's landlady, had parted her curtains and stood there with her red hair in pink rollers, glaring balefully at them.

Brock dashed after the dog and caught his leash as he came to a dead stop. In the nick of time the cat had darted under the porch. Brock gave Mrs. Carnady a friendly wave, which she ignored, and brought Quarters to his car, parked at the curb. He opened the back door and Quarters jumped inside. The Major sat erectly in the front passenger seat.

As mildly as he could manage, Brock asked, "How long is this arrangement going to last, Dad?"

The Major sighed. "As long as Mrs. Carnady can tolerate Quarters, I suspect."

Brock drove away before he said carefully, "Perhaps we should find him a home in the country."

"Never! Quarters couldn't tolerate the country."

"You can't keep moving, can you? Perhaps you should make more of an effort to get along with Mrs. Carnady."

"You mean appease her. You know me better than that!"

"Would you like to come to Seattle?"

"No, thank you, Brock. I'm too set in my ways to live with anyone, especially a swinging young bachelor."

"Me, swing?" Brock laughed. "I'm getting too old for that scene."

"A man's never too old." His father eyed him quizzically. "Something wrong with your love life?"

"It was never better. I've met someone special—a wonderful woman."

"Hah!" said his father. There was a short silence while Brock drove through the quiet Sunday streets. Then the Major asked, "What's so wonderful about her?"

"She's just . . . special. Different from other women I've known."

"Take it from me. They're all alike."

Brock said nothing. He had entered the freeway and he concentrated on his driving.

Farther down the highway, the Major demanded, "How is she different?"

"She's a little older than I am," Brock began tentatively.

"Good God!" said his father. "I thought you'd gone through that stage fifteen years ago."

Brock felt the heat that colored his cheeks. "Look, I know you hate women, Dad, and I know why. Just don't count on me sharing your bile."

"I don't hate women, Son. I love 'em and leave 'em. Just as you do, you young stud."

Brock's irritation deepened. His father had certain fantasies about his bachelor son's sex life. He didn't want to believe that for his son, casual sex could never compete with his interest in solving a problem in bits and bytes.

That magical weekend in Denver with Charlotte had been radically different. He realized that he did not want to share it with his cynical father. "'Love 'em and leave 'em,'" he repeated, softly. "But my mother left us, didn't she?"

"We were not discussing your mother," the Major said stiffly.

"Let's discuss her," Brock persisted. "Why did she leave us?" He had never been able to understand how his mother could abandon him. It still hurt.

"That subject is closed." The old man's lips snapped shut and remained clamped.

Brock's mouth was just as tightly set. Driving down, he had sworn he would not argue with his father, and he wasn't sure why he'd brought up the old trauma of his mother's disappearance from his life. He was more sensitive where Charlotte was concerned than he had realized. He kept his silence until he parked in the lot behind the *"hofbrau."*

They entered its dark, smoky interior through a back door and walked into a large room divided into high-walled booths. A plate rail running around it just under the ceiling was lined with German steins. The air was rich with the spicy aromas of pastrami and corned beef and strong beer. A waiter waved them toward a long glass-enclosed counter where huge haunches of roast beef, corned beef and pas-

trami were spotlighted. White-hatted chefs moved behind
it with long shiny knives slicing generous slabs of red meat
and piling them between the halves of sliced rolls.

They carried their heaped plates to a booth. After their
first bottles of beer were open on the scarred wooden table
between them, and the cheerful waiter had brought jars of
both hot and mild mustard, Brock asked, "What kind of
'threats' has Mrs. Carnady made?"

The Major shrugged. "Eviction. If my big ugly dog
doesn't stop chasing her obscene cat. I told her Quarters
was every inch a gentleman and simply wanted to play. You
should have heard her. She screeches, Brock. Most unfortunate habit. 'My Queenie thinks he wants to gobble her up,
and it wouldn't surprise me if he did!' "

The Major mimicked his landlady's whine so accurately
that Brock chuckled in spite of himself.

Encouraged, his father went on. " 'Mrs. Carnady,' " I
said, " 'It's well known that the female is the more deadly
of the sexes.' *That* really made her screech!" he said with
satisfaction. "She threw me out of her apartment."

"I've no sympathy for you," Brock declared. But he was
remembering a winter in Germany when he'd caught a vir-
ulent flu that was going through the military colony and
how his father had taken sick leave to stay in their quarters
with him, nursing him as tenderly as any woman could have
done. He said, "If you promise not to aggravate her again,
Dad, I'll speak to your landlady for you."

"You'll do nothing of the kind," the Major retorted.
"I'll handle her."

Brock gave up.

When he took him back to his apartment Brock guessed
that his father was wanting to take the afternoon nap he still
tried to deny that he needed. Brock decided to start the long
drive back to Seattle.

His father insisted on accompanying him—with the dog, of course—back down the two flights of stairs. Mrs. Carnady, still in the pink rollers, was at her window to watch them walk to his car.

"Be kind to her, will you?" Brock said, and surprised both of them by embracing those straight, unyielding shoulders before he got into his car.

"Kind!" His father drawled the word with such loving contempt that it seemed to say, *My son, the fool,* but there was a look of anxious affection in his eyes that made it difficult for Brock to leave.

His heart torn between exasperation and love, Brock wondered what Charlotte would think of the Major. For a moment, as he drove north along the freeway, he tried to see his father through her eyes: white-haired and erect, with that challenging, sometimes fierce gaze from under overgrown white brows—a distinguished and rather intimidating elderly man whom women still found attractive.

But trying to imagine Charlotte's reaction had opened the door to his memories, and the image of her, lying naked in the curve of his arms with her hair spilling over his pillow and her eyes shining with joy, drowned out all others.... It seemed weeks instead of days since he had held her, and he suddenly missed her so keenly that he turned off the freeway to the first pay telephone he saw and called her house.

In his mind he could see her answering the phone, her hair piled softly on top of her head, wearing something loose yet revealing, like that sinuous white dress he'd seen. He could already hear her light musical voice and the special way she said his name, and he was forming the words he knew he would blurt out. *I'm on my way home, and I've missed you like hell. I want to see you, Charlotte, I want to hold you.*

But it was Wade Emlyn's deep voice that answered.

It was like a dash of cold water in his face. Brock hesitated, while that hulking shadow on the garage wall rose vividly before him, bringing back all the doubts and uncertainties that unexpected confrontation had raised about deeper involvement with Charlotte.

"Hello?" Wade repeated more loudly. "Hey, anybody there?"

He had waited too long, Brock realized in acute embarrassment. To speak now would be too revealing. Very quietly he replaced the phone.

IT WAS MONDAY EVENING. Charlotte had finished washing the dinner dishes, Wade was studying in his room down the hall and she was wondering despondently whether to turn on the television or pick up a novel when the doorbell rang. She firmly squelched the leap of her pulse as she thought, *Brock?*

The past weekend, with no word from him, had been sheer torture. Not since she was a teenager had she listened with so much longing and anxiety for the ring of the telephone. Finally she had taken herself in hand.

It was a relationship that was not going anywhere. Hadn't she known that from the beginning? Their weekend in Denver had been special, very special—but it was something fleeting and evanescent. Brock had realized it, and that was why he was staying away. Best to end it before it hurt them both.

But she was hurting now.

Rising reluctantly from her chair, she told herself that she did not want him coming to stir up the fires of passion she had been trying so hard to bank.

The bell sounded a second time, and Wade called over the music by which he studied, "Are you getting that, Mom?"

"Yes," she called back. It was probably one of his friends, she thought, and opened the door. Brock stood there, holding out a box of fancy chocolates.

"Candy?" Charlotte said in confusion. She was betrayed by her immediate sensual response to the sight of him—the windblown hair, the slant of eyebrow that her fingers had traced while she lay in bed warmed by his body, the easy curve of his smile. But part of her emotion was anger that just seeing him could do this to her. She said in an accusing voice, "You brought *candy*?"

His grin teased her. "I would have brought wine but I was afraid you'd think I was trying to seduce you."

Charlotte fixed him with a clear gaze. "*Are* you?"

She saw a flicker of change in his expression, and sensed he was as emotionally keyed up as she was. In response she felt her own fragile equilibrium shift.

"I've missed you, Charlotte," he said in a low, serious voice. "More than I . . . thought I could."

"But you stayed away."

"I've been working in Tacoma. I drove down to Portland to see my father over the weekend. . . ." He hesitated. "May I come in?"

She stepped back and let him enter. Wade's radio was playing a tender love song that muffled their voices and pulled at her heartstrings.

"Your father doesn't have a phone?" she asked pointedly.

So she had missed him! Brock thought.

His mouth curved tenderly, and in spite of herself Charlotte responded to its warmth. He leaned forward and touched her lips with his. The brief contact was electrifying. He laid the candy box on a mahogany shelf under a small mirror in her entry, pushed the door shut behind him, and took her in his arms.

"I'm sorry, love," he murmured against her hair. "I should have called, but . . ."

Charlotte hadn't really known until he pulled her close how starved she had been for the touch and taste and feel of him. She slid her hands up around his neck, and parted her lips for his kiss. His hands were in her hair holding her head, his thumbs lying along her temples, while he drank in her sweetness. The nagging anxiety and resentment was slowly draining out of her.

When he raised his head he said, "Where's your son?"

"In his room, studying."

His eyebrows rose. "To music?"

She smiled slightly. "He says it helps keep him awake."

"Maybe this is a good time for us to talk."

She murmured, "I can think of better things to do."

He groaned. "So can I, darling, but we have to talk, Charlotte. I . . . I don't want to hurt you."

Strange how those very words could send pain slicing through her. "You don't like Wade, do you?" she said in a tight voice.

He looked shocked, but also a little guilty. "I like Wade," he protested. "Why wouldn't I like him? It's us I want to talk about—you and me."

"Well?" She felt as if she were on the edge of a sheer precipice, her knees shaking at the thought of falling.

"I think I know what kind of woman you are—"

She saw that his hands were clenched into fists and knew exactly what he was going to say: He wanted to end their relationship, because he was afraid she was going to ask for more than he could give.

In desperation she interrupted him. "You do? Then let's talk abut you first, because I don't know what kind of man you are. Tell me," she ordered in a light, bright voice, leading him to the sofa. "Tell me first about your father. What's he like?"

She wondered why he had gone to see his father without telling her he was going away. Had it anything to do with her? She forced herself to wait in silence.

Brock sat down beside her, cocking an ear toward the hall from which flowed the music from Wade's radio. "He's a retired army officer." Brock smoothed a small pillow that somehow had fallen between them. When he caught himself doing it, he picked it up and threw it into a corner of the sofa. "He's seventy years old and still an officer."

Charlotte was not sure what that meant. "You mean he's still in the military service?"

"No. I mean he's spit-and-polish, and if you don't know military life you won't understand that."

"I don't," she admitted wryly, although she had a good idea what he meant.

"It means if the Major were feeding pigeons in the park, he'd line them up and make them salute."

In spite of herself, Charlotte laughed. "And your mother? Does she line up and salute?"

"She ran out on us when I was twelve."

"Oh, no!" His calm emotionless tone wrenched her, and her thoughts began to churn. How had this affected Brock and how would it affect her? "That's awful! Did you have a stepmother?"

"No. The Major raised me."

Anyone else, she reflected would have said "my father." "Why do you call him 'the Major'?"

"Because he's that kind of man."

She was beginning to have a glimmer of understanding. "You must have traveled a lot."

"I grew up on army posts all over the U.S., with two years in Germany and two more in the Philippines."

"With a father who made you salute him, and no woman in the house."

Brock shrugged. "We had housekeepers."

Charlotte thoughtfully observed the tip of one shoe, which she was gently moving up and down beyond the hem of her skirt. What Brock had told her explained a lot, she thought. His ease with people came from long practice at meeting new neighbors, making new friends. *And conquests?* And then moving on. She ached for him.

"Since you know what kind of woman I am," she said slowly, "suppose you tell me."

"You were made to love—for me to love." His voice deepened with desire and his hands clenched again as he fought the urge to pull her close and kiss her until their bodies fused in that surrender that had been haunting him. "You attract me more than any other woman I've known."

She sensed that he was holding something back, and she pressed her lips together to hide their trembling.

After a moment, he continued, "I know that you don't offer yourself lightly, and that I'm a very lucky guy. So lucky I can't quite believe what is happening. I think," he said, after another pause, "that you would naturally expect a relationship like ours to . . . to progress toward a commitment. Am I right?"

Charlotte's heart moved up into her throat, but her instinct for caution was growing. She swallowed and said slowly, "I don't think I'm ready for a commitment, Brock."

"Neither am I." She could not miss the relief in his voice. "But what are we to do? I can't keep my hands off you,

Charlotte. I want you this minute more than I've ever wanted anything in my life."

"No more than I want you, Brock," she confessed over the lump in her throat.

It was true. What she felt for Brock—for the grace of his lean body, his casual, quiet humor and his seeming ease with himself—was beginning to feel a lot like love. But she still couldn't believe this was happening to her. She put her hand on his cheek and turned his face toward her.

When Brock saw her eyes, filled with affection, he breathed her name and pulled her close. When he kissed her it blew everything out of his mind but her fragrance and the feel of her skin and the warmth of her body in his arms.

Down the hall a door slammed and steps muffled by the carpet of the hall approached the living room. Brock let her go and Charlotte moved away from him. Wade appeared in the entry. In spite of the unfortunate timing of his appearance Charlotte let her gaze wander over her son in loving examination, reminded forcibly—as she was so often since he had reached six foot two and had filled out—of his father. Wade had the same steadiness of purpose, the same surprising grace of movement despite his size. Even as a baby, he'd been big. In high school the coach had wanted him to go out for football but his paper routes had made that impossible.

"Hi!" he said, grinning at them. "I need a cuppa coffee, Mom. I'm falling asleep over my books tonight."

Charlotte stood up. "I'll make a cup for all of us. You remember Brock Morley, don't you?"

"Yeah, sure," Wade said, and stuck out a hand.

Standing, Brock took it and with mixed feelings saw his own long narrow hand disappear into Charlotte's son's big grasp. He sensed an easy relationship between mother and son such as he had never known. He was envious of the kid's size and youthful self-confidence, and the look of love that Charlotte had lavished on her son brought Brock a stab of pure jealousy.

Wade dropped into a chair across from the sofa, and Brock resumed his seat. They looked at each other until Brock began to feel uneasy under Wade's frank scrutiny. It was the scrutiny of a grown man. "So," Brock said. "What are you studying so conscientiously?"

Wade grimaced. "Math. It's not my best subject."

Brock, who had been fascinated by mathematics, said mildly, "I enjoyed it."

"Yeah? You some kind of freak?" Wade joked.

In the kitchen, filling the coffeepot and setting out her oversize coffee cups—Wade liked large cups or mugs, and Brock certainly drank enough coffee to appreciate their size!—Charlotte found herself comparing her emotional memories of Wade's father with what she felt for Brock. She had been deeply in love with Garth Emlyn, but when she thought of their passion it seemed pallid in comparison with what she felt now.

Garth and I were so young, she thought. She had been sure she couldn't love anyone any more than she loved Garth Emlyn, and perhaps at that time it was true. But the passion of a mature, aroused woman was powerful and its satisfaction deeply fulfilling.

Was it the relentless time clock in a woman her age, telling her to take joy when it was proffered? Was that what made her natural hunger for fulfillment so fierce? Well, her maturity also advised caution.

The insights she had gained from Brock's brief revelations about his mother's defection and his early life with his father made her realize how little she really knew about him, and how little he knew about her. Even though they had both felt strongly that the attraction between them was more than physical, their intimacy had come about too swiftly. It had come like a flash flood. No wonder neither of them trusted it.

Learning more about each other would help them understand this incredible thing that was happening to them, Charlotte decided. For instance, the fact that Brock had never known a mother's love seemed significant.

Charlotte got down a tin of Danish cookies and put them on a plate she covered with a paper doily. Pulling out her largest tray, she arranged coffeepot, cups, cookies and cream and sugar on it, and carried it into the living room where Brock and Wade were exchanging wary comments on their favorite musical groups.

She opened the box of chocolates Brock had brought, and Wade exclaimed, "Hey, great, man!" and selected a truffle. He was the only one of the three of them who seemed completely at ease, Charlotte thought as conversation lagged. For some reason, Brock's natural poise had disappeared.

Wade ate two cookies and his truffle, finished his coffee, and then rose casually. "Back to the numbers," he said, and picked up another truffle from the box on the coffee table to take back to his room.

Brock heard his door close firmly. He pulled Charlotte into his arms and kissed her. Her lips tasted of sweet chocolate. He slid one hand up underneath her blouse and she shivered, her nipples hardening in anticipation as he reached for them, lightly rubbing first one and then the other.

She unbuttoned his shirt and laid her hand on the wiry curls of hair and through her fingers felt the rapid rhythm of his beating heart. Obeying an urge to touch him more intimately, she lowered her head until her lips were on his skin, and she was breathing in the fragrance of his warm body and tasting its slight saltiness.

"Charlotte." Her name was a caress in his voice. "I can't stand this. I want to lay you down on that rug and love you. Now. This minute."

"I want it, too," Charlotte whispered. She had a dazzling vision of lying on the soft-toned area rug, opening herself to Brock—and imagined Wade coming down the hall. Reluctantly she drew back from Brock's urgent embrace and warned, "But Wade could come back to refill his coffee cup—"

Brock let her go instantly. He had heard the firmness with which Wade had closed his door, and was sure that the door had stood open when he arrived, because he had clearly heard music. Didn't she realize that her son had given them a deliberate gift of privacy?

"Does Wade figure in all of your decisions?" he asked with some irritation.

A pain squeezed her heart as she heard jealousy in his tone. "I'm a mother, Brock. It isn't something I can change."

Was her son always going to come first? *But I need you, too.* He held back the words that sprang to his tongue, sensing he must go cautiously in the matter of her son. "I don't want you to change," he insisted. "You're wonderful just as you are."

He thought about ways to get her alone, to insert himself between her and this son who was no longer a child.

"Would you like to go sailing with me this weekend?"

The change in subject was welcome to Charlotte. "That sounds lovely, Brock. Are you a weekend sailor?"

"Not really. But I have a friend who's always asking me to crew. I can get his boat. How about Sunday?"

"Wonderful!"

They talked for an hour longer, then Brock kissed her and left, feeling both frustrated and happy—an emotional state that was new to him.

ON SUNDAY MORNING Charlotte met him at the door dressed in white sailcloth slacks and jacket. "I've got coffee in a thermos," she said, "and I'm making sandwiches. Come in and say hello to Wade while I finish."

He followed her back to the kitchen. Wade was eating his breakfast and he looked interested when Brock asked him if he would like to go along.

"Thanks, but I can't. I've got a date with Kate."

"Bring her along," Brock said impulsively and was rewarded with a beautiful smile from Charlotte.

It seemed to her a wonderful idea. But she saw a strange expression cross Wade's face, one she couldn't decipher before it was gone.

"Sorry," he said. "Kate's made plans."

They took the lunch and drove in Brock's car to a small harbor near Des Moines. The boat was a nineteen-footer with a small cabin with two bunks that was entered from a low hatch in the cockpit. The day was fresh with a blue sky clotted with puffy clouds that moved leisurely across it.

Charlotte was seeing a different Brock as he rigged the sails and prepared to cast off. There was strength in his lithe grace, and beauty in his movements about the small deck. The boat had a stately, unhurried air; the breeze that filled her sails ruffled Brock's hair as he sat at the tiller, and swept strands from Charlotte's topknot across her cheeks.

Gulls followed them hopefully, then turned back. In the distance a ferry boat was crossing to McNeil Island, and white and red sails dotted the Sound. They did not talk much but enjoyed a sense of privacy and a communion born of sharing the beauty of the day.

After lunch, though, the sky darkened. The wind rose and the water became choppy. "Better put on one of those life jackets," Brock suggested, "and hand me one."

When she did as he asked, he added, "Watch the boom, now. I'm bringing her around. Hang on!"

The sails snapped in the spanking wind, and they raced toward shore as several big drops of rain fell on their faces and splashed on the surface of the water.

"There are slickers in the cabin," he told her.

She lowered herself into the hatchway and found the rain gear, and they donned the yellow oilskins for the final race to shore. When they finally made it, Brock secured the boat and they ran to shelter in a small café. Brock ordered coffee and doughnuts and while the rain ran in streams down the windows they talked—about mutual friends at the clinic, about Brock's life with his father on army posts, about Charlotte's experiences raising a fatherless boy. It was a very satisfying conversation. When the shower moved inland and the sun came out, she helped Brock wipe down the boat and spread the sails to dry.

They drove back to Charlotte's house in the early dusk and found Wade at home, studying.

Brock could not conceal his disappointment. "I'd hoped we'd be alone," he muttered as they stood in the hall. He took her face in his hands, his thumbs gently rubbing her cheeks. He kissed her deeply. "But this has been a perfect day."

"Perfect," she agreed. It was incredible that two people so different should find such magic in just being together. "I keep asking 'Why me? Why you?'"

She carried the food basket out to the kitchen and Brock followed her.

"Just think," she said, over her shoulder, "if you hadn't aroused my maternal instincts—"

The look in his eyes, darkening with shock, stopped her. She carefully placed the basket on the kitchen table. "In the beginning, I mean, when I started worrying about all those cups of coffee you drank instead of eating—"

"Maternal?" he said, with a violence that startled her. "God, what a thing to say!"

She was surprised to see that he was genuinely angry. "Brock! I didn't mean—"

"Can you call what you felt in Denver *maternal?"*

"No, of course not!"

"Then what are you trying to say? You think the reason I wanted you was because my mother abandoned me twenty-one years ago? Is that it?"

"Brock, you're putting words in my mouth!" she protested.

Looking at his face, she realized that she had fallen over the precipice without even seeing it. She had touched a most vulnerable spot, and she was devastated by what she had done.

It had been a mistake to mention his mother the other day and she would only make it worse by trying to explain how that nebulous dream in which he had seemed a contemporary of Wade's friends had disturbed her. It was all part of her insecurity because her fortieth birthday was just around the corner, and her fear that because of that, his interest in her would be fleeting.

When he started for the door, she ran after him and caught his arm but he jerked away. She watched from the doorway as he walked rapidly toward his car, rigid with anger.

She couldn't let this happen.... She ran down the walk and grabbed his arm again, twisting him toward her. "Brock, what does it matter why I first noticed you or why we came together, as long as we hold on to what we have?

We have something very special together, but we need to work on it." When he said nothing, she wailed, "Oh, sometimes you do seem so young!"

He stopped then and looked at her. A half-moon was positioned just above the roof of her house and its pale light illuminated her face, her finely boned, narrow face with its passionately curved mouth and beautiful, anguished eyes.

"It's the age thing, isn't it? Haven't I told you it doesn't mean a thing?"

She watched the darkness drain out of his eyes, and some of the anguish left her. But she said, "I know it makes no difference, Brock—at least my mind knows it. That's not really it."

He was very still. "Then what is it?"

"I've been thinking about it, and it's not just a little difference in age. It's . . . it's that I've been so totally a mother these years since my husband died. It's difficult for me to think of myself as a . . . a desirable woman again. It's been so long. . . ."

"Oh, Charlotte." He experienced a second pang of jealousy and was not sure whether he envied Wade the mother's love he himself had missed, or whether his subconscious recognized it as a threat to his lover's claim on her. In either case, the emotion was an unworthy one.

Rejecting it, he pulled her close in a desperate hug. "I'm sorry I yelled at you," he breathed against her hair. "You're right, we do need to explore this thing between us. And I'm going to enjoy doing that, every minute of it. The sooner the better. How about I pick you up after work tomorrow and we have dinner at my apartment?"

She pressed her cheek against his slightly scratchy jaw while joy flowed through her veins. "Yes, darling," she said unsteadily. "Oh, yes."

CHAPTER SIX

CHARLOTTE WAS IN HER BEDROOM, dressed in her lavender wool suit with the trapunto trim on the cardigan jacket. She had written a note for Wade and left it on the refrigerator door telling him Brock was picking her up at work for dinner, and had returned to her room for the one thing she had almost forgotten.

Carried away that night in Denver, she and Brock had taken a reckless chance. Fortunately, she was not pregnant but she did not intend to take such a chance again. An illegitimate child at thirty-eight? She had visited her doctor immediately on her return to renew a prescription that she had not needed for a long time.

She found her plastic container of contraceptive pills and was holding it in her hand, when she heard a sound and turned her head. Wade, clad only in his sleep-rumpled pajama bottoms and looking so much like his father that it startled her, was standing in her bedroom doorway, his eyes widening on what she held.

She saw recognition and instant comprehension in his expression. Then a mask slid over his young face, so like Garth's. "I'll be late tonight, Mom. I'm playing 'til one."

She recovered from the momentary paralysis of her shock a second too late. "Wade," she began urgently, but he had already gone into the bathroom. The lock clicked.

Charlotte glanced at her watch and knocked on the door. "Wade! Can I talk to you?"

Almost immediately she heard the sound of the shower running. For a moment she hesitated there, wanting badly to say something to soften the awkward moment, and feeling quite helpless.

The look she and her son had exchanged had said everything. Wade knew that she was sexually active, and he knew that she had read his knowledge in the startled expression he had instantly masked. She was equally sure that Wade intended to stay under the shower until she had left the house to avoid any discussion of the subject. For the moment, she'd have to go along with that, or be late to work and let her patients, some of them very ill, wait for their appointments.

She poured a glass of water and took her pill, then went out through the kitchen back door to the garage, passing the refrigerator where the note she had already left under a red star would tell Wade exactly who would be loving her tonight.

Charlotte assumed that at nineteen Wade was no longer a virgin. It had been over five years since she had given him the lecture about sexual responsibility that would have come from his father if Garth had lived. Wade was a grown man now—but how was he going to feel about his mother taking a lover?

She drove her car into the medical parking lot, saw that Dr. Ferdie's Mercedes was already in its slot, and tried to put the unsettling speculations out of her mind. Her anticipation of the evening with Brock was now mixed with anxiety because her happiness with him was still so fragile, and the encounter with Wade had cast a shadow over it.

But as the morning wore on, her longing for Brock began building. Why should she feel guilty because Wade knew that she had a lover? His father had been gone a very long time. The dread that she was going to be faced one day with the end of something that was assuming more and more importance to her only strengthened her burning need to be with Brock. She needed him, and not just to shiver under his touch. She needed to see him look at her in that tender, teasing way that made her feel so young and vulnerable.

It was a busy morning, but in between her scheduled tests, her thoughts returned again and again to Brock's anger the evening before. It had hurt, and she found its intensity difficult to understand. She tried to visualize the mother who had abandoned him and could not. How could any mother walk away from her son? The thought of a twelve-year-old Brock, shocked and lonely, sent a pain through her heart.

When she was not trying to understand his mother, she wondered what kind of man a son would call "the Major." Was the Major to blame for the breakup of Brock's home? She recalled Brock's little story about the Major lining up the pigeons in the park, and sensed the affection glowing through his humorous comment on his father's idiosyncrasies.

Five o'clock came and her last patient and his mother were sent home. It was a case that cracked her carefully cultivated emotional detachment wide open. Five-year-old Jeddy Flagler was a milk-pale boy with the smile of an angel and an unconquerable spirit shining out of blue-shadowed eyes. He was also a candidate for heart surgery, and the little boy's clear-eyed acceptance of the odds as Dr. Ferdie explained them to him and his mother broke Charlotte's heart.

He was willing to put his life in Dr. Ferdie's hands in the hope of one day being able to go to school with his friends. In order to keep her composure, she had to remind herself that his youth gave him a better chance of survival than many of the doctor's older patients would have in similar circumstances.

So she was subdued when she walked out of the clinic's rear entrance and found Brock waiting in his car. He leaned over to open the passenger door for her and his smile lightened her mood immediately.

"Hi," he said, and when she slipped in beside him he gave her a lingering kiss before he straightened up and started the engine.

"You're changing my work habits," he told her. "My boss said he's never known me to leave a job on time before." He grinned at her. "That's a compliment, lady."

"Then I thank you—or him."

He pulled out of the parking lot and onto the street, driving easily and swiftly, like a man who knew where he was going, and she asked, "Where are you taking me?"

"Do you like Chinese food?"

"Yes. Wade and I love the Golden Dragon. Do you know it?"

He was looking straight ahead. "I said I'd fix dinner, remember? There's this great take-out place—"

She began to laugh.

"You said we should get to know each other," he reproached her. "I never promised you cordon bleu."

She was laughing again when he pulled up at the Shangri-la. It was another restaurant that she and Wade knew well. "At least we share a liking for Chinese food," she told Brock.

"We've a lot more than that in common," he said soberly before he left her, and as she waited in the car she felt the tide of her desire rise strongly. *I won't think of Wade and his Katie,* she promised herself. *I won't think about Dr. Ferdie retiring. Tonight is mine. Tonight I will think only of Brock—and us.*

He came back with a large brown paper bag, which he put on her lap. She peered into it at the assorted cartons with fine wire handles. "You expect us to eat all this?"

"Of course not. I'll be eating it for three days."

"Don't be too sure," she said. "It smells wonderful."

When he pulled into the underground parking garage at his apartment building, he took the sack from her. They went up in the elevator to the twelfth floor and he unlocked the door of his apartment. Charlotte entered and looked around with an intense curiosity.

It was a large room with one wall of windows framing a magnificent city view, with the glimmer of the gray Sound under a cloudy sky in the distance. The room was furnished with a noticeable lack of clutter that made it look surprisingly spacious. A row of framed posters on the wall caught her attention. They were mostly from European ski resorts, labeled in French and German. Garmisch-Partenkirchen, said one, under a laughing young Nordic man on skis, with the snow-covered Zugspitze towering at his back. Large and colorful, the pictures lightened the dark paneled walls.

"Well?" Brock said expectantly.

"You're very neat."

"Don't open any closet doors," he warned.

Charlotte laughed.

"My father's so damned neat that I had no choice but to become an unregenerate litterbug," he explained. "I wouldn't tell you that, except that you're bound to discover it for yourself."

He had dropped the food sack on a counter as they passed a kitchen alcove and now he took her in his arms. "I could try to be neat for you," he whispered, and her heart lurched. They kissed and she savored the innate sweetness.

It was not a word she dared use aloud when speaking of a man, because men tried to hard to keep it hidden, but it was there. Wade had the same quality.

Dr. Ferdie, too. It was what made Dr. Ferdie's patients love him, and what made him consider retiring from his lifework because his wife was unhappy. *Men are unappreciated,* Charlotte thought fiercely and her eyes, gazing up at Brock, were suddenly misty with emotion.

"If you keep looking at me like that, I can't guarantee you'll get anything to eat," he warned her.

She moistened her lips, and he groaned.

"Sorry. I'll try to look hungry."

He filled a copper teakettle with hot water and put it on the stove to boil for tea, leaving the tap running and putting two plates under it in the sink to warm. In a large carton he found the appetizers—cheese-stuffed fried wonton and foil-wrapped teriyaki chicken wings—and arranged them on a plate that he carried to a round table in front of the window. He dried the warmed plates and filled them with cashew chicken, beef broccoli and sweet-and-sour pork from the food cartons, and took them to the table. After he seated her, he went back for a large bowl of rice.

The odors rising to her nostrils were rich and tantalizing. The teakettle whistled, and Brock strode to the kitchen. In moments they were enjoying a first-rate meal and drinking green tea from small cups.

"Do I get marks for my cooking?" he asked her, little golden lights dancing in his eyes.

"Your method is unorthodox, but the result is highly edible."

"Downright unappreciative, aren't you?"

"I wouldn't say that. Look, I'm cleaning my plate."

After they had finished eating, he sent her to the sofa from where she could hear him putting the leftover food into his refrigerator and rinsing their plates for the dish-washer. When he joined her, she had picked up a small gold frame from the lamp table. Brock looked over her shoulder at the picture of the Major in uniform. "I took that the day he retired from the army after thirty-five years."

Charlotte examined it in silence. His father's eyes were alert, but his expression was stern and unyielding.

"That's his executive officer look," Brock told her. His father's hair was almost white, even then, but he was clean-shaven. It was after he retired that he cultivated the trimmed Vandyke beard and mustache he wore with pan-ache.

"Thirty-five years?" Charlotte's voice held wonder.

"He rose from the ranks to warrant officer, and finally a commission. That may be why he was always so spit-and-polish."

She was staring thoughtfully at the picture and Brock wondered what she thought of his father.

"I can't see you in him, Brock," she finally said.

"I'm supposed to look like my mother."

"You don't know?" she heard herself ask with dismay. She had sworn she wouldn't mention his mother tonight.

But he answered her with no emotion in his voice. "I was twelve when I last saw her. I remember *her* but not just how she looked."

"But you have pictures of her, don't you?"

"No," he answered shortly, and she was silent with shock. *No pictures?*

She opened her mouth to demand to know how that was possible, but Brock forestalled her by sitting down beside her and putting two fingers on her lips. "Your turn," he said gently.

Instantly she was totally aware of his presence, as if the fine invisible hairs on her arms were miniature antennae, sensing his body warmth and signaling his nearness. Inhaling the soapy fragrance of his hands, mingled with a faintly spicy aroma that she had come to associate with him, she felt a familiar tingling in her breasts and a stirring of desire that quickened her breathing.

Brock put his arm around her and drew her closer. "What kind of a child were you?"

"Right now it doesn't seem important," she murmured, obeying an urgent need to touch his face. She traced the tender curve of his smile, letting her forefinger rest in the tiny hollow at its corner. His mouth felt surprisingly soft.

He turned slightly and kissed her fingertip, then reached up and pulled away her hand and lowered his lips to hers. Warmth spread down through her body while the kiss went on and on, fanning the deep glow of her desire until it burst into flame. He slipped a hand into the neck of her dress and found the front clasp of her bra. She sighed in pleasure as he caressed her breasts.

In a little while he stood up, pulling her to her feet. Holding her beside him, he walked across the room and moved a chair. Now she saw why his one-room apartment seemed spacious. He pressed a panel and a portion of the wall slowly opened and lowered a bed to the floor. It was so easy, so convenient that she had to wonder how often he brought a female guest here, and felt a painful twinge of jealous doubt.

"This is where I dream of you every night," he told her, and with his gentle hands that she had watched him use with beautiful precision when he was at work on her machine, began unbuttoning her dress.

As he removed the layers of loose clothing that she moved within so seductively, Brock marveled at how beautiful she was. Her slender body seemed perfection itself to him—straight of back and lusciously curved where curves counted, with long legs and well-shaped calves. One would never realize, he thought, that she had borne a child nineteen years ago. His desire rose in a blinding haze that threatened to shatter his control. He sat on the bed and pulled her down onto his lap and kissed her, and with his tongue still passionately exploring her mouth, fell back on the bed with her in his arms.

Murmuring endearments, he caressed and explored her beautiful body until she rolled from side to side and moaned his name. He rose then, throwing off his clothes with reckless haste, and returned to lower himself over her. He was frantic to enter her, and he controlled himself only by thinking of her pleasure instead of his own.

She was here in his bed in his arms, as he had dreamed it night after night since Denver, and he exulted in bringing her with him to the heights of ecstasy. It was more wonderful than any dream. He heard himself crying out on the mounting wave of his climax, "Oh, Charlotte, Charlotte!" and he heard the tone of wonder in his voice.

Charlotte heard him through her own cry of ecstasy and gasped, "I love you, Brock!"

He rolled over on his back, pulling her with him, her head on his shoulders, their legs entwined, and they lay still while the thunder of their heartbeats slowed.

Then he said, "Did you mean what you said?"

"What?" But she knew what he was asking.

"Do you love me?"

"Yes." She could answer that without qualification. Brock had broken down all her defenses and stolen into her heart. No matter what happened, whether their passionate union was short-lived or not, he would always be there.

"I'm glad, because I think I'm in love with you," he said softly. "I've never said that before, Charlotte."

"Oh, Brock..." she murmured, unable to conceal the joy that suffused her. She lifted one hand to his cheek and kissed him sweetly.

He tightened his arms around her. "What are we going to do about it? Shall we get married?"

"Oh, Brock!" she said again, with an entirely different intonation, and he felt a painful suspense.

"Isn't that what people in love do?" He knew he could easily spend the rest of his life with this woman.

For the first time she lowered all the barriers she had built up in her mind. Could there be a future for them? Wade was in college and starting to build his own life. She could think of her own happiness now, couldn't she? And Brock's?

The thought of his unhappiness as a boy returned to haunt her. Abandoned by a mother who was so hated that all pictures of her had been destroyed? She longed to lavish her love on him.

"Are you sure, Brock? Can you accept a wife with a grown son?"

She was perceptive, Brock thought. She had known what a jolt meeting that big jock of a son had been. He cursed himself for allowing her to see that. "What's five years and a grown son?"

She laughed breathlessly and buried her face in his shoulder. Over her head Brock met the Major's cool eyes in the gold-toned frame. "Say you will," he urged, defying that stern gaze, wanting to make a commitment before he found himself looking at the wonderful woman in his arms through his father's cynical eyes. "Promise me," he ordered.

"I will," she said, and when his arms tightened around her, added in a squeezed-out breath, "think about it."

"Not good enough." He brushed his lips lightly over hers, sensitively memorizing the feel of them, the tiny ridge along her upper lip and the slight dent at its center. Nothing—no one could make him give up this woman, not the Major nor anyone else. "Promise?"

The whispered word sent a soft breath into her mouth. It was faintly scented with wine and ginger.

"If. . ." she began.

"Don't say 'If Wade approves,'" he warned her with a mock severity. "If you do, I'll ask my father's permission, and he won't give it."

"I'd hoped he would like me," Charlotte said, suddenly serious.

"Oh, he'll love you," Brock assured. "It's marriage he doesn't like."

She was silent for a moment. Then she said, "I'd like to meet him, Brock."

"After we're married."

"Before."

"No. Negative, no."

Charlotte considered that. "I suppose I could call on him and introduce myself as his future daughter-in-law."

"You wouldn't!"

"I would."

"Look, darling, you'll be sorry if you do anything like that. You'll need support when you face the Major."

"Is that a challenge?"

"Dammit, no! It's the truth."

"What's he got against marriage? Or is it just *your* marriage?"

"He says it's a form of slavery."

Amused, she said, "That's a woman's line, darling."

He ran his hand over her hip, his eyes alive with exciting speculation. "Will you be my slave?"

"If you'll be mine."

"You've promised," he exulted, glowing. "I'll hold you to that." He lowered his head and put his lips to one breast, teasing and suckling the nipple until she felt an answering contraction between her thighs. She reached down to caress him and drew in a sharp breath as she felt the strength of his arousal.

"Love me," she whispered urgently. "Love me now!"

CHAPTER SEVEN

BROCK LAY ON THE BED, his relaxed body brown against the white sheet, his sleepy eyes following Charlotte as she gathered up her clothes. She lifted one foot to step into a shoe beside the bed and he rolled over lazily and reached down to catch her ankle.

"Brock!" She teetered on one foot.

"My arms feel empty."

"Darling." She sank down awkwardly on the bed beside him, her arms full of clothing.

He ran his hand up her smooth calf. "Stay with me, Charlotte. I want to hold you in my arms all night. I'll take you to the clinic in the morning."

She was torn between her longing to stay in the warm nest of his arms and her strong reluctance to risk Wade's wakening in the morning to discover that she had not come home. It wouldn't be fair, when she had always insisted that he let her know if he was going to be home late.

"Wade will worry...."

Brock let her go. "Doesn't he know where you are?"

"He's probably guessed," she admitted, and escaped into Brock's bathroom with her clothing. She had not wanted to tell him that Wade knew exactly where she was. That revealing look she and her son had exchanged just before she left the house was something that still troubled her.

Swiftly she showered, surrounded by evidence of Brock's personal habits—a curiously intimate experience. When she returned to the other room, Brock had put on his clothes. They went out into the silent hall and took the elevator down to the garage, meeting no one. He drove her through almost-deserted streets to the hospital parking lot to pick up her car. There was activity around the emergency entrance, but the medical building that housed the clinic was dark and silent.

"I'll follow you home," Brock said.

"It's so late," she protested. "It will be daylight when you get back to your apartment."

"Uh-huh. You see why we have to start living together, don't you?"

"Yes." She kissed him, then unlocked her car.

To her relief, no lights showed when she pulled up at the house with Brock's headlights just behind her. But Wade was home. His van was parked on one side of the driveway. She drove past it into the garage, and Brock came up to walk with her across the dark yard. Wade had left the back porch light on for her.

He caught her by her arms at the door. "You'll tell Wade we're going to be married." It was not really a question.

"I'll tell him, darling."

"When?" he asked, between kisses. "Now?"

She shook her head, laughing softly. "I'm not going to wake him if he's sleeping. If you're afraid I'll change my mind, there's not a chance! I'll tell him, I promise."

He kissed her one last time. "G'night, sweet."

She let herself in the house quietly, and he went back to his car.

Wade's bedroom door was ajar and she could hear him breathing heavily, as if his sleep were troubled by dreams. She pushed on the door until she could see him. A dim light from the street lamp fell across his face. She was so happy that she felt a twinge of guilt because he looked so exhausted.

He worked so hard! As she carefully closed his door she heard him grind his teeth, and wondered what he was dreaming. He was growing away from her these busy days, which was inevitable. Soon Wade would no longer need her. And that made marriage to Brock logical and not the wildly improbable coupling it had at first seemed to her.

She thought she would not sleep the few hours left before daylight, but she sank into dreams of Brock almost as soon as she lay her head on the pillow, and the alarm seemed to go off in the next moment.

Wade was still sleeping when she left for the clinic, and she couldn't help reflecting that she could have stayed with Brock. How important being with him had become to her! Now that she had taken the big step, their marriage could not come too soon. All her thoughts revolved around Brock and their coming union.

All morning she hugged her secret to herself, not wanting to share her happiness with anyone before confiding in Wade. Just before noon she was giving a cardiac echo test to a frail, elderly black woman when she saw the light flashing on her telephone. When she could leave her machine she picked up the receiver and heard a woman's voice that she recognized after a startled moment.

"Charlotte, this is Ellin Ferdinand. I was wondering . . . can you lunch with me Wednesday of next week?"

Charlotte's heart sank. She was sure Ellin had called because her husband had insisted on it. The clinic was closed on Wednesday afternoons and she could think of no excuse that would not sound like a rebuff.

"I'll be happy to," she lied.

"Good. I don't know what this is all about, but my husband says that you are plotting something for me." Ellin laughed pleasantly. "I promised him I'd at least listen."

"Wonderful!" Charlotte tried to put some enthusiasm into her voice. What on earth had Dr. Ferdie told his wife? Did Ellin expect to be asked to plan a party? Somehow the implication was there in the light, amused voice.

"I hope you like seafood. Ferdie and I have discovered a great new place on the Sound, not far from the airport. I enjoy the selection there, and Ferdie thinks you'll like it."

So his wife called him Ferdie, too. "Sounds great!"

Ellin described the location of the restaurant and asked, "Can you meet me there at one?"

"Okay."

Charlotte went back to her patient and the pulsing image on her monitor, putting the luncheon engagement out of her mind until she saw Dr. Ferdie a few minutes later and told him about his wife's call.

"That's settled, then," he said with satisfaction. "I've got some material from the local heart research team I'll give you so you can prepare your approach." He added with a shade of wistfulness in his voice, "My fate's in your hands, Charlotte."

"Don't count on me, Dr. Ferdie," she warned. "I'm not a persuader."

"You'll do fine."

A little after twelve she finished with her last patient. She had thought she would use her afternoon off to catch up on the sleep she had lost the night before, but she was too keyed up to nap. At five Brock telephoned.

"Have you told him yet?"

"Brock! Wade isn't home from school yet. I haven't even seen him since yesterday morning!"

He chuckled. "Now that you've said yes, it's not going to be easy to wait. It seems an age since I saw you."

"It's been exactly fourteen hours, give or take a few minutes, since you kissed me good-night," she teased him. "What about you? Have you told your father?"

"God forbid!"

She was silent for a moment. Then she sighed. "I still think I should meet him, Brock."

"In good time, sweetheart. Wade, first."

"Why?" she demanded.

"Because he's here, and the Major's in Portland," Brock said with indisputable logic.

"I think Wade's going to be home this evening," she said tentatively.

"Perfect. Call me later. I'll be home after ten. Here's a kiss, love. Got one for me?" he asked in that easy way.

"Yes, oh, yes!"

WADE DID NOT HAVE a gig that night, and Charlotte didn't have to urge him to have dinner at home with her. He seemed as anxious for a confidential talk as she was. She had made stuffed pork chops, one of her dishes that he especially liked. Usually he picked up his plate and went into the kitchen for seconds, but this evening he was toying with his chop.

She saw that he was not only nervous, but apprehensive, so she began talking of Brock in casual and cheerful tones, telling Wade about his work at Echo and how it had brought them together, and how they had met again in Denver. "He's a sweet guy, Wade. You'll like him when you know him better. Last night—" She bit her lower lip as his eyes shifted away from her gaze. "Last night he asked me to marry him."

Her heart sank when she saw the effort it required for Wade to keep his voice steady as he asked, "Did you say yes?"

"I love him, Wade," she confessed.

Wade swallowed hard, then said, "Is he going to move in here?"

"We haven't discussed that, but I suppose that's what we'll do. Brock's apartment is hardly big enough for one person, let alone three."

"Four," Wade said under his breath.

Charlotte's heart gave a loud thump. Had she really heard that? "What did you say, Wade?"

"I'm going to marry Kate."

"*Marry* her? Marry *Kate*? Oh, no!" Panic wiped everything else from her mind. The words came tumbling out and she couldn't stop them. "Oh, Wade, you can't mean it! Why, Kate's still in high school, she's still a *child*! You're both too young—"

Wade looked pale. "I was hoping we could live here with you, Mom," he said hesitantly, "until I can get a job, and get ahead a little."

"You're planning to quit school? After how hard you've worked to get into college?" The sick look of misery that came into her son's eyes stopped her.

"Kate's pregnant, Mom."

Charlotte felt the numbness of shock spreading through her arms and legs. It had never occurred to her that he and Kate…! She knew her dismay must be showing in her face.

"For God's sake, Wade," she said in angry despair, "you had sex with a sixteen-year-old girl?"

Wade stiffened. "Mom, you don't know much about sixteen-year-old girls, do you?"

Charlotte cried, "She's a *minor*, Wade. Do you realize that the courts consider that statutory rape? You could go to jail!"

He tried to smile. "I don't think she can claim rape."

"Didn't you have sense enough to take some precautions?"

"Kate said she was on the Pill."

"You relied on *her*, an irresponsible—"

"She said her aunt got them for her." He swallowed. "I'll have to get a full-time job. That knocks out college, doesn't it?"

The swift anger that had boiled up to blanket her hurt was evaporating, leaving raw pain exposed. She hurt for Wade's thrown-away opportunities—and for Kate, whose predicament was tragic. "Don't say that, Wade. Not yet. There must be a way out of this."

His mouth took on the stubborn look she knew so well. "We've already discussed abortion. Kate won't agree to that."

"Wade, dear, I wasn't suggesting—" Abruptly she closed her mouth. What *was* she suggesting when she spoke of a way out, if not an abortion? She was so agitated that she hardly knew what she was thinking.

"Mom, this is my child she's having. I'm going to marry her."

Her heart felt bruised, tenderness battling with an excruciating pain. Her first grandchild born to an immature sixteen-year-old girl? A tiny creature, owing its existence to the son born of her love for Garth and his for her, thrust into life with no choices because his father was doomed to remain at the minimum-wage level for lack of an education? What kind of a start was that?

"Wade," she began carefully, "I should be full of joy because you're giving me a grandchild, but all I can feel right now is pain. I hurt for you, darling, because it will mean the end of your dreams, but I hurt for Kate, too, because motherhood at her age will close ninety percent of her options in life.''

"She'll be getting a husband who loves her," Wade said stubbornly. "Isn't that what most women want? I can support her. I've got a job.''

"With what future? What hurts most, Wade, is that your child—my grandchild—will not have many options, either. Think about this. If someone else could give it a better home, a better start in life—''

"It's my baby, Mom!''

Their voices were rising emotionally.

"Then don't doom your child to a disadvantaged life! I'm not saying it will be easy, for you or for Kate to give your baby up, but—''

"You didn't have it easy after Dad died, did you, Mom? Did that ruin my chances?''

"No," Charlotte said deliberately, "but marrying Kate will. And we've both worked so damned hard for your chance! Oh, Wade—'' Her voice broke.

Wade stood up. "Don't go all weepy on me, Mom!" he said bluntly. "A college education won't make me a better disc jockey.''

"Are you sure about that?''

He picked up his plate and carried it into the kitchen, coming back with a large glass of milk. With studied casualness, he said, "I'm going over to tell Kate we can get married. Is it all right to tell her we can live here?''

Charlotte said just as carefully, "I'd like to go with you.''

"Mom, this is between Kate and me.''

"Not entirely. Kate's a minor, after all." She didn't say it, but "jailbait" hung unspoken in the air between them. "I think I should discuss this with her aunt.''

"Oh, for cripes' sake, Mom!"

"Will you wait while I get my coat?"

"Mom, it's no use—"

The telephone rang. Wade did not move except to begin drinking his milk, so Charlotte got up from the table. Brock's beloved voice seemed to come from some enchanted land she had left long ago.

"Brock," she said, and realized how lifeless she sounded.

He sensed a difference in her immediately. "Are you all right . . .? Is Wade there?"

"Yes."

"You told him, didn't you? Shall I come over?" When she hesitated, he said, "I finished the job earlier than I expected. I'm not far away—I can be there in a few minutes."

She heard the concern in his voice, but she knew that she couldn't tell Brock what was really wrong. Not over the telephone, with Wade listening. "No," she said. "Don't come. We're going out."

"Going out?" He was plainly surprised. "Why?"

"Brock, I can't talk now," she said desperately. "Call me tomorrow."

There was silence on the line. Then he said, "Okay, love." But she knew he didn't understand.

When she returned to the dining room with her eyes full of tears, Wade's hostility melted. He put down his empty glass and embraced her, pulling her head against his big shoulder. "Don't cry, Mom," he said, his own voice husky. "If it makes you feel any better, I'm torn up inside, too. But I've got to do what's right. And I love Katie."

"Why?" she asked, wanting to understand. "You're so much more mature than she is. Why do you love her?"

He looked at her blankly for a second, as if to say, *Why ask for a reason for love?* Then he answered, "Kate is all dancing light. I couldn't help loving her. But . . . but maybe it's really because she needs me.''

"Does she even know what love, real love, is?'' Charlotte asked in despair.

"I don't know, Mom. I sure didn't want this to happen to her,'' he added. "But it did.''

He was right. "Yes,'' she said, "and we have to deal with it, don't we? Shall we go over and talk to Kate and her aunt?''

"Okay, Mom. Maybe it's best that I have you along. Kate's Aunt Stelle has never liked me much.''

"I didn't know that.''

He gave her a wry smile before he went out the back door. She locked it, and leaving the food on the table, raced to the bedroom to grab her purse and a jacket. Wade was just backing the van out when she went out the front door. He stopped long enough for her to get in beside him, and then continued backing down the driveway.

They drove in a strained silence to the apartment Kate shared with her aunt and guardian. Charlotte was marshaling her thoughts for the coming interview. But her emotions were still churning so much that she found it difficult to think straight. Only one thing remained clear in her mind: this marriage would ruin both Wade's and Kate's lives. She was certain that Kate's aunt would agree with her. They must find a way to save the children from their folly.

The tires hummed on the wet pavement while those and other thoughts swirled around in her head. She tried to avoid thinking of the expected child—or of her own longings to hold Wade's child. She mourned for the grandchild, whom—whatever its fate—she possibly would never know. But these children were not ready to become parents.

Kate and her aunt lived on a tree-lined street in an apartment building that had been built some years ago. The brick building had a sturdy, settled look about it. There was a bank of mailboxes in the outer lobby with doorbells under each one. Wade pressed the button under the box labeled E. Drew, and presently a young voice asked, "Who is it?"

"It's me, Kate," Wade said, and a buzzer signaled the door had been unlocked. Charlotte walked through with him, and when Wade ran up the stairway instead of waiting for the elevator, she followed him more slowly.

He rang a bell on the second floor, and they waited. Charlotte could hear music from behind the door, a record player or the radio playing a tune she often heard from Wade's room when he was studying.

Kate opened the door. She was a small, fine-boned girl with long straight black hair, who held her head cocked to one side. Her dark eyes widened slightly when she saw Charlotte with Wade.

"Come in, Mrs. Emlyn. Hello, Wade." Kate moved back with a gesture of invitation and a step somehow in rhythm with the music. Charlotte was reminded of Wade's description: *Kate never walks, it's always like she's dancing.*

It was apt. Kate had the supple movements and erect posture of a trained young dancer. Her pregnancy did not seem to weigh on her spirits, and Charlotte thought that it was probably still unreal to her.

Behind her was a high-ceilinged room with bookcases flanking a fireplace on the far wall. Magazines were strewn over a large coffee table between the fireplace and a sofa with its back to the door.

"Thank you, Kate," Charlotte said, entering. "Is your aunt at home?"

"I'm sorry. Aunt Stelle has gone out."

"I'm sorry, too." She turned to Wade. "I think perhaps she should be present when we discuss this."

"What did you want to discuss with her, Mrs. Emlyn?" Kate asked innocently.

Before Charlotte could reply, Wade said, "Kate, I want you to know my mother is not speaking for me. I came to tell you we can get married. I can support you. I'll get a full-time job—"

Sudden, unexpected anger tightened Charlotte's throat. "*If* he quits school," she put in.

"Mom . . ." Wade said warningly.

"Oh, he mustn't do that!" Kate exclaimed. Her eyes, looking even wider, darted from Wade to his mother and back again. "Not on my account."

"I'm glad you agree with me, Kate. May I sit down?" Still irritated at Wade for jumping in like that ahead of her, Charlotte walked around the sofa, and sat down facing the fireplace. Kate followed her but took a chair near the hearth. She sat primly, like a little girl imitating the adults. Wade walked over to the window and remained standing.

"Kate, dear, I'm so sorry this has happened—"

Kate jumped up, crying cheerfully, "Coffee, anyone?" She started past Charlotte who was shocked to hear her humming under her breath a phrase from the radio song that seemed to be forever playing in the background whenever Wade was home.

Charlotte said, "No—please, Kate," and the girl returned to her chair and sat back down, resting her hands in her lap. She had stopped humming, but the radio played on.

"Kate, dear," Charlotte began again, "are you sure— have you seen a doctor?"

"Aunt Stelle took me. He said I'm pregnant."

Charlotte was alarmed by the trace of pride she heard in the girl's voice. "My dear, if you were older, I'd be so happy for you, but having a baby at your age is not fair to you or the child. Have you and your aunt talked—?"

"Oh, yes. She agrees with me. Completely."

"Agrees with . . . what? What do you plan to do, Kate?" Charlotte asked carefully.

Kate smiled. "Why, have my baby, of course."

And then what? The radio was still playing, but no longer in the background. Now its insistent rhythm entered Charlotte's head. Wade's bombshell had left a heaviness in her chest that seemed to be growing.

When Kate said nothing more, Charlotte asked hesitantly, "You're thinking of putting your child up for adoption?"

Kate looked horrified. "*My* baby?"

"Our baby," Wade corrected her, tight-lipped. He had been moving restlessly, but now he paused with his back to the room's one large window. It looked out on the top limbs of a large magnolia tree beside the street, its sturdy leaves shiny with rain. Charlotte wondered if Kate had seen Wade's van from that window and known he would ring her bell.

"Wade, I wish you would sit down," she said. "You make me nervous."

Wade walked over to stand deliberately beside Kate, who ignored him.

"Where will you go?"

"Why should I go anywhere, Mrs. Emlyn?" Kate asked. "I've got to get my diploma. I mean, I'll have to support my child."

"Our child," Wade said angrily. "And I'll support him!"

"You'd stay in school," Charlotte said in an uncertain voice. The feeling of heaviness was increasing, pressing against her heart and lungs and shortening her breath.

"Why not?" Kate tossed her head proudly, although her face was pale. "Lots of kids in high school are having babies. After all, having a baby is the natural thing to do, isn't it? I think it's neat."

"Kate, dear..." Charlotte faced the two of them with a choking sensation. "You did say you've discussed this with your aunt?"

"Oh, yes. We understand each other. She's a single parent, in a way, you know. I mean she's raised me. She hears what I'm saying."

"I'm a single parent, too, Kate," Charlotte reminded her. "I know all about the difficulties a single mother must face. Wade can tell you."

Kate did not look at Wade, and his face reddened. He grabbed her arms, pulling her to her feet. "Listen to me, Kate! My baby's not going to have a single parent. We're getting married as soon as possible. I'll pick you up tomorrow afternoon to get the license. I think we have to take blood tests. I'll find out."

"Wade, can't you see that Kate has no idea of the responsibilities she thinks are so 'neat'?" Charlotte pleaded. "This baby is not a new toy! Kate's not ready for marriage. She's still a child herself!"

"Mom, will you please shut up?"

Kate had slipped out of his hands. She avoided Charlotte's eyes, looking directly at him. "I've decided that I'm not going to marry you, Wade. You've nothing to worry about," she added. "I won't name you as the father."

"But I am the father!" Wade exclaimed in outrage.

Kate patted her stomach lovingly, although there was not the faintest bulge there. "This baby is mine. I don't intend to share her with anyone.'' She was pale but quite positive. ''I know what I want out of life, and it isn't marriage. Not at this point.''

It was Charlotte who found her voice first. ''Kate, dear, you don't know what you're saying. Raise your child alone! How will you feed and clothe it?''

Wade turned on her, white with shock. ''*I'm* going to feed and clothe it!'' he yelled. ''Leave us alone, Mom! I want to talk to Kate.''

''Wade, please!''

''I don't want to talk to you,'' Kate told him coolly.

Wade looked as if she had struck him.

Charlotte's heart ached for her son. ''How do you propose to earn a living for two, Kate?''

''I can stay with Aunt Stelle until I finish school. I want to be a lawyer.''

''A lawyer!'' Charlotte exclaimed, appalled. ''You're living in a fantasy, Kate, dear.''

''I *know* it'll take a long time,'' Kate said a little sulkily.

The heaviness in Charlotte's chest was moving up into her head, which was beginning to throb in time with the background music. ''Your aunt must make a very good salary if she is willing to hire a baby-sitter for you while you go through college and law school. Or does she plan to quit work and baby-sit for you? And in that case, who will pay the bills?''

''That's enough, Mom! You don't have to be sarcastic.''

Kate said seriously, ''Aunt Stelle will keep her job, naturally.''

Charlotte drew a deep breath and tried to control her temper. ''Wade, Kate, please believe I want what's best for both...for all of you. The most loving thing you and Wade can do for your baby is to find a good home with mature parents who can provide your child with the best chances in life. I'm sure if you will just think about it—"

"Have you finished, Mrs. Emlyn?" Kate was even paler, but her voice was steady. "Because you and Wade have nothing to say about this baby. She's my baby, mine alone. I've always planned to have my very own baby."

Charlotte nearly choked. "Are you saying you deliberately became pregnant?"

"I knew you'd think that, Mrs. Emlyn. I didn't, but I think it's just neat the way it happened—"

"Kate!" Wade broke in desperately, "I'm his *father*! I have something to say about his—"

Kate turned on him fiercely. "She's a girl!"

"How can you possibly know?"

"Because I'm her mother!"

The pain in Charlotte's head exploded. She put her hands over her ears and shouted, "Stop! Stop this!"

They turned to her, startled into silence.

"This squabbling—I can't bear it. You're both children! Oh, why couldn't you have been more careful? It would have been so simple, just a little forethought, a little responsibility." In that dark moment it came home to her again that the child in this immature girl's womb was her own grandchild, and she was seized by such a confusion of emotions that she felt paralyzed.

Brock, she thought—this seed that was her grandchild would be Brock's responsibility, too. Could she ask that of him? Everything was swirling around her in a kaleidoscopic pain. Brock and Wade and tragically mixed-up Katie . . . and their child. . . . Despair overwhelmed her, and she cried, "How could you do this to me?"

Wade turned on her, his face a mask of anguished fury. "To *you*?"

"Don't you realize you've ruined my life, too? I was going to be married! I had a second chance for happiness—"

Wade's square jaw flushed. "You've lived your life, Mom," he said bluntly. "It's my turn now. It's my happiness we're talking about—my future, my life! This is my child—and Kate's." He turned back to her empty chair.

Kate had quietly left them.

"Kate!" Wade bounded up the two steps out of the living room and disappeared down a hall. Presently Charlotte heard him pounding and yelling, "Open up, Kate! Let me in! *Katie, please!* Talk to me," he begged.

There was no answer. Charlotte waited, literally biting her tongue in her regret for her emotional outburst. For a moment of white heat she had been completely out of control. Now she wished desperately that she could undo the damage she had done. She wanted to run after them and take both Kate and Wade in her arms and tell them it would be all right, they would work everything out—somehow. But she knew that anything she tried to say now would only make things worse. She had already said too much.

When the pounding stopped, there was utter silence except for the music coming from the radio. Charlotte waited a moment, then walked up the two steps and looked down the hallway. Wade stood before Kate's closed door, his head bowed with his forehead touching the wood.

Charlotte finally spoke. "Tell Kate we'll talk with her another time," she said gently. "Please take me home now."

Wade joined her at last, and drove home in silence.

Still not speaking, they entered the house. Wade walked into the kitchen and went automatically to the refrigerator and poured himself a glass of milk. Charlotte followed him. "Forget what I said, Wade," she began hesitantly. "I was very upset. I want whatever's best for you and Kate and the baby. We'll work it out someway.''

"You shouldn't have gone with me, Mom," he said resentfully. "If you hadn't been there, I could have talked to her, persuaded her we should get married—"

"And thrown your life away!"

"My life is my own. I can throw it away if I want!"

"No, you can't! I made a promise to your father and I intend to keep it. I won't let you throw everything away because you made a foolish mistake."

"I'm not sorry for anything. I love Katie, and I'm going to marry her and take her away from that witchy aunt of hers. I could have had it all straightened out with her if you'd stayed out of it. Now she won't talk to me and it's all your fault."

"Wade, please listen to me."

He drained the glass of milk and set it in the sink. "No more, Mom," he said wearily. "I can't take it."

She had the bereft feeling that she had lost him. She followed him down the hall, pleading, "Wade, please understand. Truly, I want what's best for you."

He closed his bedroom door in her face.

A black cloud of despair hung over her as she undressed and got ready for bed.

CHAPTER EIGHT

SOMETIME DURING THAT SLEEPLESS NIGHT, Charlotte wondered if Brock could face finding himself a step-grandfather at thirty-three. In her heart she knew that whatever she thought of Kate or whether or not Wade was able to persuade the girl to marry him, she would acknowledge Wade's child and do everything in her power to assure his or her well-being. How was Brock going to react to that? *How would he feel about making love to a grandmother?*

Wade did not appear for breakfast, but she set a place for him. She got out the box of cereal, poured her orange juice and filled a pitcher with milk, then sat at the kitchen counter in her robe to eat. Her mind still churned with the shock of Wade's revelation and Kate's unexpected reaction to the situation and what it forboded for them all.

When she finished eating she looked up Estelle Drew's number and reached for the wall telephone beside her. She wanted to talk with this aunt of Kate's who "understood." Because *she* certainly did not understand a sixteen-year-old girl who claimed it would be "neat" to have a baby, and expected to continue her schooling as if nothing had happened. Perhaps together they could prevent a tragic early end to Kate's carefree youth and Wade's college career.

Estelle Drew was not exactly enthusiastic when Charlotte suggested that they meet at a quiet restaurant for lunch so they could discuss this pregnancy without the children present.

"Why? It's Kate who's having the baby," Estelle reminded her in a voice that was quick and decisive. "It's her right to be present at any discussion of her condition."

"But I've talked with her," Charlotte explained. "Didn't she tell you I came to your apartment with Wade last evening?"

"In that case I doubt if she would want to see you again," Estelle said bluntly.

This was not going to be a pleasant interview, Charlotte realized, affronted. Then she told herself it was natural that Kate's aunt would blame Wade for Kate's predicament, just as she harbored the suspicion that Kate had trapped Wade.

She persisted politely. "I think we should talk, Miss Drew."

After a pause, Estelle said, "I'll meet you if you like, but I can't see much point in endless discussions of what's happened."

Charlotte had to be satisfied with that. They agreed on a restaurant midway between Estelle's office and the clinic.

Leaving the cereal out for Wade, Charlotte went back to her room to put on enough makeup to camouflage the effects of her lack of sleep, and to dress in her best business suit, a soft fawn colored wool that brought out the same shade in her hair. She firmly resisted her impulse to waken Wade and reopen the discussion he had cut off by going to bed. But it hurt to leave for work with this feeling of estrangement between them.

When Charlotte arrived at the clinic, a little late, Joy handed her a memo. "Your boyfriend called and left a message," she said with a wink.

"Thanks." Charlotte put the slip of paper in her purse without looking at it. Her promise to call Brock the evening before had completely slipped her mind. How could she have forgotten that? Wade's confession had turned her world upside down, and she felt an anxious flutter of longing for Brock. But she couldn't allow herself to think of her need for him until she had worked her way through the dilemma Wade had put them in, and come to grips with it.

A chill gripped her as she realized that if she were forced to make a choice between her son and her lover she would choose her son. But it would break her heart.

She shook off the apprehension she felt. She was having trouble thinking rationally because every time she thought of Kate Parsons and her aunt, her resentment boiled up again. She simply could not accept Wade's decision to quit college in order to marry a girl who was still a child herself and who had, possibly deliberately, failed to protect herself from a pregnancy.

At the same time she resented Kate's refusal to admit that Wade had any right to be consulted in the decisions she was making about their expected child. She had seen Wade's face when Kate turned on him with "It's *my* baby!" He had looked as if he'd been kicked in the teeth.

A patient was waiting for an echocardiogram and it was not until Charlotte left the clinic at noon and was sitting in her car that she was able to take the memo Joy had given her out of her purse and read it. "Brock Morley called," it said. "Call him at this number."

It was a number Charlotte didn't recognize—probably the telephone at wherever he was working on a computer monitor today. She longed to confide in him, to have him put his arms around her and tell her they would work something out together that would help Wade stay in school. And then she remembered that black moment when she had wondered if Brock could accept this birth of a grandchild so soon after their marriage.

If she could not be sure of his understanding and support in the problems a son and his children would inevitably bring her, should she even think of marrying Brock? Her head began to ache. She dropped the memo back into her purse and drove to the restaurant where Estelle Drew had agreed to meet her.

The hostess led her to a table in the center of the elegant garden court where the sun shining through a skylight directly overhead fell on the young woman waiting for her. Estelle Drew was a younger and more attractive woman than Charlotte had expected to see, but her style was severe. Perhaps it suited the job Estelle had. Wade had said she was a legal secretary in a law firm. Her hair was just a shade away from being blond, and the fact that Estelle had had it lightened—obvious from its barely visible roots—said something about her character that was denied by the easy-care short cut of her hair and the unmistakable career woman's dress-for-success suit that she wore.

Estelle's uninviting expression did nothing to soften Charlotte's headache. Her greeting was as cool and efficient as she looked, and she didn't waste time on any preliminaries after they had both ordered salads and hot tea.

"Kate doesn't want to get married," she began. "After all, she's barely sixteen. It's important that she finish high school."

"I couldn't agree more," Charlotte said. "Wade is in no position to take on the responsibilities of a family at this time. But he is the father of her child. Kate doesn't seem to recognize that Wade has any rights at all in her decisions about this pregnancy."

"He doesn't," Estelle said, immediately raising Charlotte's hackles. "Since Wade will not carry the child, he has no more right to insist that Kate marry him than he has to insist that she have an abortion."

Well, that was blunt! Charlotte narrowed her eyes, trying to conceal the anger that was her instant response. "I'm not asking that Kate marry him, and I doubt that my son would insist on an abortion. But he does want to acknowledge his child. I find that very touching."

"Touching it may be," Estelle said crisply, "but it's Kate's body. It's her decision whether to carry this child or not, and if she bears it, whether to keep it or give it up for adoption."

The waitress came with two abundant salad bowls. Estelle had it all coolly figured out, Charlotte observed, trying to hang on to her temper. Kate's aunt was cold, arrogant, unfeeling; silently she went through a litany of epithets while the waitress arranged the teapots and hot water between them.

When she left, Charlotte said, "I agree, perhaps, that the final decision on an abortion should rest with Kate and her doctor. But when a child is born he has two parents, and his father is as important as his mother."

Estelle smiled slightly. "He was important to the child's conception, certainly, but after that?"

Charlotte thought that she had never disliked a woman so much. Her jaw clenched with her effort at self-control. Estelle Drew was insufferable!

"It's okay today for a woman to be unmarried and still have a child," Estelle went on. "Kate is too young to make the decision for marriage and I'm glad she's mature enough to realize that."

"Kate *mature*?" Charlotte exploded, too angry to be tactful any longer. "I agree that she's too young for marriage. In my opinion, she is also too young to take the responsibility of motherhood!"

"She's perfectly capable of rising to the challenge of motherhood. Bearing a child will help to mature Kate."

"But what will it do to the child?"

"We'll just have to wait and see, won't we?"

Charlotte drew in her breath in an angry gasp that Estelle ignored.

She went on, "I have friends in the corporate world who have chosen to be single mothers and have found it a most rewarding experience. A child can find such an environment congenial and even less stressful than an unhappy marriage or a condition of poverty—"

Charlotte interrupted her. "What you say, Estelle, about a single woman choosing to have a child may be acceptable for someone our age—we don't have many more child-bearing years—but for a high-school student?" A wild notion made Charlotte add, "Or are *you* the one who wants this child?"

For an instant Estelle's eyes blazed pure fury. *So now we know,* Charlotte thought. *We are natural enemies in this situation.*

Estelle said, "My first consideration is for Kate, just as yours is for your son."

"That isn't quite true," Charlotte replied. "I'm concerned about Kate. I'm also concerned about their child. Are you?"

"What's your solution, Charlotte? Have her give her baby away, tear out part of herself and regret it for the rest of her life? A mother's rights certainly count for more than yours or mine! And who can care for a child better than its own mother?"

"I can think of many in this case," Charlotte retorted.

"You don't know Kate as I do. You would feel more comfortable if you and Wade could pretend this child had never been conceived. Is that it? That's the usual male reaction."

Charlotte studied the other woman. Estelle was very attractive in a crisp, cool way. She had classic features and her eyes were large and full of fire. But there was something very cold about her.

"Why do you hate men, Estelle?" she asked, with more curiosity than rancor.

"I don't hate them. I think they're largely unnecessary. Kate has all she will ever need from Wade now that she is pregnant."

Charlotte's sense of outrage returned tenfold. That was too much, after the hour-long telephone conversations she had observed over the past eighteen months, often instigated by Kate; the times she knew Wade had left the house early so he could drive Kate to high school before he left for an early class at the university; and the hours she knew Wade and Kate had spent with their friends hanging around McDonald's! "I'd like to hear that from Kate herself, if you don't mind."

"She doesn't want to see you." Although she had eaten very little of her salad, Estelle rose from her chair. She flung a bill down on the table. "Will you take care of the check, Charlotte?" she asked coolly. "I really must get back to the office."

Charlotte nodded, barely able to suppress the rage she felt. Estelle was neurotic and she had obviously brainwashed her niece! Charlotte remained at the table and pretended to be interested in finishing her lunch.

Gradually, as she drove back to the clinic, Charlotte began to see that for Kate some of the things her aunt had said made sense. Much of her own anger was a mother's instinct to protect her son from hurt. She couldn't help feeling a rapport with Wade's desire to marry Kate and help care for his child.

But she still saw teen marriage as a disaster.

Wade had said, the night before, "She needs me," and Charlotte now knew why. He didn't want Kate to remain under the influence of the aunt who disliked not only him, but all men. Perhaps she should have waited until she was less emotionally upset to have a talk with Estelle Drew. She had not helped the situation.

But even as she sympathized with Wade's desire to take Kate away from her aunt's influence, Charlotte recognized the truth: she really did not want him to marry Kate. A marriage was forever—or if it wasn't it could seem that way while it lasted. And how could such a marriage succeed? What would it do to the child who would be born into such a situation?

That was one thing, at least, that she and Estelle Drew agreed on. But this marriage could happen, whether they liked it or not. Charlotte couldn't really believe that Kate was not still crazy about Wade. She could be experiencing a traumatic shock, perhaps, but she was, after all, still an unpredictable teenager in love. Kate could change her mind about marrying Wade in an instant.

Charlotte groaned. She was trying not to let her own selfish desires influence her thinking, but if those children married now, a lot of careful planning would suffer—Wade's and Kate's for an education, and her own and Brock's for marriage.

What were their options? Give Wade and Kate the house and move into Brock's tiny apartment? She tried to imagine sharing his efficiency with its pull-down wall bed. Even with Brock, whom she adored, it wouldn't work. Honeymooning teenagers could handle it, perhaps, but not a mature widow and a longtime bachelor! She knew she would have to keep her job at the clinic in order to help Wade financially. And that might make anything other than all of them living in her house impossible.

She doubted if sixteen-year-old Kate was physically strong enough to cope with marriage and pregnancy, and after the baby came, motherhood. Did she realize what it would mean to try to keep house, care for her baby and continue her schooling?

Only one thing was certain: Charlotte knew that she could not put off any longer telling Brock what had happened. They would have to make some decisions together.

Wade's van was gone from the driveway when she arrived home late that evening, after staying to give an emergency test to a patient who was suffering from congestive heart failure. She was relieved to find a note from him on the refrigerator, reminding her that he had a late gig that night. She dug Joy's memo out of her purse and dialed the number Brock had left. When no one answered, she called his apartment, but got no answer there, either.

She had just hung up the telephone when it rang, and she snatched it up again.

"Hello, love, had your dinner yet?"

She shivered. Brock's voice had not lost any of its magic. "No, darling," she said. "I just came in the door. I tried to call you. Where are you?"

"At a pay phone. I found the bug I've been chasing for two days, but the switchboard operator in the building went home two hours ago. Can I buy you a steak?"

She drew a deep breath. Now was the time for the talk they must have. "Yes. Bring it over here and I'll cook it."

"Umm, that sounds good." His voice dropped a note, became more intimate. "We've got some planning to do, you and I. Like where and how soon..."

She felt a painful contraction in her chest. So much had happened since she had promised to marry him.

"Yes, Brock, we have." *More than you know.*

"Two steaks or three?"

She knew what he was really asking. "Wade's already eaten. He's playing tonight."

"I'll be there in half an hour or less."

"Hurry, but don't get a ticket for speeding."

He laughed. "It'd be worth it."

His laughter and the tender tones of his voice brought back a swirl of memories—the brush of his hair against her cheek, the fragrance of his body and the sweet taste of his lips. *Oh, Brock, I need you!* she thought, suddenly feeling so near tears that she couldn't speak.

"See you in a few minutes," he said, and hung up.

She stood for a moment holding the receiver, her mind repeating his words to her. He had sounded so happy. She sent up a little prayer as she hung up the phone and went to her bedroom to discard her coat and change her clothes.

Let him still be happy after I've told him!

BROCK DROVE toward Charlotte's house with a glow of anticipation. She had told her son they were going to be married. Now it was not a possibility, but a fact. It was real. They could make plans. Questions and ideas were tumbling over each other in his head. Questions about their living arrangements bumping against intimate videos of sharing a bedroom with Charlotte—in what house? His apartment wouldn't do.

Breakfast with Charlotte facing him across a table with flowers on it—or maybe a single rose.

Did she awaken cheerful or glum? He didn't know.

How long would she make him wait? How soon could they both get away for a honeymoon? With that thought a flush of desire swept through his whole body. Hawaii? he wondered, and images of Charlotte in a bikini on a palm-fringed, surf-scalloped beach flashed across his mind.

He recognized the state he was in—euphoria. It was like going for one's first job interview, or more like accepting a dare to make the high dive into the ocean at Acapulco, a state of high excitement fraught with anxiety about the unknown.

Marriage.

And I'm thirty-three years old, he thought, in amused incredulity. Charlotte felt that was so young, but he knew that he was ready to take this next step. He'd had only one brief live-in relationship. That had broken up on the rocks of his preoccupation with computerized medical diagnostic tools.

The microcomputers that let doctors and medical technicians look into the interior of living bodies and report the perpetual activity occurring there were endlessly fascinating. Working with them was like a drug he was addicted to; when he was on a search for the cause of some program glitch, he couldn't let it lie until he'd found it.

He'd had several girlfriends who hadn't been willing to put up with that. *Workaholic,* one of them had called him. Would Charlotte eventually tire of his obsessive work habits, too?

He pulled up in front of her house, noted the absence of Wade's van, and with the package of steaks in his hand ran up to her front door. She opened it wearing a crisp shirtwaist of pale pink that made her a vision of delight. He put the steaks behind him and leaned forward to kiss her. If he once took her in his arms in his highly charged emotional state, he wouldn't be able to let her go.

She reached up to put her arms around his neck and kissed him with an abandon that verged on hysteria—that was his first hint that something was wrong. But some instinct warned caution. He produced his package and said, "New York cut. Will they do?"

"Wonderful!" She took them and retreated so abruptly to the kitchen that his alarm grew. He followed her, wanting to ask why she hadn't called him and what was bothering her but sensing that it would be better to let her tell him in her own time. A mixed green salad stood on the counter with dressing at the ready. A glimpse into the dining room showed him a table set for two.

She busied herself with opening the package of steaks and preparing them for the broiler. "We're having a simple meal—just steak and salad and some crusty French bread I can warm while the steaks are broiling." She took out a bottle of good Beaujolais and handed it to him to open. "I'm ravenously hungry. How about you?"

"I can eat." He noticed that her movements were jerky, suggesting either extreme nervousness or some strong emotion.

While he tore the foil from the bottle, Brock remarked, "I was thinking pleasantly sexy thoughts while I was driving over. About our honeymoon. How about Hawaii, sweetheart? Would you like that?"

Her hands stilled on the cutting knife with which she was trimming the steaks. Looking down at them, she said carefully, "Yes, Brock. Very much."

What was wrong, he wondered. Aloud, he said, "As soon as we set a date, I'll arrange for some time off. Do you think your Dr. Ferdie will cooperate?" He grinned and added, "He'd better!"

Without warning, Charlotte asked, "Do you think you could face honeymooning with a grandmother, darling?"

Startled, he didn't reply at once.

She whirled to face him, knife in hand, and another strand of her fine hair slipped out of the loose knot at her crown to slide down in front of one ear. "Tell me straight,

Brock, and don't try to be tactful! How would it make you feel to know you had just made love to a grandmother?''

He felt a strange quiver of apprehension run through his body. ''Very, very old,'' he said with a slightly nervous laugh.

He saw that she was very tense. Carefully he took the knife from her hand and laid it on the counter. ''Now, tell me, Charlotte. I feel safer.'' He expected her to smile, but she didn't. ''What's this all about?''

''About me,'' she began. ''About us.'' She took a deep breath and said, ''Wade's teenage girlfriend is pregnant.''

''What the hell . . . !'' He didn't say anything more, not sure what was expected of him. These things happened, he told himself. Wade was old enough to father a child, certainly; in fact, old enough to have known better, Brock thought.

He'd foreseen this, but had not expected it until some time in the indefinite future. He was not sure how he felt about it. But he could see that Charlotte was taking it hard.

Before he could frame something to say that might console her, she said, ''Wade wants to marry her and bring her home to live with me—'' she swallowed ''—with us.''

''With us?'' he repeated, hastily revising his image of their marriage. Not just Charlotte sitting across from him at the breakfast table but Wade, whom in his euphoria he had almost, but not quite, forgotten. And not only Wade, but a very pregnant teenager, and soon an *infant*?

He had never been around babies; the very thought of them terrified him. They were so small and fragile—and so unpredictably noisy!

Color was returning to Charlotte's face. She began to talk, rapidly and nervously. ''It's impossible, of course. Wade must stay in college, or he won't be able to support a family. I'll have to help them if he marries her.'' Her words tumbled over each other in her rush to get them out. "Kate's determined to have the baby but refusing to get married. She's saying 'It's my baby,' as if it's a possession, something to play with."

"Then why are you worrying?" All the while something in his head was saying, *Grandfather? Grandfather?* and trying to reconcile the image that that suggested with his perceived identity as a young bachelor about to take the plunge into marriage.

Charlotte rushed on: "Wade's insisting on marriage. She's too young, of course. But he might be able to persuade her to go through with it. I don't think we could really stop them...." She pushed aside a strand of hair that had fallen down over one eye. "I know I'm too upset over this to make much sense, but—I'm going to have to go along with him, Brock. I've got to see him through college, no matter what he does."

Brock held up his hands against her torrent of words. He'd never seen Charlotte so worked up about something before. "Now, wait a minute," he said. "Calm down, will you? Let me sort this out. Are you saying that we can't get married?"

Charlotte looked at him with something akin to fear in her eyes. He read it as a deep subconscious rejection, and felt the chill of fear himself. What was happening?

"Can you see yourself as a thirty-year-old—"

"Thirty-*three*!" he corrected her, growing annoyed in spite of his determination to remain cool.

"*—grandfather?*" She hadn't even heard him. "Your sleep disturbed? Babies cry a lot, you know," she said fiercely, "and this one could very well be an unhappy baby, because its parents are so young and know so little about what will be demanded of them. And because they are young, their friends will run in and out of the house and stay late, not very considerate of the older generation—and—and of course they'll be asking us to baby-sit.... Does that fit your picture of our marriage, Brock?''

Thrown off guard by her impassioned attack, Brock admitted, ''Well, no, not exactly, love.'' He gave her a rueful expression. ''Mostly, I've been picturing you in a bikini with me on the beach at—''

''You see?'' she said despairingly. ''It just isn't going to work.''

He was experiencing a devastating letdown from his previous euphoria. He tried cajoling her. ''Look, darling, aren't you being hysterical about this? Wade isn't the first young blade to get his girl in trouble. These things happen all the time. He'll live through it. We all will.''

''But the money!'' she protested.

''Charlotte, what are you doing? You've no sooner agreed to marry me and now that a problem crops up you're ruling me out? You're not even willing to give us a chance?''

''Are you?'' she countered. ''Do *you* think it will work?''

Her lack of trust in his love seemed a continuation of her hangup over the difference in their ages, which he had not been able to understand. It was the hint of a break in her voice that deflected his rising anger.

''Look, take it easy!'' he said. ''It's not the end of the world. So the situation will take some getting used to. Give it time, love. You said a little while ago that you were hungry. Why don't we put those steaks in the oven? It will be easier to talk about this after we eat something, won't it?''

Charlotte gave him an absolutely furious look. Pat her on the head, would he? Then she heard his chuckle.

''Did you hear me just now? I'm the one who's scolding you about not eating. Have you forgotten how you got on my back about going without lunch?''

"Oh!" she wailed then, and flew into his arms. He nuzzled her neck while she held him tightly. She smelled of flowers and herbs and he felt his love for her well in a tender flood. She was really on edge over this thing. So what if she was going to be a grandmother, he told himself recklessly. She was still his Charlotte.

"On second thought," he said, caressing her back with little circular motions, "let's leave the steaks out a little longer." He kissed her then, a deep kiss of quiet demand that sent a tingling message down through her body to the very core of her existence. It said, *This is important, too. You and I are important.* She surrendered to her need to be held close, and relaxed in his embrace.

When he raised his head, she saw the warm glow of love deep in his eyes. Her worries receded and her happiness swelled.

"Do you want me, Charlotte?" he asked in a husky voice.

"Yes, Brock, my love. Oh yes!"

Leaving the makings of their dinner on the kitchen counter, they walked down the hall to her bedroom, where he began slowly and sensuously to make love to her.

CHAPTER NINE

CHARLOTTE WAITED FOR WADE the next evening with some anxiety. There was no note saying he wouldn't be home for dinner, which usually meant he expected to join her. Tonight, she was unsure what it meant.

Theirs had been a close relationship since his father's death, and she found the estrangement from him painful. She didn't know how she was going to end it because the argument with him about getting married was still going on in her head. She knew it would be folly to bring it up again, but it would be difficult not to. How else could she convince him she was right?

She listened in vain for the sound of his van. But there was no sign of him and he didn't phone. After her solitary dinner, Charlotte lit a small fire in the fireplace and sat beside it in the living room, wondering where he was, carrying on an imaginary conversation with him.

About ten o'clock Brock telephoned to say good-night. "Are you in bed, sweetheart?"

"Not yet. Wade hasn't come in and—"

"Isn't he working tonight?"

"No. He'll be home soon. I want to talk to him."

"Go easy, love," Brock said. His voice softened. "I wish you were here, in my arms—like last night."

"So do I, darling."

"Good night, my love."

"I love you," she murmured.

Wade came in the back way about eleven o'clock. Charlotte knew he could see the lights were on in the living room, but he headed for the refrigerator without speaking.

"Wade?" she called out. "I didn't know you had a gig tonight."

"I didn't," he answered shortly. The refrigerator door banged shut.

She waited.

When he came into the room he had a piece of cake she had brought home in one big hand and a glass of milk in the other, but he glared at her. "I went to see Kate."

"You did?" Charlotte asked in quick apprehension. "What happened?"

His mouth tightened with anger. "Did you put her up to it?"

"What are you talking about?"

"Her aunt threw me out."

Charlotte's rush of intense anger at Estelle Drew brought the blood to her cheeks. How *dared* she! "Oh, Wade! That woman—that—"

"Barracuda," Wade supplied through gritted teeth. "She said you had lunch with her today. Why?"

"I thought we should talk," Charlotte said with a sigh. "Wade, I'm on your side, dear. I just think marriage is a bad idea for you and Kate right now."

"Well, you sure fixed me with Kate," he said bitterly. "She wouldn't even come out of her bedroom, and her aunt wasn't about to let me go back there without forcing me to knock her down so she could call the police and accuse me of being violent."

"Wade, I'm so sorry Kate feels the way she does."

"Are you?" he challenged her. "I'm going to marry Kate, Mom. I know Kate loves me, and she knows I intend

to raise my son. If she didn't know it before, she knows it
now," he said. "Her witchy aunt can't change any of that.
Neither can you, Mom."

He stalked down the hall to his room and slammed the
door shut behind him, while Charlotte tried to adjust to
being tossed into the dump with the "witchy" aunt. She
wondered just what kind of scene had taken place in Estelle's apartment. Whatever had happened, it had
strengthened Wade's resolve to marry Kate and made it
impossible for her to talk any sense into him tonight.

Sighing, she got up from her chair, closed the fire screen
and went to bed. She spent another sleepless night honing
arguments with which to make her son see how irresponsible his insistence on marriage was, especially if he truly
loved Kate and wanted the best for her and their unborn
child in the years ahead. But how was she going to make
him listen? He already knew all the reasons she could mus-
ter why it was important for him to finish school.

As usual, Wade was still sleeping when she was ready to
leave for work the next morning, but she left a note for him
on the refrigerator door that said: "Think!"

She went on her way to the clinic before she realized that
it was Wednesday, her half day—and the day of the luncheon date she had made with Dr. Ferdie's wife. It was too
late now to change it. She tried to put a brake on the helpless circling of her thoughts around those two children,
Wade and Kate, and turn them outward again.

She was not at her best, she thought that noon as she
drove along the coast to the restaurant they had chosen,
with literature on the goals and accomplishments of the local Heart Association tucked in her purse. She was afraid
that Dr. Ferdie was going to be disappointed in her.

The seafood establishment where he had made the reservation for her and his wife was an unimpressive but neat

gray-and-white building on the water's edge south of the airport. Once inside, her impression was one of light and space. On two sides, windows looked toward views of the Sound. Low planters containing green foliage divided the large dining room into more intimate areas.

Charlotte asked for Mrs. Ferdinand and was shown to a table beside a window where the doctor's attractive wife was sitting with a glass of the palest of pink wines at her place. Beyond her, Charlotte could see a white ferry making its way across the sparkling water toward the islands on the horizon.

"Am I late? I'm sorry."

Mrs. Ferdinand's smile was warm. "Hello, Charlotte. No, I'm early. Will you join me in a glass of wine?"

"Thanks, I'd love to."

"Do you want to try this white zinfandel? It's lovely."

Charlotte nodded her acceptance to the waiter, and seated herself across from Ellin Ferdinand. She was a woman who carried her years well. Charlotte knew that she and the doctor had three children, one married and two away at college in the East. Her hair was a pale blond because of the silver strands blended with it, but her eyes were the lively eyes of a youthful spirit.

"Ferdie said you liked seafood," she said, taking up a menu. "They make wonderful shrimp cocktails here. I suggest we start with those."

They ordered, and as they chatted over their wine, Charlotte found herself relaxing somewhat from the painful tensions that had ruined her sleep the past two nights. She felt more comfortable with the doctor's wife than she would have believed possible. The view beyond the window was one of leisurely activity, noiseless sailboats gliding at a distance, gulls swooping down to perch on the posts of a dock near the restaurant.

"How is your son, Charlotte? Isn't he in college this year? Ferdie has told me how hard he's working for his education."

Charlotte was not prepared for the genuine interest Ellin was showing. To her chagrin, tears flooded her eyes. "Yes, he's a freshman at the university," she managed to say before her voice broke.

Ellin looked devastated. "What did I say?" she exclaimed. "Is something wrong?"

"Please forgive me," Charlotte murmured, pulling a handkerchief out of her purse. "Yes, something's wrong, but I didn't mean to—I should have canceled my appointment with you, Mrs. Ferdinand, but I thought I could handle myself better than this."

"Nonsense, my dear. And call me Ellin, please. Is your son in some kind of trouble? Maybe the doctor and I can help."

"It's kind of you, but I don't really know how you could help. Anyway, I wanted to talk to you about something else—"

"Ferdie has always admired your son," Ellin said seriously. She leaned forward and put her hand on Charlotte's arm. "I've heard him say more than once what a good solid young man he is. If it will make you feel better to spill it out, Charlotte, I'm a good listener."

"It's an old story. His sixteen-year-old girlfriend is pregnant, and he wants to quit school and get married."

"Oh, dear," Ellin said, her expressive face showing her distress. "They're very young to marry, aren't they?"

In spite of her resolve to forget them for a few hours, Charlotte's worries about Wade and Kate spilled over. It was a relief to talk to another mother, and especially one as sympathetic as Ellin.

"The girl is very immature. She insists she doesn't want to get married, but she's as excited about having a baby as a kid with a new doll. I don't think she has any idea yet of what it will involve, or how it will change her life. And Wade is making all the noises of a young father—planning to quit school and find a full-time job so he can support his family. I'm heartbroken at the thought of his leaving college."

"So am I," Ellin said, immediately winning Charlotte's undying love. "I have a friend who teaches in high school. She's been telling me that teenage pregnancy, with or without marriage, is happening more often than we realize. It's sad to think of something like three million of these children having children of their own."

"I thought I married young," Charlotte confessed, "but I was nineteen and Wade's father was twenty-one."

Now I'm thinking of marrying again—a man who is tender and sweet but who may not be ready for this. But that was a private worry.

"And if that child also bears a child at fifteen," Ellin mused, continuing her line of thought, "I mean, if the pattern is repeated from generation to generation—do you realize that a woman can end up a *great-grandmother* in her forties!"

Charlotte flinched. "The prospect of becoming a grandmother is quite enough of a shock!"

Ellin laughed in sympathy, and some more of Charlotte's tension fell away. While they ate delicately buttered grilled sole and sipped their wine, they continued discussing teenage pregnancies in a general way as a social problem.

"The bottom line, according to my friend, is that many of these girls end up on welfare because they haven't been trained to earn a living," Ellin said. "And that includes the

ones who get married," she added, "because most of the
marriages end in divorce."

"I don't think either Wade or Kate will have to choose
welfare, and I'm afraid I can't think of them as statistics,"
Charlotte said. "Right now, I'm being made to feel like an
ogre standing in the way of Wade's freedom to conduct his
own life. One would think the whole situation was my
fault."

Ellin chuckled. "I know, my dear. I've been there."

By the time the waiter had returned for their dessert orders, Charlotte was able to look at her son's dilemma with
more objectivity. But the luncheon was almost over and she
had forgotten her purpose in coming! In fact, she was
finding it hard to believe that Dr. Ferdie had any difficulties with this warm and generous woman.

"I've burdened you with my worries," she said with remorse, "and I haven't even mentioned the favor I planned
to ask of you."

"Yes?" Ellin smiled so encouragingly that Charlotte felt
like an imposter.

But she produced the heart research literature from her
purse and handed it across the table. "I've been asked to
sound you out about volunteering for the heart-research
support auxiliary," she improvised. "They need more
workers, volunteers on whom they can depend to donate
regular hours. They need people who can type and keep
records and whom they can train to man their free blood-
pressure-check vans. . . ."

Ellin was regarding her thoughtfully. "Ferdie keeps urging me to become interested in some community work now
that the children are all away," she said, and Charlotte
wondered if his wife had seen through Dr. Ferdie's subter-
fuge in suggesting this luncheon.

"I'll look the material over, Charlotte, and thanks for thinking of me." She drank the last of her wine and added, "I'm thinking of other possibilities as well."

Charlotte had a sinking feeling that one possibility could be her husband's retirement. If Ellin guessed Dr. Ferdie had confided their personal problems to another woman, this luncheon could do more harm than good.

"I'm not a very good saleswoman for heart research, am I?" Charlotte said lightly. "I've talked of nothing but my own problem. But it's really helped. Thanks for letting me unload on you."

"I told you I was a good listener. In fact, our talk has given me some food for thought. We must do this again, Charlotte."

"I hope we can, Ellin."

They parted in the parking lot. Charlotte waved goodbye as the other woman drove off, gazed once more at the glittering blue Sound and its tranquil sailboats, then headed back toward town herself, depressed by the thought of Wade's estrangement. It was true that talking to Ellin had relieved some of her tension, but Wade's accusations still hurt. She feared that his resolve to marry was stronger than ever.

When she arrived home, she was sure of it. Her son had scrawled a defiant "THUNK!" in heavy black letters beneath her note on the refrigerator door.

BROCK CALLED LATE THAT EVENING, and she immediately accepted his offer to come over. For the second day in a row, Wade had not come home nor called to tell her where he was having dinner, and that was enough unlike his usual thoughtfulness to shake her.

When Brock came, he was carrying a sheaf of purple irises starred with white and yellow narcissi, and she exclaimed over them with pleasure. Taking the bouquet from him, she tilted her head and he framed her face with his hands while he kissed her.

"Feeling better about things tonight?"

"Not much," she confessed.

He looked at her with concern. She was calmer, certainly, than she had been when he last saw her, but the shadows under her clear eyes were evidence of her lack of sleep.

She took the flowers out to the kitchen to put them in water and he followed her. Taking a tall crystal vase out of a cupboard, she began arranging the irises in it, dropping a narcissus in here and there like a sparkle of dew among the green blade leaves. He watched her, taking pleasure in the graceful movements of her hands and arms and the subtle shifting of her breasts as she worked.

When she had finished, Charlotte made coffee and while it was brewing, carried the vase into the living room. Behind her, Brock said, "How do you feel about a June wedding?"

Immediately the many emotions that had broken her sleep for three nights began churning. She waited a long moment before replying, "I don't want to saddle you with debts, Brock."

"What kind of debts?"

She went back to the kitchen, where she busied herself getting down cups and saucers, setting out cream and sugar.

Brock had followed her again. His eyes fell on the note on the refrigerator door: "Think!" and below it, a bold "THUNK!" His look was quizzical.

He took the tray from her and carried it back to the living room. He waited until she was seated and then took the cup she poured and sat on the sofa at right angles to her chair and said firmly, "I want to set a date, sweetheart."

"Brock, listen to me. Before we can do that, there are things we have to discuss."

"About debts," he prompted her.

"A baby is expensive."

"I know that, love."

"And there's Wade's tuition. Kate's aunt probably won't help them if they marry.... I could take out a mortgage on this house—it's paid for—but it isn't large enough for five of us. And it isn't fair to ask you—"

He brushed that aside. "I thought you said the girl doesn't want to get married."

"She did say that, but Wade doesn't accept it. We can't count on it." She looked down into her cup. "He went to see Kate last night, and her aunt ordered him out. It only made him angry and more determined to go through with it."

He spread his hands. "Let it lie, Charlotte," he advised her. "The girl refused him. So he's not going to get married. Not yet, anyway. So why borrow trouble?"

"Brock, I know my son. He's determined. He's certain he's doing the right thing. He'll keep going back unless her aunt calls the police. And Kate won't stand up under that kind of pressure. She's as unpredictable as a spring breeze, anyway. They could elope at any time."

"So until it happens, why should we worry? We'll figure out how to live with a baby and pay for it when the time comes, okay?"

She had always liked his easy manner. But in her anxious state, it seemed more like irresponsibility. And she didn't quite believe him. She had seen the uncertainty flicker across his face when she had first mentioned Wade bringing Kate and the baby to live with them.

"That's all you're concerned about?" she demanded. She raised her hands to her head, which was beginning to ache. "Brock, I've spent every night thinking about this. I've been thinking about Wade, who's absolutely torn up over this. And about poor Kate who has no notion of what she's facing. But mostly I'm wondering what kind of life can this baby she's carrying look forward to, whether those children marry or not? And it's my grandchild!"

An edge crept into his voice. "But you don't really want it cluttering up Wade's life. Why don't you admit it?"

His blunt challenge threw a spotlight on the guilt she felt because she did resent, not the innocent unborn child, but the timing of its arrival.

"'It'?" she flung back at him. "'It'? Brock, whether we like it or not, a living human being has been conceived. Oh, I know, giving the baby a sex and an identity makes it become too painfully real to bear. But Brock, we can't just wish this baby away."

"Oh, love, love, I'm not wishing your grandchild away! I'm saying you've got to let go. Wade's no longer your little boy; he's a man."

"You think I'm being hysterical over this. But this could ruin his whole life. I'm so dreadfully afraid Wade will quit school—" Charlotte put down her cup and stood up. "You're hard, Brock," she said, almost in tears. "He needs my help."

"You can help Wade get his education, but you can't live his life for him." Brock set his own cup down and stood beside her. "You are one very mixed-up lady, and I do understand," he said tenderly. "But try to look at the facts. The girl has said no. If a man's girl won't marry him, well, that's her privilege and his problem. It's not yours. If he persists and persuades her to marry him in spite of their age and your opposition, well, that will be his problem, too. Not yours."

"That's so hard," she cried again.

"You've got to let go," he repeated, and reached for her.

When she took an involuntary step back, evading his embrace, a strange thing happened. It turned him off. As suddenly as that, his patience snapped, and the jealousy of her close ties with her son that he thought he had overcome early in their relationship returned, along with a surge of disappointment. Where had he lost the fine euphoric happiness with which he had driven through the streets to her house after she promised to marry him? She was obsessed with her son's happiness, not his.

And with this infant, who was not yet real to him.

"All right, Charlotte, sleep on it." He turned and started for the front door, then paused with a qualm of shame for his jealousy and a suspicion that he was being chauvinistic.

"I'll call you in a day or two," he promised.

She looked woefully after him, but this time she did not urge him to stay. Feeling a definite hurt, he left her house.

When Charlotte heard the engine of his automobile roar into life, she ran to the front door with the sudden conviction that she couldn't let him go like this. His abrupt departure had come so suddenly that she hadn't realized at first that he was angry.

Bewildered and remorseful, she was just in time to see his rear lights grow smaller in the light fog that had moved in from the Sound.

DRIVING BACK TO HIS APARTMENT, Brock recalled the clean, woodsy smell of Charlotte's hair, the silken softness of her skin and the misery in her eyes, and he regretted the way he had left her. Replaying the evening in his mind, he realized that beneath her apparent calm she had been anxiety-ridden when he arrived and not herself. Their sudden quarrel had probably been caused as much by her sleepless nights as by his reaction to her problem with her son.

It was nearly eleven, and there was little traffic on the streets. He drove automatically, wondering how Charlotte could accuse him of being hard. He thought he was just being realistic.

He had been the only child of a man who keenly valued his privacy. It had been a lonely house for a growing boy. There had been a time when he had wished fervently for brothers and sisters. But that was in the past. For years now, he had been living alone—coming and going at his own convenience, rising early or late, working as late as he chose. He didn't really know how he was going to adjust to the kind of family life Charlotte had pictured.

He admitted that he had taken comfort in his conviction that the situation wouldn't lead to marriage between Wade and his pregnant girlfriend. There were other solutions to their problem, even if they did marry as Charlotte feared.

But Brock decided that his response had shown little understanding of the travail Charlotte's son had brought her, and he resolved to call her as soon as he reached his apartment and apologize for his bluntness and apparent lack of sympathy.

His thoughts moved on to the other time he had blundered into a quarrel with Charlotte. He had been the one who was upset that evening. Wondering why it had so angered him when she had confessed a "maternal" feeling in her first attraction to him, he was surprised to find himself remembering a certain lady love of the Major's he had particularly disliked.

He could see her face plainly: a pretty, earnest young woman who had an annoying habit of cooing over him as if he were the Major's lapdog, as Brock had scornfully told a young friend. She had been one of a bevy of young women who had hoped to marry the Major after his divorce and had thought to get to him by mothering his lonely son.

Brock was assailed by a surge of suffocating anger and resentment—unmistakably a replay of those painful confused adolescent emotions he had struggled with after his mother left them.

As an adult, he had not consciously realized before just how unhappy and resentful he had been in those days. Charlotte had managed to breach the armor he had built over that old wound. He was a little frightened by this proof of how deep his love for her ran. It was sinking deeper and deeper, dredging up layers of long-buried emotions he had deliberately forgotten. It terrified him that she could do this to him. What if he lost her?

The telephone was ringing when he unlocked his apartment door, and he had an uncanny intuition that it had been ringing for several minutes. A certain heaviness of guilt in his chest began to lift with the thought that Charlotte, too, was already regretting their quarrel. He felt thankful for her forgiving love, and remorseful that he had let her concern for her son get to him.

He crossed the room and picked up the instrument. "Hello?"

The words that came without preamble across the wires to his ear were not in Charlotte's soft voice. He recognized the unmistakable nasal tones of the Major's landlady, the lady of the pink hair rollers.

"Thank God I've reached you, Mr. Morley. Your father fell down the stairs trying to hold back that big ugly dog of his. I've called an ambulance and sent him to the hospital."

CHAPTER TEN

IT TOOK BROCK four hours to drive to Portland. As he sped along the dark freeway, his tires singing on the wet pavement, he was assailed by memories of his father, a lonely, punctilious man who had raised him with disciplined love while maintaining a stiffly guarded privacy.

Curious, he thought, how certain he had been of the Major's love, in spite of the distance there had always been between them. The few times he could remember being lifted in his father's arms were related to illnesses or childhood hurts. His father had never embraced him. As a consequence he could recall vividly a few times when in extreme emotion, his father had laid a hand on his shoulder and gripped it. One was when he had told him his mother was not coming home, ever again.

"Why, Dad? Why did she go?" he had demanded.

"That's her business," the Major had said gruffly. And that had been his last word on the subject.

Pictures flashed between him and the rythmically moving windshield wipers and the rising and then waning lights of passing cars: a flash of memory from their vacation in Greece when the Major had taken him up the Acropolis and told him the history of the Parthenon. There had been a woman there, an American tourist.

There had been a woman tourist when his father had taken him to see the Michelangelo frescoes in the Sistine chapel in Rome. They were always encountering women—

the Major had cut a dashing figure, especially in his uniform. But there was always a hint of contempt under the cloak of charm he had worn for them.

He wondered if his father was going to die.

It was three in the morning when Brock entered Portland in a light misty rain that hid Mount Saint Helens and most of the city from his view. He drove through quiet, deserted streets to the hospital where Mrs. Carnady had said his father had been taken. An ambulance turned into the emergency entrance, siren wailing, while Brock was making his way in from his parked car, and he imagined the Major lying broken and still on the stretcher two attendants removed from it. With a feeling of dread, he pushed through the glass doors into the lobby.

His father was still in surgery, the impersonally efficient woman behind the information desk told Brock. "There's a waiting room up there. Third floor."

Brock thanked her and found the elevators. He had to wait another hour in a nearly deserted lounge before he was able to talk to the Major's doctor, a brusque but kind young man with gray pockets of fatigue under his eyes.

"Your father took a bad fall. He has fractures in both legs, compound in the right one. There were some injuries to the arterial system that needed immediate attention."

"*Both* legs?"

"Besides a cracked rib or two, and a broken wrist. Unfortunately, he hung on to the dog's leash instead of letting go."

Brock experienced an unsettling dizziness at this revelation of just how serious was the damage the Major had suffered.

"An old man's bones are fragile," the doctor said. "There were certain tests we had to make before we could complete the repair work. So he's had a night of it. A remarkable man, your father. There was no concussion. He was conscious and able to sign his release for surgery."

Brock took a deep breath and asked, "Will he be disabled?"

"It's too early to make predictions, but if all goes well and there are no complications, I see no reason why he won't walk again. It will be a long, slow convalescence. Casts for several months and then physical therapy."

Brock's worst fears were relieved by the doctor's matter-of-fact attitude. But the Major in casts, plural, was a daunting prospect. "Can I see him?"

"He'll be in the recovery room until he wakes up. I'd like him to know you're here, but make it brief."

Brock thanked him and went to find the recovery room. Through its glass doors he could see several gurneys with IV stands attached, and nurses moving among them checking the patients, who were of various ages and both sexes. He waited outside.

Several times a gurney was moved out through the doors and down the hall to a large service elevator. He waited, lounging against the wall, until two young nurses wheeled the Major out. His father's skin was almost as white as his beard, but his eyes were open and directed toward the ceiling. The bulk under the light cover revealed his casts. One extended from his ankle to his hip. There was also a cast on one forearm. Brock breathed thanks to whatever fate had made the Major attempt to bring Quarters to heel with his left hand.

Seeing his father lying helpless and looking old and thin inside his bulky casts was a more traumatic experience than he had anticipated. "Hello, sir," Brock said, not surprised at the huskiness of his voice because his throat had almost closed up.

One of the nurses smiled at him, and they paused for a moment to let the Major turn and focus his eyes.

"Brock..." It was a dry whisper. The pale blue eyes acknowledged him gratefully, then closed again.

Shaken, Brock asked, "Where are you taking him?"

"Second floor. Orthopedic surgery ward. Ask at the nurses' station."

He thanked her and walked beside the gurney until it was swallowed by the elevator.

He found his own way to the second floor where a crisply starched young woman consulted her list and said, "They took Mr. Morley to the intensive care unit. Down that way. Through those doors."

Intensive Care was a semicircular unit arranged around a nurses' station, so that the nurse on duty could look into each cubicle and keep watch on a half-dozen seriously ill patients. Curtains separated the heads of the beds from their close neighbors. Brock looked in at his father's pale form. A sheet was pulled up to just under his arms, which lay exposed. An IV tube was hooked up to the arm that was not in a cast. Another thin tube connected an oxygen tank to his nose, and the suction cups of monitors on his chest were visible above the cover.

He lay so still.

"You can stay for just one minute," the nurse warned Brock as she admitted him to the cubicle that was barely wider than the Major's bed. "He's heavily sedated."

Brock leaned over the inert figure. "Dad? Sir?"

His father's eyes opened. Recognition came slowly, and with it a cloud of anxiety. "Quarters," he whispered.

"Right." Brock understood immediately. That old gal with the cowardly cat was fully capable of sending Quarters to the pound. She certainly couldn't be counted on to feed him. "I'll take care of Quarters immediately," he promised.

His father's eyes closed.

"Your minute's up," the nurse said pleasantly.

Brock touched the pale, veined hand lying on the coverlet and left.

Outside the hospital he discovered, to his vague surprise, that the sky was lightening with dawn. The rain had stopped and the mountains formed a dark silhouette on the horizon behind the skyscrapers of downtown, except for Mount Saint Helens, which was blanketed with snow.

He was beginning to feel his lack of sleep as he drove to the Major's apartment building. He rang Mrs. Carnady's bell, waited three minutes, then rang it again. Finally she came to the door in a shapeless blue bathrobe with the familiar pink rollers in her hair. She kept the chain on the door and was ready to bite his head off before she recognized him. Her expression softened noticeably.

"I've just come from the hospital, Mrs. Carnady," he said. "Thank you for acting so quickly."

She took the chain off the door and opened it a little wider. "How is Major Morley?"

"He's had emergency surgery. Both legs and one arm are in casts."

"Poor man." She looked genuinely sorry and launched into a dramatic account of hearing the terrifying sounds of a tumble down a whole flight of stairs and the crazed barking of the frightened dog.

"Where is the dog now, Mrs. Carnady? Up in my father's apartment?"

"You crazy?" she demanded. "We had to call the animal shelter to come and get the beast before the ambulance team could get near your father with their stretcher."

Brock shook his head. "Dogs can be very protective. It will kill my father if anything's happened to that dog! Can you give me the address of the shelter you called? I'll have to go and get him."

"Where you gonna take him?" she asked suspiciously.

"I'll be staying here for a few days—"

"Not with that dog, you won't!"

Brock smiled at her. "Mrs. Carnady, my father won't be able to negotiate those stairs for months, maybe never again. So he'll be giving up his lease when he leaves the hospital. But until I can make other arrangements for my father, the dog and I will occupy his apartment." He sounded like his father, he thought. Seeing her hardening expression, he added, "Or do you want to try to evict a sick man who was injured on your property?"

She bristled. "It was the damn dog that pulled him down. *I'm* not responsible!"

"Of course not—if you say so, Mrs. Carnady. But I've noticed that stair carpet is worn very smooth."

"Well!" she said, and glared at him while he watched her quickly think that one over. He had learned more than a few things from the old man.

"Well, okay," she relented, "but only until you find a home for that mutt."

Brock climbed the stairs, trying not to visualize the Major's crumpled body lying at their foot with a frightened Quarters barking over him. He unlocked the apartment with his key and looked at his watch. It was still too early to call anyone. He made a mental note of the calls he must make when the day got rolling: first to the animal shelter to describe Quarters and guarantee the cost of his keep until he could pick the dog up; next to his supervisor in Seattle to request a few weeks off. And Charlotte.

Charlotte. Just the syllables of her name could pierce his heart, but now it was not with desire but with a dagger of anticipated pain as he had a flash of insight into what his father's accident could do to their plans to marry.

But he was too exhausted to examine the consequences. He walked into his father's bedroom, yanking off his tie as he went, and fell on the bed. Almost immediately he was asleep.

He wakened several hours later, a little disoriented to find himself lying fully dressed on his father's bed, surrounded by pictures of himself growing up on military bases all around the world, sometimes alone, sometimes standing at attention beside the Major. He saw the familiar framed certificate of his father's commission as second lieutenant among them. But a mental picture of his father, as pale as the plaster casts on his body, leaped to Brock's mind, and his next thought was, *Quarters!* He got off the bed and went into the kitchen to brew some coffee.

When it was made, he took his cup of coffee into the living room, looking around the apartment as he drank it. His gaze moved over the Japanese samurai sword that was his father's most prized possession, his antique guns and the old furniture, some of it picked up in England and some of it in Hong Kong. It would all have to be moved, perhaps put in storage until the Major had recovered enough so that they would know how well he would be able to manage.

Brock foresaw that he was going to have his hands full in the near future. He cringed at the thought of hiring someone to take care of the Major in the crucial months after his release from the hospital. If he couldn't get along with a landlady, what chance was there of finding a practical nurse who would take his verbal abuse?

What was the answer? Move the Major to another apartment here and try to find a nurse, or take him to Seattle where he could at least oversee his care? He felt the strongest urge to talk to Charlotte. He looked at the telephone. She would be at work now. He remembered how near hysteria she had been the night after she had learned her son's girlfriend was pregnant, and decided he could wait to tell her about his father's injuries. She had a heart full of her own problems right now.

He would call her later, after he had a chance to think things through. He didn't want to believe yet that they would have to postpone making wedding plans.

He called his supervisor at Echo, then picked up his keys and went down to his car and drove to the animal shelter. There he picked up Quarters, who was frantic with joy to see him, and continued on to the hospital. He found the Major fighting for breath, with two doctors and two nurses trying to save him. He did not go back to the apartment until far too late to make any more calls.

THE SKY HAD FALLEN IN for Charlotte, but life went on as if Brock had not just walked out of her life.

He had left her Wednesday night saying, "I'll call you in a day or two," and she hadn't heard from him again. She knew he had been angry with her. She had felt the abrupt withdrawal expressed by his turning away from her and the effort with which he had pulled himself up to say he would call. Perhaps he had intended to, then.

When the weekend came, with no word from him, she tried to reach him. But there was no answer at his apartment. On Monday she called his number at Echo from the clinic, and was told that Morley was taking a few weeks off. She wondered why he was taking time off now, when he had spoken of taking a vacation for their honeymoon. After that, she was sunk in misery.

What made it harder was her estrangement from Wade. She never saw him or knew exactly where he was. Their routine was pretty much the same. Charlotte got up and went to the clinic, leaving notes for Wade on the refrigerator door, and he went out, she assumed to school—and she knew to the radio station, because she could tune in to his program—leaving polite little notes for her saying he wouldn't be home for dinner. She had no opportunity to talk with him, and she felt painfully excluded. She had no idea whether or not he was seeing Kate.

As the days passed, she was forced to conclude that the picture she had drawn for Brock of their life together if Wade married Kate had been too much for a confirmed bachelor to accept.

The only bright spot in that dark two weeks was little Jeddy Flagler's recovery from heart surgery to correct a valve that had been faulty from birth. When she saw him on his postsurgery examination, he had already gained some color in his skin and his big eyes glowed. His simple faith had been rewarded—he was going to be able to join his friends at school after a few weeks of rest, and his parents and Dr. Ferdie were almost equally happy for him.

It was shortly after that day when she had taken a computer picture of Jeddy's repaired five-year-old heart that she picked up the ringing telephone one evening and heard a familiar voice.

"Hello, Charlotte."

"Brock!" She almost choked over his name. She was torn between anger at his neglect and relief at hearing from him at last—and had a tearing hunger to hear more. So many words rushed to her tongue and tangled there that all she could get out was, "I . . . I've missed you!"

"I've missed you, too." His voice was deep with truth, and she believed him.

She wanted to shout, *Why? Why?* But she said, "Where are you? Have you been very angry with me?"

"Oh, love, I'm sorry!" he said remorsefully. "I'm in Portland, and I wish you were with me right now. There was an accident—" He told her about his father's fall and how he had learned of it the night he left her house.

Appalled, Charlotte asked, "How is he? Was it very bad?"

"Pretty bad. He's like a mummy encased in plaster. An infection developed after surgery and it was touch and go for a few days. That's the main reason I haven't called, sweetheart. He's stable now, on the mend."

"I'm so glad, Brock." And guilty, too, because she had doubted his love.

But her immense relief at hearing from him was short-lived. He said hesitantly, "I'll be staying down here for a while. I've asked for my vacation time."

The vacation he was going to use for their Hawaiian honeymoon. Her heart sank, and she began to wonder about the other reasons he'd implied he had for not calling.

"I'm packing the Major's things. It will be a long time, if ever, before he'll be able to climb a flight of stairs. So I have to move him before he's released from the hospital."

"Where will he go?"

He paused for so long that a chill came over her. When she began to wonder if he was still on the line, he said, "It depends. He'll be in a convalescent hospital for a while. After that he may need help for a long time to come, Charlotte."

What did he mean? What was he planning? "That's so sad," she managed. "How... how long will you be in Portland?"

"It's hard to tell. What about Wade's problem, darling? What are those two going to do?"

"Wade and I are not talking right now," she said painfully. "I think Kate is still insisting she won't marry him. He's very unhappy."

"Well..." Brock's voice died away.

She waited, but he had no comforting words for her.

"I'll probably be looking for another apartment in Seattle when I leave here," he said at last. "I may have to have the Major with me. I doubt if I can find a nurse who would put up with him."

"Oh," she answered lamely. She drew in a large gulp of air, realizing she had been holding her breath. At least he was coming back to Seattle. But her thoughts were whirling around visions of a household that included a cantankerous old man Brock had not wanted her to meet until after they were safely married.

As if he could read her thoughts, he said, "Our prospects for an early marriage seem to be pretty slim right now, don't they? Think we'll make it next year?"

A whole year? Only a short time ago he had been urging her to set a date in June. Did he want to back out? Her life seemed to be suddenly flying apart, instead of going down the happy road that had stretched ahead of them when she promised to marry Brock. She tried to keep her voice steady. "We... we do have a lot of problems to work out, don't we?"

"Yeah." He sounded discouraged.

For a moment she could find nothing to say. At last she said, "Brock, I'm so sorry about your father."

"Thanks. Well, love I'll call again."

He could have called before. He could have spared her those two unhappy weeks of ignorance. After she hung up

she was very alone in the house. There was no one to see her
cry.

In Portland Brock went wearily back to his exploration
of his father's strongbox. He was looking for Medicare
supplement insurance papers, because the hospital had
asked about it. The Major's bills for doctors and drugs and
hospital care were mounting rapidly. His father was still too
weak to be consulted about such things, but Brock was well
enough acquainted with military regs to know that retirees
were transferred to Medicare from free military medical
care when they reached sixty-five.

Searching for medical insurance policies was his excuse.
Scarcely admitting it to himself, and ignorant of the sig-
nificance of what he was doing, Brock was also looking for
a picture of his mother, for letters from her, for anything
the Major might have saved. Over the years he had accepted the fact that he was not allowed to remember even
what his mother looked like, but Charlotte's shock that he
had no pictures had stirred up old hurts. The need for his
father's insurance policies offered an opportunity, which he
took. But so far he had found nothing.

The Major's papers were neat and in businesslike order.
There was a will lying in an unsealed envelope in the
strongbox. Brock scanned it, but his mother was not even
mentioned by name. On the Major's death everything he
owned was bequeathed to his "only offspring, legitimate or
illegitimate, Brock Morley." The woman named Elizabeth
Rexler Morley—who, according to Brock's birth certificate, had borne him—might never have existed.

It was a long time ago, and Brock told himself he had
come to terms with his mother's departure well before this.
But it aroused his curiosity to find her twelve-year presence in his life so completely erased by his father. It was as

if she had stepped off the edge of the world the day she left their apartment in Frankfurt. He found it hard to believe that his mother had never even inquired about him after she left.

His father must have cared a great deal for her, Brock thought. He must have loved Elizabeth Rexler the way he loved Charlotte.

But what had Elizabeth Rexler Morley felt for her husband? Had she loved him not enough—or too much?

Brock tried in vain to shake off the depression that had gripped him. He was too exhausted after these past trying days to think straight. At least he was now sure that his father would live, for at this point he was sure of nothing else.

CHAPTER ELEVEN

CHARLOTTE HUNG UP THE TELEPHONE and laid her head on her arms on the kitchen counter, surrendering briefly to her emotions. She felt immense relief at knowing Brock was all right and that he missed her, and an aching sympathy with his obvious concern for his father—the father she hadn't met but with whom she sensed Brock had a curious but apparently close relationship.

But his words, "Think we'll make it next year?" tolled like a sad bell in her head. His father's accident was too much, she thought. She saw, more clearly than ever before, that a marriage was not just between two people, it inevitably involved others who also had claims on them. And that was the way life was. But it was too much.

She raised her head and saw Wade's note on the refrigerator.

It was different from the others he had been leaving over the past two weeks. Like most of them it said, "Home late." But this time he had signed it with a small round face with three dots for eyes and nose, and a sad little drooping mouth, like a smile turned upside down.

Charlotte laughed through her tears. They had not signed their notes that way since Wade was thirteen. The face had almost always worn a happy smile in those days. But it had also been a way of communicating their feelings when things were bad. She added a little note to his before going to bed, drawing an even sadder face and scribbling: "Me, too."

He was still sleeping when she left for the clinic the next morning, but that night when she came home he was on the telephone. She paused in the doorway, because the tone of his voice told her he must be talking to Kate, and his pleading made her cringe for him.

"Well, sure you're going to be busy with all that stuff," she heard him say uncomfortably, "but I could . . . Look, if you're going in the evening . . ."

They were arguing.

"But, Katie, if I could take the class with you, I could help you. . . . I *want* to!" It sounded as if he were trying to interrupt the flow of Kate's raised voice coming thinly through the receiver.

"Look, Kate," he said hotly, "I schedule my own gigs. I won't accept one on those nights!"

Charlotte slammed the door behind her to let him know she was home. By the time she reached the kitchen he had hung up the phone, but he hadn't had time to erase the hurt and anger from his face. She put her purse on the counter beside his books. He was still going to classes, she thought with relief.

"Hi, honey," she said. She dropped her sack of groceries on the counter, and began taking out the bread, the carton of milk, the plastic bags of vegetables. Wade lounged against the counter, watching her, trying to be casual. When she brought out the package wrapped in butcher's paper, he said in a voice still roughened by emotion, "Uh, what's for dinner?"

"Lamb chops."

"Got one for me?"

She smiled at him, warmth flooding her heart. "How about two?"

Wade hesitated. "Did you buy them for your guy?"

"Nope. Hadn't you noticed? He isn't coming around much these days."

A look of shared misery flashed between them. "I'm . . . sorry, Mom."

She held out her arms. He took two long steps toward her. For a moment they clung to each other, wordlessly expressing their love and their relief at ending the painful strain of their disagreement.

When he let her go, he warned, "I'm not giving up on Kate, Mom. Sooner or later, we're going to be married so I can raise my son. But I've decided not to crowd her."

"Very wise. How is Kate?"

"She's into something she calls natural childbirth, something about doing breathing exercises and stuff like that, but she doesn't want me to go with her. She says her aunt's going to be her birth coach." There was such pain in his voice that Charlotte didn't trust herself to speak.

She patted his arm and went to put the meat and the milk in the refrigerator. Tonight she would listen, she resolved. Just listen and be thankful that the lines of communication were reopening.

"Why isn't Morley coming around?" he asked after a moment.

"He's out of town." Charlotte told him about Brock's father.

He listened without interrupting and commented, "That's tough."

Charlotte went into her bedroom to change from her suit. Before she returned to the kitchen to start dinner, she heard Wade in the bathroom, whistling as he washed up. His father had whistled in just that tuneless way.

After they had eaten, he began returning some calls that were waiting on the answering machine and making playing dates for later in the month. Things were almost back to normal except for the new note of maturity Charlotte heard in his businesslike tones. Kate was not the only one this baby was going to force to grow up fast.

She knew Wade too well to assume that he had turned his back on what he saw as his responsibilities as a prospective father. As he had said, he was giving Kate some room and waiting for his moment. She felt a certain pride in this son she had raised alone and was thankful he had been given to her to share her years of widowhood.

Best of all, he was not yet quitting school. She was happy about that. But Brock, her love, seemed a million miles away in Portland with his own family priorities, and she missed him with an ache that wouldn't go away.

AT THE CLINIC ONE MORNING, in the middle of a diagnostic discussion Charlotte was having with Dr. Ferdie about one of her tests, he said unexpectedly, "By the way, Ellin has never mentioned heart research to me."

"Oh?" Charlotte said guiltily. "I guess I didn't do a very good job of selling her on volunteer work."

"Oh, I don't know. She hasn't mentioned retirement to me lately, either. And she has been volunteering, but in a different project. It's a strange thing—all of a sudden she's upset about the number of high-school girls who are getting pregnant these days. Do you know anything about that, Charlotte?"

"I'm learning," Charlotte said dryly.

He gave her a sharp look, but apparently thought better of asking questions. "At least she's stopped haranguing me about taking it easy so we can travel. I don't have the slightest interest in traipsing through Italy's painted churches with her."

The remark was so typical of his single-minded devotion to his profession that Charlotte couldn't help laughing. "I thought not."

He grinned sheepishly, and they returned to the subject of her test. Later that day, when she had a few minutes free because her patient was late, she telephoned Ellin Ferdinand.

"You gave me a push in an entirely new direction, Charlotte," the doctor's wife admitted. "Thinking of your son's dilemma and what was ahead of his girlfriend led me to look into community agencies that are trying to help those teenagers who get pregnant too soon. Often it's through a lack of knowledge of their own bodies or because they don't understand the new emotions they experience at that age."

"That age is rough for boys, too. I remember thinking it must be easier to raise a daughter." Charlotte shook her head, trying to imagine her feelings if Kate were hers.

"Girls that inexperienced are ill-equipped to raise a child," Ellin said sadly. "I'm devoting some time each week to a workshop at the hospital that tries to prepare pregnant teenagers not only for their delivery but for motherhood."

"That sounds worthwhile," Charlotte said. "I'd like to know more about it."

"I'm simply soaking up information for you!" Ellin said in her enthusiastic way. "Let's lunch again, Charlotte. I'm dying to tell you some of the things I've learned."

They made a date, and Charlotte went back to work, pleased that Ellin sounded content to have Dr. Ferdie continue working for a while longer.

BROCK'S DAY WAS LIKE all the others since the Major had been moved out of intensive care: a morning run with

Quarters, a couple of hours after breakfast spent in going through his father's papers—he had finally found his supplemental health-insurance policies—a visit to the hospital, another walk with Quarters.

Then an afternoon of packing boxes and another visit to the hospital, stopping somewhere for an early dinner on the way back to the apartment. And then a final walk and more packing until he was tired enough to sleep with a dog used to curling up on the Major's feet.

He was working against time. He had to get back to Seattle if he wanted to keep his position with Echo. But he had to be patient until his father was well enough to be moved to a convalescent hospital where he could stay until his casts were removed.

The Major was better off financially than Brock had been led to believe. But his father had always been close-mouthed about his affairs, so Brock wasn't surprised. After his retirement from the army, the Major had joined an investment firm as a customers' representative. Apparently he had made some profitable investments of his own. Brock found some bills to be paid and some letters to be answered, took care of the things he could and laid aside papers that must await the time when his father could help him attend to them.

As he worked, he kept looking for a picture of his mother, but the Major had obviously kept no pictures of anyone except those of the boy Brock had been, and they were becoming an embarrassment, grinning back at him from every room in the apartment. He had never before realized how many there were. Brock began to feel the weight of his prickly father's undemonstrative devotion.

As the Major began to regain some strength he became a troublesome patient. His doctor insisted on getting him on his feet twice a day, a difficult task for the nurses who had to help him bear the weight of his casts. The only weapon the Major had was his tongue and he used it so vituperatively that he had one little nurse in tears. The only one who ever bested him was a feisty black woman, a nurse's aide, who could match his salty language, insult for insult.

"Callin' me names don't scare me, you old rascal," she told him with a sunny smile. "You nothin' but a bag o' broken bones. I could throw you over my shoulder and toss you out that door if you riled me. But you don't rile me that much."

She was a large woman, probably big enough to carry out her threat, Brock thought. When he complimented her on the way she handled his father, she laughed. "Oh, I know it's nothin' personal. Your father's just mad at the world 'cause he's so helpless."

She was the perfect nurse for him, but when Brock approached her about taking full-time care of the Major when he was released from the hospital, she said emphatically, "No, sir, not for a winnin' lottery ticket could I be talked into doin' that! I can take a patient like your father because I know he'll be leavin'. Besides, I've got other patients who're nice to me. I'd be crazy to go out of here with him and give him a full-time punchin' bag to work on."

Reluctantly Brock decided that he would have to take the Major to Seattle when he was able to travel. Otherwise he would be driving back to Portland to replace the nurses his father badgered into quitting. He might even have to keep the old man with him until he recovered sufficiently to take care of himself. Would that time ever come again? Brock found it very painful to think of the Major dependent on anyone.

That night he dreamed he held Charlotte in his arms while they slept and he woke up swollen with desire and even hungrier to hear her voice. He looked at his watch and picked up the telephone beside the Major's bed. One ring, and Charlotte's low questioning voice said, "Hello?"

Immediately he could picture her, clad in her white robe, perhaps, with her golden brown hair falling loose on her shoulders the way it did when he took her to bed. He imagined her having a lonely breakfast at her kitchen counter and instantly picking up the telephone at her elbow so it wouldn't waken her sleeping son.

"I love you," he said, and heard her draw in her breath.

"Brock! Where are you?"

"I'm still in Portland, love, missing you like hell."

"I miss you, too, darling. How is your father?"

"Ill-tempered and wanting to tear off his casts. I guess that means he's getting better. They'll soon move him to a convalescent hospital, and then I'll come home."

He heard another soft intake of breath, but before she could say anything, he went on, "I'll be looking for a larger apartment so I can bring the Major home with me when the casts come off. I'm working night and day to get his stuff ready to move or go into storage. In my spare time I'm filling out his insurance forms and walking his dog."

She was silent for a moment. "I see," she finally said. "So your father's going to be living with you?"

"Yes. It won't be easy, but I owe him that."

"Of course." He had warned her it might happen.

Brock thought she sounded remote, and he knew she had instantly grasped the change that meant in their plans to marry. She must know why he was no longer able to urge her to marry him as soon as possible. How could he ask her to take in an old misogynist like the Major, with his tart tongue and gleeful insults?

As soon as he had that thought, he felt such an overwhelming sense of loss that he knew he could not live without her. "How are you, sweetheart?" he asked softly. "How are things there?"

"About the same."

"God, I miss you! What about Wade?"

"He's still in school, and that's a relief. Kate won't even see him."

Then the marriage she opposed was still just a threat hanging over her head. But he heard the note of anxiety in her voice. Thoughts of the expected grandchild were still weighing on her. "Give it time, love."

And give me time, he prayed silently. Surely, with time, they could sort out something.

"I don't have much choice, do I?" Her laugh was sad, with a bitterness that hurt.

He wanted to beg, *Don't stop loving me*. But what right did he have to ask her to wait? The Major could be dependent on him for years to come!

THE EVENINGS WERE LONELY with Brock away, and Charlotte was doing a good deal of thinking about her expected grandchild. For one thing, it kept her from dwelling on the problem that was keeping Brock away and the growing worry of his long silences, which could not be entirely explained by his father's accident. He had sounded lonely and loving when he phoned, but that had been a week ago. No matter how busy he was, there had to be moments when he could have phoned her. Was he falling out of love with her?

That was a possibility she couldn't face. So she pushed it out of her mind and thought about the child growing in Kate's womb, and worried about Kate. Since Wade was no longer seeing her, Charlotte had no way of knowing whether the girl was exercising and eating proper foods, whether or not she smoked or drank or took other substances that would harm the baby.

She was fairly certain that Kate was innocent of such destructive habits, but she knew that like Wade and most of his friends, Kate was a latchkey student with a great deal of freedom. She, too, had taken many of her meals at fast-food outlets and was probably overly fond of sweets. Her baby deserved better nutrition.

The things Charlotte learned from Ellin Ferdinand during their second luncheon date, about what she saw being taught in the hospital workshop, only alarmed her further. She didn't think Kate was getting such information.

"The girls learn that alcohol and even coffee can cause birth defects," Ellin told her over a delicious dish of baked flounder at her favorite seafood restaurant on the Sound. "The nutritionist on the hospital staff tells them how much weight they can gain and about the difficulties being overweight can cause in the delivery room. She gives them nutritious diet plans. A nurse then tells them about the changes taking place in their bodies, the hormones and all, and shows them a film of an actual birth. Charlotte, you could have heard a butterfly's wings in the room during that film! And afterward, so many questions from the girls!"

It was that conversation that prompted Charlotte, after much thought, to call Kate on her next half-day Wednesday, at a time when she knew Estelle Drew would still be at work. Luckily she caught the girl just as she arrived home from school.

"What do you want, Mrs. Emlyn?" Kate asked politely enough, but with a faint tone of suspicion.

"Just to know how you're feeling, and if your doctor says everything is going well. I'm truly interested, Kate, and since you and Wade have disagreed, he can't tell me anything."

"I'm okay." Her laconic tone was not encouraging, but she didn't hang up. When Charlotte let the small silence grow, Kate offered, "I'm taking natural childbirth classes."

"I'm glad, Kate." She resisted the impulse to tell her she'd had Wade in natural childbirth. "I guess that puts you in touch with other young women who are having babies?"

"Yeah. I'm in a special class for teenage mothers. I'm in a continuation class at school now, too."

Somewhat reassured that Estelle Drew was looking after her niece, Charlotte prodded, "Is there anything you need, Kate?"

"My aunt gets me everything I need."

"I heard from a friend about an organization that provides a free workshop to young women your age who are having their first babies. It's a program about nutrition and birth and baby care—"

"At one of the hospitals? Yeah, I've heard about that, but it's in the daytime."

"Oh, you do know about it . . . ? Is there any way I can help you?"

After a brief hesitation, Kate said, "Well, as a matter of fact—but you're working, too, aren't you, Mrs. Emlyn? Like my aunt?"

"It's my afternoon off. What can I do?"

"I need a ride. I have an appointment at the lab at four, and my aunt can't take off." Kate paused. "I could call a taxi, but . . ."

Charlotte looked at her watch. She just had time to make it. "I'll be right over."

When she rang the bell above the mail slot, Kate answered through the intercom, "Mrs. Emlyn? Wait right there. I'm coming down."

She must have run down the stairs, Charlotte guessed, when Kate burst through the door a few minutes later, her cheeks and eyes glowing with health. Charlotte looked at her in pleased surprise, immediately dropping her gaze to Kate's waistline.

Kate didn't miss the look. "Not many people notice yet," she bragged, "but I have to fasten my skirts with a safety pin. Aunt Stelle and I are going shopping for maternity clothes next weekend."

"Already?" Charlotte said lamely.

"Well, I'm close to four and a half months. I didn't tell anybody but Wade, and I didn't show."

Charlotte forced herself to remember that this was reality. In just a few short months this baby would be a real person whose very existence would be in Kate's inexperienced hands. It was still hard to believe.

As they walked to the car, Charlotte noticed the young girl's natural quick grace and the way her eyes darted about, taking notice of everything happening in the neighborhood. She waved to a woman who looked up from the flower bed she was working in across the street, and gave the postman just entering her walk a bright smile. He responded with a cheery, "Afternoon, Miss Kate!" As she climbed into the passenger seat of Charlotte's car, her eyes followed a small terrier who trotted along, nose to the sidewalk.

"I wonder if that dog's lost."

"He looks very businesslike," Charlotte said. "I think he knows where he's going."

"Yeah, I guess."

Keeping her tone carefully neutral, Charlotte asked, "Who is your doctor?"

Kate turned bright eyes to her. "Dr. Packard. He's great. Do you know him?"

"No. Most of the doctors I know are cardiologists."

"That's right, you work on Pill Hill, don't you, Mrs. Emlyn?"

Charlotte grinned. "Where did you hear that? I thought it was only the hospital employees who talk about Pill Hill."

"Oh, Wade tells everybody that's where you work."

Charlotte looked at Kate closely as she spoke Wade's name, but there wasn't a hint of any emotion in the bright young face. A resentment she could not control built in her because she knew how far from casual Wade was about this butterfly of a girl.

Kate directed her to the building that held both Dr. Packard's office and the laboratory where she was scheduled for some routine tests. It was in the area where Charlotte worked, where at least five hospitals and clinics were clustered near the same intersection. She asked Kate when her baby was due and what her doctor recommended and listened attentively to Kate's nonchalant replies. After a few minutes Kate, sensing her listener's genuine interest, began letting her enthusiasm bubble up.

It was soon apparent that she was totally engrossed in the experience of having a baby. "I've picked the hospital," she confided. "A friend of mine had her baby there and it's really neat. They've got a new maternity ward, and it's like checking into a fancy hotel. Fabulous rooms with wallpaper and carpeting and a color TV. There's a table and chairs by the window where the champagne dinner for the new mother and her visitors is served. That's after the delivery, of course."

Inevitably Charlotte thought of the months when she was carrying Wade, and her intense interest in every change she noticed in her body. She and Garth had been so happy!

But as Kate chattered on, Charlotte was reminded of a child playing house, pouring tea for her little friends and gravely discussing the childhood diseases of her dolls. She tried hard not to let Kate see how the girl's naive pleasure in her condition was affecting her—because this little girl's fantasy didn't include a husband who would return home from his business to kiss his children good-night.

Garth had been with Charlotte every minute of her delivery, and it had been an incredibly moving experience, one that brought them infinitely closer together. But Kate did not mention Wade again. It upset Charlotte to realize Wade was going to be denied those privileges his father had enjoyed at his birth. Knowing how much he wanted them, she immediately decided that she couldn't tell Wade she had seen Kate.

She waited for the girl in a small room filled with pregnant women, none of them as young as Kate, and wrestled with her mixed emotions.

Finally Kate reappeared. "I'm progressing nicely," she announced cheerfully. "At least the tests were okay. I don't have to see the doctor until my regular visit next month."

"That's great," Charlotte said, conscious of the eyes of the other women following them as they left the waiting room. Some were smiling; other eyes questioned her about Kate's obvious youth, and held a hint of sympathy.

"The nurse showed me some more exercises I should be doing. And she told me about a course called Parenting for Teenagers. It's given at a hospital near here at several different times. Is that the one you told me about?"

"I think it is. Would you like to attend?"

"Yeah, if I could. But Aunt Stelle works long hours, and it's too far to walk."

"If there's a session on Wednesday afternoons, I could take you," Charlotte offered.

Kate stiffened. "I don't want to be obligated to you."

Charlotte said softly, "What would be best for your baby?"

Kate shot a quick glance at her.

"That's all that really matters, isn't it?"

"Yeah," Kate finally murmured, and added, "You don't have to tell Wade you're taking me, do you?"

"Not if you ask me not to."

On the way home, they arranged that Kate would enroll in the Wednesday-afternoon session of Parenting for Teenagers the following week, and that Charlotte would drive her to and from the hospital where the workshop was held.

"I'll give it a try" was all that Kate promised.

CHAPTER TWELVE

THE FOLLOWING WEDNESDAY Charlotte picked up Kate and took her to the parenting course. Ellin Ferdinand welcomed them at the hospital's small lecture room and introduced them to the pert young nurse who was the instructor. Nurse Peabody looked little more than a teenager herself, and it was immediately obvious that she had a warm rapport with her students. During the class discussion, Charlotte and Ellin sat in the back row and observed the reactions of the young expectant mothers.

With her outgoing personality, Kate fit easily into the group and was already making friends. She was vivacious and uninhibited, her reactions were mercurial and she revealed a sense of humor that cheered the girls, some of whom were shy and obviously depressed.

"She's a charming child," Ellin observed.

Kate would attract notice wherever she went, and it would mostly be favorable. "But still a child," Charlotte pointed out. "Immature, possibly even unstable."

"What Kate is experiencing matures a woman fast," Ellin said.

The program that day was on feeding the baby, and the benefits and disadvantages of breast-feeding compared with bottle-feeding. The young women were intensely interested in the subject and asked many questions, most of them thoughtful. What about the mother who works? Did she have a choice?

"Only if her employer furnishes a day-care nursery," the nurse replied. "Child care is expensive. If you have a friend who has children the same age, you may be able to arrange something between you and find part-time work."

"Will breast-feeding make my breasts sag?" one young woman asked.

"Not necessarily."

Sitting in the rear, Charlotte and Ellin listened with great interest. "There are immense satisfactions in this work," Ellin said quietly. "I'm glad that you nudged me into volunteering. I've become very involved with the problems some of these young women are facing."

"I'm glad," Charlotte said, and added with a grin, "Selfishly glad, and for Kate's sake."

A half hour later, as Charlotte and Kate were leaving the hospital together, Charlotte stopped dead just outside the double glass doors. Approaching them on the concrete walk from the street was Brock Morley, walking slowly beside a white-haired gentleman who was using two metal canes strapped to his arms, and moving with obvious pain.

The sun was low, breaking through the clouds. It illuminated the pale branches of trees along the sidewalk against a background of black rain clouds over the Sound. In that strange light Brock looked wonderful and somehow unreal.

"Brock!" she gasped. She hadn't heard from him all week, and she'd had no idea he was back in Seattle.

He seemed as startled as she was. Color came into his face, but he said with his natural ease, "This is my father, Charlotte. Father, this is Mrs. Emlyn."

Charlotte looked into icy blue eyes shaded by heavy white brows drawn into a bushy scowl, and was stunned by the fury she saw in them. It didn't even occur to her that he might not know who Mrs. Emlyn was. She felt the force of his fury directed at her. Her smile faded before the intense hostile emotions emanating from him.

"How do you do?" She heard herself introduce Kate. "I didn't know you'd returned," she said pointedly to Brock.

"No. Well, we're still getting settled," Brock said. His father remained silent.

She was seething inside, smarting with the memory of the evenings she had spent waiting in vain for Brock to call. She wondered just how long he had been in his apartment, only a few miles away. How dared he do this to her?

Brock smiled at Kate, unaware of Charlotte's anger. "Hello, there. I'm glad to meet you, Kate. You're Wade's friend, aren't you?"

Kate flashed Charlotte an accusing glance and muttered a curt "Hi."

Brock's attention switched to his father who was moving on again with difficulty, having barely acknowledged the introductions. He experienced a flash of pure rage. After a month of devoting all of his time to the old man, he'd had about all of his thorny temperament he could handle. He turned back to Charlotte, who looked elegantly desirable, and wished he could carry her off and love her all afternoon. Instead he was trapped in a situation of stifling intimacy with his father.

"I'm taking the Major to his new doctor. I'll call you when I can, Charlotte," he said in a low voice, and hurried after his struggling father to open the hospital door for him.

Furious, Charlotte walked with Kate to the car. Kate sat in the far corner of the front seat, brooding. It was only after Charlotte's temper had cooled a bit that she realized Kate was upset, too.

"Are you angry with me, Kate?"

"Yes!" Kate hissed.

"What did I do?" Charlotte asked, bewildered.

"That man knows I'm pregnant, doesn't he?"

"Yes."

"You told a man I don't even know about me and Wade? Why did you tell him?"

"Why does it bother you? You've given me the impression that you don't much care what people think."

"You have no right to gossip about me!"

Charlotte parked in front of Kate's apartment building and turned squarely toward her. "Kate, he knows because what you and Wade do affects us, too. Brock Morley is no stranger. He and I were planning to be married until—" She stopped.

Kate's eyes had shifted away from her as if she didn't want to hear more, and Charlotte remembered with regret her emotional outburst about her marriage plans the night she and Wade had come to talk to the girl. She reminded herself of her resolve to listen and not talk.

"I'm s-sorry," Kate mumbled.

At first Charlotte wasn't sure what Kate was attempting to say. Then she realized that Kate was trying to muffle laughter! Talk about mercurial moods! She stared at the girl, deeply offended.

"I'm s-sorry, but did you ever see f-four angrier people? Mr. Morley's father was in a r rage, I have no idea why. And Mr. Morley was furious with him for being rude to us. And you simply f-f-flamed! And I was mad at you—" She broke down in giggles.

Charlotte felt surprised and chastened. Kate was a lot more perceptive than she had given her credit for. When she thought about it, she could see a comic side to the encounter, her first with the legendary Major. She gave Kate a slow grin.

"It was funny, wasn't it? All of us mad—and for different reasons."

"Yeah." Kate laughed again and this time Charlotte joined in. She felt infinitely better.

"Thanks for the ride." With another swift change of mood, Kate jumped out of the car and ran to her door.

"I'll come for you next Wednesday," Charlotte called after her.

"Okay!" Kate shouted back. Afterward, driving home, Charlotte's anger at Brock returned—a baffled anger mixed with anxiety. *Why* had Brock failed to call her as soon as he returned to Seattle? She knew bringing his convalescent father home with him must have complicated his return considerably, but how much time and effort would it have required to dial her number and tell her that he was back?

If she had been the one who had been away caring for an injured parent, she couldn't have waited to tell Brock she had returned. That he had failed to do that simple thing signaled a withdrawal from her that she couldn't understand and that deeply frightened her.

All through the rest of that afternoon and evening, she expected to hear from him, but the telephone didn't ring. She was losing Brock, and she didn't know why. Hurt and anxious, she was too proud to call him.

WADE HAD WHAT HE CALLED a gig the next evening, playing his records for a party on the university campus, and Charlotte was alone in the house. She had driven home from the clinic through a light but steady rain, and it was still raining when she had finished her lonely dinner. She had kicked off her shoes and settled down with her aching misery and a glass of white wine before the television set when the doorbell rang.

The sound of water running through the downspouts had masked the footsteps of whoever had come up on the porch. She put down the wineglass and went to open the door. Brock stood there, pale and unsmiling, with raindrops sparkling in his hair and on his shoulders.

He looked at her with a desperate hunger in his eyes and said simply, "I'm glad you're home."

Charlotte felt a constriction in her heart and at the same time a rush of the anger she had bottled up since the afternoon before.

"I shouldn't even let you in!" she exclaimed.

He stepped inside and she was a little startled to find him several inches taller than she was, until she remembered that she had discarded her high heels. He didn't say anything more, just reached for her. She breathed in his scent of wet wool and spicy cologne and the faint tinge of someone else's cigarette smoke that clung to his jacket, and surrendered to the familiar strength of his embrace. His lips found hers with a passion that told her he had suffered all the pangs of loneliness and longing that their separation had caused her.

"Why didn't you let me know you were back?" she demanded when he came up for air.

He kissed the question away, but after a moment she pulled back. "I'm still angry with you, Brock," she said. "I'm sorry about what happened to your father, and I know it's been difficult for you, but I didn't expect to be completely forgotten."

"You think that?" He nuzzled her neck, dripping cool raindrops on her warm skin. Her breasts were still tingling from the presence of his body. "I didn't forget you for one minute. I thought about you constantly."

"How was I to know that? You could have called me."

"I did call you. From Portland," he murmured in her ear.

She fought against her desire to surrender completely. "Twice!" she scoffed.

He released her but left his hands lightly encircling her waist. "I tried many times when your line was busy. You could have called me. I did give you the Major's telephone number, didn't I?"

"I did try. You never answered."

"I spent a lot of time at the hospital. And walking Quarters."

"'Walking Quarters'?" she repeated, baffled.

"The Major's dog. And your line was always busy. I just didn't have the time to call and call until it was free."

"Wade hasn't been home that much," she objected, and confessed miserably, "He's been freezing me out, too."

"Oh, Charlotte!" Brock said remorsefully. "Is that what you thought? I'm not trying to make excuses, love, but I've been spending eighteen-hour days straightening out my father's affairs, packing up his effects and sending them to storage...."

Warmth was stealing back into her heart. How she had missed him! She pulled his head forward and kissed him, and the last droplets of water ran off his hair onto her cheek, like tears.

She led him into the living room and took his wet raincoat, continuing to reproach him softly. "I can understand that, Brock. What I can't understand is why you didn't let me know you were back in Seattle. How long have you been home? All you had to do was pick up the phone and dial—"

"I brought my father back with me, Charlotte. I hired a nurse and went straight back to work because my boss was beginning to make unpleasant noises. As soon as I did, the Major fired the nurse.''

"Oh, no!" she said with a rueful laugh.

"*I* didn't think it was funny. He still needs a lot of help, Charlotte. I've been spending every spare minute feeding and dressing him. I can't leave him alone very long, but I had to see you, to try to explain—''

He stopped talking and pulled her close again. He kissed her for a long, long moment, dipping deep into the sweetness of her mouth. She responded with her hands in his hair, caressing his neck and ears and pressing herself against him as if she could merge her body in his.

She felt his powerful arousal and her passion rose strongly to meet it. Arm in arm they moved toward her bedroom where they feverishly discarded their clothes. This was no sensuous slow-motion ballet toward a culmination of lovemaking, but a compulsive coming together to fill a desperate mutual need to reaffirm their love and heal the scars of their separation.

Hungrily, she let her eyes devour his body, long and lean, with fine black hairs on his arms and legs and matting his chest. Her hands stroked his strong shoulder muscles, his flat stomach, and caressed his neat buttocks when he bent to kiss her breasts. The fragrance of his hair rose to her nostrils. She loved his body. This arrangement of smoothly working muscles, with angular curves and flat planes that made him a man, was her utter delight.

His urgency made him masterful. With one hand he tossed back the coverlet, and with one knee behind hers, he toppled her on the soft bed, coming down on top of her. He kissed her again, and she lifted her hips to meet him. Their need was so great that the climax they shared came swiftly, soaring in its intensity, welding them together. For long moments they held each other while racing hearts returned to a normal beat.

Brock sighed. "Oh, sweetheart, I've missed holding you like this. I love your eyes," he murmured, and traced the line of her brow with one finger. "I love everything about you. Don't ever change." He kissed the tip of her nose. "I want to stay and make love to you again, slowly and beautifully, but I can't. I shouldn't have left the Major this long. I've wanted to come before, but I've been searching for another practical nurse for him—"

"Oh, Brock! Couldn't I have helped?" She laid one hand on his cheek.

"—and looking for an apartment large enough for the two of us and his physical therapy equipment—and packing up my things for the move."

"You're moving from your apartment?" The apartment where he had proposed.

"It's done." He disengaged his arms and sat up on the edge of the bed. She felt strangely alone. Already his thoughts had moved beyond her. So soon. They had been so close. She could not imagine being closer to another human being. Yet Charlotte had the feeling that he was slipping away from her.

He dressed quickly, talking while he pulled on his clothes. "Luckily, a larger apartment became available in the same building," he told her. "I was glad because of the elevator. It wasn't going to be easy to find something on the ground floor."

"You could have let me help you," she said again. She slipped out of bed and put on a robe.

He was leaving the bedroom, apparently as eager to leave it now as he had been to bring her to it. Some part of her mind resented that. They stopped in the living room and she gave him his raincoat. They stood near the front door, and he kept his hands on her. She stood in the circle of his arms, her hands on the lapels of his jacket, not willing yet to be physically separate form him.

"Can't I help you find a nurse?"

"I'd appreciate it, love, but I've got a request in at several agencies." He paused, then said miserably, "I've been telling myself I should get out of your life."

She caught her breath. "Brock, no!" The instinct that had warned her their relationship was in trouble had not been false, it seemed. The thought was wrenching. She clung to him. Now she could not let him go.

"Then yesterday when I saw you . . . I couldn't sleep last night, Charlotte. I've got a problem that's going to be with me for a long time, darling. How can I ask you to share it? It isn't fair to you."

Her throat clogged with fear, thickening her voice. "Do you trust my love as little as that?" she demanded.

He pulled her closer, cradling her head against his shoulder. "I remember thinking the same thing about you when you were worrying about the difference in our ages."

When she lifted her gaze she saw the warm shine in his eyes in which love and longing and regret were all mingled. The regret chilled her. Was this the ending that in her most vulnerable moments she had visualized from the beginning of their unexpected relationship? Her breath caught with panic.

"I guess we can admit that we're crazy in love, can't we?" Brock said quietly. "But what are we going to do about it?"

No teenager's emotions could be more volatile than hers were since she had fallen in love with Brock, she thought. Loving him had made her vulnerable again, sometimes filling her with self-doubt. But now her heartbeat quickened with hope.

"You asked me to marry you," she reminded him. "I seem to remember saying yes."

"Charlotte, since this happened I'm afraid that marrying me means taking on my father, too. You saw him yesterday. Ever since my mother left us he's needled women and mocked them. When he's feeling well he's more civil about it, he can even be entertaining. But right now he's like a wounded bear. He'd eat you alive!"

Charlotte laughed shakily. "Brock, I'm not afraid of your father." She was filled with such a deep, urgent need that she knew she couldn't let him go. Not if he loved her. The obstacles to their happiness might be great, but surely they weren't insurmountable. "What do you think I am? I see sick and cross elderly patients every day!"

"Not to live with. And not old woman-eaters like the Major."

"I want a chance to meet him and talk with him. I can't believe he's as awful as you paint him. Why don't you bring him over here some evening?"

"He wouldn't come. He's too miserable right now."

"Your father needs visitors," she persisted. "He needs to be taken out of his preoccupation with himself and his injuries."

Brock shook his head. "You just don't know the Major."

"Then give me the chance to know him! You're not being fair to me, Brock."

"Drop it, Charlotte. I'm sorry but you don't know what you're getting into."

Suddenly her anger and hurt were back, in a flood so strong that she heard herself lash out, "Are you sure you're not using him as an excuse, Brock? You've been thinking it over, and you can't take the fringe benefits of marriage, is that it? A step-grandchild would make you feel so 'very, very old,'" she mocked him.

Color crept up from his collar. "You can't forget that five years between us, can you? You're a hundred-and-eighty degrees wrong, Charlotte."

She was horrified at herself, but she had to go on now and get it out. "Have you ever told your father that you asked me to marry you?" she said bluntly.

"I told him I was thinking of getting married. He called me a fool. Maybe I am." While she stilled with shock, he glanced at his watch and said shortly, "I've got to go. He needs me, Charlotte."

This hurt was too deep. He had come to make love to her. Now he was leaving her behind, not admitting her into his troubled life with his father. She was not going to offer her help again. "Yes, go!" she cried. "Let's forget the whole thing. Admit we made a terrible mistake."

His eyes implored hers. "Charlotte, I didn't mean what I said. It's been a strain. Look, I don't want to leave you like this. I love you so damned much—"

"Just go!" she cried, feeling the tear spill over her eyelids. "Just go away!"

He left her and she sank down in a chair and covered her eyes. Why was loving so difficult? Loving Brock seemed to leave all her nerve ends raw and exposed. He could hurt her too easily.

Already she deeply regretted the things she had said. She herself had provoked the quarrel, and she hadn't really wanted Brock to go. His last words rang in her ears: *I love you so damned much* . . .

Suddenly she was sure that Brock knew she hadn't really meant it when she sent him away. He knew that she had given him her heart. She felt humble and very loving. But perhaps what they needed was to have some time apart, at least until they could resolve their family problems.

CHAPTER THIRTEEN

ON THE FOLLOWING WEDNESDAY Charlotte went into town and wandered through the infants' wear department before going to pick up Kate. With a clutch at her heart, she looked at tiny dresses and romper suits, inevitably reminded of her own pregnancy with Wade. Would Kate have a boy or a girl? She yearned over the dainty dresses with their fairy-book frills.

She finally selected a sleeper of fine white cotton flannel suitable for a newborn infant and had it wrapped as a gift. The pretty package was lying on the passenger seat of the car when Kate came running out of her building and climbed in. She picked it up and gave Charlotte a suspicious glance.

"What's this?"

Charlotte put the car in gear and drove off without looking at Kate. "It's a little early to be starting a layette," she said carelessly, "but I thought the baby's grandmother should launch it." *So,* she told herself wryly, *you're already staking your claim!*

Kate didn't say anything. She opened the package and sat gazing at the tiny arms and legs of the sleeping garment, then rubbed her fingers over the soft material.

"It makes it seem so real," she murmured. She looked up at Charlotte with a quick lift of her head and said shyly, "Thank you, Mrs. Emlyn. I . . . I haven't bought anything yet. This is the first—"

"I'm glad," Charlotte said.

She shopped for groceries while Kate attended her class. When she came back for her, Kate began talking animatedly about the program as soon as she got into the car. She had learned a lot about the physical changes taking place in her body and was fascinated with every detail, eager to share them.

Charlotte remembered how enthralled and also terrified she had been in those first months of her pregnancy by the things that were happening quite outside her control.

But Kate's mood shifted, as it could do without warning. "We talked about choices today," she said with a sidelong glance at Charlotte. "Of course, everybody in the class has already chosen not to have an abortion, even though delivery is more dangerous for someone my age. But we talked about marriage versus single parenting. Some of the couples are already married."

"Oh?" Charlotte said noncommittally. "Are there fathers in the class, too?"

"Yeah. There's two or three guys in the class, and they're not all married. One's going to Lamaze classes with his wife, learning how to be her birth coach. Aunt Stelle's going to be mine." Kate began chewing on a thumbnail. "Did you know that when a couple gets married before the girl is eighteen or the boy twenty, one-fifth of 'em get a divorce within a year? One-third get it by the second year, and in six years sixty percent of them are divorced! Wow!"

"That's a lot of failure," Charlotte commented.

"Yeah. Mostly it's because there isn't enough money to go around. Besides that, most of 'em who're my age get pregnant again right away and end up divorced anyway because they can't cope. Only by then they've got several children to support instead of just one. So they go on welfare."

Kate was painting a very dark picture, but Charlotte knew it was statistically true. She said nothing.

"Or if they stay married, they end up with a dozen kids and never do anything besides have babies. For some girls that's all they want—lots of kids," she said quickly. "But I want an education, too."

"It won't be easy to get."

"I can do it," Kate stated confidently. She flashed a look at Charlotte. "I think my baby should have an educated mother."

Charlotte smiled at her. "So do I."

After a little silence Kate said soberly, "Wade still doesn't understand why I won't marry him."

Charlotte's heart cramped in sudden pain for her son. She knew that Wade was every bit as unhappy as she was since she and Brock had quarreled. "I think I understand, Kate. And I think you're right to postpone marriage until you're older. But Wade's facing a tremendous challenge, too, the challenge of becoming a father. And he feels shut out."

Kate said nothing, looking straight ahead as they drove along. Charlotte stole a glance at her fresh peach cheek and the long dark lashes that swept down to hide her eyes. At that moment she would have given much to know what Kate was thinking.

"He keeps calling me. All the time."

"That doesn't surprise me. I remember how you used to talk for an hour on the telephone almost every evening. I think Wade misses that."

"Yeah. Well..."

"But I guess you do, too, don't you?"

"Things change," Kate said shortly. "I want him to stop calling me."

Charlotte said carefully, "You don't have to plan marriage now in order to share this experience with him, Kate. Do you have to shut him out completely? Wouldn't his support and caring make it easier for you in the coming months?"

"No!" Kate said explosively. "I told you! I'm not going to put Wade's name on the birth certificate, because I don't want any child support from Wade, and I don't want my baby pulled this way and that by joint custody like some of my mixed-up friends. I just want my baby. Tell Wade to stop calling me."

She turned to face Charlotte. "Because if he keeps asking me to marry him, I'll probably do it." Her tone made it a personal threat, establishing that there was no question in her mind what Charlotte wanted. "That would be a complete disaster. *That's* why he's got to stop bugging me."

Charlotte was startled into silence. She realized two things. First, that Kate was not as shallow as she had assumed. Her rapid shifts of interest possibly indicated a quick but untrained mind instead of a short attention span. Second, her own ambiguity wasn't helping the girl. Charlotte needed to sort out her conflicting emotions, which seemed daily to become more cloudy instead of clearer.

She wanted Wade to experience the joy of becoming a father, but as Kate plainly saw, she didn't want him to marry Kate in spite of a reluctant growing affection for the young girl. And once again she had failed to mind her tongue.

Kate was leaning forward like a racer waiting for a starting gun. As soon as Charlotte stepped on the brake in front of her building, she flung open the car door, yelled a brief "Thanks" over her shoulder and ran up the walk. She had not forgotten to pick up the present for her baby.

Charlotte drove home feeling depressed. Her life, like Kate's, was a fouled-up mess. And only a few short months ago, it had seemed wrapped up in a gift package of luminous dreams! There was only one clear road ahead, and that was to see that Wade's child made a healthy and auspicious entry into this mixed-up world. She hoped Kate would hold fast to her resolve not to marry so young, but her baby's health and well-being must come before all other considerations. To that end, she must keep Kate Parsons's friendship and give her what support she could along the rocky road she knew lay ahead for the girl.

Nor would she give up on Brock! Somehow their love must survive these strains.

When Kate called to tell her not to come on her next Wednesday afternoon because her Aunt Estelle was taking time off from work to go with her for her monthly check with her doctor, Charlotte made a daring resolve. She determined to call on Mr. Morley while Brock was at work.

Brock had phoned after their quarrel and they had exchanged brief apologies, but the breach had not been completely healed, and in the unhappy week since then she had not heard from him. As far as she knew, he hadn't been able to hire another nurse. She decided she would assume that his father was alone during the day and take him something to eat, and she thought long and hard about what it should be.

Portuguese bean soup. It was a recipe she had inherited from Garth's mother and Wade loved it. She could make it ahead of time and warm it at Brock's apartment.

On Monday she bought the beans—navy whites, pink and kidney beans—washed a cup of each and put them in a large Crockpot to soak overnight. In the morning she drained them, added three cups of water for each variety of

bean and set them to simmer at a low temperature while she
was at work. Tuesday night she added two cups of chopped
onion, a cup of chopped cabbage and two *linguiça* sau
sages sliced in thin rounds.

When Wade came into the house, he exclaimed with a
pleased grin, "Bean soup!"

"Right. I made enough so I can take what's left over to
Brock's father tomorrow. Do you think he'll be pleased?
He's a world traveler and Brock says he's a pretty good chef
himself."

"If he doesn't like this," Wade said, moving toward the
stove and sniffing the aroma appreciatively, "give up on
him. You're wasting your time."

Charlotte laughed and took the corn-bread muffins she
had baked out of the oven.

On Wednesday Ellin Ferdinand called her just as she was
preparing to leave the clinic. "Any chance you can lunch
with me before you go to pick Kate up?"

"I'm not picking her up today. She'll miss this session
because her aunt is taking her to her doctor."

"Does she like the workshop?" Ellin asked.

"She seems to enjoy it. At least she is learning things."

"I've talked with her counselor. You'll be interested to
know that she's not the most immature girl in the group.
Actually, she is considered to be coping quite well with the
emotional problems of her pregnancy."

"I'm sorry to hear that there are some who have even
more growing up to do...! Ellin, forget I said that. Kate is
typical for her age, I suppose. And she can only take half
the credit for her condition. Perhaps I've been forgetting
that."

Ellin laughed. "Perhaps that's to be expected, in your
circumstances."

"Actually, I may have underestimated her. She was telling me last week how many teenage marriages end in divorce, adding to the single mothers on welfare. The figures appall me. She's determined not to be one of them."

"Some of the teenage marriages do succeed," Ellin said, "but it's a very small percentage. The few who make it have the unquestioning support of both families, and I'm not talking about just help with the money, although that makes a big difference. Shall we lunch, anyway?"

"How about next week? I've got another appointment today."

They made arrangements to meet, and Charlotte went out to her car to go and pick up the soup and take it to Brock's father.

She checked the mail slots in the lobby and found that Brock had moved from the twelfth down to the eighth floor. She was carrying the Crockpot and a long loaf of crusty French bread, and a smiling woman who was just leaving the building held the door open for her so she did not have to ring.

When she knocked on the apartment door, she was startled to hear a dog bark loudly. She hadn't realized Brock was keeping the Major's dog in his apartment, and wondered if that was allowed.

"Quiet, sir!" shouted a man's voice. The dog stopped barking. In the same commanding tone the man called, "Come in, the door's open."

She entered and faced the white-bearded, shaggy-browed man who had stalked rudely by her outside the hospital two weeks ago. He was sitting in a chair facing the door, with his two metal canes fastened to his forearms, one hand grasping the collar of the barking dog. Lightning flashed from his keen blue eyes as they traveled from her slightly untidy hair down the lines of her loose jacket and flowing skirt.

"Who the hell are you?" he asked bluntly. "You're not the therapist."

"I'm Charlotte Emlyn, Mr. Morley. I've brought your lunch."

"Do I know you?"

He was holding back the panting black dog with some difficulty, but she noted with relief that its tail was wagging madly. "I'm Brock's friend. He introduced us last week—or tried to," Charlotte said coolly.

The thick white eyebrows shot higher.

"Were you expecting someone else?"

"An amazon who pummels my legs for an hour. Most unpleasant creature."

Charlotte smiled at him. "I heard you fired your nurse. But I brought plenty of soup, anyway."

"Humph!" After a moment, he asked with suspicion, "What kind?"

"Portuguese bean soup. Do you like it?"

"How do I know? Never heard of it." He was studying her and pretending not to, lowering his eyebrows and drawing them together to hide his eyes from her. Charlotte decided that he knew very well who she was.

"Don't get up," she said cheerfully, although he had made no move to do so. "I'll find the kitchen." She turned and called back over her shoulder, "You can let the dog go. *He* seems friendly enough."

She heard a muffled expletive as she set the Crockpot on the counter and plugged it in. The dog bounded after her and sniffed at her ankles, tail still going madly, then stood back and barked while she opened cupboards to find some plates and bowls.

"You're an old fraud, Quarters," she told him. "Just like your master."

When she carried dishes and silverware for two to the small round table at one end of the living area, the Major said with icy challenge, "So you think I'm a fraud?"

"Your hearing is very acute for your age," Charlotte told him.

"And you're too skinny for yours," he retorted with a flash of gleeful malice.

Charlotte laughed. It came out of her in a spontaneous burst of enjoyment and rang musically in the open rooms of the apartment. For just a second, the Major could not conceal his surprise.

"Are you always so much fun, Major Morley?" Charlotte asked him. "Or just when you break a leg?"

He looked at her and then in a calm and deliberate way he began to curse her—without anger but with a shocking explicitness, watching her hawkishly from under those eyebrows.

Charlotte continued to arrange the silver and napkins on the table, paying him little attention. When the flow of colorful army profanity slowed, she said, "Feel better now? Don't let it worry you. I've heard all those words before."

"Are you a goddam nurse, too?" he demanded.

"No, but I'm a medical technician, and I've been married. Doctors curse sometimes. So do husbands. I think the soup is warmed. Come and get it."

She turned her back and went to the kitchen to avoid watching him struggle up from his chair with his two canes. She returned with steaming bowls of thick brown soup and put them on the table. The rich spicy odor filled the room. She went back for the sliced French bread and the butter she had found in the refrigerator. Then she sat down opposite his chair.

He walked slowly across the room, freed his arms and sat down after propping his canes against the chair. One leg apparently still stiff at the knee extended out into the room. Charlotte waited until he had finished the difficult maneuver, then lifted her spoon.

For a few moments they ate in silence. She did not try to make conversation. She buttered several slices of bread and returned them to the bread tray. Before long he picked up one, then another.

"How do you like the soup?"

"It's edible."

When they had finished eating, she washed the few dishes, leaving him sitting at the table. She wasn't going to offer to help him back to his chair. She knew intuitively what his reaction would be and she knew, too, that it was important for him to become independent, even though he was finding it painful to move around. When the dishes were done, she returned to the living room and asked, "Is there anything I can do for you?"

"Yes," he snapped, blue eyes flashing under a menacing scowl. "Get the hell out of here and leave me alone. And take Quarters with you. He needs a walk."

She had seen the dog's leash hanging in the kitchen. When she went to get it, she saw that Quarters had indeed been in need of a walk. While they were eating he had made a puddle in the middle of the linoleum.

Charlotte gasped, "Oh, Quarters!" and grabbed some paper towels. The Major could have slipped and fallen again!

She was on her knees scrubbing the spot when a sharp feminine voice said, "I'm glad you're taking care of that. I draw the line at cleaning up after a patient's dog."

"You shouldn't have to," Charlotte agreed, looking up at the large athletic woman who stood watching her out of opaque brown eyes.

"If it happens again, I'm not coming back. I'm surprised the manager allows animals in this building."

"Yes," Charlotte said ambiguously. "You're the therapist?"

"Right. I'll be busy with Mr. Morley for the next hour," she warned.

"I'm taking the dog for a walk. I'll keep him out of your way."

"I'll appreciate it."

The rattle of his chain brought Quarters skidding across the linoleum toward Charlotte in his eagerness. She clipped it to his collar and called to Brock's father, "Goodbye, Mr. Morley. I'll leave you to your therapist."

"Lord deliver me from interfering females," he growled, and the therapist rolled her eyes toward the ceiling.

Charlotte felt a flash of sympathy for him. The therapist didn't look like much fun to her, either.

"I'm taking Quarters," she called, and went out the door without a backward look, the animal dragging her toward the elevators with a bark that must have resounded through the entire floor. She wondered how long Brock would be allowed to keep him and considered the possibility of giving him the run of her backyard. Could she handle that?

In the elevator she shortened the slack on his leash, forcing him to sit near her feet. "Heel!" she ordered when they got outside, but it was obvious that he had not been trained. She jerked hard on the leash and repeated the command.

Quarters sat down and gave her an astonished and somehow reproachful look that made her laugh.

"You're going to have to learn," she told him. "The Major can't put up with your bad manners anymore."

As if he understood, he got up and guided her with a more sedate urgency to the tree that shaded the walk, which he watered liberally. Then they started down the block, Charlotte using all her strength to keep him by her side.

The squeal of a car braking startled her. "Charlotte!" Brock exclaimed, pulling his car to a halt beside her. Their eyes met in mutual anguish and love. Quarters yelped in excitement and dragged her over to the curb where he stood up and barked ecstatically into Brock's face.

"Quiet!" Brock shouted. "What are you doing here?" he asked, softening his tone.

"I brought your father some lunch."

"So did I. I've got hamburgers."

She swallowed. He looked so unbearably dear and wonderful. "You're actually taking a lunch break, instead of trying to exist on coffee all day?" she asked lightly.

"I've got no choice. I haven't found anyone to stay with him yet," he confessed. "I try to get home to feed him and take Quarters out for a little run."

"Maybe your father's accident has a silver lining, after all. I made soup. There's some left for you, if you want it."

The grateful look in his eyes warmed her. He turned off the engine and got out of the car. "Let me," he said, reaching for Quarters's leash.

"I'm trying to teach him to heel."

"I wish you luck," he said wryly.

"Your father won't be able to control him otherwise," she pointed out, hanging on.

"I know, but—" He sighed and surrendered the dog's chain. "How did you get along with the Major?"

"He has a choice vocabulary, doesn't he?"

Brock grimaced.

"Don't tell him so, because I told him I'd heard them all before."

Her face was flushed with the exertion of holding the dog, and little strands of shining hair had escaped from her careless topknot. She looked very young and very beautiful. Brock gazed into her laughing eyes and said with intense conviction, "I love you."

Her eyes shone with moisture. "I know. And I love you."

He took her free hand and they ran breathlessly down the block together, letting Quarters stretch his legs. At the intersection they turned and walked slowly back to Brock's building.

He asked about Kate. "She's an attractive girl. Do you like her?"

"Yes. There's more to her than I thought. I'm beginning to believe that she cares for Wade but she won't admit it."

"Maybe that's the reason she won't marry him," Brock said. He knew, because that was exactly how he felt about Charlotte. He loved her too much to marry her, the way things were.

"I think she's making more sense than he is," Charlotte went on. "He's still begging her to change her mind."

"What if they elope?"

"They'll live with me," she said flatly. "They have no other option. Kate must know that her aunt won't offer to let Wade live in her apartment."

He didn't say anything for a moment. "Imagine them and their kid and the Major all living with us!" he said in a whimsical tone that told her he couldn't.

"And don't forget Quarters," she put in dryly. For a few seconds she was seeing it all in brutal full color: an impossible situation.

They had reached his building. Brock looked at his watch. "I've got fifteen minutes," he said, "and the Major's therapist is due."

"She's up there with him now."

"Already?" He added ruefully, "I'm not used to checking the time until after I've finished patching a glitch, and then it's always too late for anything else."

"Things change, as Kate says."

Charlotte felt very weary. They could never go back to the euphoria of those first days after Denver when they were intoxicated with the joy of finding each other. Brock could never go back to the uncomplicated bachelorhood he had enjoyed before his father's accident, or before they met. And this pain she felt now was probably the inevitable other side of the bright coin of love. And they did love each other—far too much to stay angry.

"I won't go upstairs again, then. You can bring my Crockpot over sometime. And I'll try not to quarrel with you if you can't come tomorrow night."

He put out his hand for the dog's leash, but she stepped out of his reach with it. At the curb she opened the door of her car and Quarters bounded joyfully into it. "I'm taking him home with me, Brock. He'll be happy in my fenced backyard."

Brock looked alarmed. "You can't do that. The Major won't sleep a wink without that mutt lying at his feet."

"The Major is too used to having his own way," Charlotte said flatly. "Tell him I fell in love with his dog and kidnapped him. Tell him he'll lose both his therapist and his apartment if I bring Quarters back. Tell him anything you like."

Quarters barked his impatience to be driven off. Obviously the promise of riding in a car outweighed any loyalties he might have. "A fickle friend," she commented.

"You don't know what you're taking on, to say nothing of what you're letting me in for," Brock complained. "The major'll have my hide." But there was the shadow of a grin on his lips.

They kissed, oblivious to Quarters's barking and the honking of a carful of teenagers. It was a very satisfactory kiss.

CHAPTER FOURTEEN

THE PACIFIC NORTHWEST was approaching its loveliest season. Azaleas and camellias were in bloom and the roses were in bud. Frequent showers kept everything shining clean and sweet-smelling. Between the rains the clouds parted to reveal a hauntingly blue sky reflected in the deep waters of the Sound, both sky and sea made more blue by the white sails dotting the water and the snowy peaks of the Olympic peninsula beyond it.

It was the season for love, and Brock ached to hold Charlotte and make slow and consuming love to her. Instead, he was driving his father to a doctor's appointment.

That was the pattern of his days, he thought bitterly. He couldn't give Charlotte up, yet he was able to see her only in hurried visits, when what he wanted was to carry her off forever. Their quarrels and the mutual frustration had forced them to an unspoken understanding that until they could set a marriage date, it was easier not to see each other so often. Brock sometimes felt as if she were drifting out of his reach.

The Major had discarded his metal canes with their forearm cuffs and was getting around, rather awkwardly, with one sturdy walking stick. Quarters was still with Charlotte, thank heaven, but his father had not forgiven either of them, although the arrangement had undoubtedly saved him from further spills as well as prevented their eviction from the building.

Today the Major was scheduled for a final X ray of his slightly stiffened but functioning legs. Brock had traded his Saturday for the day off to drive him to the medical building. He delivered the Major to the lab and left him with the radiologist and went down in the elevator to refill a prescription for him at the drugstore.

As he crossed the lobby of the building, his attention was caught by an attractive young girl with long straight black hair who was sitting by herself on one of the sofas. She seemed vaguely familiar, and when she caught his glance she smiled shyly at him, he paused and took a second look at her. It was Charlotte's son's pregnant girlfriend. And yes, she was definitely bulging.

"Hello," he said, stopping near her. "You're Kate, aren't you?"

"Yes. You're Mrs. Emlyn's friend." She looked even younger than sixteen, but her eyes were clear and self-confident, and she had an air of well-being. "How is your father now?"

"Better, I think. At least, he's more polite when I introduce him to my friends."

She laughed. "You were angry with him that day, weren't you? We were all angry. Mrs. Emlyn was mad at you, I was mad at her and your father was mad at all of us."

He looked at her with interest. So she had been aware of Charlotte's anger? He hadn't known until the next evening just how upset Charlotte had been with him that day. "A very wise nurse explained to me that my father was simply mad at his fate, but it's more likely he's been furious with himself. He loves his dog too much to blame him for his accident."

Kate's dark eyes danced. "That's rather nice of him, isn't it?"

Brock felt a strong liking for her. "Are you here to see your doctor, too?"

"I've seen him. I have to wait for my aunt. She's picking me up after she gets off work."

"What time will that be?"

Kate sighed. "Five, if I'm lucky."

Brock looked at his watch. It was a quarter of three. "Where do you live?"

"On Beacon Hill."

"I'm on Beacon Hill, too. Why don't I drive you home?" he offered. "Can you let your aunt know?"

"Sure. I can call her at the office."

"You do that while I get this prescription filled at the pharmacy. Then I'll go up to the radiology lab and bring the Major down."

Kate nodded happily and got up rather awkwardly to find a pay phone.

A half hour later Brock escorted them both out to his car. The Major was in a good mood. He was walking more jauntily now with his one cane, he had enjoyed getting out of the apartment and he had sharpened his wits, gleefully insulting his radiologist by comparing reading X-ray films to seeing pictures in tea leaves.

He looked Kate over with a connoisseur's eye and said, "Where did we pick up the intriguing stray?"

Kate said pertly, "At my gynecologist's," rolling the word off her tongue with obvious pleasure.

Brock hid a grin and wished he could see his father's expression. Presently he heard the Major say, "Am I getting older or are expectant mothers getting much younger?"

Kate said, "Both, probably," and began telling them artless stories about the other teenage mothers in her parenting class. In the back seat the Major listened in what Brock assumed was an appalled silence.

A little later, just as Brock was pulling up before her apartment house, Kate exclaimed in a startled tone, "Oh!"

"What is it?" Brock asked. "Is something wrong?"

"She moved." Kate's tone was awed. "Here." She grabbed his hand from the steering wheel and put it on her stomach.

Brock jumped and his foot jammed down on the brake. He had felt the tiny kick of the thing in her womb against its warm wall and it produced a sensation in him he had never before experienced.

"Isn't that amazing?" she breathed, her eyes wide as she gazed at his face.

Coming from anyone else, her action would have embarrassed Brock. But he was strangely touched. He said gently, "Thanks for letting me feel it, Kate."

A beatific smile spread over her face. In the back seat, the Major said, "My God."

"Goodbye, Mr. Morley. Thanks for the ride," Kate said, and got out of the car. She looked back at his father and added, "Goodbye, sir."

As Brock drove away, the Major muttered, "Cradle snatcher!"

Brock couldn't believe his ears. "You don't think *I*—hey, I'm not responsible!"

"Thanks for letting me feel it," his father mocked.

"You're crazy, you know that?" Brock said angrily. "You're a dirty old man."

His father laughed.

When he got out of the car at the apartment, Brock noticed a slip of paper on the front seat. He picked it up. It was a prescription for Kate Parsons, which must have dropped out of the wide-open tote she had been carrying.

Damn! He put it in his pocket and turned to offer a hand to his father.

The Major had been tired by the excursion, and when he got him upstairs, Brock helped him into bed for a rest, and then prepared some meat and vegetables for their dinner. He couldn't find a telephone number for Kate, and he decided he would have to drive over to her apartment later and deliver the prescription.

After warning his father, to the Major's intense annoyance, to stay in bed while he was gone and not to try to answer the door if anyone came, he went back down to the garage for his car.

When he arrived upstairs at Kate's apartment after buzzing from the lobby, the door was opened by a slender woman with cropped blond hair and wearing a tailored suit, who welcomed him with a wide smile when he told her why he had come.

"Come in, Mr. Morley. Kate has been simply combing her possessions for that piece of paper!"

He stepped inside the pleasant apartment and Kate came forward, her dark eyes warm. "I'm so relieved!" she exclaimed. "My doctor already thinks I'm spacey, and if I had to go back for another prescription, he'd give up on me. Mr. Morley, this is my aunt, Estelle Drew."

Brock smiled at the attractive blonde. Her figure was smashing and her skin was as fresh and smooth as her niece's, but there was something so fastidiously polished about her that she reminded him of chrome and glass. She extended a hand and when he took it, gave him a firm handshake. "Will you come in for a cup of coffee?" she invited.

"Thanks, that sounds good." He was curious about this woman whom Charlotte had accused of "brainwashing"

Wade's girlfriend to choose the questionable challenge of single motherhood at her age.

"Sit down, Mr. Morley," Kate said. "I'll bring the coffee."

She brought in two cups of coffee and two pieces of cake. Beside her aunt, she seemed womanly, even if she was barely grown.

"None for yourself, Kate?" Brock asked her.

She shook her head. "It's not good for Baby."

"Kate is very careful about her diet," Estelle explained. "I'm proud of her."

Estelle was a legal secretary, Brock learned, in a prestigious law firm, and subtly she made him understand that hers was a responsible and very taxing position. He enjoyed her conversation, but Brock was uncomfortable with the hint of steel he sensed beneath that silken exterior.

He felt a somewhat protective sympathy for the pregnant teenager who was her ward. It was a novel and surprisingly tender affection he felt for the young girl—stronger than friendship, yet not what the Major had crudely suggested that afternoon.

That was why he found himself, before he left them, offering his help if Kate needed any service he could give.

Estelle Drew accepted his offer with no hesitation. "If I could call you sometime to take Kate to her doctor," she suggested briskly. "On a day when we have to be in court, it's impossible for me to get away."

He wondered if she actually went to court with her lawyer boss, or if the "we" was a sort of royal convention.

"Kate has to call a taxi," she concluded, "and it's sometimes difficult for her to get one, especially on a rainy day."

Brock shook his head with regret. "I'm afraid I can't get away, either. But there is one possibility. My lunchtime is pretty flexible. If I should happen to be working at one of the local hospitals and her appointment is near the middle of the day—"

Kate clapped her hands and cried, "You're so *nice*, Mr. Morley!"

"I might be miles away," he warned her. "But I'm often working in the hospital district." He told them how to get in touch with him through the dispatch secretary in his maintenance department. He also gave Kate his home phone number.

They were both flatteringly grateful, and he left feeling pleased with himself.

CHARLOTTE WAS FINDING THAT boarding a standard poodle in her rather small backyard posed some problems, since both she and Wade were away for most the day. Wade felt sorry for the dog and began taking him with him in his van when he could. One day he took him to the hamburger stand, which resulted in Quarters's introduction to shoestring fries; from that time on, he was almost embarrassingly Wade's dog.

"We'll be sued for alienation of affections," Charlotte ruefully told her son. But Quarters was happy.

The dog was almost alone in that, she thought. Everyone else was lonely, frustrated, or angry at someone. Except Kate who, Charlotte noted as she continued to drive her to the parenting classes on Wednesday afternoons, watched her body balloon with total narcissistic absorption, happily regaling Charlotte with every physical development.

She never admitted fear or talked about the birth itself. Charlotte had the impression that the delivery didn't loom as large in Kate's mind as the complimentary champagne dinner her friend had described as its aftermath, which she saw as a festive occasion with herself, the new mother, in a central position, receiving honors and gifts.

Sometimes Charlotte wondered just how realistic Kate's visions of motherhood were, in spite of all the advance instruction she was getting in her pregnancy and parenting classes. Could she imagine the nights of inadequate sleep, the steady pressure of twenty-four-hour care, without letup, that having a baby brought to a young woman? Perhaps no one who had not experienced it could. And perhaps that was a good thing.

One Wednesday when Charlotte had come home for lunch and was doing some housecleaning while waiting until Kate would be home from school, she saw a taxi drive up and stop in front of her house. The Major got out of it with some help from the driver and began a slow approach up her driveway. Without stopping to wonder why he had not chosen to come to the front door, Charlotte flung it open and exclaimed, "Major Morley!" She was about to add a delighted "You came to see me!" when she realized that he was looking utterly surprised.

She noticed that the taxi was waiting for him, and guessed that he hadn't expected to find her in. "You came to see Quarters, didn't you?"

"I came to take him home," the Major said in clipped tones meant to establish his authority as the dog's owner.

"I'm sorry," she said truthfully. "He isn't here."

The Major's skin flushed pink under his white beard, and his eyes flashed. "I'd like to see for myself, if you please."

"Quarters is fine," she assured him. "Come in and let me explain." She held the screen door for him after he had laboriously crossed the grass to her walk and climbed up on her porch. Slowly he lifted his stiff leg over the threshold. She could see a pulse beating in a tiny vein in his forehead.

"Come, Quarters!" he called sharply, advancing into the room.

When there was no response, he turned to her and snapped, "Where is he? What have you done to him?"

"Quarters is perfectly well, Major Morley. He will be returned to you as soon as you are able to handle him. He's with Wade, my son."

His voice became steely. "I'll be the judge of my ability to handle my dog, young woman! By what right—"

"My son is in college, and I'm at work all day most days. Quarters was lonely here."

"I should think so!"

"My son has been taking Quarters to school with him in his van. It's full of sound equipment and Quarters is a good watchdog."

While she talked, she was leading the Major through the house and toward the back door. "That way Quarters doesn't get as lonely, and his barking doesn't annoy the neighbors. Wade goes to the parking lot between classes to take him out for a run." She opened the back door. "Come and see the doghouse Wade built for him."

He stood on the back porch and stared at Quarters's new home.

"I know you miss him," Charlotte said gently, "but he's really quite comfortable and happy here."

A suspicious moisture appeared in the Major's faded blue eyes, but with it was an anger that blistered her. Intuitively Charlotte realized her mistake. Brock's father was a proud man who would not willingly allow his emotional dependence on anyone, human or animal, to be seen, and she had witnessed his terrible longing for the dog that had been his constant companion.

He left her side to tackle the steps that led down to the grass. There he paused again to catch his breath and stare at the sturdy doghouse.

"That is quite an *edifice*," he said finally, his tone reducing it to lath and shingles. "I don't suppose Brock has seen it yet?"

"Why, yes, I believe he has," Charlotte said innocently. "Why?"

The Major shrugged. "He's pretty busy these days—looking after me and his little pregnant friend, too."

For a moment Charlotte could say nothing, she was so startled. Was he talking about Brock and *Kate*?

"He's helping her with some kind of exercises. Do you suppose he's training for Lamaze coaching with her?" He shot a keen look at her from under the bushy brows.

Lamaze? She didn't believe it. They scarcely knew each other. As far as she knew, Brock had met Kate only once—the day she had introduced them outside the hospital.

The Major was watching her closely. She caught the malicious little gleam of satisfaction in his eyes, and knew that her shock had delighted him. Well, the joke was on him! Brock's father obviously didn't know who was responsible for Kate's condition. But Charlotte didn't feel like laughing, because she knew that he had deliberately meant to hurt her.

She wouldn't give that vindictive old man the pleasure of knowing he had come anywhere near the mark. But she was furious with him. She thought, *I'm not going to take his abuse!* and heard herself say, "Major Morley, since you're here, will you tell me something? Will you tell me what happened to your photographs of Brock's mother? He told me he doesn't have a single picture of her. I find that very strange."

He flung his head back with an incredulous jerk of anger and said coldly, "What's strange, young woman, is your audacity in digging into what is no business of yours."

She looked him in the eye. "Anything that hurts Brock is my business. He told me that his mother left you. From what I've seen of you, I think I can understand why."

His answer was to return her level look and repeat his deliberate and impersonal litany of highly original curses, designed, she knew, to shake her and shut her up.

She listened as calmly as she could, and then said, "I'm sorry Quarters wasn't here. Perhaps Brock will bring you over some evening for a visit with him."

He replied to that with a wordless grunt and began walking across the yard.

She went as far as the garage with him, and from there watched him make his way slowly down the driveway toward the waiting taxi, her compassion for his disability poisoned by her hurt and disappointment. She felt almost ill. How could she ever welcome that bitter man into her family circle with Brock? Was it hopeless, after all?

At that moment Wade's van swung into the driveway and both the Major and the van stopped, confronting each other. Quarters, on the front seat beside Wade, set up a noisy barking. When Wade opened the van door, Quarters leaped over him and out, and dashed toward Brock's father, who braced himself on his cane to receive the dog's leap.

But Quarters only swiped his hand with his tongue, then ran back to Wade, who was stepping down to the pavement. The dog gave Wade an ecstatic lick, then whirled around again and ran toward the backyard, passing both the Major and Charlotte with a bark of greeting. He headed for his water dish, where he lapped enthusiastically between barks of joy at this gathering of his friends.

When Charlotte saw the Major turn to follow the dog, she turned, too, and hurried into the house. Grabbing her purse from the kitchen counter where she had left it, she ran out the front door, paid off the taxi driver, thanked him for waiting and told him she would drive Major Morley home. Then she went back through the house.

Brock's father, exhausted from his exertion, had dropped into a garden chair and was watching helplessly as Wade tossed a ball and Quarters chased it, working off some of the energy that he had stored up during the day in the van. Charlotte stood unnoticed in the back door until Quarters—panting and eager eyes begging—brought the ball to the Major and dropped it at his feet. After a heart-stirring hesitation, the old man obediently bent over to pick it up and threw it. There was something pathetic about his exhaustion and his response to the dog's plea.

Charlotte beckoned to Wade, and he bounded up on the porch.

"Will you stay with Brock's father while I go on an errand? Keep him here visiting with Quarters. Don't let him leave, under any circumstances. I'll call Brock to come for him when he gets home from work."

Wade grinned. "Got it," he said.

His cheerful acceptance of the situation and unquestioning cooperation turned her cloud of depression inside out. She wouldn't let the Major defeat her and spoil her right to happiness with Brock! Once again she took heart.

Charlotte picked up her purse and jacket and went out to the car, which she had left at the curb, to drive to Kate's. If she hurried, she could still get her to the class at the hospital. And she was going to ask her about those Lamaze exercises!

Kate was waiting for her, eager to be on her way. She was getting quite large now, but her balance was still good. She had not slowed much in her movements, which still had a light, quick quality that was part of the mercurial personality Wade loved. There was something to be said for having babies when one was very young, Charlotte thought.

"How are you progressing with your natural childbirth training?" she asked casually as they drove to the hospital.

"Great!" Kate said with typical enthusiasm. "Aunt Stelle is going to be my labor coach, so she goes to the classes with me when she can. Trouble is, she's so busy. Sometimes she has to work evenings, and I don't have a way to get to class." Her quick frown almost immediately disappeared, as she said, "But Mr. Morley offered to help out when he could. He gave me his phone number."

Indeed! Charlotte thought.

"I didn't know you knew him that well, Kate."

Soon she was hearing the story of the lost prescription and of Brock's generous offer of transportation when and if he was available. She listened incredulously to Kate's account of how she could get in touch with Brock on the job. He had never suggested that she call him at Echo. No one but a teenager, she thought, would take him up on an offer like that and think nothing of interrupting his work!

And on his lunch hour? Brock, who never used to take one? Of course, she reminded herself, he had been fixing lunches for his father, and the Major was now able to fix his own.

"Wasn't it great of him?" Kate exclaimed. "Aunt Stelle was so pleased! Just a few nights later Aunt Stelle's boss kept her late when she was supposed to go to natural childbirth class with me, and she called Brock."

So he was "Brock" to Estelle Drew! "Did he go?"

"Oh, yes. He was a good sport about it. He didn't know anything about it, see, because it was his first time. Everybody laughed at us. But we were just practising breathing and he soon caught on. It was fun."

Fun and games! Charlotte thought, imagining Brock's hand just under Kate's ripening breasts to check her diaphragm breathing.

"And when we got back to the apartment Aunt Stelle was there, and she'd brought a chocolate cake and ice cream, even though I couldn't have any." She made a nice face of revulsion. "Baby doesn't like."

Remembering that super secretary's crisp good looks was enough to further shake Charlotte's composure. Was she jealous? Darn right she was! And that was just what the Major intended, wasn't it?

"I thought your Aunt Stelle didn't like men."

Kate giggled. "She says they're useful for some things. So she uses 'em."

It was all Charlotte could do to conceal her anger. So Estelle Drew thought her looks would enable her to "use" Brock Morley? Charlotte was not only jealous, she was furious, and her anger was directed at Brock as well as at Kate's aunt. How could he fall for that woman's ploy? How *dared* he spend his precious spare time with Estelle and Kate Parsons, when he had so little for her?

Worst of all, how dared he give his father the weapon with which he had attacked her, by telling him about it!

BROCK ARRIVED HOME a little after six o'clock. Since he had brought his father to live with him, for the first time in his life he was keeping nine-to-five hours, like any desk jockey. The apartment seemed strangely silent. He strode to the bedroom that was his father's and found it empty, and his heart sank. What now?

His father was ambulatory at last and could leave the apartment if he chose, although it would not be easy; and the risk of his falling was still great. Brock flinched as he visualized the Major lying sprawled somewhere, unable to get up. Anywhere, because he was quite capable of calling a taxi and going wherever he took a notion to go.

Brock wondered where to start looking. He would need help, and he might as well enlist the police who could keep an eye out as they patrolled. The police could use dogs. That thought brought Quarters leaping to his mind, and then he knew where his father had gone. At almost the same time the telephone rang.

He snatched it up, knowing in an intuitive flash what he would hear. Sure enough, it was Charlotte. "Your father is here, Brock, playing with Quarters. I sent his taxi away. Can you come for him?"

"Damn him, anyway! I'll be right over."

"Relax," she said, sounding surprisingly cool. "Every thing's under control. But you may have to convince him he shouldn't take Quarters home with you."

He forced his taut muscles to let go and took a deep breath. "I'm on my way, love. I'm not only relaxed, I'm very relieved."

He drove to her house through the gathering dusk in record time and walked swiftly up the path to her door. I surprised him when she opened the door and, stepping into his arms, gave him a lingering and very satisfying kiss, because even in those first seconds he had seen that both Wade and his father were seated in the room. His father was holding a highball glass and looking half dead with fatigue. Quarters was lying between his chair and Wade's completely limp.

As Charlotte's warm lips eloquently communicated her frustrated desire, his whole body took fire, and part of the heat was generated by frustration at their lack of privacy. But he also had an intuition that she had done it not in spite of their audience, but because of it. She was defiantly proclaiming their closeness to the others in the room. His love for her at that moment was unbounded, but a warning prickle told him that something had happened to upset her, and he wondered what the Major had done.

"Darling," she said, "Quarters and your father have worn each other out. I think your father would like to go home, so I won't keep you longer than it takes for him to finish his drink. Can I offer you one?"

"No, thank you." His practised eye had expertly assessed his father's strength and he knew the old man was near to collapsing. He wouldn't have the energy to insist they take Quarters with them tonight, thank heaven!

"Major?" he said, offering his hand. He turned to Wade. "Thank you for taking such good care of Quarters. We'll come back again."

"Sure," Wade said. "See ya."

Charlotte walked to the door with them and ostentatiously kissed him again, whispering, "Come back soon?"

He was light-hearted with love and longing and wondered how he was going to sleep that night, as he guided his father's stumbling steps across the front porch and down the walk to his car. His frustration was as great and as painful as ever, and in addition there was that uneasy feeling that Charlotte's display of affection had been defiantly aimed at his father.

They were going to have to resolve this situation soon, but how? The Major was less trouble but even more of a worry now that he was ambulatory than he had been when he was helplessly bedfast.

CHAPTER FIFTEEN

TWO DAYS LATER Brock called Charlotte at the clinic to say that a medical employment agency had sent a practical nurse who would come for a few hours a day to help the Major get dressed—it was surprising how difficult a stiffened knee made it for a man to put on his trousers!—and prepare food for him.

"The Major promises he will charm the woman into staying with us. He assures me he'll have her eating out of his hand," Brock told her, and she felt a resentment of the old man's power that armed her against Brock's next words. "So we've got a night out," he said. "What would you like to do? Shall I get tickets for a play? Or shall we hear some jazz and maybe dance?"

"Wow!" she said. "Should I go shopping for new clothes and have my hair done?"

Her tone vaguely disturbed him. Charlotte did not ordinarily "have her hair done," and he loved the casual yet bold way she twisted a knot on top of her head. "Wear that sexy white dress that I like," he told her. "We'll do whatever you want, sweetheart. But let's dance. All I can think about is holding you close."

The ice around her heart was melting. His voice, deepened by desire, could do that to her no matter how discouraged or angry she felt.

They discussed the possibilities and decided to start the evening at a popular club that featured jazz musicians. "

want to dance with you. Like Denver," he said, his tone roughening.

That brought to her mind images so inflammatory that she had to remind herself she was sitting beside her monitoring computer, with another patient in the waiting room. "I think something can be arranged," she murmured.

She put down the phone with a little prayer that nothing would go wrong before nightfall.

It was one of Wade's evenings at the radio station. Charlotte was ready when Brock came, and his eyes lit with pleasure as his gaze traveled over the curves revealed by the dress he had asked her to wear, loose yet clingy and revealing. He held out his arms and she walked into them, drinking in the sight of him as she came, and glorying in the warm strength of his embrace. She could hear the strong rhythm of his heart beating in syncopation with her own, and when their lips met, his kiss was familiar and deeply satisfying, like a long drink of water on a hot day.

"I could stay right here," she murmured against his lips.

"We'd better go before I take you up on that."

She picked up her clutch and light coat, and they left the house.

The jazz club, in an old waterfront building, was intimate, with a minuscule dance floor. They ordered a dinner of veal medallions with mushrooms and a Caesar salad, and a light California rosé wine. For dessert they chose Oregon huckleberry pie. By the time their coffee came, the musicians had set up their equipment on the small stage. The bandleader tapped his toe three or four times and a saxophonist began wailing "Sweet Georgia Brown" in classic New Orleans style.

Brock pulled her to her feet and into his arms. Their bodies touched lightly, yet they were close enough so that she felt the supple play of his muscles as they moved in time

with the music, and there was intense pleasure in moving
with him.

At first there were few other couples on the floor, and
they whirled apart and back together with an exuberance
that was exhilarating. But the music was loud and the
rhythm insistent, and the room filled quickly. The floor was
soon packed.

It was an ambience very different from that they had
shared that night in Denver, yet dancing with him in the
rhythm-charged intimacy of the dusky room brought back
the magic of that encounter, and Charlotte felt as if she
were falling in love with him all over again. All the problems that had beset them since then were dimmed by the
desire that flamed when their bodies touched.

The jazz lovers crowding the dance floor gradually
stopped dancing and just stood listening to the insistent
African beat and the inspired variations the soloists built on
the traditional blues and jive melodies. Charlotte and Brock
stood swaying with their arms around each other. The air
grew heavy with perfumes and cigarette smoke as the room
pulsed with the emotional response of the audience to excitingly new versions of classic jazz favorites.

Oblivious to the enrapt listeners surrounding them in the
semidarkness, Brock pulled her closer. He lowered his head
and took her lips in a deep kiss. Her breathing nearly
stopped as she felt the caress of his tongue, and the emotion of her passionate response almost closed her throat.

"Let's go," he urged, and began pulling her through the
crowd to their table to signal the waiter for the check.

She sat very close to him in the car, with his hand on her
thigh burning through the fabric of her dress. When they
reached her house, he kept his arm around her and walked
her into her bedroom. In minutes they were out of their

clothing and murmuring frenzied words of love as they caressed each other and exchanged passionate kisses.

For an hour nothing mattered except the sensual pleasures of their intimacy, and their delight in each other's bodies. When the sharp hunger of their desire had been satisfied, they lay entwined and began to talk. There had been even less time for talking than for loving in the past stressful weeks, and it was a luxury to indulge in it now. They talked of their first meeting and explored their emotions. They confessed what they most loved about each other.

"You're so altogether," Charlotte told him.

"What does that mean?" he asked, lazily tracing circles on her breast.

"Comfortable within yourself."

He shook his head as if baffled. "I'm not sure I'm flattered. I wouldn't call you 'comfortable.' In fact, sometimes you're uncomfortably disturbing!" He looked at her soberly for a moment and said, "Maybe what I love most about you is your caring. You care deeply about things. It's wonderful that you care about me."

"You love me for loving you?" she teased.

"That, too. I love your body." He ran his hand over her hips. "I love your skin and your hair and the way you talk and the way you dress. Most of all I love your eyes because they tell me you love me."

She laughed softly. "I'm besotted with you, too. Isn't it wonderful?"

After a moment Brock said, "The Major asked me if I could make Portuguese soup. He still remembers that."

She made a slight but revealing movement away from him.

"He really enjoyed it."

"He hates me, but he likes my soup?"

Brock raised his head. "He doesn't hate you!" he protested.

"No? Then why did he hint that you're the father of Kate's baby? He doesn't really believe that, I'm sure."

"Bloody hell, Charlotte! Did he do that?"

"Deliberately—with a great deal of pleasure, I think." Not until she said it did she realize that she was still allowing some of her anger at Brock's father to spill over on him because he had given the old man the weapon with which to hurt her.

He related his meeting with Kate at the hospital and his offer of a ride home. "The Major was needling me. He keeps up this stupid running joke that I'm a great stud."

"Oh?" Charlotte drew back to look at him. "What gave him that idea?"

He was not sure she was just teasing, and he silently cursed his father's sense of humor. His annoyance put an edge to his voice. "Look, I can't explain the Major. It's just something he's always done, teasing me about my...my masculinity. Sometimes he gets pretty explicit."

"What gave him the idea you were training to be her birth coach?"

"Her *birth coach*? You're kidding!"

"I'm not. He mentioned Lamaze."

"What the hell is that?"

"Natural childbirth. He said you were helping her with her exercises."

"Exercises," Brock said limply. "Well..." The conversation had got way out of hand. He sighed and began to explain. "Kate left a prescription on the seat of my car, so I had to take it over to her that night. I met her aunt and she made coffee and, well, she'd been helping Kate practise some breathing exercises. Kate's enthusiastic about anything she's doing, isn't she? She pulls everyone else into it—"

"Even having a baby." Charlotte sighed.

He looked at her. "You're not jealous of our little Kate?" he teased.

"How about her attractive aunt?"

"Estelle? Hey, she's pure steel!"

Charlotte lay on her side, facing him, and considered his words. So it was 'Estelle' and 'Brock.' Naturally it would be, given Brock's easy way with people. She said thoughtfully, "Yes, Estelle's a man-eater. Wade called her a barracuda."

Brock laughed softly. "Oh, she's not that bad."

"A female version of the Major."

Brock said, "You're calling my father a barracuda?"

"Didn't you say he was woman-eater?"

"Yeah," Brock said, after a moment.

She waited, but he didn't volunteer anything more. The room was dim. Occasionally a light from a passing car threw a wheeling reflection across the ceiling.

"He made me so angry," Charlotte said regretfully, "that I asked him about your mother."

Brock raised himself on one elbow and stared down at her. "You *what*?"

"I asked him why you had no pictures of her. And why she left you."

"Why in the world did you do that?" Brock asked, deadly serious now.

"I wanted to hurt him—the same way he tried to hurt me," she confessed.

"An old man who is totally dependent on me?" he said incredulously. "I know he's difficult, but—"

"He's my enemy."

Brock lay back down, his arms at his sides. He was silent for long seconds, while she waited in a deepening hurt for him to contradict her. At last he said, "He won't even tell me why she left. One day she was there and the next day when I got home from school she was gone. When I tried to ask questions, the Major barked at me as if I were a noncom, and he looked so terrible that I thought he was going to die. I was sure that's what had happened to my mother. It frightened me so that I didn't question him again, not until much later.... He still won't talk about it."

"And you're still frightened."

"No, just exasperated," he said wearily. "It no longer matters. You have to understand, Charlotte. He didn't dump me in a boarding school. He took me with him everywhere, wherever he was stationed. He nursed me through my childhood mishaps and adolescent crises, saw that I had everything I needed—"

"Except love?"

"You're wrong there. He wears a prickly coat, but it hides a lot of love. I've never doubted that, even though it embarrasses him if I hug him and I'm often exasperated enough to yell at him. He's my only family and I'm stuck with him."

Charlotte watched him with troubled eyes. That had sounded like an ultimatum. *Love me, love my father.* Just as she had said, in effect, *Love me, love my son.*

"I know, darling," she said helplessly. "I guess I'm stuck with him, too. Forget I complained, will you? I really like the old porcupine, you know, just because he's yours. I'll try harder to make him like me."

Brock turned toward her. "We could just get married," he suggested, tracing with his finger the fine blue line of a vein between her shoulder and her breast. He lowered his head and kissed it, sending a healing balm of pleasure radiating from the spot.

"And hope our responsibilities go away?" Charlotte asked dreamily.

"Oh, they won't go away. But we could continue to live apart. That would be one solution," Brock mused. "I could stay all night once in a while without offending your son's sensibilities. It's getting harder all the time to get up at midnight and leave you." He pressed his lips against her shoulder again, and murmured, "Your skin is so soft...."

"What about your father's sensibilities?" she asked. "It seems to me you're pretty careful not to offend them by staying out after midnight. Or doesn't he know why you left him alone tonight?"

"If we were married, we could send the Major over here for the night. Hey, maybe that's the answer," he said lazily. "Let them live here! We'll take my apartment."

Charlotte's laughter was wry. "You tempt me."

Brock rolled on his back and put his hands behind his head, staring up at the ceiling. "The Major's getting more mobile all the time."

"But will he be able to live alone?" Charlotte asked. "Ever?"

He was silent for a long time. "I'd always worry about his falling again, and he would hate that. But he hates my taking care of him even more."

She sighed. "I can see the scenario. We marry and buy a three-bedroom house, so your father can have a room that he hates. We take Quarters's doghouse with us, but Quarters prefers to go with Wade in the van. Then Wade comes home one day with Kate and the baby and they say, 'Of course, Wade's room is large enough for the three of us!' And the circus begins. It would make a great sitcom."

Brock sat up and put his legs over the side of the bed. "I wish we were as young as Wade and Kate are. We'd get married anyway, and *make* it work."

She flinched. "Don't try to be prophetic. So far, Kate's holding out."

Brock kissed her, then got up and began to get ready to leave her.

Charlotte watched him with both love and misery in her eyes. At least they were not parting with a quarrel this time. But how long could their love survive, sustained only by these snatched hours together—wonderful hours but far too brief and ultimately frustrating?

Yet, what else could they do? Marry and let the chips fall? Brock was right. At eighteen, when she married Garth, she might have done that. Now she tried to calculate the emotional cost to each one involved if they failed to make it work.

After a while he kissed her tenderly, then left. Charlotte didn't urge him to linger. Wade would be home in less than an hour.

CHARLOTTE CONTINUED TO DRIVE Kate to her Wednesday-afternoon parenting class at the hospital. Sometimes she met Ellin Ferdinand there and they had a cup of coffee together while Kate was learning new mothering skills.

Ellin looked positively radiant the day she told Charlotte, "Ferdie is taking a vacation!" They were sitting at a small white table in the hospital cafeteria with their coffee and Danish between them. "We're going to Ireland! He's finally agreed to go farther than the nearest medical convention because when he was a boy he had a fantasy about owning a castle in Ireland with his own pony." She laughed delightedly. "At least he's willing to leave his patients with another doctor for two weeks. It's a start."

"I hope he enjoys it so much he'll do it again," Charlotte said.

"I'm going to see to it. I don't want him toppling over with a heart attack himself!"

Charlotte smiled at the woman who had become a close friend. She knew now that Ellin had not been urging her husband to retire because she was bored, but because she worried about him. She hoped Dr. Ferdie realized it, too.

At the end of their pleasant hour together, she picked up Kate, who was getting very large and finding her new weight awkward, but loving the attention it brought her. She was still enjoying her role as expectant mother, and Charlotte listened tolerantly as Kate instructed her in the best way to hold an infant.

"The nurse is wonderful," Kate told her. "She answers all my questions without making me feel like a nerd. So many things are happening that I don't understand. My body makes noises and I go from happy to sad like a bouncing yo-yo. I thought I was coming unglued, but she said it's my hormones. All those symptoms—" She waved her hands in the air.

"Like heartburn? Backache?"

Kate looked at her in pleased surprise. "Yeah. She said they don't mean I'm going to drop dead."

Charlotte laughed. Then she frowned slightly and said, "But you must report anything that alarms you to your doctor, so he can prevent things from going wrong."

"Yeah," Kate said again. "When I see him he's the one who asks the questions."

They were on Kate's street now. Charlotte felt Kate stiffen beside her and glanced at the girl. She was staring straight ahead, her eyes fixed on the van parked on the wrong side of the street in front of her apartment building. Charlotte followed her gaze. It was Wade's van, and he was sitting behind the wheel, with Quarters next to him on the front seat. Just sitting there, waiting.

Charlotte was already pulling to the curb, facing him. For a few agonizing seconds as their eyes met, Charlotte felt as if she were actually inside her son, sharing his emotions as intensely as if they were her own. His look focused on her face, at first incredulous and then with a terrible accusation of betrayal.

He gunned the motor. The van shot forward and zoomed recklessly around her car. She watched in her rearview mirror, helpless, as it roared away from them, down the street. She heard the squeal of tires as Wade turned the corner sharply and the thud of his precious sound equipment slamming against the side of the van.

Her fear was so paralyzing she could scarcely breathe. She should have told him she was seeing Kate. He would kill himself—her steady, sober Wade. It would be their fault—hers and Kate's. Kate must be made to see what she was doing to him.

She said urgently, "Kate—"

But Kate was out of the car and running awkwardly, with small steps, her head bent and her arms folded as if to protect her unborn child. Charlotte slipped out of the car and ran after her but she was through the door before Charlotte reached it. It closed and locked. Charlotte began pressing on the buzzer before Kate had time to reach the second floor. But she knew even then that Kate wasn't going to let her in.

BROCK HAD FINISHED INSTALLING the monitoring equipment in a cardiologist's new suite of offices in time to stop at a delicatessen and pick up a carton of his favorite sandwiches—hot sliced pastrami in good Italian buns, with a side of sauerkraut—for his and his father's evening meal.

It was about six-thirty when he reached their apartment. He heard Quarters barking as soon as he left the elevator.

The Major must have brought him home again! That damned dog was going to get them evicted yet. Quarters had been allowed in the apartment on a temporary basis in the beginning. When Charlotte had taken Quarters home with her, the manager had thanked him for making other arrangements.

Brock unlocked the door and immediately inhaled a strong odor of beer. An excited Quarters leaped at him and almost knocked him down.

"Quiet!" he shouted above the barking to no avail. "What the devil?" he yelled. "Have you been feeding your dog beer?"

"Quiet, sir!" the Major commanded from the living room, and Quarters stopped barking and began washing Brock's hands with his rough tongue.

"Well, Quarters, have you been kidnapped again?" Brock asked resignedly.

"Do I have to kidnap my own dog?" the Major demanded.

Just then Brock rounded the corner and saw Wade Emlyn sitting across from his father in the dining area, the table between them littered with empty beer bottles.

Wade's body was sprawled over a dining-room chair in a relaxed position that suggested he was in danger of sliding under the table. His eyes were red, and he squinted up at Brock as if he were seeing two of him. "Quarters was lonesome. I brought him home. Jus' for a l'l' visit."

"Well—fine," Brock said, his hand trying to pat the dog who was still lavishing licks of his tongue on him. This was an entirely new side of Charlotte's son.

"We've all been lonesome," Brock's father told him, his keen glance going significantly to Wade's flushed face. "We've been drowning our sorrows together."

"I can see that. I won't even ask what sorrows. How about—"

"You don't need to ask. We'll tell you," the Major said. "Our sorrows are all women." He lifted his beer bottle, which Brock had a strong suspicion was empty. "To women, those mysterious bitches we love and hate and will never understand."

"To the mishterious witches," Wade echoed.

His father was not entirely sober, either, Brock realized. "I'll drink to that, if you'll both switch to coffee with me now. I've brought food. Pastrami and sauerkraut."

"Cheers!" said the Major, lifting his empty bottle again. But Wade got up precipitately and headed for the bathroom. In seconds they heard sounds of someone being violently ill.

The Major smiled slightly and said nothing. Brock hesitated. He realized that Wade would never forgive him if he followed him now and offered to help him, so he went into the kitchen and got out dishes and silverware.

In a few moments, a paler Wade came back to the dining room. "Sorry," he said in a chastened voice. He sat down at the table. Brock brought in three plates on which he had divided the sandwiches and the container of sauerkraut. He and his father began eating. Wade sat with his food before him, looking sick and stubborn. But at least he was soberer.

"Brock, did you know that my mother was seeing Kate?" he challenged.

"Yes. I've been seeing her, too."

The Major lifted his bushy eyebrows, but kept silent.

"You've been seeing her! Why?" Wade demanded with a flash of anger.

"Your mother and I both think that she needs help," Brock answered after a moment's reflection. He was trying to answer as honestly as he could. "She isn't admitting it, but she needs all the help she can get."

"Then why won't she let me help?"

"I don't know," he said truthfully. "She could be blaming you for the condition she's in. Quite naturally, I'd say, overlooking her own part in the conception."

"I could blame her," Wade said darkly. "She claimed to be safe."

"Never trust a woman," the Major advised.

"The trouble with that theory," Brock said slowly, "is that she seems quite happy with her condition. Frankly enjoying it. Like the Major says, Wade, the other sex is often something of a mystery."

Wade slammed his hand on the table. "I thought she loved me. I thought she would want to marry me."

"I know something about your mother, Wade, that's no mystery."

Wade looked up at him with a scowl.

"Your mother cares for you, very deeply. And she is also deeply concerned about Kate Parsons, about her welfare and that of your child. Do you believe that, Wade?"

"Yeah, I guess," Wade said finally. He stood up, unsteadily. "I better go home." Quarters sprang up with an expectant look.

"Coffee, first," Brock said gently.

"Yeah, right." Wade sank into his chair again, and Quarters collapsed at his feet, disappointed.

The Major was watching both of them sourly.

By the time Wade had sobered up enough to make it safe for him to drive home, it was very late.

CHARLOTTE WAS WAITING UP for her son. The telephone kept ringing—for Wade. Each time she heard it she froze, afraid it was the police calling to tell her that there had been an accident. She sat in the living room, unable to go to bed before Wade came home . . . if he came home.

She called one of his friends, but he said he hadn't seen Wade in weeks. She was afraid to tie up the telephone in case the police should call her. She wanted to call Brock, but she asked herself what he could do besides call the police. He was not well enough acquainted with Wade to know where to look for him! She wanted Brock's support, his comforting presence—but she didn't want to add to his own worries.

The telephone rang again. This time it was Brock. "Wade wanted me to let you know he's on his way home."

Charlotte felt the tension drain out of her. "Is he all right?"

"A little the worse for drink. But we gave him some coffee and made sure he was sober before he left."

Just then she heard Wade's van as he turned into the drive. "He's here," she breathed. "Talk to you later. Thanks, darling."

It seemed as if she had been waiting a fortnight, but it wasn't late, only eleven o'clock. The van's engine died. Moments later she heard Wade's steps on the back porch. Brock said he had been drinking—probably ever since that confrontation with her and Kate that afternoon! It was the first time, as far as she knew, that her hardworking, level-headed Wade had done such a thing. She sat still, waiting.

He came into the living room, red-eyed and reeking of beer, and went unseeing past her on his way to the bathroom where she heard him being sick. Charlotte got up and went out to the kitchen and brewed some mint tea.

He looked pale and miserable when he came out. She had expected him to still be angry with her, but he looked too sick. Charlotte placed a steaming cup and saucer before him.

"You haven't eaten, have you?"

He shook his head in revulsion, but after a moment he raised the cup of tea to his lips and tasted it. Charlotte made a thick sandwich of pot-roasted beef and brought it to the table. Then she poured herself a cup of the tea and sat down opposite her son.

They sat and drank the healing, aromatic liquid in silence. After a while Wade gingerly began eating. When some color began stealing into his cheeks, she said, "Would you like to know where I took Kate this afternoon?"

He didn't answer her.

She told him anyway. "I drove her to the hospital where she learned how to bathe a newborn infant. She doesn't have a way to get there—her aunt drives her car to work—and even if Kate were willing to ask you to drive her, you're over at the university all day."

"I'd cut classes!"

"Maybe that's what she's afraid of."

"How long have you been doing this?"

"About two months. Once a week."

"Why didn't you tell me you were seeing her?"

"Because she asked me not to."

He made a sound of frustration. "What's wrong with her? Why is she doing this to us?"

"She has her reasons, Wade. One of them is that she's determined that when she marries it will be for something more than to legitimize her baby. She has several close friends whose parents are divorced. She told me that a divorce hurts too much; she wants to protect her baby from that."

"Does Kate talk to you about me?"

"Hardly ever," Charlotte told him reluctantly.

He hit his fist on the table. "I know she loves me! Why is she so stubborn?"

"I believe that she thinks she's doing the right thing," Charlotte told him. "For you and for the baby. But someone has to look after Kate. She needs all the support she can get right now. These classes are giving it to her. All I can do is see that she gets there. Her aunt is too busy. Kate's baby is important to me because he is your child, and my grandchild. I want to see that neither Kate nor your baby is neglected. Okay?"

Even as she spoke the words, she was aware of the truth she didn't want to face—if Kate never married Wade the baby she carried could be lost to them. Kate could marry someone else. She could move a continent away and the connection would be broken. This child could grow up a stranger to both Wade and herself. The thought was painfully distressing.

Wade chewed methodically on his sandwich.

"I think Kate cares for you, Wade," Charlotte ventured.

"She sure isn't giving me any signals," he said bitterly.

"Right now there's no room in her life for anything but the changes taking place in her own body and all the new things she must learn before the child she's carrying arrives. It's a tremendous challenge, because it is going to change her entire life."

"It's changed *my* life," Wade protested.

"It's taking her in a totally new direction. That's why you feel cut adrift."

"I feel used!"

"Remember how young Katie is. If you can be patient you may be able to win her back when all this is over."

Wade looked at her curiously. "I thought you didn't like her, Mom."

"Kate's very likable. I thought she was too young for you, darling—" she sighed "—and not very stable."

"Are you changing your mind about her?"

Charlotte considered her feelings toward the girl for a moment. "She's going through an experience that usually matures a woman in a hurry, and so far she's coping pretty well." She smiled at Wade. She didn't think it would help to remind him that Kate's toughest tests were ahead—not only the birth but the unending demands of an infant's care afterward. "Yes," she said, "I think I'm beginning to be fond of her."

Wade swallowed the last of his tea and said wryly, "I'm going to bed."

CHAPTER SIXTEEN

THE BREACH BETWEEN THEM that had been widened by the encounter at Kate's place had not been healed by their talk. As the weeks of Kate's pregnancy dragged on, Charlotte seldom saw Wade. He was taking a summer session at the university and did his studying at the library. Apparently he was accepting more playing dates than he had in the winter, because he was never home.

Charlotte worried that he was working too hard, trying, perhaps, to fill the emptiness Kate had left in his life. But she could only surmise that. Always, before, they had been able to maintain a feeling of communication even though they were seldom home at the same time. Now that feeling of closeness was gone. She might win in her struggle to keep him in school, but she was losing him, and her heart was heavy.

Some weeks after it happened, Brock told her about the evening he had arrived at his apartment and found Wade and his father drinking beer together. Charlotte had not taken it well.

"That's the first time in his nineteen years that my son has come home in such a state, and your father gave him the beer?" Her chin jutted out and her eyes were full of fire.

"Now wait a minute, love. Wade was no stranger to beer."

"I didn't say that. I know he and his friends managed to get it even before they were of drinking age, and I've allowed him wine at home. But he's never before come home in that condition!"

"He had provocation," Brock said mildly. "He thought he'd caught you and Kate conspiring against him."

"But why did he go to your father? They're practically strangers."

"You're forgetting Quarters. That's what they have in common. Your son has inherited your caring, love. He's been bringing Quarters for regular visits since the Major came over here to take his dog home. That's compassionate and very decent of him."

"*Wade* is visiting your father?"

Brock grinned. "I was home when they came one day. I don't know who was the most excited, Quarters or my father. He really misses that old mutt."

Charlotte was dumbfounded, and Brock said, "You didn't know?"

"I'm just surprised that Wade finds the time. He's away from home from early morning until late at night, not just three or four nights a week, but every day. He takes Quarters with him everywhere. I never see either of them."

"It's very thoughtful of him," Brock said.

Charlotte felt warm inside. It was the first time she could remember Brock volunteering praise for her son.

"Of course the Major is trying to make a misogynist of him," Brock told her with a glint in his eye. "They sat around for an hour swapping scurrilous comments about women."

She refused to be baited. "It was probably good therapy for both of them."

Brock kissed her, and they talked no more of family matters.

But by August, Charlotte's relationship with Brock had also reached an emotional impasse. Too many of their rare evenings together were ending in frustrations and pointless arguments, and Charlotte suggested they take her own advice to Wade, and just let some time pass until their situation became clearer.

Now and then Brock reminded himself that he would be a happily married man now, if it were not for the Major's dog and Kate's unborn child. The child had become a real person to him that first afternoon he'd talked to Kate. It had happened in that moment when the young girl had taken his hand and laid it on her stomach and he had felt the tiny bit of life move inside her.

Since then he had experienced a reluctant but growing interest in the progress of her pregnancy, and as he found excuses to see her again he knew he was developing a strong affection for the young girl. He found solace from his loneliness in observing how cheerfully Kate, in her untutored but rapidly maturing mind, was accepting the challenge of her situation.

He had driven her to her doctor once, but he had stopped by the apartment several times when he was on his way home after working late, so her aunt was usually with her.

Brock got on well with Estelle Drew. He thought on the whole Estelle had taken a sensible approach to Kate's teen pregnancy; but that was one of the things he and Charlotte disagreed about so often that they had agreed not to discuss it any more.

"She's encouraging Kate to keep Wade's baby, but when it comes to the bottom line," Charlotte had insisted darkly, "Estelle will put her own priorities ahead of Kate's or the baby's needs. She's a completely selfish woman."

"Perhaps," he said, "but that doesn't necessarily make her a monster. She's very bright. She's simply another ambitious career woman who is projecting her failed desires on her niece, and Kate is young enough to be malleable."

To him, that explained Kate's determination to become a single mother, no matter what the consequences, and her pie-in-the-sky dream of becoming a lawyer.

Charlotte conceded that Estelle was very bright. That had been her own impression of the woman. So why did Brock's rational analysis of the situation rankle her? She still could become very emotional over her expected grandchild. "It's pie in the sky, all right," she said of Kate's dream, and added, "Poor darling."

"The mystery to me," Brock said, "is why Kate is treating Wade so badly, when they were lovers. If she were unhappy about being pregnant, I'd say she blamed him for it, but she seems to glory in her condition."

"Something happens to a woman, even as young a woman as Kate, when she becomes pregnant," Charlotte said dreamily. "It's something a man can't really understand."

"Obviously," Brock said rather shortly, because he was a little ashamed of his intense curiosity about Kate's condition, and that led to more words, which led to their agreement not to discuss it.

The one thing they both agreed on was that Kate would need support to enable her to cope with the additional changes motherhood would bring into her young life. She was not likely to achieve any other of her goals in the near future. Right now, they agreed, she was still hazy about what they were.

So Charlotte continued to drive her to her parenting classes and now and then Brock stopped in just long enough to have a cup of coffee with Estelle and listen to Kate's latest discovery about how her body was going about its current mission.

ONE EVENING in the first week of August the telephone
rang while Brock was helping his father, who still found it
difficult to remove his socks, get ready for bed. He got out
a pair of pajamas and flung them at the Major, then went
to answer the insistent ring.

Kate Parsons said, "Can you come over, Mr. Morley?"

Her voice sounded unnaturally high, and he responded
quickly. "What's wrong, Kate?"

"Nothing's *wrong*! I just need someone to help me do
my exercises."

He had been drawn into helping her with her breathing
exercises gradually. Estelle would be coaching Kate when
he arrived. She would suggest that Brock take her place
while she prepared coffee and cake for them, or while she
worked on a brief she had brought home from the office.
Kate had enjoyed instructing him in the difference between early-contraction breathing from the lungs, and the
diaphragm breathing that was supposed to help relieve the
pain of delivery; but he still felt quite ignorant.

"Where's your aunt?"

"I don't know. She said she was working late, but no one
answers at her office."

"Do you feel all right?" he asked anxiously. Kate must
be in her eighth month.

"Yeah, but I don't want to be alone. Will you come?"

"Of course. Can I bring you some ice cream or something?"

"No," she said resignedly. "My doctor has me on a diet.
Just come."

Brock hesitated, feeling fresh reservations—or was it an
intuition? "Maybe you should call Mrs. Emlyn, Kate."
Charlotte knew he was helping her keep an eye on the situation, but he wasn't sure how she would feel about his
spending time alone with Wade's girlfriend.

"Mrs. Emlyn's not home, either. Besides, she's farther away," Kate objected. "You've helped me before."

Had she called Charlotte or not? "Wade won't be there to answer the phone when you call," he reminded Kate gently, guessing the reason for her reluctance to call Charlotte. "This is one of his nights at the radio station, isn't it?"

"Mr. Morley. Brock." She sounded very young, with an almost desperate note in her voice. "Just say yes or no, will you? Are you coming or not?"

His alarm signals were going off again. He wondered if his father had picked up the extension by his bed. The old man was quite capable of listening in.

"I'll be there in no time," he promised.

He made sure the Major had everything he might need on his night table, placed the telephone and his cane where he could easily reach them, and told him where he would be. His father made no comment other than to pick up his remote control and turn on his television set. Brock grabbed a jacket and went down in the elevator to the parking garage.

It was a balmy night. A fog bank lying offshore concealed the mountains of the Olympic peninsula but stars were shining overhead, clustered around a sliver of new moon. Inland the moonlight fell on Mount Rainier, a pale snow-topped triangle low in the midnight-blue sky, a distant cold place reminding one that the summer still joyously a-bloom in the city on the Sound was impermanent. As impermanent as youth. Winter always came.

He parked in front of the thirties-era apartment building, remembering that Charlotte's Dr. Ferdie had told him how the Great Depression of that time had caught Seattle with hundreds of new apartment buildings that stood vir-

tually vacant until America began preparing to enter Worl
War II.

"Brand-new apartments went for a song," Dr. Ferdi
had said. "A medical student could get one free just fo
sleeping in an empty building in those days."

Brock wished it were as easy today. For a few seconds h
played with a fantasy in which he and Charlotte woul
marry and rent three adjoining apartments and stash eac
one of their looming responsibilities in a separate one, s
they could have privacy in their own. He walked up unde
the old magnolia tree to the entry of the building, buzze
Kate, and was admitted to the foyer.

Upstairs, Kate opened the door as he stepped out of th
elevator, and greeted him with a wide smile. Her figure wa
grotesque now and the contrast between her youth and he
condition struck Brock anew as tragic. This was a girl wh
should be out playing tennis with her contemporaries c
rehearsing the lead in a school drama.

Instead she was carrying a skein of fine wool and as h
walked with her into the living room she showed him som
laboriously practised knitting stitches. She laughed. "To
morrow night Aunt Stelle will rip out everything I've don
tonight. I've given up learning how to knit in time to mak
a carriage robe for my baby!"

"I'm afraid I can't help you there," Brock said, grin
ning. "Now, if you wanted to learn how to whittle a whi
tle..."

"'Whittle a whistle!'" she echoed, giggling, as de
lighted as a child would be with a tongue twister. "M
Morley, whittle me a whistle, will you, please?"

It was this side of Kate's personality that he found en
dearing—the part of her that was still a wondering child
"Actually," he said, "I have to have a willow wand."

She clapped her hands and chanted, "Whittle me a whistle from a willow wand!" Her joyous laughter pealed. "What's a 'willow wand'?"

"It's a tough flexible branch from a willow shrub, very slender. In Idaho where my father was stationed one year, my friends taught me how to slip the bark from the smooth core of a straight section of a wand and cut a notch in it, and then replace the bark to make a whistle. It took a certain skill. The end you blow has to be shaped like the mouthpiece of a wood instrument."

"Can you still make one?" she demanded.

"I'm afraid I don't remember exactly how we did it. It was a long time ago." He felt a twist of nostalgia. Idaho had been while his mother was still with them. "In Idaho," he went on, "there are many streams that run all year long, in winter under the ice, with willow shrubs growing thick along the banks. In summer the water is so clear you can see the stones on the bottom as if you were looking at them through a pane of glass, and the stones are all colors of the rainbow."

"That's beautiful," Kate said with a sigh. Her expression of wonder changed, as quickly as one of his monitor screens could dissolve, to a look of pure fun as she began chanting again, "Whittle me a whistle from a willow—" Another expression wiped the glee just as swiftly off her face and she cried, "Oh—oh—oh—"

Brock leaped to his feet. "What is it, Kate?" he said, with a terrible feeling that he already knew. "Take deep breaths!" he ordered. She turned wide, unfocused eyes on him and opened her mouth obediently, while he drew in breath with her, trying to still his own panic. *Not now! Where was Estelle? Charlotte! Help!*

In a few seconds Kate relaxed, and comprehension came
back into her eyes. With it was stark fright. "But it isn'
time!" she protested.

"I think you'd better call your doctor," he said shakily

"Yes," she said, rising to her feet. "He'll probably tel
me it's false labor. Everybody talks about that." She tried
to smile at him as she went to use the phone in the kitchen
but stopped. "You won't go?"

"I'll be here, Kate. Don't worry."

In a few minutes she was back. "The doctor said to ge
off my feet. If I have any more contractions, call him again
and he'll meet me at the hospital. If I don't have anothe
one, I can wait and come in to his office tomorrow. He say;
he can give me something to stop premature delivery."

She looked a lot calmer than Brock felt. She sat down or
the sofa and swung her feet up, then picked up her knit
ting. Brock thought how pretty she was. Pregnancy ha
made her bloom, but tonight he thought she was a trifl
pale.

"I don't want to have a preemie," she said, fear makin
her dark eyes look black. "The nurse said teen mother
were more likely to have premature babies. More preemie
die in infancy. If they live, some of them who're very pre
mature have fits or low IQs." She let out a hiccupin
breath. "I don't think I could handle it if I had a pree
mie."

"Here, now, don't be thinking such negative thoughts,
he scolded her. "That's the kind of thing that can happe
if they weigh less than a pound or two." He was improvis
ing, because he knew nothing about such things excep
what he read in the newspapers. But he said, "Look at you
You're already too big to have a kid that tiny."

She giggled.

"Besides, you've been taking care of yourself. Some girls don't, you know."

"Yeah," she said. "I guess the nurse was trying to scare us into taking care of ourselves." She picked up her needles again, but she was clearly in no state to practise knitting stitches.

Brock himself was just a hairbreadth away from panic. "What's your aunt's office phone number? She should be home with you tonight."

Kate told him and he went to use the telephone. There was no answer at the law firm where Estelle worked, so he dialed Charlotte's number. There was no answer there, either.

A half hour later he looked up Estelle's boss's home number and was nonplussed when his wife answered and said her husband was at the office. Another call there confirmed that neither he nor Estelle was there. No doubt they were together somewhere, Brock thought angrily. And Charlotte was still not at home.

No matter. Kate hadn't had another contraction. But Brock felt a responsibility to stay with her until Estelle arrived. He would be leaving the Major alone in his apartment. The practical nurse had lasted only a little longer than the one he had hired in Portland, but in a way her defection had been good for the Major. Alone all day most of the time, he had been forced to exercise his weak legs, and he had become more self-sufficient.

Brock called him and told him that Kate was having premature labor pains and he was going to stay with her until her aunt came home. "I might have to take her to the hospital," he explained, "and if that becomes necessary I'll likely be away most of the night."

"You dog," the Major said. "Have a good time."

Brock swore and heard the Major laugh gleefully.

When he returned to the living room, Kate was experiencing another contraction. She was breathing through her mouth and looking scared.

"You're awfully tense, Kate. Remember all the things you told me you'd learned about the importance of relaxing?"

"But I don't know whether to relax and help her come or to hold back!" she wailed. "She's not supposed to come yet!"

Brock took out his watch. "We'd better start checking the time between contractions, hadn't we?"

"Yeah."

He went to the telephone and tried again to reach Estelle and Charlotte—without success. When another contraction came within ten minutes, Kate was calmer than he was. When her face contorted with pain, she opened her mouth and took several quick deep breaths. Brock watched her trying not to let her see how nervous he was. He felt increasingly helpless.

During the next hour he tried to reach Charlotte again but there was no answer.

"You'd better call my doctor again," Kate told him. The contractions were coming irregularly, from six to ten minutes apart, but one interval was only four minutes. "I don't think she's going to wait."

"Of course." He was proud of her young strength. He got hold of the doctor and reported that the contractions were coming more frequently, even though he was keeping Kate flat on the sofa.

"I'll call the hospital and make arrangements. It looks as if that baby may surprise us."

"She's very worried about a . . . preemie."

"Tell her not to worry. It's not that premature. Very young mothers frequently deliver at seven months and the pregnancy is over eight. We can probably treat it as a natural birth, although I'll want to examine her first. I'll meet you at the hospital.''

Brock was made even more panicky by this unfamiliar talk, but he was impressed by the controlled way Kate began making her plans. "I was going to pack my hospital bag next week," she mourned.

"You're to stay off your feet, remember?"

"Okay," she said, "then I'll have to tell you what to pack."

She stiffened with another contraction, which was obviously painful, and then made a visible effort to relax, breathing deeply through her mouth. "It hurts more than I thought it would," she whispered when it was over, and he ached with tenderness for her naïveté and youth.

"Mr. Morley—Brock—do you remember anything about how we breathed together the night you drove me to my natural birth class? That's just one of the things you may have to do for me if Aunt Stelle doesn't come home in time. Can you help me?"

He tried to keep the wild panic he felt out of his voice. "Sure, Katie. If you can tell me what to do."

When he saw Estelle Drew again, he would likely break her neck.

Following Kate's directions, he packed some personal things for her and the expected baby in the suitcase she told him to get down from the closet shelf, and they were ready. She stopped to put a pale pink salve on her lips and write a note for her aunt, telling her where they were going. Another contraction interrupted their preparations.

When it was over, she pulled Brock down beside her on the sofa and talked to him about what he would be expected to do in the role of birth coach. "Let's practise it once

more," she suggested. "Just in case Aunt Stelle doesn't ge
there in time."

Brock agreed, secretly praying that Estelle Drew woul
walk into the apartment before they left. They had hardl
finished the exercise when Kate gasped and grabbed hi
wrist, digging her fingernails into the skin. Brock said, "Al
right, now, begin relaxing from your head. Take a dee
breath...another...from the diaphragm...another..
another... Now several quick breaths!" He was breathin
with her. Perspiration broke out on his upper lip.

"Okay?" he asked when she sighed and began breath
ing normally again. "Now let's get the hell over to the hos
pital!"

IN BROCK'S APARTMENT the Major put down his bedsid
telephone and lay looking up at the ceiling for a few mir
utes, fingering his beard. The apartment was too quiet, bu
he scorned television. Even the bed was too still—n
squirming of a warm perspiring body at his feet.

Presently the Major sat up in bed and reached for h
cane. He got up and walked to where Brock had hung h
trousers over the back of a chair. Taking them with him, h
lay down on the bed again, and with some struggle mar
aged to get them over his feet.

When he had pulled them up over his legs, he sat up o
his bed and called a taxi. He finished dressing, except fc
his socks and shoes. Wearing his slippers, he sat in the li
ing room and waited. When the buzzer sounded, he walke
out of the apartment and took the elevator down to th
lobby. A very short man with an impudently turned-u
nose, who was wearing his billed cap slightly offsid
looked him over. "You called for a taxi?"

"Yes," said the Major. He gave the driver Charlotte Emlyn's address and followed him out to the cab.

It was a ten-minute ride. "Wait here," the Major told him. "I'll be right back with my dog."

The driver eyed him suspiciously, and when the Major started up the driveway to the backyard instead of going up the walk to the front door, he slammed out of his cab and followed him. "I'll go with you if you don't mind."

"Not at all," said the Major.

The house was dark, and the backyard was inky. "Come, Quarters!" the Major ordered softly.

There was no answering bark, except that of a disturbed dog several backyards away. The Major felt his way over the grass with his cane, and rapped it sharply on the doghouse. The sound it made was hollow.

The Major clumped over to the lawn chair and collapsed in it.

"What now?" asked the taxi driver.

"We wait."

"Not me. I want my money."

The Major stood up and took out his wallet. He counted out some bills, said, "Keep the change," and sat down again, his hands on the cane propped up before him.

The taxi driver looked down and seemed to see his slippers and bare feet for the first time. "You going to be all right here?"

The Major waved him off testily, and after a moment the driver left, shaking his head.

IT WAS ONLY ten-fifteen. To Brock, it seemed as if he had spent an eternity in Kate's apartment, trying to get in touch with Estelle or Charlotte. Now he was walking Kate down to the curb and helping her into the car for the drive to the hospital. It could have been his worst nightmare but unfortunately it was real. He was taking Kate to the hospital and there would be no one there to meet her except her doctor. And she expected him to be her birth coach.

Brock Morley, bachelor-about-town, a *birth coach*? No way. The doctor would just have to use anesthesia.

The night was still balmy and dry; he was thankful for that. It could have been raining and the roads slick. He started for the hospital, trying to stay calm and fighting his natural impulse to drive with his foot heavy on the accelerator. Beside him Kate inhaled sharply, and he knew another contraction was on the way.

"Oh—oh—oh!" she gasped, and Brock turned a corner so sharply that his rear wheel went up on the curb. When it bounced off, he lost control of the car for a few seconds—long enough to graze the fender of a car parked near the corner. There was a horrendous metallic screech.

"Oh!" Kate said more loudly.

Brock brought his car to a stop. Several men ran out of the store on the corner, and a police siren sounded behind him. He was in the lane of traffic and horns began blowing in the intersection. Brock glanced over at Kate, whose face was very white. An angry-looking man was thrusting his face in at her window. Brock's own hands were shaking.

A police officer walked up on Brock's side of the car. "Get out," he said. "Let's see if you can walk a straight line."

"Officer, I'd like a drink right now," Brock said desperately, "but I haven't had one. This young woman is about to have her baby, and I'm a little nervous."

The officer took one look at Kate's anguished face, and said, "What hospital, ma'am?"

It was Kate who answered him.

"Follow me," he told Brock. To the angry owner of the swiped fender, he said, "Get in touch with headquarters."

The police officer left, and Brock reached into his jacket for a business card, which he gave to the man whose car he had struck. Moments later, the police car passed them and Brock pulled out after it. That was the way they arrived at the hospital, with siren wailing.

Kate was having another contraction. Brock pulled up behind the police car at the emergency entrance and hit the brakes so sharply the tires squealed. Two attendants ran out with a gurney, but the police officer waved them away and charged into the emergency entrance.

"A deep breath," Brock reminded Kate. He could almost feel the pain with her. "Blow! From the diaphragm, Kate," he begged.

"Yes," she gasped.

When it was over, he helped her out of the car. The officer returned with a nurse and Brock turned Kate over to her, mentioning her doctor's name. "I'll park the car, honey, and be right back."

"I'll take her up to OB," the nurse said, smiling. "You can sign her in when you come back. Don't worry. You've got plenty of time."

He had never felt so inadequate as he drove his car over to the main parking area. Walking back, he remembered driving to Portland in the middle of an anxious night to find the Major trussed up like a mummy. *I seem to have a fatal attraction for hospitals,* he thought.

When he returned to the emergency entrance, he saw a pay telephone and he stopped to call Charlotte's number once more. There was still no answer. It didn't help his nervous state when the white-capped woman at the nurses' station on the obstetrical floor asked brightly, "Are you the father?"

"N-no!" he stuttered, and surprised himself by volunteering, "I'm the grandfather."

Wait until I tell Charlotte that one!

He found the room number the nurse gave him. The door was closed and he knocked before entering.

"Just a minute!" a woman's voice said. "Kate is putting on her gown."

Brock waited in the hall, wishing he were someplace, anyplace, else.

WADE DROVE UP HIS dark street with Quarters sitting on the front seat beside him. The dog's dusty black hair was matted in curls and his tongue was lolling with pleasure as he surveyed the pavement unrolling before them as intently as if he were driving the van. Late as it was, he had no intention of curling up in sleep as long as the van was moving.

Quarters was great company, Wade thought with affection, and he had an amazing affinity for automobiles. He could happily live in the van, waiting for Wade's infrequent visits between his classes and other appointments. Too bad Major Morley didn't have a van.

He was approaching the house, and he saw that it was completely dark. Turning into the driveway he pulled up close to the garage before he stopped and turned off the engine. When he opened the door on the driver's side, Quarters leaped over him and out in his usual rude fashion, began barking loudly as soon as he hit the pavement and tore off into the backyard. That was not unusual because he was always thirsty enough to head for his water dish, but it was not like him to make such a racket. Wade got out of the van and started across the yard. Quarters was standing up before one of the white garden chairs, barking like crazy. Wade stopped, as he realized that a man was sitting in the chair in the dark.

"Hey!" he said. "Who is it?"

Whoever it was was talking to the dog. "Hello, Quarters, old boy. How are you doing, sir?" The dog's bark was one of excitement, not of alarm.

Wade relaxed. It was the old soldier, Quarters's master. "Hey, man! This is a little late to come visiting, isn't it?"

"I'm not visiting," the old man said testily. Wade's eyes were adjusting to the inky darkness and he could see the pale white-bearded face above the outline of the white chair. "My jailer left me alone tonight, so I took the opportunity to come after Quarters."

"And found him gone, yeah? Quarters rides with me a lot. Where's your taxi?"

"He couldn't wait, so I dismissed him."

Wade had reached the chair. He looked down at the defiant old man. "I'd better call Brock and tell him where you are, hadn't I?"

"No need to call, son. Brock's likely to be away all night. He took his little pregnant girlfriend to the hospital."

Wade stiffened. "*Pregnant* girlfriend?"

"Very pregnant. Do you know her? Little girl with long dark hair?"

"Kate?" Wade exclaimed, his voice rising. "He took *Kate* to the hospital?"

"She's in labor."

"Oh, my God!" Wade started for the van. Quarters broke away from the Major's stroking hands to run ahead of him, anticipating him as usual. Wade stopped and turned back.

"Come on," he said. "You'd better go with me, Major Morley. I can't leave you here."

CHAPTER SEVENTEEN

KATE WAS SITTING UP in bed, an enormous pink blob in the quilted satin robe Brock had packed for her. She looked relaxed and expectant now that they were actually here. "Isn't this a gorgeous room?" she greeted him.

He hadn't noticed. He was still too nervous, and becoming angry with Estelle, who should be here. And where was Charlotte? But at Kate's urging, he looked around at the cheerfully painted walls and carpeted floors and thought that it was a far cry from the white instrument-filled room in the Portland hospital that the Major had inhabited for nearly a month.

The doctor came, still in his street clothes, booming a hearty greeting as he advanced into the room. "Well, Kate! Contractions, is it?" A young man with a shock of red hair that showed a tendency to curl and a pleasantly casual manner, he held out a hand to Brock and asked Kate, "Is this your father?"

She giggled and gave Brock a bright, teasing glance.

Brock said, "I hope she's going to be my daughter-in-law."

Kate sobered immediately, her fine black brows coming together in a scowl.

The doctor looked from her to Brock and back again. "Where's your aunt, Kate?"

"Working."

"We're trying to get in touch with her," Brock explained. He was conscious of the dampness of his hand compared to the doctor's firm dry grasp. *Where* were Estelle and Charlotte?

"I left a note for her," Kate said.

"How far apart are your contractions, Kate?"

"Four to eight minutes."

"Baby's impatient, isn't she? Let's see if we can persuade her to wait a while longer." A nurse entered the room, exchanging a glance with the doctor, who said, "If you will wait outside, Mr.—"

"Morley."

"I'd like to examine my patient now."

The room was homey and attractive, but once outside the door, Brock was back in the cold harsh light of a hospital hallway. He walked down to a foyerlike square next to the nurses' station where there was a pay telephone. He tried both Estelle Drew's and Charlotte's numbers. Neither answered, although he hung on for a long time.

When he went back to Kate's room, the door was open, and she was watching television. "The contractions seem to have stopped," she informed him, "but the doctor isn't sending me home. He said I'd better spend the night. Especially because Aunt Stelle isn't home. He thinks the baby is ready to come." She said anxiously, "You won't leave me, will you?"

"Not until your aunt comes," he promised. He sat down in one of the overstuffed leather chairs, feeling greatly relieved.

His reprieve didn't last long. Soon the contractions were back, and coming more frequently. Kate buzzed the nurse, as she had been instructed. The petite young woman who came in was a pert brunette who looked only a few years older than Kate.

"I suggest you get out of bed and walk." She smiled at Brock. "You can time the contractions for me. Have you practised your breathing/blowing routine, Kate? Now's the time. This baby's on her way."

Brock stood up and looked at his watch. When he put a hand up to push back a lock of hair, his forehead felt damp.

"It will help if you walk with her," the nurse said. "Put your arm around her waist. It will support her back." She stood in the doorway for a moment and observed their progress with interest.

"When the contractions are closer together, we'll move you to the birthing room." She flashed another smile at Brock. "I'll give you a surgical gown, and show you where you can scrub up."

"Me? Scrub up?" he said, alarmed.

"You're the birth coach, aren't you?"

"No!"

Kate looked at him and giggled. "My aunt trained with me. I think she'll be here before the baby comes."

"God, I hope so!" Brock said fervently. Both Kate and the nurse laughed, and Brock wondered how he had ever got himself into this incredible situation. "Look, I'd better go telephone again."

He wanted to bolt for the pay phone, but Kate cried out, *"Oh*—oh—oh—"

He put his arm around her. "A deep breath, Kate. Another one. Keep your mouth open," he reminded her.

The nurse watched for a few seconds, nodded and then left. Brock thought he could cheerfully wring Estelle Drew's neck, and prayed Charlotte would be home the next time he called.

Fifteen minutes and two contractions later, the door swung violently open and Wade strode into the room.

"Oh!" Kate said, and began breathing in and out, very fast.

Brock held his breath, waiting for some kind of explosion. He tried to imagine what had happened to bring Charlotte's son here at this time, and could not.

Wade had stopped just inside the door, his eyes moving past Brock as if he were part of the furniture and fastening on Kate's pale face. "That's it, Katie," he said softly. "From the diaphragm," he urged, coming to gently elbow Brock out of the way and put his strong arm around her.

As she looked up at him, Brock saw the surprised expression leave her face. It was replaced by a look so naked, so filled with raw need, that he turned away, deeply moved. It was a look too intimate for a third person to share. These were kids but they were not too young to know an aching love.

He felt a warm flood of almost painful sympathy and liking for the two young people that he imagined was something like fatherhood. At that moment he was startled to see his own father appear in the open doorway and pause hesitantly.

"Oh, there you are," the Major said with the testiness of fatigue.

"Dad! What in hell are you doing here?" Brock was completely confused. He felt as if he were in a world suddenly gone crazy.

"It wasn't my idea. I was brought here." The Major's pale blue eyes were drawn to the young couple, and Brock saw them soften with a reflection of his own emotion. He was still confused, but exchanged a look with his father that shared a flooding warmth for the young expectant mother and the awed young father.

Brock indicated the armchairs and his father made his way across the room. Brock sat opposite him, and realized only then how his ordeal had exhausted him. He should go and try telephoning again, but for the moment he couldn't bring himself to move.

Wade and Kate began a leisured arm-in-arm pacing of the room while they carried on a low, intimate conversation, ignoring everyone else.

"You know what to do, Wade!" Kate marveled.

"You're not the only one who's been taking classes," he said softly, smiling down at her.

"Not in natural birth?" she murmured incredulously.

"Yeah. I told the instructor you couldn't come with me and she let me sit in without a partner. Sometimes she played your part for me. But I was chatting you up all the time in my head. I can coach you, Kate. I'm going to see my son born!"

She laughed softly. "Your daughter, you mean. I took the test, Wade, the one with the long name."

"Amniocentesis," said the nurse, who was back. "Who are you?" she asked Wade, looking interested. "I thought Kate's aunt—"

"I'm the baby's father," Wade replied, his voice deep with pride.

"Well, welcome aboard," the nurse said with a grin.

Wade and Kate resumed their walking. "We have to have a name for your daughter by the time she arrives," she reminded him.

"I've been concentrating on boys' names," Wade said "Like Mark. And Jim."

"I've been calling her Candy," said Kate.

"Nope. We can do better than that. How about Madonna?"

Kate laughed. "Be serious! How do you like Carla?"

Before he could answer, she was concentrating on another painful contraction. They paused and he rubbed her back gently, murmuring, "Relax, Katie, relax."

The nurse had looked at her watch. Now she said to Brock and his father, "It will be a while yet."

Brock sighed and turned to the Major. "All right, now. Tell me why you aren't home in bed where I left you."

"There's a hell of a lot more going on here," the Major said, his eyes bright.

CHARLOTTE AND ELLIN FERDINAND stood up as the lights came on in the theater, still applauding the ballerinas and other dancers who had just taken their bows. Ellin had invited Charlotte to use her husband's ticket to the ballet when Dr. Ferdie had been called away on an emergency.

"That was very enjoyable," Charlotte told her friend as they made their way out with the rest of the audience.

"I'm so glad you could come with me," Ellin said. They walked together to where Ellin had left her car and joined the traffic lane of departing vehicles.

While Ellin drove through the warm night toward Charlotte's house, they recalled highlights of the ballet just performed and compared it with other performances they had seen. It was an interest they hadn't known before that they shared, and they were enjoying the conversation so much that Ellin said, "Shall we stop someplace for a cup of chocolate or an ice cream? It's still early."

"I'll make a cup of chocolate for you at my house," Charlotte offered.

"Great," Ellin said. "I can phone from there to see if Ferdie is home."

Wade's van was not in the driveway, and there was no welcoming din from Quarters. "That dog lives in Wade's van," she told Ellin.

They went inside and Charlotte walked into the kitchen to prepare hot chocolate. As usual, there was a note on the refrigerator door from Wade, though it was longer than usual: "If anybody's looking for Major Morley, I'm taking him to the hospital with me. Kate's in labor."

Major Morley here again? Wade was taking him to the *hospital*? Then the second part of his note hit home. "Oh dear heaven! Kate!" she gasped. "She's in labor!"

"So soon?" Ellin exclaimed. "It isn't her time, surely?"

"No, it isn't. I'm not sure but it must be at least between two and three weeks early. Something's wrong! I've got to be there, Ellin. I don't care if her aunt does think I'm unnecessary!"

"Of course you must go, my dear. I'll drive you over."

"If there's something wrong with the baby... I'm the grandmother, after all!"

"Of course," Ellin said again. "Just let me call my answering machine first, to tell Ferdie where we're going."

They went out to Ellin's Cadillac and she drove expertly over the shortest route to the hospital. Charlotte was in a state that was near shock. "If she's miscalculated, it could be nearly a month too soon. The baby's premature, Ellin."

"Doctors don't miscalculate, Charlotte. But Ferdie always says that babies are unpredictable. Kate's in good hands, Charlotte."

"She's so young. Everything's more of a risk than it would be if she were only a little older. Her doctor told her teenager mothers are more apt to be premature."

"A normal preemie can make it okay in today's hospitals."

"I'm glad you're driving, Ellin. My hands are like ice."

They reached the hospital. It was around eleven o'clock. The rooms were dimly lit but in the bright hallways there was the muted bustle of the night routine. A nurse directed them to Kate's room.

Charlotte's first impression was of a softly lighted, attractive bedroom, decorated in shades of terra-cotta and blue. Her eyes were drawn first to the lamp hanging over a large round table at which Brock and his father sat, quietly playing checkers. Then she saw Wade and Kate. They were walking slowly across the carpeted floor, their arms linked, their heads together, oblivious of everything except each other and this moment in their lives.

Charlotte knew the words Wade was murmuring in Kate's ear were love words, and the look on Kate's face made her eyes mist with emotion. She remembered walking with her husband like that the night Wade was born. It seemed like yesterday.

She wondered why Brock was here, but she was glad to see him. Her eyes sought his, wanting to share what she was feeling with him, and she was shaken by the emotion she saw in them. The inexpressible joy and relief they revealed told her how moved he was and how very glad to see her.

The two young people stopped and Charlotte tore her gaze from Brock's and stared when Wade looked at his watch and murmured, "Relax. Okay, now breathe with me. From your stomach." Kate was having a contraction, and taking it in stride. Wade was coaching her with total assurance. Kate looked up at her and smiled.

"The doctor's not stopping your labor, Kate?" Charlotte asked, in some anxiety.

"No, he says she'll be born sometime this morning." She lifted a radiant face to Wade, then asked Charlotte, "Did you know that Wade was auditing a natural birth class? He can coach me, since Aunt Stelle isn't here."

"No, I didn't know." Charlotte asked, "She?"

"We're talking about naming her Carla. Do you like it?"

"Carla," Charlotte said experimentally. Suddenly her anxiety was suffused with excitement. She felt almost numb with the conflict of her emotions.

Behind her, Ellin said, "That's a very pretty name."

Kate and Wade resumed their walking. Charlotte thought she had never seen two happier faces. Her eyes met Brock's again across the room, and she was warmed by the welcome on his face. He and his father had both risen from their chairs and she said, "Major Morley, I'm so glad to see you here. Ellin, this is Brock's father, Major Morley."

"I've been trying all evening to call you," Brock told her.

"We were at the ballet," Ellin said. "I'll leave you now Charlotte. Kate, my dear—and Wade . . ."

Kate paused. Ellin took her hands and kissed her cheek then kissed her again. "That one's for Carla. And one for the happy father." She rose on tiptoe to kiss Wade's cheek Kate beamed at her.

In seconds they were walking again, totally absorbed in each other and their whispered conversation. Charlotte thought, *We're all acting as if nothing can possibly go wrong, and I'm scared to death.*

She sat at the table with Brock and his father and surveyed the abandoned game of checkers. "How do you happen to be here, Major Morley?"

"It was not by my choice. I was trespassing in your backyard again," he told her, with the air of defiant satisfaction that always amused her. "I was looking for Quarters when Wade found me. He brought me here."

"I believe you thoroughly enjoy being an old reprobate!" Charlotte said. "Otherwise you wouldn't work so hard at it. Where is Quarters now?"

"In the parking lot. In Wade's van, which he vastly prefers to that pretentious doghouse Wade made for him."

"Yes," Charlotte said ruefully. "He'll never be content just to run after cars again. He'll always try to jump aboard."

"Completely corrupted!" complained the Major, but there was no malice in his voice.

It was obvious that everyone's thoughts were focused on the young couple walking to and fro in the softly lit room. From time to time, Wade looked at his watch and coached Kate through another contraction. They were coming more often, but the young parents remained calm and relaxed.

Presently the nurse entered and consulted quietly with Wade and Kate, then announced that it was time for Kate and her birth coach to move to the birthing room. "The family can remain here," she told them. She smiled at the Major and said, "Let me guess. You're the baby's great-grandfather?"

His head jerked back. Charlotte waited for the explosion, remembering the salty names he had called her when he let go. But to her surprise his lips quirked. "That will be a new experience," he told her, fingering his beard.

She smiled at Charlotte and Brock. "Later, I can give the grandparents surgical jackets and show you where to scrub, if you want to observe the birth. You won't actually be in the delivery room, but I can put you in a viewing room. You'll see the baby as soon as the mother does."

Charlotte's heart swelled until her excitement nearly spilled over. She sent a glowing glance at Brock, who looked more frightened than excited. He said, "Estelle, Kate's aunt will be coming. I'm sure she'll, uh, want to be with Kate."

The nurse shrugged. "If she isn't here, you're welcome."

"Thanks," he said hollowly.

IT WAS AN HOUR later when Estelle Drew arrived at the hospital and came storming into Kate's room. Charlotte had obtained a deck of cards from one of the nurses and she and Brock and the Major were playing gin rummy.

"Where's Kate?" Estelle demanded of Brock. "I found her note. Why did she call you? It's not her time yet! It can't be her time!" Her hair was windblown, and her neck scarf disarranged. In her distress and her haste, she had lost the polished appearance of the successful career woman and looked like any mature woman whose daughter—or ward—was in premature labor.

"She's in the birthing room. The doctor thinks she will deliver tonight," Brock explained.

"Where is it? The room, I mean. I have to be with her—"

"Wade's coaching her," Charlotte told her.

"*Wade?*" Estelle's eyes opened wide in shock. "But he can't! I'm her coach! I trained with her." No one answered her, and she turned on the Major. "Who are you?"

"The *great*-grandfather," the Major said, taking obvious pleasure in the thought that he was shocking her still more. "And where have you been?"

"Uh, working, then we went out for something to eat." But Estelle's concentration was elsewhere and Charlotte realized that she was more concerned about Kate than angry, and for the first time felt a surge of sympathy for her. Before Charlotte could speak, however, Estelle turned on her high heels and soon they heard them clicking rapidly along the vinyl floor of the hall toward the nurses' station.

"Perhaps," she murmured to Brock, "Kate's aunt is human, after all."

"Haven't I told you?" he said with a grin.

She wasn't sure when it had happened, but they were holding hands tightly.

In minutes Estelle was back, accompanied by the doctor, who was talking loudly as they entered the room. "Kate absolutely must not be disturbed in the transition stage. I must insist that she have complete privacy and relaxation to do her work: It's fundamental to natural birth. She is being coached very well by the baby's father, which I consider an ideal situation. When the final stage begins, Miss Drew, the nurse will allow you and Mrs. Emlyn, as the closest relatives, to observe. Until then, wait here."

Estelle's face was still flushed with anger, obviously from an argument she had lost, but she did not persist. She sank into the fourth chair at the comfortable round table. The Major picked up the cards. "Do you want a hand, Miss Drew?"

"It's apt to be a long night, Estelle," Brock warned her.

"Why not?" she said, and the Major began dealing. Estelle's hands shook as she picked up her cards.

Charlotte leaned across the table and touched her arm. "Kate's going to be all right."

Estelle gave her an uncertain smile.

"I remember the night you were born, Brock," the Major said, and Brock looked at him in surprise.

"I wasn't allowed anywhere near your mother. I was made to feel like the enemy by her guards—the matron and her iron maidens. I spent the night on vinyl chairs in an ugly waiting room, hearing your mother's screams. When they finally let me in to see her, they had already taken you away from her, and she was half out of her mind. She looked up at me and said, 'Never again, do you hear me? Never again!' Afterward she told me they had strapped her to the delivery table."

Charlotte exclaimed, "Oh, no! How awful!"

Brock felt a nausea in his stomach and a roar of wind in his ears. His father had never told him anything as revealing as this about his marriage or the mother who had left him.

"I had to go down the hall to the nursery and look through a glass wall at a dozen babies to find you. They all looked alike to me."

Brock stood up and mumbled, "I've got to find a drink—a drink of water, that is."

"There are paper cups in the bathroom," Charlotte told him. She looked after him anxiously, sensing his distress.

The Major did not seem to notice it. He picked up his cards, one by one, apparently engrossed in his hand.

TWO HOURS LATER, Brock and Charlotte returned from the coffee machine with four cups of coffee, which they hoped would keep everyone awake. Brock had offered to take the Major home and return, but his father had indignantly refused. "I wouldn't miss this for a measly few hours of sleep!"

Estelle had made two trips to the birthing room and had been turned away each time with the word that things were "progressing." For someone who had trained with Kate to coach her, Estelle was taking it hard. She was pale, her hands trembled, and she was so nervous that she was constantly dropping cards.

They had just finished their coffee when the nurse came with "hatching jackets" for Estelle and Charlotte to put on before entering the viewing room. She instructed them to scrub up and follow her. "It's 'push' time," she said. "It won't be long now."

Masked, with hair and clothing covered, Charlotte slipped into the viewing room with Estelle. Kate and Wade gave no sign of noticing them, but the nurse assured them that the young parents knew they were going to observe.

"They want you here," she said, "but they are very busy now."

The delivery room was dimly lit and the area where they stood was in darkness. Gradually Charlotte's eyes became accustomed to the scene before her. Kate was lying on a hospital bed, in a half-sitting position. Wade sat at Kate's head, and was rearranging pillows behind her so that she was more comfortable. Her face, red with effort, was running with perspiration.

"Oh, my God!" Estelle gasped. "Something's wrong!" Her hand, touching Charlotte's, was icy.

"Remember your training, coach," Charlotte admonished her. "You were told she would be 'laboring,' weren't you?"

"Yes, yes," Estelle said. "It's just that she—it's hurting her so much—I'm so excited I can't remember a thing. I've never seen a birth before, not even when a cat of mine had her kittens. She had them in the night, in a box of expensive wool fabric I was going to take to a tailor! But you—?"

"I've been there," Charlotte whispered. "I had Wade the natural way."

"Wade. Yes," Estelle said strangely. She was watching, wide-eyed. Wade was supporting Kate with his arm around her, and whispering in her ear. From the expressions on their faces, it was easy to read what was happening. He was whispering love words, and she was leaning into him, drinking in the sound of his voice as she concentrated on her painful task.

Now and then he wiped the perspiration from her brow with a damp washcloth. It was obvious that Kate was totally concentrating on what she was doing, and on Wade's signals to her to fill her lungs with air. It was also obvious that she was shuddering with the pain of the passage of the baby in its journey, and Charlotte recalled her own pain in shattering empathy. Beside her, Estelle trembled.

"I couldn't have coached her as well," she admitted. "I couldn't have stood it—"

The doctor, sitting on a stool at Kate's feet, had his back to them and it concealed what was happening at the foot of the bed, but they could read it in Kate's agonizing efforts, and they could hear the doctor's calm words of encouragement. "Good, good. You're doing great, Kate. All right, now, *push*!"

Charlotte knew the moment the baby slipped though the difficult passage into the air of the real world. Kate's face was suffused with a look of utter relief and she cried out in pleasure, Wade's face mirroring her emotion. It was the most moving thing Charlotte had ever experienced, even— and this surprised her—surpassing her memory of Wade's birth. She was so completely sharing this moment with Kate that she felt the girl's utter fatigue. But she could not relax yet.

She felt Estelle tense beside her as they waited in absolute stillness for what would happen next. The doctor stood up, still obscuring their vision. But he was holding something in his hands. When he moved aside, making a smiling remark to the nurse, they could see the baby lying across Kate's abdomen. Charlotte held her breath until she heard the tiny coughing sounds and then a wail as her newborn granddaughter spontaneously drew in her first breath.

She didn't feel the tears running down her cheeks until she turned to Estelle and saw her eyes brimming with tears. She opened her arms and they embraced tightly, sharing an emotion too deep to be put into words. Then they stood with their arms around each other and watched in silent fascination as Kate leaned forward to stroke her tiny child with two fingers, making a weary but smiling comment to Wade, who looked dazed with happiness.

Everything seemed to be moving in slow motion. Everyone was very relaxed now, enjoying the drama of the arrival of a new personality. The doctor and the nurse seemed to share the pleasure of the young parents.

Presently Charlotte saw the doctor clamp and cut the cord, then lift the baby and put her in a small bathtub filled with water on a low table beside Kate's bed. "It's her natural environment," the doctor explained. "It will make her feel at home in her new world."

Again there was no hurry. Everything was done leisurely with no alarming sudden movements. Charlotte realized with belated wonder that the baby had not been spanked or dangled by the heels. They could see her plainly in her warm bath. The room was still fairly dim and very quiet.

Carla stopped crying and looked around her. She raised one tiny hand to break the surface of the water. The other followed, and the incredibly small fingers reached to touch each other, then made delicate swimming motions in the air. The baby's head turned toward her parents.

"She's playing!" Estelle breathed.

Charlotte's response choked in her throat. She and Estelle would always have the memory of this shared moment in common, she knew, and it would be impossible, ever again, to think of Estelle as other than a friend.

CHAPTER EIGHTEEN

THE EVENTS OF THE NIGHT had left Brock shaken. He wa[s] humbled by Kate's trust in him, and he was not at all su[re] he could have measured up to what she had expected [of] him. It was a relief to know that Charlotte and her au[nt] were with Kate now.

Left alone with his father in unaccustomed surroun[d]ings, Brock was conscious of a certain shift in his vie[w]point. He was seeing himself and his life and the peop[le] close to him from an unfamiliar angle, and it seemed to hi[m] to signal profound changes in his life.

When Charlotte had asked him how he would feel abo[ut] becoming a step-grandfather, he had quipped, "Very, ve[ry] old." Was that what was happening to him now? Was th[e] disorientation he was experiencing a case of premature a[g]ing?

The joyous sense of well-being that had enveloped hi[m] when Charlotte appeared in the doorway had underlin[ed] the strength of his commitment to her. He saw clearly ho[w] their lives were joined; they were two halves of a whole, an[d] he was comfortable with acknowledging his need for he[r.] That had not changed. But what he had seen tonight ha[d] completely altered his attitude toward Charlotte's son.

He no longer accepted Wade as part of his life wi[th] Charlotte simply because he was hers. It wasn't just that [he] had come to like Wade; the serious young man and the g[irl] he loved had become in some way intimately related to hi[m]

Brock had found himself cheering for Wade for the way he had handled himself when he calmly assumed his rights as the baby's father.

Across the table from him, the Major was shuffling the cards, apparently absorbed in his own reactions to the situation that had brought them to this particular bedroom in a strange hospital. Watching him, Brock realized that something had changed in their relationship. He closed his mind to what was happening in the birthing room, which was now by the grace of God out of his power to affect, and turned his thoughts to the implications of his father's unexpected revelation about his own birth.

"You and my mother had a miserable marriage?" Brock hazarded.

Perhaps it was the casual tone of his question that disarmed his father, who answered, just as casually, "On the whole, yes. But it had its moments."

That, at least, was an admission from the old cynic! "What happened?"

The words just slipped out. Brock held his breath while his father favored him with a frosty stare that told him the Major knew very well what he was asking for: the details of that final quarrel that had been kept from him all these years.

"Nothing scandalous." The Major shrugged. "She was one of those women who couldn't take the military life. It's not an easy one, you know. We lived like princes with a retinue of servants in a place like the Philippines, and like second-class citizens in Alabama. Moving every two years, with every move ravaging the last two years' savings."

It was the same old evasion Brock had heard for twenty years. "That won't wash, Dad," he said bluntly. "There has to be a reason why I never heard from her, or saw her again."

The Major riffled the cards and began dealing for two handed gin.

Brock studied the familiar face. His father's color was good, his skin showing pink and healthy through the white beard, the extra weight he'd gained evident in the cheeks that were no longer hollow. Contrasted with that in his mind was the image of Charlotte's face, tense with worry when she burst into the room with Mrs. Ferdinand, and suddenly glowing with a light that exploded in his heart when she saw him.

"You're getting around pretty damn well these days," he commented. "Out of bed and into your trousers without my help."

The Major glanced down at his extended stiffened leg with its exposed bare ankle and scuffed slipper. "Except for my socks and shoes."

"What were you planning to do with Quarters if you found him in his doghouse at Charlotte's?"

"Bring him home, of course."

"And find yourself out on the street with him?"

The Major slapped down the last card and muttered a few choice curses. "Dog-haters are people-haters. Ever noticed that? They have no humanity. Why should I allow people who don't appreciate dogs to run my life?"

"Unfortunately, many of them are landlords and land-ladies," Brock said, "who don't like their carpets and their furniture ruined by inconsiderate pet-owners."

"Humph! Cigarettes do twice as much damage."

"Maybe. But there's something you should be thinking about, and that's where you're going to be living when Charlotte and I get married."

The Major picked up his cards and began arranging them in his hand. "So you're going to marry her."

"We would have been married now if you hadn't held on to Quarters's leash when you fell. That was a stupid thing to do, as you must realize now."

His father glared at him. "You don't have to tell me. The doctor has already taken care of that. But that doesn't mean I won't do the same thing next time. I'm too old to change my habits."

"I don't want a next time," Brock warned him.

His father raised his gaze from his cards and gave him another hard look. Brock was not smiling. "You young studs are ruthless!" the Major said bitterly.

"As ruthless as you were when my mother left."

There was a silence in the room. The television in the corner, soundless, threw a moving rainbow of colors onto the opposite wall. There was the faint hiss of a fan from the air-conditioning conduit, and the muffled quick steps of nurses moving in the hall outside the room.

The Major sat looking at his hand for so long that Brock knew he wasn't seeing the cards he held. Finally he laid them down, face up. "I've regretted it," he said in a voice that cracked. "I would take back everything if I could.... She's dead, Brock. She died within a year, of pneumonia, in France."

His hands were trembling, and he put them in his lap, below the table.

Brock gave a heavy sigh. He wasn't surprised at his father's words. He had felt the total absence of his mother for many years now. He realized that he had known the truth for a long time, too—sensed it, perhaps, or unconsciously put it together from a hundred small insights gleaned while he was living with his father.

"There was another man," his father began. His voice shook.

"You don't have to tell me, Dad. There are some thing I don't think I want to know."

But his father continued, "He was a wealthy man with large vineyard and a house that was a hundred years old. I meant giving up her American citizenship, but he offere her a stability I couldn't, and she wanted it badly."

Brock made a gesture of protest that was ignored.

"I made a pawn of you, Brock," his father said, an Brock jerked his head up.

"I gave her her freedom in exchange for you. I did it be cause I couldn't face losing you, too."

The silence was heavily weighted, but Brock could no break it. His father was staring down at the cards fanne out in front of him.

"I've regretted it every moment since it was done. Be fore we left Germany I had written to tell her so, to offer t send you to her for the summer and go to my new assign ment in the States without you. My answer was the news o her death." He raised his eyes to Brock and said, "I've ha to live with that."

Brock drew another deep breath. The pale eyes were sti proud, daring him to offer pity. Brock wanted to weep fo him.

He made a quick, restless gesture and said, "Rememb the circus you took me to see in Munich that year before w left? I've never forgotten that wonderful weekend. Thos incredible Yugoslavian acrobats, or beautiful Olga on h trapeze, or the elephants with the harem girls riding in the gaudy howdahs... Remember?"

The Major opened his mouth, but didn't speak. Broc reached out and grasped his father's arm. "It was all s long ago," he said gently. "What matters now is the lov you gave me. We were a family, we two. And now I'm goin to be married to a wonderful woman and I want you to be happy for me."

His father's eyes and mouth were tightly closed. He reached blindly for Brock's hand and clasped it tightly.

"You'd better deal another hand," Brock said, looking down at the Major's exposed cards.

IT WAS NEARLY DAWN when a nurse appeared in the open door of the room. She gave them a smile and went to the bed and swiftly turned down the cover and sheet. Behind her Wade came in with one arm around an exhausted Kate, who proudly carried the smallest baby Brock had ever seen, wrapped in a light blanket. It was so tiny it filled him with panic.

Behind them came Charlotte and Estelle. His father reached for his cane, and Brock helped him get to his feet. Brock was struck by the look of wonder that lay like a luminous curtain over the fatigue on the five faces; even the nurse wore a pleased, proprietary air. Charlotte's eyes sought his. She appeared to be ready to drop, but the look of joy and fulfillment she sent his way made Brock move to her side and put his arm around her, needing to touch her.

For a moment Kate stood in the center of the room, looking down at the baby in her arms, while everybody hovered around her. It was a scene Brock thought must be reenacted in homes and hospitals over and over again, a scene that made him think of paintings of the adoration of the magi.

"She's perfect," Kate breathed. "She's got all her fingers and toes and the most beautiful eyes. She's even got some hair!"

Brock looked at the mouth, like the tiny bud of a tea rose, and at the fingers that curled like delicate bird claws, and his heart echoed, "Perfect."

Charlotte leaned into the blessed comfort of Brock's arr
around her and felt that life could give her no more joy tha
this moment held. When she could raise her eyes from th
incredible miracle of her granddaughter, she saw tha
Brock's father's pale old eyes had filled with tears. Glan
ing around the circle, she realized that there were no dr
eyes and she felt a great love pouring out of her heart t
encompass everyone in the room. They were all joined, i
a way, by this new life.

The tableau lasted only a moment. Then the nurse cam
over and took Kate's arm. Kate handed the baby to Wad
who held it tenderly with a look of happiness Charlot
knew she would never forget. Kate gratefully let the nurs
help her into bed and then reached for the baby.

"You can all go home now," the nurse said briskl
"Mother needs her sleep."

"It was a gentle birth," Charlotte said later, resting h
head wearily against Brock's shoulder as he drove throug
the dawn-misted streets. A few early risers were already c
their way to work. Brock had asked Wade to take his fa
ther home so the Major could ride with Quarters besic
him, panting happily.

"I'm glad," Brock said. "What a night! I was never s
glad to see anyone as I was when you walked in."

"No, I mean," Charlotte murmured, "that the docto
called it a 'gentle birth.' It's the method of delivery he use:
It's only possible in natural childbirth when the mother
awake and cooperating. What it means is that the baby
not spanked and made to cry, but is treated like a gue
from another world, given semidarkness and privacy ar
quiet in which to become accustomed to her new enviro
ment."

Brock smiled tenderly. She was so weary, and at the sam
time so exhilarated, that she was on one of her highs, tal

ing as if she had to communicate with him and couldn't get it all out fast enough.

"The doctor took little Carla so gently, Brock, and laid her on Kate's stomach. Carla gave just one little cry when she took her first breath. He let her lie there a few minutes before he clamped the cord. And after a few minutes she stopped crying. And that tiny little girl raised her head and looked around—I swear she looked at her parents! Oh, darling, I wish you could have seen it!"

"I don't think I'm quite ready for that," Brock said. "Let me get used to being a grandfather before you arrange anything more, okay?"

Charlotte laughed softly. "It's not going to be all that bad, is it?"

"It's going to be wonderful," he said, "especially when we're married. I told the Major tonight that it won't be long now."

"Oh, Brock!" For a moment her spirits sagged. "How are we going to manage . . . ?"

"I think we can leave that until another day, sweet, since it's now nearly morning."

He pulled up in her driveway, walked her to her door and kissed her. "I have to be at a clinic in Tacoma by ten at the latest, but I hope you'll call in sick."

"Not a chance," she said. "But, oh, Brock, I'm so happy! Crazy, isn't it? Nothing's changed except we've one more little problem, and I've never been so happy. I'll wonder why when I wake up about thirty-six hours from now. I'm afraid I'll be asleep on my feet until then!"

SOMEHOW CHARLOTTE GOT THROUGH her morning of computer diagnostic tests, and left the clinic on her lunch hour for a quick dash over to Kate's hospital room. With the conspicuous burden she had been carrying gone, and her long raven hair tied up with a crimson ribbon in a ponytail that fell over her shoulder, Kate looked like the high-school student she was.

She was sitting up in bed, nursing Carla. Wade sat on the bed beside her, with one arm around her. Carla's tiny hand was making opening and closing movements near one of his big fingers.

"Hi, Mom," he said without embarrassment. "I'm cutting classes today. It's my daughter's birthday."

"That's reason enough, I suppose," she said, and meant it. "Kate, how are you and Carla this morning?"

"Wonderful." Kate's eyes were shining. She and Wade were still riding on cloud nine, Charlotte judged. She couldn't help thinking of the depression that could follow this euphoria when Kate experienced the fatigue of night feedings and nearly twenty-four-hour care that lay ahead. How would she and Estelle cope with that?

Perhaps a young mother could take it better than an older one could, Charlotte thought, looking at Kate's healthy color and bright eyes. Certainly she was less daunted by the prospect ahead of her. But then neither books nor well-meaning older women could adequately prepare one for that difficult time.

Wade didn't look nearly as fresh or as happy, Charlotte belatedly noticed. "You're looking tired, Wade. Miss your sleep?" she teased gently.

"Very funny," he said.

"Wade is surly this morning," Kate said pertly. "He still wants to get married."

"And you still don't?" Charlotte asked her.

Kate shook her head firmly. "I'm not ready for marriage, Mrs. Emlyn." She caressed Carla's almost hairless head with a tentative but infinitely tender touch.

"Motherhood is quite enough to cope with for now. I'm going to take one thing at a time."

"Did you ever hear such rubbish?" Wade groaned. "Kate has admitted she loves me and wants to marry me someday. Seems to me she's got things backward."

"Seems to me you had some things backward, too," Charlotte told him, tartly. "Have you asked Kate *when* she will be ready for marriage?"

Kate answered without waiting for Wade's question. "When he graduates from college. I just may go to college myself after I finish high school!"

"There's your answer, Wade," Charlotte said, saluting the young girl with her eyes. "And it sounds pretty good to me."

Wade said soberly, "As long as you don't shut me out, Kate."

"I promise, Wade. I know you think I've been hateful, but I didn't want you to quit school," she confessed.

"If I stay in school, what then? Will your aunt let down the bars?"

"She doesn't run my life," Kate said with a flash of spirit. "It was my choice. I just couldn't think of any other way not to give in to you, Wade. It wasn't easy to say no when you were begging me to marry you."

Charlotte felt like a mother-in-law for the first time in her life—but probably not the last, she thought wryly. She wasn't needed in this room just now. In fact, Wade would never need her again in quite the same way he had in his first nineteen years. She was filled with a regretful pride, mixed with a little envy of the young couple, who had a lifetime in which to build a good marriage.

"I've got to get back to the clinic," she said, and wasn't sure they noticed she was leaving the room.

She had reached the nurses' station when she met Estelle Drew just coming in. Miss Chrome-and-Glass looked the worse for a sleepless night, too, but she greeted Charlotte warmly. "How did you find Kate?"

"Nursing Carla. Wade's with her and they're cooing like lovebirds."

Estelle hesitated. "Perhaps I should give them a few moments more alone?"

Charlotte gave her a sharp look. "You're changing your tune about him, aren't you?"

Estelle threw her hands out in a helpless gesture that said it all. It was out of her hands.

"Wade will be with her all day today," Charlotte said dryly.

"I took the day off, too," Kate's aunt admitted. "Please come with me to the cafeteria for a cup of coffee. There's something I'd like to tell you, Charlotte."

"I'm on my lunch break. I really should get back...." But some need in Estelle's eyes made her hesitate. "Oh, I can steal another fifteen minutes," she said with a grin. "After all, I don't become a grandmother every day."

They descended to the basement cafeteria and walked through the line to the coffee machines, picking up some fresh berries on the way. Estelle paid, and led the way to one of the white enameled tables in an almost deserted corner of the big room.

For a few minutes they talked about the sleep they had lost and the night they had shared. "I'm still too keyed up to be very sleepy," Estelle confessed.

They ate their fruit and sipped hot coffee.

"What is it you want to tell me?" Charlotte asked.

"You're direct, aren't you?" Estelle said wryly, stirring more sugar substitute into her coffee. "I want to tell you something I can't tell anyone else. I'd like an hour to work myself up to it, but I'll blurt it out instead because it's become impossible for me to keep it to myself."

"I'm very curious," Charlotte said, "but are you sure you want to do this?"

"Oh, yes. I'm bursting with it, and if I don't tell you I'll blab to someone who shouldn't know. You're the logical person, because you're proud of being a grandmother, too." Her smile was defensive, a little frightened. "Do you understand what I'm saying?"

Charlotte was afraid she was staring. "I hear you, but I'm not sure I can believe what I hear, Estelle."

Estelle looked swiftly around. They were still almost alone in their corner of the room. "I thought you might have already guessed. I'm Carla's other grandmother. Kate is my illegitimate daughter."

Charlotte saw moisture in the other woman's eyes, but she still felt a disbelief. It seemed to her that the relationship between Kate and Estelle was the least motherly one she could imagine. "You said last night that you'd never seen a birth before—"

"I didn't see Kate born. It was a cesarean birth and I was out cold."

"Does Kate know?"

"She has no idea. It was a dreadful time for me." Estelle's tense fingers played with her cup. "I couldn't tell my parents I was pregnant. I lived in a small Bible Belt town— never mind where—but it was very conservative. The feminist revolution of the seventies was only a rumor. You must remember how it was. Most young women were made to feel such shame over an out-of-wedlock pregnancy."

"I know," Charlotte murmured, trying to picture Estelle in that situation, and compassionately imagining how she must have felt when Kate faced the same problem.

"I decided to have my baby, but secretly, not letting my family know. So I left home, pretending I was working in the city when I was living in a charity home for unwed mothers, planning to give Kate up for adoption. Then my sister and her husband, who had no children, were killed in an automobile accident." She paused, the shadow of a painful memory passing over her expression.

"My sister left me some jewelry. I didn't go home. I had her things sent to me. They enabled me to keep Kate, and after a while I managed to get a forged birth certificate that said she was my sister's child."

Charlotte was aghast. "But you could have been found out at any time! How come you haven't been?"

Estelle shrugged. "A lie lived long enough becomes the truth for most people. I never went home again. There are some relatives who would know I'm living a lie if they knew about Kate. Some may even have guessed, but they're so far removed from my life now."

Charlotte was shocked. "You severed all your connections?"

"I thought I had to. I was ambitious and I thought Kate's illegitimacy would hold me back. But my secret hangs over me, and it gets heavier each year. Someday it will drop of its own weight. That's one reason why I had to tell you. I will have to tell Kate one day, and it looks like that will mean telling Wade, too."

She managed a smile. "The other reason is that I found I couldn't bear letting you think you were the only grandmother." She laughed ruefully and said, "You're hogging my space, you know."

Charlotte regarded her with thoughtful sympathy. "It does look as if we're joined in a relationship by young Carla. I'm trying to reconcile what I know about you with the way you encouraged Kate to openly espouse single motherhood. Was it your secret that made you a feminist?''

"That's part of it. Over the years, so many innocent children have been stamped with the stigma of illegitimacy and carried a shame they didn't deserve all their lives! I didn't want that for Kate or her child. Yet I knew that she wasn't ready for marriage. I've got over blaming Wade for what happened, but I still believe that if she and Wade can complete their education before they marry, their marriage will have more chance of surviving.''

"And I've got over blaming Kate. What you said made sense, but I was so angry at you that I couldn't admit that.'' Charlotte smiled at the tense woman across from her. "I'm glad we can be friends, Estelle. I think together we can help them work out their problems.''

CHAPTER NINETEEN

WHEN SHE RETURNED to the clinic, Charlotte found Dr
Ferdie talking to Joy at the receptionist's office. "Well, and
how is your granddaughter?" he asked, gray eyes twin
kling behind his rimless glasses. "Ellin wants to know."

"Granddaughter!" Joy shrieked.

Charlotte discovered that she didn't mind the teasing that
followed her admission that she was, indeed, a grand
mother at thirty-eight—well, nearly thirty-nine—and she
loved the outpouring of warmth and goodwill that came her
way as word flew through the clinic. The birth of a child
seemed to touch everyone in some special way.

It was a day that would always loom very large in her
memory, but as the day wore on, she began looking for
ward more and more to a night of uninterrupted sleep.

Brock called from Tacoma soon after she arrived home.
The timbre of his voice was thrilling in its familiarity; it
could always move her. His first question was "How is our
little Carla?" and her heart flooded with love at the accep
tance evident in the way he had worded his question.

"She is unquestionably the most beautiful baby in the
world," she told him, laughing at herself as she said it.

"How could she fail, with such a beautiful grand
mother? And how are you, my love?"

"Tired and sleepy. But everything would be fine if you
were here."

"You'll be sleeping with me tonight," he murmured.
'You're always with me. You know that, don't you?"

"I feel that, too, Brock. You are always in my heart."

"I love you, Charlotte."

"I love you, Brock."

"I'll be home in a couple of days. We'll talk about plans
hen."

The happiness welled up from her heart and spread until
t pulsed through her whole being. Brock was ready to make
a commitment with no reservations, and so was she. The
ime was right and somehow it would work. For the first
ime she let herself believe it.

"Is your father going to be all right while you're away?"

"If he can go chasing around at night looking for his
log, he can take care of himself for a couple of days. I'm
going to call him now."

"I'll try to see him on my afternoon off."

"I hope I'll be back by then. Give my love to the new
amily. As for you, my dearest . . ."

They murmured love words for another minute or two
before breaking the connection. No more doubts, Char-
otte thought as she sank into sleep.

Brock was still in Tacoma when Wednesday, Charlotte's
alf day, arrived. Kate had left the hospital but Estelle was
aking a week off to be at home with her and the baby, and
Wade was going to their apartment every day after his last
lass. Charlotte felt unneeded and a little lonesome. She
vas looking forward to calling on the Major and went
ome to prepare a lunch she could take to him.

But she had barely hung up her suit jacket and put on an
apron over her blouse and skirt when the doorbell rang.
When she opened the door the Major stood on her porch,
ooking very smart in a light-colored shirt, his white hair

and beard newly trimmed, his cane at a jaunty walking stick angle. He was smiling.

"Hello, Charlotte," he said with a gleam in his pale blue eyes. Below her sloping lawn, at the curb, was a waiting taxi.

"When the cat's away!" She sighed. "Major Morley, you've not come for Quarters *again*? What do you and Wade see in that ugly hound?"

"He's not a hound. He's a standard poodle. Nobody recognizes the breed anymore," he said, with his own look of elegant contempt, "because everybody wants a yapping toy. But I haven't come for Quarters. This time I've come for you, my dear." He made a little bow of invitation. "Charlotte, will you do me the honor of having lunch with me?"

She blinked. "Why, that sounds delightful, but I was on the point of preparing a lunch to bring over to you."

"Very kind of you," he said, opening the screen door and swinging his leg inside with considerable skill. "But I'd prefer to take you out. I thought after lunch you might be willing to go for a spin with me."

"A spin? By taxi?"

"That's my only means of transportation, unfortunately."

"If you want to go for a ride, I'll take my car," she offered. "Just let me send your taxi away—"

He raised his cane to block her way to the door. "No again, young woman! This time I'm in the driver's seat. Will you honor me with your company?"

Charlotte put her hands on her hips. "May I ask in what direction we will be spinning? What's our destination?"

"You may ask," he said, "but you will have to wait until after lunch to see."

She looked him up and down. "Just what are you up to?"

"There's one sure way to find out." His shadowy smile and the gleam in his eyes challenged her. "If you want to know, get your coat and purse. We're wasting valuable time."

She was rising to his challenge, asking herself, *Why not?* Amused, she said, "Brock told me you were great with the ladies. I begin to see where he got his charm. Just give me a minute, Major."

She left him standing at her door and went down the hall to her bedroom, very curious as to what was behind this unexpected gesture. Swiftly she touched up her makeup and repinned her hair and, once again in her tailored suit, picked up her purse and went to rejoin Brock's father.

She preceded him down the walk to the taxi. The driver gave her a grin and a nod of recognition. He was the same man she had paid off for going away without the Major. Charlotte got in the back seat and waited while Brock's father backed in with what must have been some discomfort to his leg, to sit beside her. He gave the driver the name of a restaurant she was not familiar with.

It wasn't far from the hospital area. "Where did you hear about this place?" she asked him when the taxi pulled up before it.

"I used to patronize it when I was stationed at Fort Lewis. It's been in its present location for a good many years. A small family restaurant that serves French food."

Charlotte waited on the sidewalk while he paid the driver and told him, "I'll be wanting a taxi again in about an hour and a half."

"Don't know if I can make it, Major," the man said cheerfully, "but somebody'll pick you up." He winked at Charlotte before he drove off.

The restaurant was divided into two long rooms plainl furnished with banquettes and white-covered tables alon; each wall. They shared a common foyer where both th maître d' and the cashier stood behind their high counters

"Major Morley," Brock's father announced.

"Good morning, Major, we have your reservation." Th maître d' beckoned a young waiter and handed him tw menus. They followed him to a banquette. There was mouth-watering aroma of subtle sauces in the room. Th tables held miniature bouquets of fresh flowers.

The Major was handling himself very well, Charlott thought, although it took him considerable time to sea himself beside her and dispose of his cane.

"Have you a good Beaujolais?" he asked the hoverin; waiter.

"Our customers tell us it is excellent, sir."

"Bring us a litre, please."

"Don't you even want to know what I'm planning to o; der?" Charlotte demanded.

"All women like a good Beaujolais."

"Oh. Do you know all women?"

He looked at her sharply. "What would you prefer?"

"A white wine." She was being deliberately contrary. Sh liked Beaujolais. "Perhaps a sauvignon."

"Bring us your best sauvignon, also," the Major told th waiter, waving away Charlotte's protest.

"There is no need to be extravagant," she reproved him

"Let me be the judge of that."

The waiter came promptly with two bottles of wine in freestanding wine cooler. He opened both bottles and wit great ceremony the Major sampled both before allowin; their glasses to be filled.

When he lifted his glass to her, Charlotte picked hers up and laughingly shook her head at him. "Do you expect me to drink a litre of wine?"

"Only if you want to."

"You're tipping your hand, Major Morley. What is it that you want from me?"

"I have something to show you. Later. That will be time enough to talk of favors. After we enjoy our lunch."

"And you have weakened my principles with liquor?"

"Could I?" He chuckled at her expression and asked, "How is my great-granddaughter?"

"She's gained a couple of ounces."

"She could use a few."

"Right," Charlotte agreed. "She just missed being classed a preemic, did you know that?"

"I realized that she was considerably less sturdy than Brock was when I first saw him. And he was not a sturdy boy."

Charlotte saw that he was really concerned, and something stirred in her heart. She remembered Brock telling her that he had never doubted his father's love, and felt a wave of emotion that embarrassingly tightened her throat. When she could speak she said, "Carla's going to be fine."

"I hope you're right."

They sipped their wine. After a moment she said, "I love your son very much."

He studied her with a penetrating gaze. "Yes, I believe you do."

"In fact," she continued, "I love him so much that some of it is spilling over on his prickly porcupine of a father."

"Humph!" he said in obvious disbelief, and promptly replenished the wine in her glass.

When the waiter returned, he asked her, "Do you like salmon?"

"Adore it."

He ordered from the French menu. "We'll have *crème d* *cerfeuil* followed by *salade niçoise* and *terrine de saumo* *frais à l'oseille*. We'll talk about dessert later."

"It sounds top drawer," Charlotte observed.

"It is. You will be served a cream of cervil soup, a del cious salad that originated in Nice—a place that Broc loved to visit—and a terrine of fresh salmon with sorre sauce."

"Why do I feel I'm being compromised?"

"Relax and enjoy your lunch."

"I will, if you will tell me more about Brock's chilc hood. Why did he enjoy Nice?"

"Because we could drive up the mountains to Valber and find snow and he could practise skiing until noor Then after lunch we could go back down to Nice and swir in the Mediterranean. He claimed Nice was the best of tw worlds."

His eyes took on a distant look. "He was an activ youngster. Then he discovered microchips and became ac dicted. And sedentary."

"He's still in good shape," she protested.

"When he remembers to work out. You should nag hir about that, Charlotte."

She drew a quick breath, wondering if his remark mear his acceptance or his approval. She tried to frame a ques tion, but the waiter had arrived with their soup. Charlott gave her attention to her enjoyment of the meal the Majc obviously hoped would impress her, while a tiny glow c excitement added its warmth to her heart.

Charlotte begged to skip dessert, and Major Morle tipped the waiter and asked him to have a taxi waiting fc them by the time he had paid the bill.

The old gentleman had a way of getting what he wanted that was not imperious, but highly effective. They didn't have to wait long. As Charlotte climbed into the taxi, she heard him give an address to the driver that she didn't recognize but guessed it must be on Mercer Island. Her hunch was confirmed a few minutes later when the driver headed for the causeway.

The Major sat with his leg stretched out at an angle, his well-manicured hands crossed on the handle of his cane, and stared over the driver's shoulder at the street down which they were driving. They rode for two miles in a contemplative silence brought on by their excellent lunch. The taxi was taking the freeway that connected Seattle with Mercer Island, one of its attractive bedroom communities. On each side of the causeway, boats with varicolored sails were taking advantage of a brisk breeze dappling the waters of Lake Washington.

Presently the driver pulled the cab over to the curb beside a realtor's sign in front of a ranch-style house set in an expanse of lawn. Attached to the sign was a second placard saying, Open House.

Charlotte looked at the Major in surprise. "You're shopping for a house?"

"Brock told me I should look for another place to live, since he was getting married."

"Oh." Heavy disappointment settled over her spirits. "Are you trying to make me feel guilty?"

"Not at all. I would like your opinion of this house. If you don't mind?"

The driver had opened the door for her. She got out and looked at the sprawling frame house with the ornamental brick of what appeared to be a sizable fireplace between its two large front windows. It was an older home, not large, but obviously bigger than the bungalow she and Wade had inherited. There was a double entry to the right of the windows.

Brock's father followed Charlotte up the walk at his slower pace. She waited and let him press the doorbell. A smiling bearded young man opened the door.

"Major Morley?" he asked. "Please come in."

"This is Mrs. Emlyn, Mr. Scott. I've asked her to look at the house with me."

"I'll be happy to show it." Mr. Scott's smile widened as he quickly appraised Charlotte's figure.

It was a charming house, Charlotte thought, feeling sicker as she wandered through the rooms. So this luncheon was not a gesture of conciliation but an attempt to make her feel that she was responsible for Brock throwing his father out.

She had to admit it was a comfortable house, ample for a family: four good-sized bedrooms, with three bathrooms. The master bedroom had sliding glass doors that opened onto a backyard that was small but attractively landscaped, with flower beds and large shade trees.

"I've chosen this one for my room," the Major said, passing up the master suite for a smaller back room. "I like its exposure, and you'll notice it has an outside door for Quarters." Its smaller sliding glass doors opened onto a corner of the back garden made private by strategic plantings of privet and laurel.

Charlotte looked at him suspiciously. "You chose the smallest bedroom? Why?"

"I thought you and Brock would like the master suite," he said without even blinking. "As for the other two—the smaller one would make a lovely nursery for little Carla someday, don't you think?"

Charlotte sucked in her breath. "Are you proposing to rent out rooms?"

"No. I have another proposition. How much is your house worth, Charlotte?"

She calculated swiftly. "Eighty-five to ninety thousand, perhaps."

"Then if I contributed, say, fifty thousand dollars, which you could use for a down payment, you could make an offer of a hundred and forty for this, right?" He turned to Mr. Scott. "How would that be received?"

"I think it might be considered," the realtor said cautiously, his shrewd eyes on Charlotte.

She said, also cautiously, "Are you talking about joint ownership, Major Morley?"

"I would be willing to put the ownership in your name and my son's if you and I signed a personal contract."

She eyed him skeptically. "Such as?"

"Quarters lives with me until he dies, and I live with you. Contingent, of course, on my ability to put up with your bossy ways."

"And mine to put up with yours?"

She saw the twinkle in the frosty eyes then. "There's another clause I want in our agreement, Charlotte. Portuguese soup at least once a month."

Charlotte felt her heart was going to burst. Her eyesight blurred for a second. "Major, it's very good of you, but my son is co-owner of my house. He'll have to be consulted."

"Of course. We'll get a good lawyer to work out the legal angles and protect his interest."

Would it work? Could they all live with this challenging, difficult, but strangely lovable man? She moistened her dry lips. "Major Morley, let's talk to Brock about your proposition, okay?"

"A good idea. We'll get back to you, Mr. Scott."

"I wouldn't wait too long—" the realtor began, but the Major autocratically cut him off.

"In a day or two, Mr. Scott. In a day or two."

Charlotte walked beside the old soldier back to the waiting taxi in a daze. Was it possible? Could this actually be going to happen?

"I don't know if it will work," she mused aloud. "But you're a dear to suggest it."

"*Things* don't usually work," he said with a frosty bite in his voice. "It's people who *make* them work."

I must remember that, Charlotte told herself. Suddenly she couldn't wait for Brock to return from the Tacoma job.

CHAPTER TWENTY

BROCK RETURNED TO SEATTLE late Friday evening. When he unlocked his apartment door, a night-light came on in his father's bedroom and his father called, "That you, Brock?"

"Yes." Brock set down his suitcase and paused in the doorway of the dimly lit room. "Everything all right?"

The lean form under the blanket did not move. He couldn't see his father's face. "Fine. Charlotte's fine. The baby's fine."

Brock blinked. "You've seen them?"

"Saw Charlotte. Tell you in the morning." The voice sounded sleepy, but Brock heard affection in it. His father was excited about something he didn't want to talk about. "Glad you're back," he mumbled, and then gave a loud, practised snore.

Brock shook his head and went on to his own room, knowing the futility of trying to pry anything out of the Major tonight. It was too late to call Charlotte. He had worked late in order to get home for the weekend. He quickly undressed and fell into bed.

When he did call her in the morning, his welcome home was very satisfactory. Charlotte invited him over for breakfast, saying with that thrilling catch in her voice, "I can't wait to see you!"

He was eager as any teenager to be gone, but he helped his father put on his socks and left him to make his own breakfast. When he arrived at Charlotte's bungalow, Wade was just leaving to go over to Kate's. He greeted Brock cheerfully, and watched with an air of amused incredulity as Brock kissed his mother and held her close.

"See ya, lovebirds."

"Tell Kate we'll be over later to see her and the baby," Charlotte told him as he left.

When they were alone, Brock pulled Charlotte closer and said, "I don't like being separated from you."

"I've hated it," she confessed.

"We've got to do something about that. Very soon." With one hand he unbuttoned her white blouse and found the fastening to her bra. When her breasts were exposed, he lowered his head and began kissing them, teasing them with his lips until they hardened, sending electric tingles spreading from his touch.

"I invited you for breakfast," she said in a voice shaken with her sudden passionate response.

"Shall we have it in bed?" he suggested.

"I can't think of anything nicer," she said, smiling.

Later, propped up against pillows with fresh coffee, Charlotte told him about the house on Mercer Island and his father's proposition. Brock ran a hand through his hair, his face a study in indecision.

"It worries you, doesn't it?" Charlotte asked.

"It does," he admitted. "I'd hate to see you the victim of the strategies I've seen him use on various landladies and apartment managers he's had arguments with."

"Brock, whatever else I am, I'm no victim. I can hold my own with your father."

"Can you live with his quirks and outrageous demands?"

"Can he live with mine?" Charlotte retorted.

"Sometimes they're unreasonable."

"So are mine."

Brock laughed and hugged her.

"Watch my coffee!" she shrieked.

"Under the circumstances, isn't that an unreasonable demand?" he teased.

"Not unless you don't mind being burned."

The teasing note left his voice. "You should think seriously abut entering that kind of a partnership with my father. You must be very sure you want to...to expose yourself to his kind of provocation. He likes to shake people up. He says it forces them to think—if they can."

"Arrogant, isn't he?"

"Oh, yes! I'll admit that you seem to have been able to dull the point of his barbs, but they'll always be there—he'll always be something of a porcupine. He's not going to change that much."

Charlotte hesitated. She had been doing a good deal of thinking since Wednesday afternoon. "He got me when he tried to make me doubt your love. But I feel differently about him, Brock, since that night the baby was born. I felt then that he was 'family,' and I never did before. Isn't that strange? Perhaps he was testing me?"

Brock shook his head and shrugged. "Don't ask me what makes him tick. I've never been sure."

"Anyway, I feel as if he's accepted me," Charlotte said. "But little Carla has something to do with it, too."

"And perhaps Wade's affection for Quarters?" he suggested.

"Yes. I'm beginning to feel as if we're an extended family," she said slowly. "One that includes Kate and your father, and even Estelle Drew." She thought of Estelle's confession. Someday she would be able to tell Brock, and he would understand Estelle's right to be included in the little clan of which they had become the nucleus.

"That sounds good, darling, but it has little to do wi
whether or not we should try living with that many peop
and, especially, entering into a joint real-estate venture wi
the Major."

"At first it would just be Wade and your father livi
with us. And we know they get along."

"Do they? The Major is already jealous of Quarters
affection for Wade."

Charlotte raised her coffee cup to her lips, and looked
him over it. "Well, they're both mature enough to set
that difference!"

"Are you sure about that?"

"There are no sure things," Charlotte said impatientl
"Years ago, my husband's death brought that lesson hom
to me. The difference is in loving," she said slowly. "
family that is bound together by love is not split apart by
quarrels. It takes them as they come and works throu
them. Just as you and I have done, Brock. You said on
that you never doubted that your father loved you. Th
has made a great deal of difference in the way I can rel
to him."

She returned to her original thoughts about the hous
"Kate and the baby are remaining with Estelle, at least f
the present. Maybe in another year, when Kate is seve
teen and Wade is twenty, they might consider marrying a
moving in with us, but it's not going to happen imme
ately. We can handle that when and if it happens, ca
we?"

Brock considered that for a moment. Finally he sa
"Well, hell, suppose we go look at the house?"

Charlotte put down her cup and kissed him.

Brock drove, following her instructions, and they got o
of the car in front of the ranch-style residence with the bri
fireplace wall between its two large front windows.

sandwich board saying Open House, Saturday, Sunday had been placed on the sidewalk, and Mr. Scott stood in the open double doors just ushering a middle-aged couple out.

"Oh, dear," Charlotte murmured. "I do hope it hasn't been sold."

She had been too surprised on Wednesday to notice the large oak tree on the front lawn that was already beginning to drop some leaves. Nor had she seen the asters of pale pink blooming in a brick planter below a concrete porch. A star jasmine, long past flowering, wound its dark green leaves up a porch pillar. A pair of robins were probing for worms through the damp grass.

Mr. Scott was holding the door open for them. "Mrs. Emlyn!" he greeted her cheerfully. "I'm glad you've come early. We'll have lots of visitors today and tomorrow!"

Charlotte introduced Brock and Mr. Scott offered his hand. Charlotte looked around the living room and imagined her furniture and her family in it. She conjured up Brock laying a fire in the wide fireplace, and then pictured Wade playing with Quarters before the leaping flames. Brock's father would be watching them from his armchair by one of the big windows.

Too tranquil to be true! But her imagination went on creating scenes—perhaps someday a fair-haired little Carla running ahead of them down the hall toward the master bedroom. And that room, so large and light and filled with reflections of sunlight glancing off green foliage...living in this room with her love, her husband...Her eyes met Brock's and she gave him a tremulous smile, returning the kiss she read in his gaze.

Paradise.

Was it within their grasp?

"This is the room your father chose," she told him when they came to the last bedroom.

Brock examined it critically. "It's large enough, I thinl He likes his privacy. We could put a freestanding fireplac in it for him. He would spend hours reading beside a fir The outside door makes it ideal. He could come and go he pleased, and let Quarters out without waking everyor up."

"Are you ready to make an offer?" Mr. Scott asked.

"There's once more thing," Charlotte said. "Wade mu see it."

"You shouldn't wait too long..." Mr. Scott warned.

"I'll send him over today."

They left the house holding hands, Charlotte wonderir how Wade would feel about selling the house that repr sented his only heritage from his father, the place where his memories of Garth were based.

They decided to go shopping for gifts for Carla befo going to see her. Charlotte had given Kate little items baby care and some infants' wear, but she told Brock, "I' dying to buy some frilly little-girl dresses! She won't be ab to wear them yet, but I want to indulge myself."

"I have this unconquerable urge to buy her a stuffed a imal," Brock confessed. "Something like a dinosaur, or huge teddy bear."

"Better start small," Charlotte advised.

It was just after they had found the perfect cuddly lic in a nearby mall that Charlotte saw the chambered nau lus. It was in a window display of seashells of all shapes an sizes and wondrous colors. The nautilus had been sliced half with a jeweler's saw, to reveal its many chambers th graduated in size from a narrow slit to a final spacio cavity, revealing how the sea creature outgrew its form homes and formed new ones, all of pale creamy nacre.

"People always say 'I love you with all my heart,'" Charlotte said in a voice full of wonder. "But look at this, Brock!"

His eyes questioned her, and she elaborated. "I do love you that way, darling! But hearts are like that shell." Her words came in the soft rush that he knew by this time meant she was emotionally stirred.

"At first I thought there was no more room in my heart. There was Wade in it, and his father—because you don't stop loving someone who is dead. And then you came and filled it to overflowing and I thought you were crowding everyone else out.

"But the heart has many chambers. Kate found her own room, and then your father found there was a space for him. And even Estelle. And there was still a big beautiful chamber waiting for Carla to claim as her own special place." She lifted her beautiful clear gaze. "And if there is another grandchild, someday, there will be another place made ready..."

Brock's eyes darkened. "'The heart has many chambers,'" he repeated softly. "How true, my beautiful wise darling! Carla has her own lovely chamber in my heart, too. And Wade and Kate each have made their own place. My love for them doesn't take anything away from my love for you. It simply enriches it."

He put the stuffed lion, a small one but still too big to wrap, under his arm, and taking Charlotte's hand, pulled her into the shop. He left her while he got a saleswoman and took her to the window. Some money changed hands, and he came back to Charlotte and placed the creamy chambered nautilus in her hands.

"To remember this day," he said, and kissed her, to the surprised delight of the saleswoman.

Then they went out to the car and headed for Kate an[d] their granddaughter.

When they entered the book-lined living room of E[s]telle's apartment, Wade was sitting on the sofa holding h[is] daughter with Kate beside him, leaning on his shoulder an[d] fussing with Carla's blanket. He looked up at Brock an[d] grinned.

"Hello, Gramps!"

Only a few weeks ago, Charlotte would have flinche[d] afraid of Brock's reaction. But Carla's actual presence ha[d] made a difference. How could anyone resent such a ros[e]bud of a child?

"Hi!" Brock said easily. "You the baby-sitter?"

"I'm still on probation," Wade admitted. "Kate hang[s] around with her arms curved to catch if I drop her."

They hovered over Carla, admiring the dark blue clou[d] of her eyes—too newborn to reveal their true color—an[d] the pleasing proportions of her face. "She's going to be [a] beauty!" Wade boasted, and Kate crowed, "Like h[er] mother?"

Charlotte said, "We have something important to di[s]cuss with you, Wade. Brock and I are going to be marrie[d] and—"

Wade's grin widened. "It's about time."

Charlotte felt the heat that flooded her cheeks, and bo[th] her son and her lover laughed at her.

"Kate, I'd like you to be my maid of honor. Wou[ld] you?"

Kate flushed with pleasure. "I would love that!"

"Wade, I'd be honored if you would stand up with me," Brock said.

"Thanks. I was afraid I was going to have to give h[er] away."

"Oh, if only you could wait for Carla to be your flower girl!" Kate exclaimed.

"No way!" Brock exploded. "We've waited long enough. Sorry, Carla."

"Charlotte. Brock." Estelle moved up to take a hand of each of them. "I wish you both great happiness, and I hope we will always be good friends. I've got a bottle of champagne in my wine rack, I'm sure. I'm going to put it in the freezer for a quick cool so we can toast your happiness."

Charlotte brought up the subject of selling the house in order to accept Brock's father's offer. While she and Wade discussed it, Brock took Carla experimentally in his arms, holding her as if she were made of Venetian blown glass. It was the first time he had ever held an infant, and he felt large and very awkward.

"This will take some getting used to," he told Kate.

"She won't break," Kate scoffed, but she was clearly more comfortable when Carla was once more in her arms.

Brock heard Wade say, "Sure, I can get along with him. He's a neat old guy."

"Then why don't you drive over to Mercer Island and look at the house? Take Kate with you," Charlotte suggested. "After all, you've got three baby-sitters right here."

Kate was reluctant to leave the baby, but couldn't resist the opportunity to enjoy an excursion outside the apartment where she had been almost housebound the last weeks of her pregnancy. While the young couple were gone, Charlotte and Estelle and Brock sat around admiring Carla and working out ways they could relieve Kate of some of the pressure of the first months of her care. It was not going to be easy, since all three of them were involved in busy careers. But they were all agreed that they should see that Kate had time for continuation school, and an occasional night out with Wade and their friends. That she would have

their continued love and support did not have to be spelle
out.

Late that afternoon Charlotte and Brock took both Wac
and the Major back to Mercer Island to sign a purcha
agreement with Mr. Scott.

THE CHURCH WAS BANKED with masses of white chrysai
themums. Sun slanted through tall stained-glass window
throwing rainbow lights into the pale room. The sma
chapel was filled with friends, nurses and doctors, Joy ar
the other girls from the clinic, some of Brock's co-worke
from Echo and some of Kate's and Wade's friends fro
school. In the front row the Major, looking very dapper, sa
between Estelle, holding Carla, and Ellin Ferdinand.

The organ music heralded the bride and Charlotte e
tered from the rear. She was dressed smartly in pearl gra
and carried a large spray of delicate white and green o
chids with tawny centers that the Major had had flown
from Hawaii for her. Walking up the aisle on Dr. Ferdie
arm, followed by Kate, looking stunning in a rosy pea
gown, and by Ellin's young grandson who proudly bore t
rings on a cushion, Charlotte lifted her gaze to the alt
where Brock awaited her, with Wade as his best man. H
two most important men looked back at her with pride ar
love.

Dr. Ferdie pressed her arm and murmured, "Be happ
my dear," and left her. Kate stepped to her side, her fa
alight with enjoyment of the moment. Charlotte's gaze e
countered Brock's and for a few seconds the chapel and
it held disappeared. There were only the two of them ar
their love.

It was their moment of commitment, their exchange
vows that said, "You—only you." The tremendous pow
and responsibility of that commitment shook her and at t

same time filled her with a calm, sweet happiness because it was so right.

What followed was a ritual consecration of their union. Wade took the simple gold wedding band from the cushion the young ring-bearer held and gave it to Brock who slipped it on her finger beside the matching solitaire he had given her after their rehearsal dinner.

"With this ring, I thee wed..." he murmured, and Charlotte repeated the ceremony when Kate handed her the matching gold band she had chosen for Brock. Then he kissed her—a kiss of deep and tender promise—and they were man and wife.

At Ellin's insistence, their friends and well-wishers gathered at Dr. Ferdie's beautiful formal home for a champagne reception and the cutting of the cake. There were musicians playing on a brick terrace that overlooked the gardens. There, under the presiding dignity of Mount Rainier, Brock and Charlotte received kisses and hugs of affection and the good wishes of their friends.

Kate looked so stunning that she received almost as much attention as the bride, but Wade took her home early because it was time for baby Carla to go. Charlotte cut the cake with Brock, tossed her orchids to Estelle, and they slipped out of the house and into his car just as the setting sun was casting an orange glow over sky and mountains and water.

No one knew where they were going to spend the night, but it would be the first of only a weekend-long honeymoon. Brock didn't have a single vacation day left on the books, so they had discarded the idea of an extended honeymoon in the interests of seizing the moment.

Brock headed first for Mercer Island and the house that would be their home. Although the final papers weren't yet ready for signing, he had managed to wheedle a key from

Mr. Scott. He unlocked the front door and they entered the unfurnished rooms with a faint sense of trespassing. Brock had slipped the flashlight he carried in his car into his pocket.

The house had many windows, and it was still light with the golden glow of the setting sun. Holding hands, they walked through the rooms with delight, pointing out where this or that piece of furniture would go, when they could complete the move from both Charlotte's house and the apartment Brock and his father shared.

But when they reached the master suite that would be their own private place, Brock pulled her into his arms with an urgency that made her tremble. His tongue plunged into the sweetness of her mouth while his hands caressed her body until she was clinging to his shoulders because her legs would no longer support her. There was no holding back, nothing but the consummation of their vows had any meaning or any place in this night of commitment.

"This is the beginning of my life," Brock whispered.

"Of our life," Charlotte echoed.

Their hands found buttons to release, zippers to part, satiny flesh to stroke. Free of silken wedding gown and constraining tuxedo, they sank down on the soft carpeting, arms and legs entwined, and there repeated their vows in the magic language of the flesh.

Much later, when a harvest moon shone in from the back garden on their entangled bodies, they rose and dressed and made their way eagerly to the honeymoon suite that awaited them in a hotel on the Sound.

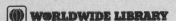

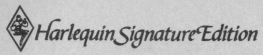

Harlequin Signature Edition

Penny Jordan

Stronger Than Yearning

He was the man of her dreams!

The same dark hair, the same mocking eyes; it was as if the
Regency rake of the portrait, the seducer of Jenna's dream, had
come to life. Jenna, believing the last of the Deverils dead, was
determined to buy the great old Yorkshire Hall—to claim it for
her daughter, Lucy, and put to rest some of the painful memories of Lucy's birth. She had no way of knowing that a direct des-
cendant of the black sheep Deveril even existed—or that James
Allingham and his own powerful yearnings would disrupt her
plan entirely.

Penny Jordan's first Harlequin Signature Edition *Love's Choices* was an
outstanding success. Penny Jordan has written more than 40 best-sell-
ing titles—more than 4 million copies sold.

Now, be sure to buy her latest bestseller, *Stronger Than Yearning*. Available wherever paperbacks are sold—in October.

Harlequin Superromance

COMING NEXT MONTH

#282 THE TENDER TRAP • Jane Silverwood
Zookeeper Faye Johnson loves working with all the
creatures at Wilderness Worlds. But animal
behaviorist David O'Neill is puzzled by the strange
goings-on there. Could Faye be involved in
something illegal?

#283 FOR ALL THE RIGHT REASONS •
Suzanne Ellison
When Nick Morales accompanies botanist Kelley
McKinney to a remote Mexican village, he knows the
journey won't be easy. But scorching desert,
rattlesnakes and smugglers are nothing compared to
the danger his heart is in....

#284 NORTHERN KNIGHTS • Bobby Hutchinson
RCMP Corporal Michael Quinn thinks Dawson City,
Yukon, is no place to have a lady as his right-hand
man. Constable Christine Johnstone disagrees, and
she's determined to make her boss see things
differently. In the land of the midnight sun,
disagreements are often settled in unusual ways—
especially when the best man for the job is a woman!

#285 DILEMMA • Megan Alexander
Shannon Gallagher is about to become Mrs.
Matthew Rossi. Her previous marriage, a very brief
union with a young sailor, is so far in her past that it
seems more like a dream. But for Shannon that
dream is about to become a nightmare....

**An intriguing story
of a love that defies the boundaries of time.**

Knocked unconscious by a violent earthquake, Lauren, a computer operator, wakes up to find that she is no longer in her familiar world of the 1980s, but back in 1906. She not only falls into another era but also into love, a love she had only known in her dreams. Funny... heartbreaking... always entertaining.

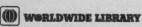